SIMON & SCHUSTER CHILDREN'S PUBLISHING
ADVANCE REVIEWER COPY

TITLE: Fire with Fire

AUTHORS: Jenny Han and Siobhan Vivian

IMPRINT: Simon & Schuster Books for Young Readers

ON-SALE DATE: 9/3/13

ISBN: 9781442440784

FORMAT: hardcover

PRICE: $17.99/$19.99 CAN

AGES: 14 up

PAGES: 528

THESE ARE ADVANCE PROOFS BOUND FOR REVIEW PURPOSES. All trim sizes, page counts, months of publication, and prices should be considered tentative and subject to change without notice. Please check publication information and any quotations against the bound copy of the book. We urge this for the sake of editorial accuracy as well as for your legal protection and ours.

Please send two copies of any review or mention of this book to:
Simon & Schuster Children's Publicity Department
1230 Avenue of the Americas, 4th Floor
New York, NY 10020
212/698-2808

Aladdin • Atheneum Books for Young Readers
Beach Lane Books • Beyond Words • Libros para niños • Little Simon
Little Simon Inspirations • Margaret K. McElderry Books
Simon & Schuster Books for Young Readers
Simon Pulse • Simon Scribbles • Simon Spotlight

Also by Jenny Han and Siobhan Vivian

Burn for Burn

FIRE WITH FIRE

JENNY HAN &
SIOBHAN VIVIAN

SIMON & SCHUSTER BFYR

New York   London   Toronto   Sydney   New Delhi

SIMON & SCHUSTER BFYR

An imprint of Simon & Schuster Children's Publishing Division
1230 Avenue of the Americas, New York, New York 10020

SIMON & SCHUSTER BFYR is a trademark of Simon & Schuster, Inc.
For information about special discounts for bulk purchases, please contact
Simon & Schuster Special Sales at 1-866-506-1949
or business@simonandschuster.com.
The Simon & Schuster Speakers Bureau can bring authors to your live event.
For more information or to book an event, contact the Simon & Schuster
Speakers Bureau at 1-866-248-3049 or visit our website
at www.simonspeakers.com.
Book design by Lucy Ruth Cummins
The text for this book is set in Stempel Garamond.
Manufactured in the United States of America
10 9 8 7 6 5 4 3 2 1
Library of Congress Cataloging-in-Publication Data
Han, Jenny.
Fire with fire / Jenny Han and Siobhan Vivian.—First edition.
pages cm.—([Burn for burn ; 2])
Summary: Jar Island teens Lillia, Kat, and Mary's ongoing
revenge plot against Reeve has unexpected consequences.
[1. Revenge—Fiction. 2. Friendship—Fiction. 3. High schools—Fiction.
4. Schools—Fiction. 5. Islands—Fiction.] I. Vivian, Siobhan. II. Title.
PZ7.H18944Fir 2013
[Fic]—dc23
2013000541

"Something of vengeance I had tasted for the first time;
as aromatic wine it seemed, on swallowing, warm and racy:
its after-flavor, metallic and corroding, gave me a
sensation as if I had been poisoned."

—CHARLOTTE BRONTË

FIRE
WITH
FIRE

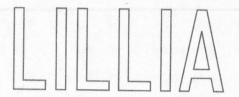

LILLIA

I COULDN'T DECIDE WHAT TO WEAR. AT FIRST I THOUGHT casual, like jeans and a button-down; then I thought no, in case his parents are there I should wear a dress, something somber like my gray scoop neck with the skinny belt. Then that looked too much like a funeral outfit, so I tried a marigold silk shirtdress, but that looked too spring, too cheerful.

The elevator doors ding open and I step out into the hallway. It's early Monday morning, an hour before school starts. I'm carrying a wicker basket of freshly baked chocolate chunk cookies and a get-well card covered in pink- and red-lipsticked lips. I'm wearing a navy turtleneck sweater and a camel-colored miniskirt, cream tights, brown suede ankle booties with a high heel. I curled my hair and did it halfway up, halfway down.

Fingers crossed I don't look as guilty as I feel.

At least it wasn't as bad as it could have been—that's what I keep telling myself. It certainly looked bad that night. It looked horrible. Watching Reeve fall off the stage and onto the gym floor in a twisted heap . . . it's something I'll never forget. But there was no spinal damage, just some bruising and soreness. His only injury was a broken fibula. Which, I know, isn't great.

He would have been released sooner if not for the hospital running a bunch of tests to make sure Reeve hadn't suffered a seizure. As far as I know, they didn't test him for drugs. I was sure they would, but Kat was pretty confident they wouldn't bother with someone like Reeve, an athlete. So no one knows about the ecstasy that I slipped in his drink. Reeve won't be suspended and I won't be going to jail. He's supposed to be discharged today.

I guess we both got off easy.

Now we go back to our normal lives. Whatever that means. After everything that's happened this year, I don't know if I'll ever feel "normal" again, or if I even want to. It's like there was the Before Lillia and now there's the After Lillia. The Before

Lillia didn't have a care in the world; she didn't have a clue. Before Lillia couldn't have handled any of this—she wouldn't have known what to do with herself. I'm a lot tougher now, not so soft and lily-white. I've been through things; I've seen things. I'm not the girl on the beach anymore. That all changed the moment we met those guys.

I used to be scared of leaving Jar Island, of being so far away from my family and my friends. But now I think about how when I go to college next year, no one there will know Before Lillia or After Lillia. I'll just be Lillia.

The woman at the reception desk smiles at me and asks, "Are you here to see our celebrity football player?"

I smile back and nod.

"He's at the end of the hall."

"Thank you," I say. Then I ask, "Is anybody here with him?"

"That cute little brunette," the woman says with a wink.

Rennie. I don't think she's left his side since Saturday night. I've called her twice, but she hasn't called me back. She's probably still annoyed with me for getting homecoming queen over her.

I make my way down the hall, clutching my basket and the card. I hate hospitals; I always have. The fluorescent lights, the smells . . . When I was little, I would try and hold my breath for as long as I possibly could. I'm good at holding my breath now, but I don't play the game anymore.

The closer I get to his room, the faster my heart beats. All I can hear is the sound of it beating and the clacking of my heels on the linoleum.

I'm standing outside his hospital room now. His name is written on the door. It's closed all but a crack. I set my basket down so I can knock, and then I hear Reeve's voice, defiant and husky. "I don't care what the doctors say. There's no way my recovery time is gonna be that long. I'm in peak physical condition. I'll be back on the field in no time."

She sniffles. "We'll show them, Reevie."

Someone brushes past me. A nurse. "Excuse me, hon," she chirps, and open the door wide. The nurse pushes through the curtain that divides the room in half and disappears into the other side.

And then there's Reeve, in a faded hospital gown. He hasn't shaved, there's a bit of scruff on his chin, and there are black circles underneath both of his eyes. He's got an IV drip in one of his arms, and his leg is in a huge cast, from his foot up to his thigh. His toes, what I can see of them poking out of the cast, are purple and swollen. His arms, too, are all cut up and scabby, probably from the broken glass that fell down on top of everyone that night. A few of the bigger wounds are sewn closed with thin black suture strings. He seems strangely small in the hospital bed. Not like himself.

Rennie's eyes are red-rimmed, and they narrow when she sees me. "Hey."

I swallow and hold up my card. "It's from the girls on the squad. They—they all send their best." Then I remember the cookies. I move to bring the basket to Reeve, but I change my mind and set it on a chair by the door. "I brought you cookies. They're chocolate chunk, I think I remember you liking them when I baked them for Key Club bake sale last year. . . ." Why am I still talking?

Reeve quickly wipes his eyes with the bedsheet. Gruffly he says, "Thanks, but I don't eat junk during football season."

I can't help it. I stare at his cast. "Right. Sorry."

"The doctor's coming back any minute to discharge him," Rennie says. "You should probably go."

I can feel my face reddening. "Oh. Sure. Feel better, Reeve."

I don't know if I'm imagining it, but when he looks at me over Rennie's shoulder, I think I see hate in his eyes. Then he closes them. "Bye," he says.

I'm halfway down the hallway when I stop and finally let out a breath. My knees are shaking. I still have the card clutched in my hands.

"IT'S DEAD," I SAY, AND LET MY HEAD FALL ONTO THE steering wheel. "Dead as a doornail."

My older brother, Pat, wipes his hands on a dirty rag. "Kat, quit being such a drama queen and turn the freaking key again."

I do as I'm told. I turn the key in the ignition of our convertible. Nothing happens. No sound, no rumble. Nothing. "This is stupid." I say it, because even though Pat knows what he's doing when it comes to any kind of engine, there's no saving this jalopy. Our family needs a new car, or at least one built in this freaking decade. I climb out and slam the door so hard the entire convertible shakes. I don't need to be walking to school, freezing my ass off this winter. Or worse, taking the bus. Hello! I'm a senior.

Pat shoots me a dirty look and then goes back to the engine. He's got the hood popped open and he's pitched forward between the headlights. A few of Pat's friends are gathered around, watching him while they pound our dad's beers. Their favorite way to spend a Monday afternoon. Pat asks Skeeter for a wrench, and then starts tapping it on something metallic.

I come around behind my brother. "Maybe it's the battery," I say. "I think the radio turned off before it crapped out on me." It happened this afternoon. I decided to skip eighth period and drive to Mary's house. I wanted to check on her, because I hadn't seen her in the hallways. I bet she was still too shaken up after what happened at the dance to come to school. She was scared out of her mind that Reeve might be hurt. Poor thing. But I didn't get far. The car died, right there in the school parking lot.

My first thought was *Is this karma?*

I sure as shit hope not.

Pat turns to reach for another tool and he nearly knocks me on my ass. "God, would you relax? Go smoke a cigarette or something."

I have been a little, um, skittish the last few days. I mean, who wouldn't be, after what went down at homecoming?

Never in a million years did I expect to see Reeve wheeled out on an ambulance stretcher. We wanted him kicked off the football team for getting caught high on drugs. We didn't want him put in the hospital.

I keep reminding myself that what happened at the dance wasn't our fault. It was an electrical fire. The newspaper even said so today. So there you have it. The explosions were what caused Reeve to freak out and fall off the stage. Not the drugs Lillia slipped in his drink. Facts are facts.

And to be honest, the electrical fire was actually a blessing in disguise. Obviously, it sucks that people got hurt. A bunch of kids had to get stitches from the falling broken glass, a freshman boy had a burn on his arm from the sparks, and one of the older teachers got treated for smoke inhalation. But the electrical fire took the heat off us—pun intended. Reeve's injury was just another casualty of the chaos. There's no way he'd remember Lillia giving him the spiked drink, with all that was going on.

At least that's what I keep telling Lillia.

Pat holds up the silver dipstick to his buddies and they shake their heads, like it's some kind of travesty. "Geez, Kat! When's the last time you checked the oil?"

"I thought that was your job."

"It's basic car maintenance."

I roll my eyes. "Did you take my cigarettes?"

"I had one or two," he says sheepishly. Pat points over at his workbench. I go grab them, and of course my brand-new pack is empty. I throw it at his head.

"You want a ride to the gas station?" Ricky asks me, helmet in his hand. "I need to fill up my bike anyway."

"Thanks, Ricky."

As we walk out of the garage, Ricky puts his hand on the small of my back. Immediately I think of Alex Lind at homecoming, how he gallantly led Lillia out of the pandemonium to safety. I wish I didn't have to see that go down. Not that I'm jealous or anything. More like the corniness made my stomach hurt. I wonder if he was being nice, or if he's actually into her. Not that I care. As I climb on the back of Ricky's bike, I inch up as close as I can to him, so we're practically spooning.

He turns his head around and says, in a low voice, "You're killing me. You know that, right?" before flicking his helmet visor down.

I can see my reflection in it, and I look pretty hot. I give him a wink and an innocent look. "Drive," I order him. And he makes his engine growl for me.

The truth is, if I want a guy, I can get him. Alex Lind included.

The sun is setting on a gray sky, and the roads are mostly

empty. This is what it's like here on Jar Island come fall. More than half the population in summertime vanishes. There'll be a few tourists that come in to geek out over foliage and stuff, but mostly it's dead. A bunch of restaurants and shops are already closed down for the season. Depressing. I can't wait until next year, when I'm living someplace else. Hopefully Ohio, hopefully in a sweet dorm at Oberlin. But I'll live anywhere, so long as it's not Jar Island.

While Ricky gasses up his bike, I buy a fresh pack from the convenience store. Smokes are expensive. I should quit, save this money for college. When I turn back to the bike, I see the big hill that leads up to Middlebury. To Mary's house.

"Hey, Ricky, are you in a rush to get back?"

He grins at me. "Where are we going?"

I point the way to Mary's house. No one answers the front door, not even her freaky aunt. There's a ton of mail bursting out of the mailbox, and the lawn is mangier than Shep. I walk around the side and find a rock to toss up to the second floor. The lights are out in Mary's bedroom, her curtains pulled shut. I check the other windows for signs of life. Every one is dark. The house looks . . . well, creepy. I let the rock fall out of my hand.

I wish I could talk to Mary for just one second so I could

ease her mind. She has nothing to feel sorry for. She shouldn't feel bad for what happened. That a-hole got what he deserved, plain and simple. Hopefully now that our revenge stuff is all over and done with, Mary can move on with her life and not waste another second on Reeve Tabatsky.

MARY

I'VE BEEN CRYING FOR TWO STRAIGHT DAYS. I CAN'T EAT; I can't sleep. I can't do anything.

I hear Aunt Bette in the bathroom, washing her face and brushing her teeth. Her nightly routine. On her way to bed, she stops in my room. She has her robe cinched tight around her waist and a newspaper under her arm.

I'm lying in a heap on my bed, staring at the ceiling. I can't even bring myself to say good-night.

Aunt Bette stands there, watching me for a second or two. Then she says, "There's an article in the paper today." She holds it up for me. The story above the fold is about the dance, the fire. There's a picture of the gym, black smoke trickling out the windows, a stream of students pouring out the door. "They think it was electrical."

I roll away from her, toward the wall, because I don't want to talk about homecoming. I don't even want to think about it. I've already gone over it a million and one times in my head. How everything went so wrong.

I was finally ready for him to see me that night, in my beautiful dress, proud and strong and changed. I had this idea of how it would go. Reeve, completely spaced out on the drugs we'd slipped him, would keep noticing me in the crowd. Something about me would seem familiar. He'd be drawn to me. He'd think I was beautiful.

Each time our eyes met, I'd touch the daisy pendant necklace he'd given me for my birthday, smile, and wait for him to figure out who I was. Meanwhile the teachers would be watching Reeve act more and more crazy. They'd sense that something was off. And as he realized who I was, they'd haul his butt off to the principal's office and he'd get the punishment he deserved.

Only that wasn't what happened. Not even close.

Reeve knew who I was as soon as he laid eyes on me. Despite all the ways I've changed since seventh grade, he saw the fat girl who'd been dumb enough to believe he was her friend. Reeve saw Big Easy. Hearing him say it knocked the wind out of me, the same way it had when he'd pushed me into the dark, cold water. I'd only ever be one thing to him. Nothing but that. I was so angry. And I snapped.

"One of the students who got hurt, it sounded like he was a big football player at the high school."

"His name is Reeve," I say quietly. "Reeve Tabatsky."

"I know." I hear Aunt Bette take a step closer. "He was the boy who used to tease you, Mary."

Instead of answering her, I press my lips together tight.

"We had that long talk about him over hot chocolates when I came for Christmas. Remember?"

I do remember. I'd hoped that Aunt Bette would have some good advice for me—a way I could get Reeve to act like he did on our ferry rides when other people were around. I thought she'd understand. But Aunt Bette told me to just grab a teacher and tattle the next time Reeve teased me in front of other kids. "That'll teach him to leave you alone," she'd said.

Leave me alone? It was the last thing I wanted.

That's when I knew that no adults could understand. Nobody would get the kind of relationship that Reeve and I had.

I can hear Aunt Bette breathing shallow breaths a few steps away from my bed. "Did you . . ."

I roll back toward her. "Did I *what*?" It comes out so mean, but I can't help it. Can't she tell I'm not in the mood to talk?

Aunt Bette's eyes are wide. "Nothing," she says, and backs out the room.

I can't deal. So I get up, wrap a sweater around my night-gown, slip on my sneakers, and creep out the back door.

I walk down to Main Street and head toward the cliffs. There's a big one I used to love to look out from, because you could see for miles.

But tonight there's nothing but blackness beyond the cliff. Blackness and quiet, like the edge of the world. I shuffle my feet until the tips of my shoes hang over the rock. Some gravel tumbles over the edge, but I never hear it hit the water. The fall goes on forever.

Instead I hear Reeve whisper to me at the homecoming dance. Big Easy. Like an echo, over and over and over.

I ball my fists, fighting to push the memory of what happened next out of my head. But it doesn't work. It never works.

There were those other times too. Like when Rennie fell off the cheering pyramid.

And the time all the locker doors slammed closed at once. Something is wrong with me. Something's . . . off.

A cloud pulls away from the moon, like a curtain in a play. Light reflects off the wet rock and makes everything glisten.

There's a path where the rocks stagger down the side of the cliff in crooked stairs. I make my way down them until I can't go any farther. I peer over the edge. Waves crash down far below me. They beat against the rocks and fill the air with mist.

One more step . . . one more step and it all goes away. Everything I've done, everything that's been done to me, it just washes away.

Suddenly there's a gust of wind and a splash of water. It nearly knocks me over the edge. I fall to my knees and crawl backward to the path.

There's one thing I can't let go of.

Reeve.

I love him in spite of everything he did to me. I love him even while I hate him. I don't know how to stop.

And the worst part is that I don't even know if I want to.

ONE WEEK LATER

CHAPTER ONE

MARY

WHEN THE MONDAY MORNING SUN STREAMS THROUGH my window, something tells me to get out of bed instead of rolling over toward the wall like I've been doing for the past week. I've known I should go back to school for a while, but I couldn't quite muster up the energy to make it happen. So I stayed in bed.

But today feels different. I'm not sure why. It's just a feeling I have. Like I need to be there.

I braid my hair and put on my corduroy jumper, a button-up shirt, and a cardigan sweater. I'm nervous about seeing

Reeve; I'm nervous about . . . something bad happening again. And then there's all the schoolwork I've missed. I haven't even tried to keep up with my assignments. My books, all my note-books, have stayed zipped away in my backpack, untouched, in the corner of my room. I pick it up by one strap and hoist it over my shoulder. I can't worry about how I'll catch up right now. I'll figure something out.

But when I put my hand on my doorknob and try to turn it, it won't budge.

This happens in our house. Especially in the summer, when the wood swells up with the humidity. The doors are original and the hardware is too. It's a big glass doorknob with a brass metal plate and room for a skeleton key. You can't even buy that kind of thing anymore.

It usually takes a little jiggling to get it to work, but I try that and it still won't move.

"Aunt Bette?" I call out. "Aunt Bette?"

I give the door another try. This time a much harder shake. And then I start to panic. "Aunt Bette! Help!"

Finally I hear her coming up the stairs.

"Something's wrong with the door," I shout. "It won't open." I give it another shake, to show her. And then, when I don't hear anything happen on the other side, I sink down to my knees and look through the keyhole, to make sure she's still standing out there. She is. I can see her long, crinkly maroon skirt. "Aunt Bette! Please!"

Finally Aunt Bette springs into action. I hear her struggle with my door on her side for a second, and then it swings open.

"Thank goodness," I say, relieved. I'm about to step into the hallway when I spot some stuff on the floor. It looks like white sand, or a chalk of some kind. To the left I can see it was laid in a thin, perfect line, but directly in front of my door it's been totally messed up by Aunt Bette's footprints.

What in the world?

I think about stooping over and touching it, but I'm a little spooked.

Aunt Bette has always been into weird things, like smudgings and crystals and channeling different energies. She used to always bring back trinkets and lucky charms whenever she went overseas. I know that stuff is all harmless, but I point down at the chalk and say, "What is that stuff?"

Aunt Bette looks up guiltily. "It's nothing. I—I'll clean it up."

I nod, like *Okay, sure,* while stepping past her. "I'll see you in a few hours."

"Wait," she says urgently. "Where are you going?"

I sigh. "To school."

With a thin, frayed voice she says, "It's better if you stay home."

All right. I haven't had the easiest week. I know that. I've done a lot of moping around the house, a lot of crying. But it's not like Aunt Bette's been doing so hot either. She hasn't been sleeping much. I hear her in her room at night, puttering around, sighing to herself. She hardly ever goes outside. And she's not painting much anymore, which might be the most worrisome thing of all. When Aunt Bette paints, she's happy, simple as that. It'll be good if I get out of her hair for the day. Give us both a some space.

"I can't stay in the house forever." I have to follow my gut. Something inside me is telling me to go. "I'm going to school today," I say again. This time without smiling. And I walk straight down the stairs, without waiting for her permission.

By the time I reach the bike rack at Jar Island High, the sun has disappeared, leaving the sky cold and wispy. The parking lot is empty, except for a few teachers and the electrician vans. Our school is being completely rewired after the homecoming incident. It looks like they've hired every electrician on the island, men working around the clock to get it done.

I'm glad to be here early, before most of the other students. I need to ease myself back into this carefully.

To my surprise, Lillia runs up beside me. She has her jacket zipped up tight and the hood over her head. Every day it's getting colder.

"Hey," I say shyly, and lock up my bike. It's the first time we've seen each other since homecoming. "You're here early."

"Oh my gosh, I'm so glad to see you, Mary." When I don't answer right away, she frowns and says, "Are you mad at me or something? You haven't called; you haven't reached out. I looked up your aunt's number in the phone book and tried calling, but nobody picked up. And Kat's stopped by your house a few times but no one's answered the door."

I sigh. I guess it was stupid to think Lillia and Kat wouldn't notice that I've been avoiding them. But I haven't wanted to see anyone from school. It's nothing personal. "Sorry," I say. "It's just been . . . a lot."

"It's okay. I get it. And things have so been crazy; it's probably good that the three of us are lying low." She says it, but she still sounds sad. "Hey, I don't know if you've heard, but Reeve's coming back to school today."

I have a hard time swallowing. Is this why I had the feeling that I needed to be here? Because Reeve was coming back too?

"How is he? I read in the paper his leg is broken."

Lilia presses her lips together and then says, "He's okay. I think he's out for the rest of the season." I guess she sees something in my face, because she quickly shakes her head. "Don't worry. Everything's going to be fine." She walks backward, away from me. "Let's talk later, okay? I miss you."

Reeve's broken. I broke him.

I got what I wanted.

Didn't I?

He'll be arriving soon. I speed walk into school. Almost every classroom has big, gaping holes sawed into the walls, for the electrical work. I need to be careful where I walk or else I'll trip on bundles of new wires running along the hallway floors.

I go into homeroom and take a seat on the radiator by the window, with the skirt of my corduroy jumper tucked underneath me. I leave a textbook open in my lap. I'm not studying. I don't look down at the pages once. I peer through my hair and watch the parking lot as it fills up with students.

The temperature dipped down past the freezing mark for the first time this weekend, and I guess the janitors didn't waste any time shutting the courtyard fountain off. It's only the smokers and the cross-country runners who can handle the cold. Everyone else is hustling inside.

I pick up the sound of bass thumping through the window. Alex's SUV pulls into the school driveway. He parks in the handicapped spot, close to the walkway. Alex gets out, walks around the front of the car, and opens the passenger door.

Everyone in the courtyard turns to look. They must know he's coming back today too.

Reeve plants his good leg on the ground. He's wearing mesh basketball shorts and a JAR ISLAND FOOTBALL hoodie. Alex extends his hand, but Reeve ignores it, holds on to the door, and swings his other leg out. A white plaster cast stretches from his upper thigh all the way down to his toes.

Reeve balances on one foot while Alex gets his crutches out from the trunk. Rennie hops out of the backseat. She grabs Reeve's backpack from the passenger-side seat. Reeve motions like he wants to carry his stuff himself, but Rennie shakes her head, swishing her ponytail from side to side. He gives up and starts hobbling toward school as fast as he can with his crutches, which is pretty fast, actually. He leaves his friends trailing behind him.

A couple of kids rush up to Reeve, smile, and say hello. But everyone's staring at his leg. One guy tries to crouch down with a pen, so he can sign the cast. Reeve doesn't stop. He lowers his head, pretends not to notice them, and keeps going.

It's just like always. Everyone wants a piece of Reeve. Most of them will never get it.

But I had it once.

CHAPTER TWO

LILLIA

I'M IN THE MIDDLE OF MY CALC EQUATION WHEN THERE'S a knock at our classroom door. It's the school secretary, Mrs. Gardner, wearing a totally unflattering navy blazer. It's way too long, way too boxy for her, with buttons that are huge and gold. It looks like she stole it from her husband's closet—in 1980. Short women should never wear blazers, in my opinion. Unless they are cropped and super fitted with, like, three-quarter sleeves.

Anyway.

I go back to my worksheet. We're solving derivative problems.

It's not even hard. All everyone said last year is that calc is the hardest thing ever. Umm, seriously?

But then Mrs. Gardner drops a yellow slip of paper on my desk. *Lillia Cho* is written on the first line. Then it says *Report to guidance office*. There's a line for the time I'm supposed to be there. It says *Now*.

Inside me, everything tightens up. I push my hair over my shoulder and pack up my stuff. Alex looks at me on my way out the door. I smile and shrug my shoulders, carefree, like, *Weird. What could this be about?*

I walk quickly down the hall. If I were in trouble, if someone figured out what I did to Reeve at the dance, I'd be sent to the principal's office. Not to guidance.

Mr. Randolph has been my guidance counselor since freshman year. He's not old. His college graduation diploma is dated ten years ago. I checked on that once. I bet he was cute, back then, but he's started to lose his hair, which is unfortunate. His parents own the stables where we board my horse, Phantom. There are equestrian plaques and medals all over the place, from when he used to compete.

I wait for a second in his doorway. He's on the phone, but he waves me inside.

I sit down and rehearse in my head what I'll say, in case he does confront me. I'll scrunch up my face and go with something like, *Excuse me, Mr. Randolph? Why would I ever, ever do something like that? Reeve is one of my closest friends. This is, like, beyond ridiculous. I don't even know what to say.* Then I'll fold my arms and stop talking until I get a lawyer.

Mr. Randolph makes an annoyed face and rubs his balding head. I wonder if that's why he's balding prematurely, because he's so stressed and he rubs his head all day. "Yeah, okay, yeah, okay. Thank you." He hangs up the phone and lets out a deep breath. "Why so nervous, Lillia?"

I force myself to smile. "Hi, Mr. Randolph."

"I haven't seen you at the barn much lately. You aren't thinking of selling that horse, are you?"

"No! I'd never sell Phantom!"

Mr. Randolph laughs. "I know, I know. But if you ever change your mind, you know who to call first, right?"

I nod, but there is no way. I'd never make that phone call. I'd never, ever sell Phantom. "Right."

"So . . . I was going over your transcripts. They look really good, Lillia. Really good. You might even have a shot at salutatorian."

Relief washes over me. "Wow. That's amazing. My dad will be happy."

Mr. Randolph opens up a file with my name on it. I'm wondering if he's going to tell me my class rank, but then he says,

"However, I did notice that you still haven't taken the swim test."

"Oh." Ever since Jar Island had the indoor pool built, it's mandatory that all students pass a swim test. It's part of graduation requirements.

"Unless that's a clerical error?"

I wriggle back in my seat. "No. I haven't taken it."

He rocks his head from side to side. "Well, you do understand that passing the swim test is required for graduation."

"Unless I get a doctor's note, right?"

He looks surprised. Surprised and disappointed. "Correct. Unless you get a note." He closes the file. "But don't you want to learn to swim, Lillia?"

"I know how to *not drown*, Mr. Randolph," I assure him. "But actual swimming is just not my thing."

He gives me a look like I'm being ridiculous. "It's a good life skill, Lillia, especially for a girl who lives on an island. It could save your life one day. Or someone else's. Promise you'll think about it."

I will think about it. I'll think about how to ask my dad to write me a doctor's note. If he won't, I'm sure I could get Kat to do it on his stationery.

As I walk back to class, someone's stapling paper pumpkins on the big bulletin board, framing the October calendar. It's only been a little more than a month since Kat, Mary, and I ran into each other in the girls' bathroom. I'm not sure if it was good luck or maybe even fate that brought us together. Whatever it was, I'm so glad it did.

We're all at the lunch table, and people keep coming over, trying to sign Reeve's cast. The Reeve I know would have lapped up the attention; he would have loved every second. But not this guy. This guy couldn't care less. All he wants to do is talk about his physical therapy plan with Rennie. They're huddled together on the other side of the table, his cast up in her lap.

"While I have the hard cast on, I'm focusing exclusively on my upper body. Chest, biceps, triceps, back, core. Bulk up from the waist up. Then three, maybe four weeks and I'm in the soft cast. Boom. Hydrotherapy."

I'm mesmerized as I watch him tear through two steamed chicken breasts and a huge ziplock bag of cut-up carrots and spinach. He's inhaling food like he's a vacuum.

"I ordered you a buoyancy belt last night," Rennie says. "It should be here by the end of the week."

Alex keeps leaning over and trying to convince Reeve to come to the football game on Friday, but of course selfish Reeve isn't having it. Alex says, "Come on, Reeve. You know it would be huge for morale. The guys are scared shitless about Lee Freddington quarterbacking for us again."

"That's 'cause Freddington can't throw for shit," Derek says, his mouth full of pizza.

It's true. We had our first game without Reeve last Friday, and it was a complete disaster. We lost big-time to a team that's second to last in our division.

PJ pipes up, "We miss you, man. And, I don't know, maybe you could give Freddington some tips or whatever."

"Yeah," says Alex. "You don't have to suit up or anything. Just be on the sidelines. I really think it'd make a big difference."

Reeve gulps down his Muscle Milk. Wiping his mouth, he says, "You guys are on your own now. I can't carry you anymore. I've gotta worry about myself. If I don't get my shit straight, I don't play next fall."

"You're still a captain of this team," Alex reminds him.

"I have to focus on my recovery," Reeve says. "I'm in bed by nine and up by five thirty to work out. You think I have time to go to a football game?"

"Just think about it," Alex says. "You don't have to decide today. See how you're feeling on Friday night." It gives me a stomachache to see Alex be so patient with Reeve's temper tantrum. If I were him, I'd tell Reeve to forget it.

Shaking his head regretfully, Derek says, "Damn, man. I can't believe this happened to you. I was looking forward to watching you throw TDs on ESPN next fall."

Reeve jams a forkful of salad into his mouth. Chewing force-fully, he says, "You're still gonna see me on ESPN. Don't count me out."

"Yeah, Derek," Rennie says, glaring at him. "From here on out, this is a no-negativity zone. Only positive thinking allowed."

Reeve heaves himself out of his seat and up onto his crutches.

"Where are you going?" Rennie asks him.

"Bathroom."

He lurches off, and Rennie watches him like a hawk, ready to spring into action if he needs her. When he's gone, she looks around to make sure no one else is listening, and then she says to Ash, "He's being so strong. He practically cried in my arms the other night when he heard Alabama was out. That was one of his safety schools! And there he was, begging the coaches to redshirt him for the first season." She closes her eyes and rubs her temples. "They don't think he'll ever get back to where he was. I can't wait until he proves those idiots wrong." Rennie takes a sip of her soda. "Sure, he might not end up at a D-one school after this is all over, but any division two or three school would be lucky to have him."

"Did you spend the night over at his house again?" Ash whispers.

Again? They're doing sleepovers now? I fully believe that Paige would let Rennie sleep over at a guy's house, but Reeve's parents have always seemed pretty traditional to me. They go to church every Sunday, and Reeve calls his dad "sir."

Running her hands through her hair, Rennie says, "I'm basically the only thing keeping him going right now."

"Did you guys finally DTR?" Ash asks her.

"What does DTR mean?" I wonder aloud.

"Define the relationship," Rennie says, rolling her eyes like I am a moron for not knowing. But she doesn't look at me. "And no, we didn't. Not yet. He has too much on his mind right now. I just want to be there for him. That's all he needs." Rennie stands up and gathers her things. "I'm going to go look for him." She leans down and gives Ashlin a peck on the cheek. "Bye, Ash. Bye, Peej, bye, Derek."

Without even a glance in my direction, she takes off. No one seems to notice that Rennie said good-bye to everyone but me.

It's been like this since homecoming, and every day it gets a little worse. I'm pretty sure Rennie's mad at me. Like, really mad.

As soon as she's out the door, I say to Ash, "Has Rennie said anything to you? About me?"

Ashlin shifts in her seat, avoiding my eyes. "What do you mean?"

"She's been acting like a total bitch to me ever since homecoming. Is it because I got queen and she didn't?" I bite my bottom lip. "I'll give her my tiara if she wants it that badly."

Ash finally looks up at me. "Lil, it's not because of that. It's because you kissed Reeve on stage at the dance."

My mouth drops. "I didn't kiss him! He kissed me!"

"But you let him. In front of everybody."

I feel like I'm going to cry. "Ash, I didn't want him to! He basically forced me. You know I don't even like him. And . . . why is she mad at me and not Reeve?"

Ash gives me a sympathetic shrug. "He's her first love. He's her Reevie. She'd forgive him for anything."

"But it's not fair," I whisper.

"Tell her you're sorry," Ashlin suggests. "Tell her you'd never think of Reeve like that."

I frown and rock back in my seat. Maybe that would make it better, but I kind of don't think so. "That's the thing," I say. "I shouldn't have to."

CHAPTER THREE

MARY

IT'S THE END OF THE WEEK, AND I'M ON MY WAY OUT of school when I hear Kat scream from the parking lot. It's a playful scream, not a scared one or anything. I glance around and spot her a few feet away, cigarette clenched between her teeth, trying to pull a flannel shirt off some guy.

I recognize the guy, sort of. I don't know his name, but I always see him wandering aimlessly around the school grounds. I don't think he has any classes. Or if he does, his teachers must be pretty liberal with their attendance sheets.

Kat could be on the Jar Island wrestling team, she's so light on her feet. She keeps moving, bouncing on her toes, twisting left and right as she works the back of the flannel up over the boy's head. I bet her brother, Pat, taught her how to do that.

The guy is unsteady, and also it seems like he doesn't exactly know how to fight back against a girl. Kat definitely takes advantage of it. She stays aggressive, tugging and pulling until she has most of the flannel free, distracting him by poking him in the ribs or pulling out the rubber band that's holding back his shoulder-length hair. It doesn't take long before all he's left clinging to is one tiny bit of sleeve.

Kat plants her feet like she's preparing for a serious game of tug-of-war. She warns him, "It's gonna rip if you don't let go, Dan."

"All right, all right," the guy—Dan, I guess—finally concedes.

Kat lets out a howl of victory and does a spin, whipping the flannel around over her head like a lasso. "This is a teachable moment, Dan. When I want something, I take it. End of story." Dan's face turns bright pink. I bust up laughing because she's so crazy.

Kat must hear me, because immediately she looks over to where I'm standing. She nudges her chin my way the slightest bit. I smile back, quick, and am about to climb on my bike and ride away, when Kat does something surprising.

She holds up a finger, like I should wait for her.

It happens so fast I wonder if maybe I imagined it. We haven't really ever done this before. Acknowledge each other in public, out in the open. I guess we can now, since our whole revenge plan is over. But I take out the book I need to read for English class and flip through it, so I don't look obvious. I watch as she grinds out her cigarette.

"Come on, Kat. Give it back."

Kat puts it on over her sweatshirt. "But I want to wear it. I promise to bring it back on Monday. And then it will smell like me."

He pretends to be annoyed, but I can tell he likes her by the way he gives in so quick. "You want a ride home?"

"Nah. I'm gonna walk. But can I bum one more smoke?" She doesn't wait for him to give her a cigarette. She takes it and tucks it behind her ear.

Then she heads over toward the bike path.

I put my book away and start walking slow, pushing my bike along, waiting for her to catch up. We probably should still be careful.

"You hanging in there, Mary?" she asks when she gets close.

"Yeah," I say with a sigh. "Pretty much."

"Did you see Reeve much this week?"

"Not really." I tuck my hair behind my ears and keep my eyes on the ground. "Hey. Um, I heard some people talking, and they said Reeve might lose all his football scholarships because of his injury." I feel my lip quiver as soon as the words are out. "Is it true?"

Kat shrugs. "Maybe. But maybe not, you know? It's not like he *lost* a leg. It's a break. And not even a bad one at that. My brother broke his femur once during a dirt-bike race. Now his left leg is half an inch shorter than his right." Her voice is strangely sober. I feel her eyes linger on me; it's like she's waiting to see if I'm going to break down. I lift my chin and manage a weak smile, even though I know I've got tears in my eyes.

Then it's Kat who looks away. She steps off the bike path and rips a handful of browning leaves off a low-hanging tree branch. "It'll all be okay. Trust me. Reeve will figure something out. The kid always does."

I nod, *yes, sure,* because what else can I say? I'll figure things out too. I managed to survive the week. That's something.

I decide it's best if I change the subject. "Who's that guy you were talking to?" I ask her. "Do you like him?"

"Please. Dan?" Kat rolls her eyes. "Mary, I don't need any boy drama, not when I've only got, like, seven months left on this island. He's a temporary cure for my boredom."

If only it were that easy. Finding a boy to like, one who'd like me back. Kat's had all this experience with boys, and I've never even had a first kiss. Probably because deep down I've been pining over Reeve this whole time, hoping he might finally think I was worthy of him.

There I go again. Thinking about Reeve, even when I'm trying not to. It's like a sickness.

"What are you doing tonight, Mary?" Before I can answer her, Kat says, "I'm heading to the mainland to see a show at my friend's music shop. They're a deathcore band, called Day of the Dogs, and they do this whole call-and-response thing with the audience where you have to scream at the top of your lungs. I know you've got a crazy set of pipes." She says this as a joke, referring back to the way I screamed on homecoming night, but neither of us laughs. "You should come. It could be good for you. Release some of whatever shit you've been bottling up inside."

I don't know what deathcore is, and though I appreciate her inviting me along, I think I should take things easy for now. "I've got so much homework to catch up on. I probably won't be able to go out for a long time."

Kat stares at me for a second, and I feel her putting two and two together. She turns her back to the breeze and tries to light her cigarette. "Okay, Mary. Look. I know you've been in a funk ever since homecoming. Things didn't work out exactly how we wanted them to, and I get it, it sucks. After my mom died, I like refused to speak for six months." She sucks in a few drags and then checks the end of her cigarette, to make sure it's lit. "You know about my mom, right?"

I nod. I think maybe Lillia mentioned it once, in passing. Cancer. But Kat's never brought her up before. And a little part of me feels happy that now she has, that she feels okay sharing something so personal with me.

"Yeah, I thought probably, but I wanted to make sure." She takes a long, deep drag and sprays out smoke. "So, anyway, that wasn't a healthy way for me to deal. Shutting down like that. It wasn't good for me. You can't be sad forever, you know? It wasn't going to bring my mom back, that's for damn sure. At some point you have to move on."

I stop walking. "How do I move on?"

She pinches the cigarette between her lips and shoves her hands in her pockets. "You should, like, I don't know. Join some clubs or something. Try to be more involved in school stuff. Bide your time until graduation."

"Like what kinds of clubs?"

Her face scrunches up. "I don't know, Mary! Clubs aren't my thing. It's whatever you're interested in. You got to put yourself out there. Make some new friends. Focus on the things that make you happy. I don't mean to sound like a bitch, but you need to get a life, because you've got another full year here before you graduate."

She makes it sound so simple. Maybe it is. "I know you're right," I say. "It's . . . it's hard."

"It doesn't have to be, though." Kat leans up against a tree. "You just do it, and you don't let your feelings get in the way." She pats her chest. "I hardly ever think about my feelings. You know why? Because if I sat there and cried over every single bad thing that's happened to me, I'd never get out of bed." Her eyes find mine, and she looks at me deeply. "I swear to you, it'll get better. You've just got to make it through this part."

I pull my coat around myself. Kat's right, I know it. I know better than to wallow like this. I lost a whole year of my life after I tried to kill myself over what Reeve did. I can't let that happen again.

"Thank you." I say it and I truly mean it, from the bottom of my heart. Because there is one big difference between then and now. Now I have friends looking out for me.

I do homework until I can't stand the sight of my textbooks, and then I go for a walk down to Main Street. A ferry pulls into the dock, and the first vehicle to drive off is a school bus packed full of football players. The windows are painted with different numbers and trash talk like DROWN THOSE GULLS!

Sheesh.

I guess we've got a football game tonight.

I make my way over to the field. I don't plan to stay for long, but it's easy to find a seat in the bleachers. There's about half the crowd, maybe even less, than showed up to cheer on the team at homecoming. I guess that's what losing your star player will do. The first game after homecoming weekend, after Reeve got hurt, we lost. Badly. Our backup quarterback, Lee Freddington, didn't complete a single pass.

A group of cheerleaders is huddled together, practicing their "De-fense! De-fense! De-fense!" clap. I figure we'll be hearing that cheer a lot more now that our team no longer has an offense. The rest of them mill about casually on the sidelines, like this is a practice and not a game night. Rennie's sitting cross-legged on the grass, looking at her phone. Lillia and Ashlin are near the players' bench, talking to each other. Lillia sees me and beams me a smile. I smile back.

The announcer welcomes the opponents, and then our cheerleaders line up and make their way toward the field-house gate, to greet our team as they take the field. I watch Teresa Cruz navigate her way to the front of the pack. I guess since she cheers for Lee Freddington, the backup QB, she's more important now.

Rennie sees this, and she positions herself right in front of Teresa.

Reeve is the first one out of the field house. He has his jersey on and a pair of warm-up pants, the same thing he wore to school today. As soon as he appears, everyone in the bleachers stands up and cheers for him. It's not the level of enthusiasm that Reeve got at the start of the season. This is more muted applause. Respectful. A courtesy.

Reeve tries to go as fast as he can on his crutches, but the ground is soft from the rain we got this week, and his crutches sink into the turf. The faster Reeve tries to go, the deeper he sinks, and it slows him down.

The other players burst out of the locker room. They try to stay behind Reeve, letting him still be their leader, but Reeve is going so slow they bottleneck behind him.

Then along the side of the pack comes Lee Freddington. He passes right by Reeve, as if he isn't even there, and takes the lead. It's like Lee Freddington grants them all permission, because then the rest of the players pass Reeve too. Reeve ends up being one of the last in the pack, with Alex, PJ, the team trainer, and the water boys who have to lug the coolers. I can see Reeve getting more and more frustrated. At one point the toe of his cast drags against the field, filling the space between it and his toes with clumps of grass and dirt. His face turns bright red, like he's about to boil over.

I stop clapping and sit on my hands. It's stupid. I know it probably makes me weak. It's just that Reeve is so completely unprepared for this. He doesn't know how to handle being on the outside. He's so used to being the center of it all. It's almost painful to watch; it's as if the moon and the stars have been banished from the heavens and forced to be mortal like the rest of us.

I wanted Reeve to get in big trouble, to lose what made him feel so confident, so superior to everyone else. And he did deserve what was coming to him, I know that deep down. But a part of me wishes it never had to get to that point. That we didn't have to break him for him to learn his lesson.

The first quarter of the game, we play as terribly as expected. Lee Freddington gets the ball back at the start of the second quarter. On his first chance to pass, he almost gets tackled by the other team. Our coach calls a time-out and starts yelling at the guys on defense.

I watch Reeve seek out Lee Freddington on the sideline and give him some tips. He's been doing this all game long. But Lee hardly looks at him. He barely even makes eye contact. And not because he's embarrassed. Because he thinks he doesn't need the help.

Right before the time-out ends, Lee Freddington walks over to Alex Lind. He drapes his arm over his shoulder and seems to whisper something. Reeve is watching this, his jaw set.

A second later, our team rushes back on the field. Lee leads the huddle, and when the ball snaps, he pulls his arm back like he's going to really go for it. Way downfield, Alex Lind is out-running another player. Lee throws the ball, a tight spiral, and it lands right in Alex's arms.

Touchdown.

I get up to leave while PJ kicks the extra point. As I pass by the sideline, the cheerleaders are lining up to do their individual player cheers for that play. Teresa Cruz steps to the front, and I see Rennie charge up and grab her by the sweater.

"What are you doing?"

"Lee threw a touchdown. I'm doing his player cheer."

Rennie gives her a look like she's an idiot. "Alex *caught* a touchdown. He's the one who scored the points."

Teresa huffs. "But we always do the QB cheer—"

"*Reeve's* our quarterback. Lee is second-string trash."

Rennie steps up and shouts Reeve's cheer so loud I see him shrink on the bench.

Rennie thinks she knows what Reeve needs, but she doesn't have a clue. He doesn't want everyone looking at him. Not any-more. Now all he wants is to be left alone.

I get up from my seat and begin my walk home. That's exactly what I'm going to do. Leave Reeve alone. Even more than that, I'll rewire my brain so that I don't think about him, don't feel anything for him. It's the only way.

* * *

Back at the house, I find Aunt Bette in the living room. She's in the dark, sitting on the floor with candles burning all around her. Wax is pooling in puddles on the hardwood. My dad would flip out if he saw that. He always says the floors are his favorite part of the house. They're cedar, the most beautiful strawberry-blond color.

"I'm home," I say, stepping into the room.

Aunt Bette startles. Now that I'm closer, I see that she has a piece of linen spread out in front of her. It's covered with piles of dried leaves and herbs. She's putting them into small bundles and binding them up with twine.

She finishes tying a knot before she says, "I didn't know you left," annoyed, like I'm interrupting something important.

"I went for a walk." And then I add, "Sorry," even though I don't have anything to apologize for. I point down at the bundles and ask, "What is that stuff?"

With one hand Aunt Bette grabs a sprig of something and rubs a leaf between her fingers. "Ancient herbs." It looks like rosemary. Or maybe thyme? I can't tell.

"O-kay," I say. "Well, good night."

At the foot of the stairs I spot a teacup on the floor. Inside is one of the bundles lit on fire. It's burning red embers and letting off a twisty curl of smoke up to the hallway ceiling.

What in the world?

My head starts to throb.

Coughing, I call out, "Um, Aunt Bette? Is it safe to leave this thing smoking in the hall?" I worry that I sound like a patronizing jerk, but really. It's kind of unnerving. And I'm feeling sick.

Aunt Bette doesn't answer me. Whatever. I step around it, careful not to breathe in any of the smoke, and make my way to my room.

CHAPTER FOUR

KAT

AFTER TALKING WITH MARY AFTER SCHOOL, I GO home, make Dad a microwave dinner and hammer a bowl of cereal, and then head to the ferry. The sun has gone down, and the wind is stinging. I zip my sweatshirt up to the neck and pull the hood tight over my head. I should have started wearing a coat weeks ago, but I hate the one I got last year. It was a peacoat, charcoal gray, a real navy-supply one. I found it at the thrift store, but it wasn't lined, and the wool made my skin itch. Maybe, if I get to the mainland early, I can stop by the thrift store and see if they have something else.

JENNY HAN AND SIOBHAN VIVIAN

Down at the ferry landing it's the opposite of what it's like in the summertime, when the parking lot is full and there are lines of people queued up to climb aboard. It's totally dead, except for a few delivery trucks and a couple of cars. Most of the workers I know have left for the season, so I'll probably have to pay for my ticket. I go up to the window, but the ticket guy is friends with my dad and refuses to take my money. Which is awesome. It happens a lot for me, but I'm grateful each and every time.

I'd freeze my ass off if I sat on the observation deck, so I find a seat inside in the café. There's a table of four old folks drinking tea and thumbing through a book of birds, marking down the ones they saw today. I turn on my music and close my eyes. I swear to God, I hope I die young, because I can't ever imagine myself doing that shit.

And then I get this tight-stomach feeling—guilt, I guess—knowing that it's been weeks since I've been to the store to see Kim. Not since our little fight, when I needed use the copy machine to photocopy Alex's gay-ass poems for our revenge scheme. I was so wrapped up in getting that done I didn't give Kim the time of day when she obviously needed a friend to talk to.

Hopefully she'll forgive me.

The thrift store doesn't have winter coats, unfortunately. Only summer crap from people cleaning out their closets. I walk the mile over to Paul's Boutique. Day of the Dogs won't come on till late, but it's better that way, because Kim and I will have a chance to catch up. I decide in advance not to talk about any of my shit. Tonight should be about her unloading on me. Maybe things worked out between her and Paul. Who knows, maybe his wife didn't actually know they were doing it. I hope so.

I walk into the store, and there's someone I don't recognize behind the counter, some skinny dude with a mullet. So I head straight to the back, where the shows are, and try to walk through the door. It's a lot darker inside the garage space, and a few people are already pushed up to the front of the stage to make sure they have a good spot for the show. Someone grabs my arm.

"Ten-dollar cover."

I turn and see Paul himself. Paul's hair is cut pretty short, and it looks more silver than I remember. He's got on an old Sex Pistols T-shirt, tight ripped jeans, and canvas sneakers. He's short for a guy, but in good shape. Kim says he's really disciplined about going to the gym since he got clean. Apparently, years ago he was into some pretty hard drugs. Like needle drugs.

Anyway, I smile, because I've met him before. "Yo, Paul."

He doesn't let go of my arm. "Ten-dollar cover."

I yank myself free and glance over to the sound booth, wondering if Kim might be in there. But it's empty.

"You deaf?"

"Where's Kim?" I say, and I know I sound pissed.

Paul looks taken aback. "You know Kim?"

"She's a good friend of mine."

He folds his arms. "She doesn't work here anymore."

"What? Why not?"

"She stole from the store, so I fired her."

I narrow my eyes. I spit out, "You're a liar."

"Excuse me?"

"You heard me." I'm so angry I'm shaking. "You're a liar. Kim would never steal from you." I know this for a fact. Kim would never, ever, ever steal from Paul. She worked so freaking hard at her job. Partly because she loved music, and partly because she loved him.

He points his finger in my face. "What do you call letting people in to see shows for free, huh? When's the last time you paid to see a band?"

"You piece-of-shit coward." I say it loud enough so that people standing near us turn around. "You fuck your employees, and when you get caught, you fire them."

He snorts like he could give two shits, but I can tell he's livid. "All right, kid. You're out of here." He throws his tattooed arm up and starts waving to Frank, the bouncer, leaning against a big amp. Frank comes over, and he looks anything but happy to throw me out.

"I hope your wife knows what a dickbag her husband is!" I'm screaming at the top of my lungs. "I'd be happy to tell her myself!"

"Come on, Kat," Frank says, wrapping his arm around me.

I start flailing and spewing all the curse words I know in one long stream.

Frank leads me into a back hallway, near the tiny room where the band hangs out until it's time for them to go onstage. I can hear them now, warming up their instruments, laughing and talking with each other.

"You okay?" Frank says.

I'm fighting the urge to cry, so I punch the wall hard. "Where'd she go?"

Frank shrugs. "They had a big fight a few weeks ago and Paul gave her twenty-four hours to pack up her stuff in the apartment upstairs. She did it in three, and on her way out she took all the cash out of the safe."

So Kim did steal from Paul? I guess Frank can see the shock on my face, because he shakes his head, like I've got the wrong idea. "Think of it more as an inevitable lawsuit settlement."

"But it's not like this place makes that much money. What

could it have been? Maybe a thousand dollars, max? That's not going to get her far. It's not like that's buying her a mansion or something. She hasn't talked to her parents in years. She could be . . . homeless."

"She'll be okay," Frank says again, but this time he's less sure.

The tears come right then. I can't stop, and Frank looks uncomfortable as shit. Wiping my nose with my sleeve, I say, "If she calls, will you tell her I came looking for her?"

Frank nods, but it's the kind of nod where we both know that won't ever happen. Kim's gone for good.

I'm straight up bawling as Frank leads me out of a side door and into the alleyway. He tells me good-bye and then shuts the door in my face. I try to call Kim's cell, but the number's disconnected. Of course.

I think of Kim, going through this shit alone. Wonder if she thought about calling me. Asking me for help. Probably not. Probably not once. Because I'm a dumb high school kid. Because the one time she tried to get real with me, all I cared about was my own life.

I feel like such a turd. To let down the person I thought of as my bestie when she needed me most. It's a sucky lesson to learn, but I make a promise to myself, then and there, to never be a shit friend like that again.

CHAPTER FIVE

RENNIE PRETENDS I'M NOT THERE DURING MONDAY'S cheer practice. She doesn't look at me, doesn't speak to me. Not a single word. Even when it's me, her, and Ashlin standing in a circle, discussing what cheers we should work on next. Rennie keeps her eyes on Ashlin, only speaks to Ashlin.

It's like I'm invisible.

I try not to let it get under my skin. Rennie loves giving the silent treatment. It's practically her signature move. What makes me mad is that I didn't even do anything to deserve it.

Not that she knows about, anyway.

So even though she's being a bitch to me, I still talk to her.

I mean, kind of. Like when I tell her, "I think Melanie is coming in late with her second roundoff." Rennie doesn't respond to me, of course. But she does walk over to Melanie and tell her to work on her timing.

In the locker room when we're getting changed, Rennie invites Ashlin to come to her house for dinner. She does it right in front of me. Ash says, "Yeah!" and then, when she remembers that I'm standing there, she frowns and asks, "What about you, Lil? Come with?"

Rennie immediately turns her back to me and faces her locker, so that I know I'm not welcome.

"Can't. I have to go to the stables." I don't really have to go, but I've been meaning to for weeks. Nadia's been riding Phantom much more than I have lately. I don't want him to forget me. Plus, I don't want to seem like I care. Monday is pizza night at Rennie's house, and I don't love the place where they order from. They put way too much sauce on, in my opinion.

Rennie snorts at my excuse. She's never liked Phantom. She tried to ride him once, but as soon as she was in the saddle, he started trotting sideways, because Rennie had her legs squeezed around him and his bridle pulled left. I told her to lift up on the reins, but instead she freaked out and jumped right off him while he was moving! She fell hard on the ground and skinned both her knees in the dirt. The stable guys ran over to help her up, but they were yelling at her too, because it is very dangerous to dismount a horse that way. Rennie was so embarrassed. She went and pouted in the parking lot by herself while I led Phantom back to his stable and got his saddle off.

I drop Nadia off at our house. At every stop sign I wait to see if she'll say anything about the way Rennie's been acting, if she's noticed the cold shoulder, but Nadia spends the whole ride texting her friends.

As I drive over to the stable, I can't help but think that Kat and Mary would never do something like this to me. Ice me out of the group for no reason. I decide to call Mary's house and throw Kat a text, to see if they want to meet at the stables and hang out a for a bit. I bet Mary will love Phantom. I'll even show her how to brush him.

Kat texts me back right away. *Horseshit?! I'm soooo in!* I laugh out loud, and it already makes me feel better.

I call Mary's house and her aunt answers. Her voice sounds groggy, like she was sleeping. "Hello?"

"Hi, is Mary home?" I ask her.

There's silence on the other end.

So I go ahead and say, "This is Lillia; I'm a friend of Mary's.

I'm calling to invite her to the stables to go horseback riding this afternoon." More silence. "So . . . if you could give her that message, that would be great."

There's heavy breathing. Then a click and a dial tone.

She hung up on me! I know Mary said her aunt's kind of weird, but geez. That was freaky. I swear, I'm getting her a cell for Christmas.

I get to the stables too late to ride, so I head to Phantom's stall to groom him. He stands perfectly still while I brush his coat. I whisper to him as I pull the bristles through, and he shines like black velvet. When I get to his neck, he keeps trying to turn his head and nuzzle me.

When Nadia comes to ride Phantom, she always asks the stable guys to brush him down and scrape the mud out of his hooves for her. But that's my favorite part of riding him. You have to build up trust with your horse. And I trust Phantom completely. I know he'd never hurt me. Even though I haven't been here to see him in weeks, he greets me like no time at all has passed. I used to be so in love with Phantom I would have slept at the barn if my mom had let me. When did that feeling go away? When I started cheering? I wonder if Phantom noticed, if it made him sad that I stopped coming around so much. The thought makes me want to cry.

One of the stable guys knocks on the door. "You've got someone here to see you, Lillia."

"Oh, great." I peer out of the stall, down the length of the barn. There's Kat, her fingers pinching her nose closed. I wave at her. "Down here, Kat!"

Kat walks directly in the center of the barn, careful not to get close to any of the stalls. "Dude. Can't we hang out somewhere else? It's rank in here!"

I take a deep, long breath. "Are you serious? I love the smell of manure!"

Kat, looking skeptical, takes her fingers off her nose and gives a sniff of the air. Then she starts to gag. "I'd stop telling people that if I were you."

"Fine. There's a pretty trail that runs down by the coast. No one else is out riding. We can walk it."

"Sure, whatever," Kat says, gasping for breath. She turns and runs back for the barn entrance.

I put Phantom's finishing brush away and give him a kiss before I leave him. Outside, it's practically dark, and kind of cold, but Kat and I start walking anyway.

"I called Mary," I tell Kat. "But I'm not sure she got—"

"Guys! Wait up!"

We turn and see Mary, running toward us. "Sorry I missed

your call, Lillia. I fell asleep. I always take a nap after school."

"Aww," Kat says.

Delicately I say, "Is everything okay at home? Your aunt was kind of weird when I called. I didn't think she'd give you the message."

Mary sighs. "Aunt Bette's on some kind of New Agey tear lately. She's more into books and crystals and stuff than interacting with actual people." She shakes her head. "So what's up? Is everything okay?"

I guess the three of us have only ever hung out when we were scheming up revenge plans. Or when we had urgent business to discuss. Except all that's over with now.

"Nothing much," I say. "I just missed you guys."

Kat eyes me. "How's things with Ren?"

"Not great," I say. And that's it. I mean, I want to let it all out. I want to tell them how much it sucks right now, but I can't. Kat went through exactly what I'm going through. Even worse. So who am I to complain?

But Kat is surprisingly sympathetic. She pats me on the back and says, "Don't worry. Someone else will piss her off and she'll forget about it. Hey! It might even be me!"

"And you'll always have us," Mary says.

I smile at them both. "Thanks, guys."

After that it's kind of quiet. It's not uncomfortable silence, exactly. More like we don't have much left to say to each other anymore. Which maybe we don't. It's still nice being with them, though.

CHAPTER SIX

KAT

WHEN THE BELL RINGS AT THE END OF THIRD PERIOD, I head to the library instead of to calc, because the guidance office is offering a workshop for seniors to help them fill out their college applications.

I'm almost positive it'll be a waste of time. I'm going early-decision Oberlin, and the materials are pretty straightforward. A basic application and a personal statement about who I am and why I want to go there. It should be a cakewalk.

But after my less-than-awesome SAT scores this summer, I need to pull out all the stops. It's a fucking broken system. With the SATs, there are tons of tricks about how to answer questions that can bring your score up hundreds of points. That's why rich kids end up doing so much better than poor kids, because they can afford special classes where they teach you those secrets.

It's not like I could ever afford a private tutor, so I got a bunch of books out of the library. Some of them were super outdated, and some dumb-ass had actually filled in the practice tests in pen. I did the best I could, but it clearly wasn't enough. I plan on talking about that in my personal statement, actually. Oberlin is a super-liberal, progressive place. I feel like they'd jive on my lower-class angst. Regardless, I'm going to have to take the SATs again next month, and hopefully improve my score by a couple hundy.

If there are any secret guidance counselor tricks I can learn, anything that will make my application to Oberlin rock freaking solid and stand out over all the others, I need to know them. I'll do whatever it takes to get off Jar Island forever. Ohio might not seem like the coolest place, but it's definitely where I want to be.

The library is dead, so dead I wonder if maybe this thing is happening in the guidance office instead. I walk over to the reference desk. The librarian there is on the computer. I hold my yellow pass up and say, "Do you know where the—" but she cuts me off with a big fat "Shhhh" even though there's no one in here but her. Then she points to the conference room next to the computers.

There aren't a lot of kids in the conference room. Maybe five other seniors, some I recognize and some I don't. I take a seat in the back, unzip my bag, and pull out the application to Oberlin. You fill it out online, but I printed a copy out so I could plan all my answers beforehand.

Ms. Chirazo, the head of guidance, comes in as the bell rings, in the flowy black pants and yarn neck scarf that seems to be her unofficial uniform. I swear, the woman has nothing but that shit hanging in her closet.

She frowns, I guess because she's disappointed with the lack of turnout. But then she sees me and her face brightens. "Katherine DeBrassio! How are you?"

I mumble, "Fine," and stare down at my papers.

"We should arrange a time to sit down in private and properly catch up!" She says it way too cheerily, and it basically confirms my worst suspicions.

I had to talk with Ms. Chirazo when my mom died. Not because I needed to. I wasn't acting out in class or crying in public or anything like that. But Ms. Chirazo saw the obituary in the newspaper. She actually showed up to one of my classes with it clipped out and asked me in this weirdly calm voice, "Would you like to talk?" She wasn't even a guidance counselor at the middle school. She worked in the high school. But I guess grief is her specialty.

I told her, "Nope. I would not."

And then bitch made it a mandatory five sessions!

I know she loved it, getting to counsel a kid over the death of a parent. I'd come in and she'd be smiling like a kid on Christmas morning. Parental death is like catnip to a school counselor. That, abusive relationships, teen pregnancies, and eating disorders. I barely said more than two words to her at each of the sessions. At our last one she gave me all these grief workbooks and crap that I chucked in the Dumpster as soon as I was dismissed.

"Well, it looks like it's just us today," she says, turning her attention back to the room. "Hopefully, you'll spread the word to your friends and classmates about how valuable this resource is." She's about to close the door, but someone stops her.

Alex Lind.

He's wearing a pair of dark jeans, and a black-and-white-checked shirt underneath a hunter-green sweater. "Sorry I'm late." Even though there are plenty of empty chairs, he slides into the one next to me. "Looks like we're officially losers," he whispers and laughs.

"Speak for yourself," I say back. It comes out kind of bitchy, so I tack on a little smirk.

Not that I even care if he thinks I'm a bitch. I'm over him. Summer was a long time ago already.

Ms. Chirazo starts going off on her spiel, breaking down the college application process into three parts. The questionnaire, the recommendations, and the personal essay.

"Personal essay is the most important part. It's the only time you'll have a chance to show the admissions board who you are, explain what you're all about. It's your chance to stand out, to let them get to know you, and proactively address any aspects of your academic record that might not be up to snuff. This will be the primary focus of our time together. Since we're such a small group, why don't we partner up."

I feel Alex's eyes on me. I immediately turn in the opposite direction, toward Gary Rotini, who's sitting on my other side. Unfortunately, he's already partnered up with some chick from my gym class. I'm surprised she's here. Maybe they require you to fill out an application for beautician school.

Alex puts a hand on my shoulder and gives it a squeeze. "You're up, Kat. Tell me your deepest, darkest secrets."

I force a swallow. If Alex only knew what I've been up to this year, he'd never talk to me again. Again, not like I'd care.

"You couldn't handle it," I say.

"Then I'll go first."

"You're a vanilla wafer. Your boring-ass secrets will put me to sleep." I look around the room for someone else to pair up with.

Alex turns his seat so he's facing me. "Hey, I've got darkness in me. I'm no vanilla wafer."

I roll my eyes. "Prove it."

He looks over both his shoulders. "One time, when I was seven, I tried to make out with my babysitter when she put me to bed."

"Oh my God!"

"What? She was really pretty! Her hair smelled like cherry Slurpee."

I lean back in my chair. "Un-tell me that right now, pervert, or I'm never speaking to you again!"

He puts his head down on the table, embarrassed.

I reach out to ruffle his hair, but then think better of it and pull my hand back. I don't need to confuse things between us. I don't need to be flirting with Alex Lind, even though it is kind of fun. I can't let myself get sidetracked from my ultimate goal, which is to get the eff off Jar Island for good.

CHAPTER SEVEN

LILLIA

AFTER SCHOOL, ASH CALLED AND GUILT-TRIPPED ME into coming over to her house. She kept saying how we haven't had alone time in ages. Which is true—we haven't. I've barely seen her outside of cheering practice.

So imagine my surprise when I pulled into her driveway and saw Rennie's Jeep. I almost turned right around and drove back home, but I didn't want to hurt Ash's feelings. And, deep down, maybe I hoped that Rennie was in on it, that maybe she wanted to make up.

But when I rang the doorbell and she opened the door, she

looked like she wanted to slam it in my face. She didn't, but I could tell she wanted to.

Now here we are in Ash's rec room watching TV and doing our nails on the beanbag chairs she won't let her mother throw away. We had to come down here because her mother doesn't like the fumes; she says they give her migraines.

Ash is trying to get a conversation going, but nobody's really talking. We're all concentrating on our nails.

"Pass me the nail-polish remover," Rennie orders. Dutifully, Ashlin hands it over.

I'm painting my toenails mint green. Ash has the best colors of all of us. I'm on my second coat when Ash asks, "Have you guys started on your college apps yet?"

"Hardly," I say, unwrapping a fun-size Snickers I found in my purse. Even though she has the best nail-polish colors, Ash's house never has any good snacks. Her mom's on a gluten-free diet. "I'll probably spend every weekend until January first working on my personal statement."

Ash turns toward me. "Are you still applying to Boston College, Lil? 'Cause I'm thinking I might apply too, for my reach school. If I get in . . . roommates?"

"Duh!" I say. "Matching comforters and everything."

Ash is a total pig, and there's no way I would ever, ever room with her. Plus I doubt she'll get in. But I don't care, because Rennie's looking at us with narrow eyes.

Doesn't feel good to be the odd one out, does it, Ren?

Ashlin squeals and claps her hands together. "Yay! Would you want to live on campus or get an apartment off campus?"

This is too easy. "I think on campus, at least for the first year. That way we won't miss out on all the fun stuff. You know, late-night study sessions and, like, flirting with boys on our hall and ordering pizza at four in the morning. We'll want to have those experiences together, you know? Then we can move off campus sophomore year." Instantly I feel mean and petty and small for trying to make Rennie feel bad. I feel like . . . Rennie.

"What about you, Ren?" Ashlin asks. "Are you done with your application?"

"Yup. My app took me, like, two seconds."

I guess the Jar Island Community College application is extra easy. I wonder if she even had to write an essay. When Rennie used to talk about going to the community college, she was sour about it. She'd say how she was the only one that was going to be stuck here. But today she doesn't look sour at all. In fact she's practically humming to herself.

She's putting on top coat, her hair falling in her face, when she says, "There's no point in me even applying to a four-year college right now. Reeve and I won't know where he's going to play until his leg is healed, and he's talking to recruiters again."

I want to say, *Oh, and there's just the small matter of how your grades suck and you have no money for college*, but I bite my tongue.

"I'm going to do a semester at JICC and get straight As and transfer to wherever he's at."

Ashlin pipes up, "You and Reeve are so gonna get married. You pretty much saved his life by carrying him through this whole tragedy."

Tragedy? A tsunami devastating an entire village is a tragedy. Reeve is a jock who broke his leg. He'll be fine.

"He'd do the same thing for me," Rennie says, and I can't believe she can keep a straight face saying it. As if Reeve would lift a finger for anybody but himself! "Oh, and speaking of that, I'm not going to be at practice for the rest of this week. Reeve's got a few appointments off island to see a sports-medicine specialist." She smiles to herself, pleased. "He's getting his hard cast off tomorrow, right on schedule."

My head snaps up. "Why do you have to miss practice for that?"

Rennie ignores me and says, "Ash, can you be in charge?"

Ashlin casts an uneasy look my way. "Sure. Lil and I can do it together—right, Lil?"

Incredulously I ask, "Are you quitting the squad or something?"

"No, I'm not quitting the squad," Rennie snaps. "That's not what I said."

"Well, you have missed, like, three practices already," I say, and my voice shakes a little as I say it, because I'm scared. I'm actually calling her out on her BS for once.

Rennie's cheeks heat up. "When I signed on to rep Reeve's number, I signed on for the whole season. I'm not abandoning him now."

Ridiculous. Abruptly, I stand up. "I'm going to get a soda."

Rennie doesn't look at me as she says, "I'll have a Diet Coke, no ice." Like I'm a waitress and she's placing her order with me.

Ash gets up too. "I'll help you, Lil. I hid some ice cream behind my mom's soy pops. It might still be there if my dad didn't find it."

As soon as we're in the kitchen and out of earshot, I go into the fridge and grab two cans of Diet Coke and say, "I wish you'd told me Rennie was going to be here."

"But then you wouldn't have come," Ashlin whines.

"Exactly," I say.

Ash hops up on the kitchen island. "I hate that you guys aren't getting along. That's why I invited you both over here today."

I know she doesn't mean it. There's nothing Ash likes better than playing the middle. "It's not that we aren't getting along.

FIRE WITH FIRE

71

It's that Rennie's being a total bitch to me for something that's not even my fault."

Ash says, "I know she misses you."

Hope flickers in my chest. "Did she say that?" I ask.

"Not in so many words. But I can tell."

Hmph. I take a sip of soda. "Are she and Reeve, like, together now?"

"Basically," Ashlin says. "She's his ride-or-die chick, you know? I think the accident is what made him realize how much she's been there for him all these years."

"I'm happy for her," I say, and I mean it, I really do. If Rennie and Reeve are officially a thing now, maybe she'll finally get over what happened at homecoming and things can go back to how they were before. And at the very least, they deserve each other.

CHAPTER EIGHT

MARY

It's Monday afternoon and I'm in chemistry, working on a lab with my group. The two boys do most of the work, while another girl and I record the results in our notebooks. This arrangement is fine by me; I've never been so great at science. We're standing around the table, waiting for some concoction to come to a boil, when I overhear two junior girls talking behind me.

One girl whines, "I'm so ready to quit yearbook. All we've gotten to do is make photo collages of freshmen. That's not what I signed up for."

What I immediately think is: Yearbook is the sort of thing Kat was talking about! I have to put myself out there, find my own happiness. I've had a lot of good days, full days at school where I've seen Reeve and haven't gotten upset. And I've had no issues with, um, my issues.

Also, I *love* making photo collages.

I used to make them all the time, back when I was a kid. I'd never throw out a magazine unless I cut out the pretty pictures first. I'd spend hours arranging them like puzzle pieces; then I'd glue them to a piece of poster board and hang them up in my room. We didn't take them with us when we moved off Jar Island. I wasn't in any state to pack, obviously, so it was up to Mom and Dad. I wonder if they threw them out, or if they might still be in the garage someplace.

I draw circles in my notebook and keep listening.

"I know," the other girl says with a huff that makes the flame on her Bunsen burner flicker. "But we have to hang in there if we want a chance at editor-in-chief next year. You know how it is. So political."

Yearbook committee. There. I'm joining yearbook committee.

After class, I pack up my textbooks and head to guidance to ask where and when the yearbook meetings are held. I end up spotting a flyer stapled to the bulletin board outside the offices. It has a picture of a camera on it and the words *YEARBOOK IS A SNAP! MEETINGS EVERY MONDAY IN THE LIBRARY!*

Today is Monday. I feel lucky, like this is some kind of sweet serendipity. It'll be good, I think, to have a club to put down on my college applications next year. College apps are all Lillia and Kat talk about these days, and they've definitely got me thinking about the future. It's not that far off, honestly. Junior year is almost half over.

I need to start thinking about what I want to be when I grow up. My mom said she always knew she wanted to be an archivist, ever since she was a little girl and found a bunch of old Zane family papers tucked away in the attic. She cataloged them and put them into a special binder between layers of acid-free tissue paper. And this was when she was seven.

By that logic, I might be destined to be a veterinarian. It's what I've always wanted to be. One time, Montessori arranged a field trip to a zoo and I got to watch a vet give antibiotics to a sick baby penguin. It was amazing. After that I used to pretend with my stuffed animals, giving them shots and wrapping up their legs with bandages I found in our medicine cabinet.

I debate calling Aunt Bette to say that I'll be home late, but decide against it. I don't need her on my case about where I've been and what I'm doing. I swear, she starts up as soon as I come home from school.

I'm halfway across the courtyard when someone almost knocks me over.

Reeve.

I manage to step out of his way in the nick of time. Thank God he doesn't see me. Actually, he doesn't seem to notice any of the people darting out of his way as he catapults himself forward on his crutches. He's too busy growling into his cell phone, his forehead wrinkled and tense. He has the phone cradled between his ear and his shoulder, since he can't use his hands, not with his crutches.

Only one thing has improved—his big white leg cast is off. Now he's got a black Velcro thing. A soft cast, I think it's called.

I end up following him. Not on purpose. He's just walking in the same general direction that I am. Even though I give him a ton of space, I can still hear what he's saying into his cell phone.

"I keep telling the dude I can do *more*, Ren," he says passionately. "Yeah, well, if he can't get with our program today, he's fired. I'll take over my PT my damn self. I'm almost a week behind where I should be according to our schedule."

Reeve abruptly stops at the chain-link fence, the one that runs along the football field. Practice is underway. The team stands in a big circle at midfield, stretching out together, clapping on beat every time they switch positions. Alex is in the center. I wonder if he's the captain now.

None of the guys notice Reeve watching them. They don't see him standing there, and they don't notice when he walks away.

Don't feel bad for him, I tell myself. *Don't feel anything for him.*

Reeve slips off the path and heads toward the pool building. There's a guy standing near the door, an older man in a full windbreaker suit. I don't think he's a teacher here; I've never seen him before. He's got a clipboard with him and a duffel bag slung over his shoulder.

"Reeve. Hey, pal. You ready to get to work?"

After clapping Reeve on the back, the man tries to get the door for Reeve, hold it open for him. Reeve gives the guy a cold hard stare. "I'm *always* ready to work. Are you?"

The yearbook committee turns out to be a pretty popular club, especially for girls. I guess because if you're on yearbook committee, you can make sure no bad photos of you get put in. That is a bonus. The library is filled with people sitting in small clusters, working on their tasks. Some are sorting through contact sheets; some are working through page layouts; some are contemplating cover treatments and working out the costs per person.

There are a few boys here too. I get the sense that they're more into the technology aspect, because they've already claimed spots at the computers. The girls mostly stand behind them and point at where they want things to go.

I see the girls from chemistry, sharing a chair with frowns already on their faces, sorting through piles of color pictures. They point and laugh at some of them, making gross-out faces and snickering to each other. "Let's put in this one of Carrie sneezing," one girl says. I sort of hope these girls do quit. They're so mean. If I'm lucky enough to work on any collages, I'll make sure not to let any unflattering photos in of anyone. Even people I don't like.

It's intimidating, though, to see that everyone already has a set job. What's a newbie like me supposed to do? I lean against one of the library shelves near the back of the room and try to think of things I can say to the adviser, Mr. Kraus, when he arrives and the meeting officially gets started. I should probably introduce myself, maybe tell him about my collage experience, if I can even call it that. I wish I knew how to use some of the fancy school-owned digital cameras that kids are passing around the room, so I could help out with the photography, too. Maybe he'll offer lessons on that sort of thing.

A few more people trickle into the library after me. One of them is Nadia Cho. She's in her cheerleading practice clothes, and she hangs out near the door, like she won't be able to stay long.

I like Nadia. She looks sweet, like a young Lillia, but with bigger eyes and freckles.

I think about going up to her and saying hi, since we've never officially met each other. But then Rennie comes in behind her. Rennie's not in her cheering workout clothes. Oh my gosh. Has she quit the squad, now that Reeve isn't playing anymore? I could totally see her doing that.

Rennie wraps Nadia in a hug. It's a tender one and it lasts for a few long seconds, definitely longer than the ones I see girls give each other between classes. Rennie peels herself away a bit and fusses with Nadia's bangs while she tells her something I can't hear. Nadia smiles up at Rennie and nods pertly. She hands Rennie a memory stick and bounds out the door.

At the stables, Lillia mentioned to Kat and me how weird and tense things have been between her and Rennie since homecoming. I bite my lower lip. It worries me to see Nadia being so chummy-chummy with Rennie. She's not a good influence. Not at all. Plus Lillia is Nadia's big sister. Nadia should be loyal to her, not to Rennie.

Mr. Kraus comes into the room. He's an art teacher, so it

makes total sense that yearbook is one of his responsibilities. "All right, everyone! Listen up!" The room quiets, but only a little bit. Most people keep talking. "We need the home-coming spread done this week, as well as foreign language clubs and fall sports." He scans the room briefly. "If you're new today, find someone and help them with their project." Then he disappears into his office and closes the door.

Oh. Okay.

So it looks like yearbook is pretty much left up to the students.

I meander my way over to some girls who are uploading photos directly from the cameras, hoping I might pick up some pointers. I end up within earshot of Rennie. She's working on the homecoming spread with another girl.

"We got more homecoming pictures today," Rennie says, handing her the memory stick.

The other girl keeps her eyes on the computer screen. "I doubt we'll need them. You've collected, like, more home-coming photos than senior pictures. It's only a one-page spread."

"We want to make sure we get the perfect shot," Rennie insists, her voice sharp.

"I think I have," says the girl, with a smile. She clicks the mouse, and a picture of Lillia and Reeve pops up on the computer screen. Them dancing onstage. Him holding her tight, gazing at her with a big grin. Before he saw me. Before I went . . . crazy.

I force myself to look away.

The girl taps the screen with her pencil tip and says, "I say we build the entire page around this shot."

Rennie shakes her head, takes over the computer mouse, and clicks onto another picture. One of the entire homecoming court. "This one is better. But, really, we should wait until we get all the pictures in before we make the final choice. We've got to be thorough."

"But the photo you want doesn't show who won king and queen!"

Rennie spins to face the girl. "Are you kidding me? The picture you want is going to make everyone remember the accident, okay? It's going to be a *trigger*." For the first time, I agree with Rennie. Actually, I wish they'd skip that page all together. "Not to mention that it's completely disrespectful to Reeve."

Defiant, the girl says, "We've always featured at least one picture of just the king and queen in the yearbook."

Rennie shoots her a nasty look and then softens her tone. She crooks her finger at the girl, wanting her to lean in close. "Look, I didn't want to say anything because it's on the DL, but the homecoming queen title is still somewhat in dispute. Coach

Christy is considering a possible recount. So let's not settle on a photo until we know for sure, all right?"

The girl nods, her eyes wide. "Okay," she whispers back. "That's a different story."

I get a squeeze in my chest. Could Coach Christy somehow figure out that Kat and I snuck into her office to mess with the homecoming ballots? I shake my head. Nope. No way. We were careful. We didn't leave a trace.

I take a seat near a group of students voting over which superlatives categories to include this year. Best-looking, most popular, nicest eyes, most athletic. I force myself to think of a different boy, a boy who isn't Reeve, for each one.

After the meeting, I'm heading home when I hear a shrill whistle coming from the school pool. Is Reeve still there? Even though I know it's probably not the best idea, I can't help but be curious. How much is Reeve improving? Is there a chance for him to maybe get those football scholarships after all?

I sneak in and watch him. Reeve's in the water in his swim trunks. His big black soft cast is up on the bleachers. The man is sitting up on the side of the pool, his legs dangling in the water. He's not in a swimsuit. He has his track pants rolled up to his knees.

"All right, Reeve, now I want you to hold on to the side here and kick your legs frog-style for fifteen-second intervals for the next three minutes." He puts his coaching whistle back in his mouth. "Set . . ."

Reeve lets out a groan.

"Unless you can't do it," the man adds, teasingly.

And Reeve loses it. He snaps, "Of course I can do it. That's not the issue."

"Then what is?"

Reeve seethes, "The issue is, I can do it for sixty-second intervals."

"So?"

"So why aren't we in the gym, putting me on the treadmill?"

The man blinks a few times. "You're not ready for the gym yet, buddy. That's why you're in a soft cast, not a walking cast. You've been pushing yourself too hard as it is. "

"You don't know that. You haven't even tried to push me. Trust me. I can be doing so much more than I am right now."

The man shakes his head. "Son, you need to accept your injury, not fight it. It's going to take time to heal."

Reeve pulls himself half out of the water. Even though he's dripping wet and shivering, his cheeks are bright, fiery red. "I found this article online about a guy who broke his fibula and five weeks after, he was running seven-minute miles. That's the kind of 'Eye of the Tiger' I need you to have. That's the level I want you to push me."

The man sighs. "Reeve, look. There's no way you're getting back on the football field this season. I want you to get that out of your head."

Reeve tightens every single muscle. "I know that! I know I'm not playing this season. But college camps start in February, man. I need to be able to hold my own. If I don't play football, then I don't go to college. End of story. It's a wrap."

The guy calmly puts his clipboard down and folds his hands in his lap. "It's a process, Reeve. One step at a time. If you get there, you get there. But you need to prepare yourself for the *if*."

Reeve recoils at the word, and then shakes his head, like he's trying to forget he ever heard it. "You know what? I'm going to do this on my own."

"Reeve—"

"Did you not hear me? You're fired. Your services aren't needed." Reeve hoists himself out of the water. He tries to put a little weight on his leg, but can't. So he ends up hopping over to his towel. Under his breath he mutters a few curse words.

The physical therapist shakes his head and packs up his stuff. He walks out of the pool, right past me in the hallway.

Reeve sits on the bench a while longer, dripping puddles of

water on the concrete floor. I'm thinking he'll pack it in and head home, but instead he slides back into the water and assumes the position at the shallow end. He does the exercise he was told to do, the frog kicks, but without stopping for a full minute. And then he does that five more times.

It's crazy, how similar we are. Here's both of us, working through our stuff, trying to make something positive out of something really bad.

CHAPTER NINE

LILLIA

TRICK-OR-TREATING ON THE ISLAND ISN'T REALLY a thing; there are too many dead spots—vacation houses that are empty all fall and winter. So the elementary school has an "alternative Halloween" that they call Fall Fest. After school, the kids go home, change into their costumes, and come back to find the entire school decked out all spookily. There are a bunch of fun Halloweeny activities, like apple bobbing and face painting and a candy scavenger hunt. Officially, the elementary school PTA runs it, but there's always a senior liaison who is basically in charge of finding high schoolers to man booths and drum up support. This year it's me. Rennie was supposed to cochair with me, but once actual planning meetings started, she bailed.

It's Friday, and we're at the lunch table, and Ashlin's begging Rennie to tell her what her costume is. "Come on, Ren!" Ash wheedles. "I told you mine."

Rennie shakes her head smugly. "You have to wait and see."

I stir my frozen yogurt around with a spoon. I'm too stressed out about organizing Fall Fest to be hungry. I've got my to-do list out, and there are still a bunch of to-dos not ticked off. I have today, the weekend, and then two days next week to get everything set. I'm still waiting to hear back on how many cupcakes Milky Morning is going to donate. And Sutton's might not donate as much candy this year, so I need a backup plan if they don't come through.

But my biggest problem right now is that I don't have enough booth coverage. I got Nadia and her friends to do the scavenger hunt, and I got the drama kids to do a campfire story hour, but I still need judges for the costume contest.

And then there's the face-painting booth.

Ever since freshman year, Rennie and I have manned the face-painting booth. We'd paint butterflies and stars and tiger stripes on the little kids' faces. It was our thing. I think it will be a perfect opportunity for us to talk, away from Ashlin and Reeve and everybody else. Just me and Rennie, like it used to be.

I take a deep breath and say to her, "We're still doing the face-painting booth, right?"

Rennie scrunches her face up. "I don't think I can. Sorry." Except she doesn't look sorry.

"That's okay," I say, trying not to sound disappointed. I shouldn't have gotten my hopes up.

"I need time to get into my costume. Fall Fest is at what, five? And over at eight? There won't be enough time, even if I rush home after school." Rennie shrugs. "Plus, some of us are going to pregame at Ash's before we head over to the haunted maze."

What? Everybody's pregaming at Ashlin's and nobody told me about it? I whip my head around to look at Ash, who's suddenly preoccupied with her salad. "Does this mean you can't do the dunk booth with Derek?" I demand.

Her hair hanging in her face, she says softly, "No . . . sorry, Lil. Ren scored some spicy rum from her job, and she found this yum cocktail we can make with it and apple cider. You should come too!"

"How am I going to do that?" I cry out. "I'm supposed to run this thing, and you guys said you'd help me!"

"I'm so, so sorry," Ashlin says, her eyes fluttery and regretful.

From the end of the table Alex says, "Lil, I'll be there."

"Thanks, Alex," I say. In a louder voice I say, "It's nice to know that I can count on somebody."

Ashlin pouts at me. "Forgive me, Lil."

Under his breath, Reeve mutters, "What are you apologizing for? If you can't do it, you can't do it."

I cast a spiteful look in Reeve's direction. For the past three years he's come to Fall Fest dressed up like Jason in *Friday the 13th*. Back when we were freshmen the senior girls asked him to do it, and it became kind of a Jar Island tradition. Reeve wears a white hockey mask and chases the kids around with a chain saw. The kids *love* it. They love him. I've asked him repeatedly, but he won't do it. Fine, he is on crutches, but he could at least show up in the costume.

"If Fall Fest sucks this year, it's on us," I warn.

"You mean it's on you," Reeve corrects me.

I glare at him. "It's on all of us. Including and especially you. You know how much the kids love your Jason routine. I don't get why you can't at least—"

"What's not to get?" Reeve snaps, pointing at his crutches.

"How is he supposed to run around the gym chasing after kids on crutches?" Rennie asks, and then lets out a groan. "I mean, hello!"

In a shaky voice I protest, "He exercises, like, every day!"

Rennie leans over Reeve to say, "Yeah, in the pool and in the weight room! He can't put weight on his leg, Lillia. Don't talk about things you don't understand."

Reeve puts his hand on Rennie's shoulder and she relaxes back in her seat, shaking her head in disgust. Then she turns away from me and starts talking about her costume again.

That's when it hits me. Rennie did this on purpose. She made it so no one would help me, so I'd be all alone. She convinced Ashlin to have people over when she knew I couldn't make it.

I finally understand what's been staring me in the face. It's not that Rennie's mad at me. It's that she doesn't want to be my friend anymore. She is officially through with me. And if Rennie's through with me, she's going to make damn sure that everybody else is too. How many times have I seen her do this exact same thing? Edge somebody out of the group because they pissed her off in some way? I've seen it happen, and I've stood by and said nothing, because I was afraid, and it was easy. Never ever did I think it would be me on the receiving end.

Alex is looking around the table in disbelief. "Are you guys serious? We can't help Lil out for one night?" When nobody answers, he tosses his fork down on his tray. "You guys suck. Lil, what can I do? Tell me what you need."

Keeping my head down, I gather my stuff together as quickly as possible. Quietly I say to Alex, "If you have time this

JENNY HAN AND SIOBHAN VIVIAN

weekend, will you come over and help me put some candy bags together for the prizes?"

Alex nods. "I'll come over tonight, straight from practice." He says it really loud, and gives everyone else a look. He turns back to me and grins. "But don't worry, I'll shower first."

It takes a lot of effort to smile back, but I do. "You better," I say.

Then I sneak out to the parking lot and cry in my car. So this is how it all ends, after everything Rennie and I have been through.

Nadia, Alex, and I have an assembly line set up in the dining room. Nadia is Reese's Peanut Butter Cups and Sour Patch Kids and Snickers; Alex is FireBalls, Lemonheads, and Starbursts; I'm Nerds and lollipops, plus I tie the ribbon onto the bag in a bow. It's the most boring Friday night ever, but I couldn't be happier this task is getting done.

I hold one up for inspection. "Does this one seem a little light on sweets to you?"

"Alex didn't put enough FireBalls in," Nadia tattletales.

"Snitch," he says, poking her in the side. "It's fine. I'm doing the kid a favor, less cavities. Besides, you already tied the ribbon, Lil."

"Yeah, I know." I bite my lip, weighing the bag in my hand.

"I don't want the kids to feel cheated out of anything."

"Maybe we should open up the Starburst packs to make the bags look fuller," Nadia suggests.

I clap my hands together. "Perfect!"

Alex gives her a high five and Nadia grins at both of us.

"Alex, you be in charge of that," I tell him, and he salutes me.

"Oh, I talked to my mom, and she said she was going to call Joy tonight," Alex says, carefully opening up a candy bag. His hair is still wet from his shower. He really did come right over.

"Who's Joy?" Nadia wants to know.

"She's one of the owners of Milky Morning," Alex tells her. "My mom knows her from book club. She says she can get her to donate as many cupcakes as you need." He hands me another bag.

Suddenly I'm feeling so much gratitude and love and friendship for Alex, I can't even. I don't know what I would have done without him today. "You're the best, Lindy," I say.

Alex gives an embarrassed shrug and says, "It's nothing." He points at me. "Hey, you're slowing down the assembly line."

After he leaves, Nadia helps me clean up and pack away the leftover candy. She doesn't look at me when she says, "Alex likes you, you know."

I open my mouth to deny it, but I stop myself. I can't lie to Nadi, but I don't know what the truth is anymore. So all I say is, "We're friends."

Nadia makes a show of rolling her eyes at me. "So do you?"

"Do I what?"

"Do you like him?" The expression on her face—a little bit plaintive, but mostly trying not to care. It breaks my heart.

"Do *you*?" I ask her.

There's a pause, I can see her thinking this over. "No," she tells me. "He's—nice. He's so nice. But I don't like him like that anymore. I did. For maybe a second."

I reach out and touch Nadi's hair. It's soft, like a baby's. She lets me for a second before shrugging away. She says, "Be nice to him, okay? Don't hurt him."

"I won't," I say. In my head I add, *not again*. That's a promise.

CHAPTER TEN

TODAY, WHEN WE RAN INTO EACH OTHER IN THE HALL, Lillia mentioned how she'd asked some of her guy friends if they could help her sort through the sound equipment and drive it over to the elementary school. It's for her Fall Festival night, the event she's running for the elementary school kids. But they all had practice.

"And of course Reeve pretended like he didn't even hear me."

I shook my head knowingly. "Of course he did."

Lillia looked ready to cry. "It's going to take me forever to load up my Audi by myself."

"Lil! I'll totally help you."

Lillia's whole face brightened up. "Thank you so much, Mary."

So now I'm scurrying over to the side entrance by the theater. I'm not very strong, but with two of us it should go a little bit faster anyway.

Instead of fighting the after-school rush inside, I cut across the back parking lot—which is when I see Alex's SUV parked by the side door right behind Lillia's Audi. He's already there, taking boxes out of her trunk and loading them into his. The back door is open, and Lillia comes out the door, wearing an ivory-colored coat and a long scarf around her neck, struggling with a big cardboard box. Alex rushes over to help her.

"Alex!" she says, looking up. "Oh my gosh."

I hang back and watch.

Alex takes the box out of her hands. "Here, Lil. You don't want to get your coat dirty."

"I've got it," she insists, and he tries to take it from her, and they both laugh because she almost drops it. "You have to get to practice."

"Give it to me," he says, but in a sweet way. Lillia finally lets the box go. I think Alex is surprised at how heavy it is. It almost falls out of his hands, but he adjusts his grip before it can.

Meanwhile, Lillia scans the parking lot. I step forward

and smile, but she waves her hand, like I don't have to worry about it.

"Thank you," she says breathlessly, when Alex lifts his head. "There are only three more inside." She turns to go back into the theater door, but Alex stops her.

"Wait here. I'll get them."

Lillia leans against the car. The wind has picked up, and her hair is blowing around her face. "I owe you one, Lindy!" she calls out. "Thank you so much!"

I start to back away, and that's when I notice it—about fifteen feet away to my left, Reeve, pulling up in his truck. He's seen them too. He has a scowl on his face, and he puts the truck in reverse. He's gone before they even notice.

When I get home, Aunt Bette's Volvo isn't in the driveway. And I hate to say it, but it's kind of a relief.

I wish I could tell someone about how strangely Aunt Bette's been acting. I've been meaning to have a conversation about her with my parents, but it's scary. My mom is Aunt Bette's sister, after all. I don't want to get her mad, or have her confronting Aunt Bette over what I'd say. I'm just . . . worried about her.

I set my book bag down in the kitchen and head upstairs, calling her name a few times in case she's home. She's so easily startled lately. I've been trying to be careful with her, give her space. I don't want to make things worse.

At the top of the stairs, I notice Aunt Bette's bedroom door is open the skinniest crack. She's been keeping it closed. I walk up slowly and peek inside.

There are books all over the floor. At least a hundred of them, piled in teetering stacks on top of Aunt Bette's Moroccan rug. Musty, cloth-covered books. The kind that sit and gather dust at the library. The kind that you find at a garage sale.

I step inside, careful not to touch anything, because I have a pretty good feeling that Aunt Bette would lose her mind if she knew I was poking around her room. I crouch down and try to read some of the spines, but most of the titles aren't written in English. It looks like maybe Latin. And some Spanish, which reminds me that I am so far behind in Señor Tremont's class it's not even funny. There are a few books split open, but to pages that don't have any words. Only, like, hieroglyphics. Symbols and numbers that make no sense to me.

Aunt Bette's Volvo putters into the driveway. I jump up and turn to head out the bedroom door. That's when I notice the shared wall that separates Aunt's Bette's bedroom from mine. The one to the right of her bed.

It used to be a wall full of art. Pictures. Paintings. Photographs. But everything's been taken down, except for the tiny nails left in the wall. Even Aunt Bette's dresser, the low four-drawer one that sat against the wall, has been pushed aside.

The whole thing is stripped bare.

Or at least I think it is. But when I take a step closer, I see that Aunt Bette has laced string, string the very same color as the eggshell wall paint, around the picture nails. I think it might even be the same stuff she used to wrap those smudge bundles. She's woven them into some kind of pattern. Like a lopsided, crooked star.

The same star that's in one of the pages of her opened books.

Oh God. What's going on?

I dart out of her bedroom and into my own. Aunt Bette opens the back door and calls for me.

"Up here!" I say in a voice that I hope sounds normal. Then I pray she won't come upstairs. Thankfully, she doesn't. I hear the faucet come on, probably for her teakettle.

I take careful steps over to my bed and sit on the mattress. It's pushed up against that shared wall. I reach out and touch it, feeling for I don't know what. Energy. Heat. Something coming through from the other side.

Has Aunt Bette been putting spells on me?

I don't think she'd try to hurt me, but I can't say I feel totally safe. Especially when I don't know how long that thing in her room has been up. And what it might be doing to me.

But there's nothing coming through, nothing to feel besides a wall. A plain old wall.

Of course. What else would it be?

I guess when you live with a crazy person, it's hard not to feel crazy sometimes too.

CHAPTER ELEVEN

LILLIA

HALLOWEEN NIGHT IS BEAUTIFUL. CLEAR SKY, NOT too cold, and a big full moon.

Kids are starting to file in with their parents, and my heart is thrumming in my chest. I'm standing by the entrance in my ballerina costume, greeting people and passing out raffle tickets. I'm wearing a pink leotard that crosses in the back and a tutu on top, with sheer pink tights and pink ballet slippers with ribbons that wind up my legs. My bun is so high and tight it's pulling on my scalp, but I don't dare mess with it because it took me forever to get it right.

Alex walks in, and he's got on black framed glasses and a button-down and khakis.

"What are you?" I ask him. "A nerd?"

Alex wags his finger at me, and then he rips open his shirt with a flourish, and underneath is a Superman tee. "Clark Kent, at your service!"

I laugh and clap my hands. Alex used to wear glasses, but he never does anymore. I like him all geek chic like this. "Alex, you're my hero," I say. Then I point him in the direction of the apple-bobbing booth and he takes off.

The kids look so cute in their costumes. There are a few Iron Mans, a Harry Potter, a little boy who is dressed up as a chef, a girl who is a bottle of ketchup. My favorite is three boys dressed up as Snap, Crackle, and Pop from the Rice Krispies cereal box. I'm totally giving them the costume award.

My sister and her friends are setting up the scavenger hunt, hiding clues around the gym. They're Santa's reindeer—Nadia is Vixen, and she's got on antlers and a fur shawl of our mom's that she never wears and crimson-red lipstick. Alex is dropping more apples into the apple-bobbing pail.

I'm by the food table arranging candy-corn cupcakes on a big black tray when I see him—Reeve, swinging in on his crutches and his soft cast. He's wearing a flannel shirt and his Jason mask and has a chain saw strapped to his back.

I can't believe it. I can't believe he showed.

I watch as Reeve sets up a folding chair for himself under the basketball net. He drags another chair over, plops down, and props his leg up on the second chair. A bunch of kids run over to him. "Reeve!" they shriek. "Chase us!"

Reeve shakes his chain saw at them menacingly. But he doesn't chase them. He can't. I watch the kids collectively deflate when they realize this, and they walk away to the other booths, and then Reeve's just sitting there alone. He looks bummed out, marooned in his chair. All alone.

I can feel a little lump in my throat. I basically harassed him into coming, and now he doesn't have anything to do. I head over, making a show of stopping and checking on the sound system along the way, so it doesn't look like I'm coming over just to say hi.

I stop in front of him. "Hey," I say.

"Hey," Reeve grunts from behind his mask.

I clear my throat. "Um, so . . . I feel bad I made you come when you can't really do anything."

"Which is what I tried to explain to you in the first place," he says, pushing his mask on top of his head.

"I know."

"How am I supposed to run around with the kids here and

then go to a freaking maze with you guys?" Reeve huffs. "My leg should be elevated pretty much at all times."

"I know," I say again.

We stare at each other for a second. And then he says, "Nice costume."

I wait for him to make a crack, maybe ask me where my tiara is, but he doesn't. He reaches out and touches my tutu. I can feel my insides heat up.

Then Alex comes up behind me and Reeve's arm drops. "Hey, man," Alex says.

"Hey," he says.

"It was decent of you to show," Alex says with a nod. To me Alex says, "Lil, if you want, I can trade jobs with Reeve since he can't run around. I don't mind. Reeve, for the apple-bobbing station all you have to do is sit there."

Reeve stares at him in disbelief. "Jason is *my* thing."

"I know, man, but the kids want you to chase them around. It's not scary if you wave the chain saw at them from your chair. . . ." Alex's voice trails off, and he looks at me like he's hoping I'll back him up.

Before I can say anything, Reeve rips the mask off his head and tosses it at Alex. "Here, take it, then. Have at it. You won't do as good a job as me, but whatever." Jerkily, he gets up on his crutches. "Go show off for your girl."

Alex's face goes red, and I look around the room, pretending like I didn't hear him.

Reeve stalks off, and at first I think he's leaving, but he's not; he's moving toward the apple-bobbing booth. Alex leans in to me and whispers, "I think maybe Reeve's still channeling Jason."

I let out a guilty giggle. "Thanks for everything, Lindy."

Alex puts on the Jason mask. "You're welcome," he says in a creepy serial-killer voice.

I laugh again, for real this time. Then I walk back over to the refreshment table and set out the spider cookies I baked the night before. I arrange it so the good ones are on top and the broken ones are underneath.

This has actually turned out okay. The kids are having fun, the booths are more or less running themselves, and some of the parents stayed behind to help chaperone, so it's not just me in charge. I'll be able to put this on my college application with pride. And the best part is, I did it without Rennie.

I watch Alex chase a group of girls with the chain saw. He almost trips but catches himself. Across the room I can hear Reeve's guffaw. It echoes throughout the gym.

I bite a piece of candy off my candy bracelet. In an hour

and a half it'll all be over. I wasn't going to go to the haunted maze because I didn't want to see Rennie, but now I think I *will* go. I have as much right to be there as she does. They're my friends too. Look how Reeve and Alex showed up for me tonight. They're not in her pocket as much as she thinks.

CHAPTER TWELVE

MARY

I don't think I ever understood the power of a Halloween costume before tonight. Probably because I never had a very good one.

When I was a kid, my mom made my costumes herself. Other kids would buy theirs at the drugstore, the kind that came with a mask and a plastic suit to put on over your clothes. Those kids would run around, breaking sticks as Superman or shooting pretend webs out of their wrists like Spider-Man.

Mom wouldn't allow it. "There's no creativity in that," she'd say.

Really, she wanted to make them herself because my grandmother had made costumes for Mom and Aunt Bette when they were little. My grandmother was a very accomplished seamstress. We still have a bunch of her quilts in the attic in a cedar chest. It's crazy to know that something so perfect could be made by hand. Mom liked that tradition. "When you grow up and have a little boy or a little girl, you'll do the same for them," she'd tell me, usually with tears in her eyes.

It was hard to argue with that.

So at the beginning of every October I'd tell Mom what I wanted to be for Halloween that year—a princess, a gypsy, a bat. We'd draw up plans together with colored pencils, and then we'd go to the fabric store to get supplies.

The only problem was that Mom wasn't very good at sewing. In fact Halloween was the only time of year when she'd take her sewing machine out of the box. She'd taken a class in high school, but that was about it. And though the whole thing started out as a fun endeavor, by the week before Halloween she'd be upstairs in the attic, working through the night. Usually she had to go back to the fabric store a few times because she'd cut the material wrong or run out of supplies because she kept starting over.

The end result was never what I'd imagined. The seams were always off. Some places the thing would fit me tight;

some places it would be too loose. Lots of times it wasn't clear what I was supposed to be. Like my dragon costume. People thought I was some kind of beanstalk. I never had that feeling of actually becoming someone else.

Not like tonight.

I was so happy when Kat invited me out with her. I was already having nightmares of having to spend the night in complete darkness, not answering the door, because Aunt Bette didn't buy candy for the trick-or-treaters.

So I'm in the bathroom, putting the finishing touches on my costume, which means adding as many safety pins as I can before Kat pulls up and beeps the horn for me.

I went through an old trunk in the attic, full of Aunt Bette's things. Inside, there was a pair of skinny leather pants. The tag was for an Italian brand, I bet from when she was twenty-one and living in Milan. She had a great pair of black stiletto heels, too, and a tight, lacy tank. Everything fit perfectly. All dressed up, I looked like a hot biker chick.

I teased out my hair so it looked wild and dramatic, and used a crimper that was underneath the sink in our guest bathroom to add a few wavy sections. I braided a few strands and clipped in some fake pink streaks.

Last I put on heavy eye makeup from Aunt Bette's vanity. Black eyeliner, sparkly shadow, and layers and layers of mascara. I'll probably need to borrow some turpentine from Aunt Bette to get it off.

I stand in front of the mirror. I don't look like Mary tonight. I don't even feel like Mary tonight, if that makes any sense. Everything's completely, utterly different. I feel lit up from the inside. I feel . . . alive.

When I turn around, Aunt Bette is behind me.

I gasp. "How . . . how long were you standing there?"

"Not more than a minute," Aunt Bette says. "I didn't mean to frighten you." She cocks her head and then takes a step toward me. With a shaky hand she reaches out and touches the leather. "My pants."

I look down and realize that I didn't ask her permission for borrowing her clothes. I say, "I'm sorry. I should have asked first. I can take all this off if you mind."

"It's not that, it's not that . . ."

"Don't worry. I won't take candy from strangers. Unless they've got Kit Kats."

Aunt Bette doesn't even crack a smile at my joke. Instead she says dazedly, "The line between the living and the dead is blurred on Halloween."

I nod, as if I'm taking her seriously, but what I really think is . . . Aunt Bette needs to quit reading those weird books. She sounds like a witch! And she's been looking more and more like one too. Her hair is so crazy and wiry, her eyes sunken and dark. If I were a trick-or-treater and she came to the door, I'd probably run. It's crazy, to think she was once a cool, fun girl who'd wear leather pants from Italy.

It's a mean thought, and I immediately feel bad for thinking it. Aunt Bette's so lonely; her life is so sad. She never visits with friends or gets a night away from the house.

She's like how I used to be.

That's when I wonder . . . did something happen to Aunt Bette? Something traumatic that I don't know about, that made her into this person? Maybe it was a fight with my mom? Maybe she never wanted us to leave Jar Island?

I don't know what it is, but I step forward and I hug her. I haven't done that once since coming back here. Aunt Bette has never been big on physical displays of affection, but that doesn't mean she doesn't need one every so often.

Her whole body goes rigid. She's so alone, who knows the last time she got a hug from anyone? "It's all right, Aunt Bette," I say, and then Aunt Bette melts, her head drops, and I feel her squeeze me back, tenderly. I can see in the mirror that her eyes are closed.

Kat's car horn sounds from outside. I peel away from Aunt Bette and tell her, "Love you. Don't wait up!" before bounding down the stairs.

"Holy shit. Look at you!" Kat says, flicking her cigarette butt out of the driver's-side window.

"I guess we're opposites tonight," I say with a laugh as I climb into her car, because Kat's got a nun's outfit on. It's a full habit that covers everything but her hands and her face, and a heavy wooden cross around her neck. Kat isn't wearing any makeup. I've never noticed before, but she has amazing skin and a couple of teeny-tiny freckles.

"I'm an evil nun," she clarifies. She twists in her seat and looks me up and down. "You look hot, girl."

"I do?" I feel like clapping like a little kid, but I restrain myself.

Kat gives me a look like I'm crazy. "Hell, yeah, you do. Good thing Sister DeBrassio brought you a chastity belt."

I stick my tongue out, buckle my seat belt, and crank Kat's car radio up as loud as it will go. She's got a wild band on, and I start thrashing my head around, rocking in my seat.

"Dear Lord, please shine your light down on this clunker and keep it running tonight." Kat makes the sign of the cross, lights herself a new cigarette, and then peels out so fast her tires squeal and smoke. "It's still early," she yells above the music. "Let's stop by my friend Ricky's house and bum some of his booze before we go to the maze."

I nod and keep dancing. I've never hung out with anyone

besides Kat and Lillia since I came back here. And I've never drunk before, not even one sip. I can tell it's going to be a crazy night. Not bad crazy, either, thank goodness. Crazy wonderful.

I'm sitting on the couch in this guy Ricky's basement. It's dark and smoky, and the TV is on. It's some horror movie. I've got a beer in my hand, but I'm not drinking it. It smells funny, like yeast.

Next to me, Kat is straddling the sofa armrest, swigging from her beer till the last drop. "I'm out," she announces. "Ricky, help me bring down some more beers." She leans in close to me and whispers, "He's cute, right?"

I nod. Ricky has these sparkly brown eyes and thick black lashes. "Very."

"Why did I ever waste time with a tool like Alex Lind?"

I'm not sure if I'm supposed to answer her question. Alex and Ricky are very different guys. I come up with *Alex Lind seems nice*, but before I have a chance to say it, Kat and Ricky head up the stairs. I watch them go, and then turn back to Kat's brother, Pat, who's watching them too. He's in a grim-reaper costume, sprawled out on a La-Z-Boy, a glass bong between his legs.

I hope Kat comes back soon. I feel out of place and kind of

awkward here, and the excitement I felt earlier on is starting to fade away. On the couch with me there's a guy wearing a monster mask, and he's breathing heavily through the rubber.

I turn and watch the TV. A guy is chasing a girl with an ax, and when he finally catches up to her, I can't help but let out a shriek. Kat's brother finally looks away from the stairs and laughs. "You scared?" he asks me.

"I don't like horror movies," I say, holding the beer bottle to my lips but not actually drinking.

"How do you know Kat?" Pat asks me.

"Um, we're friends from school."

"I thought Kat didn't have any friends at school," the guy in the monster mask says, and Pat snickers.

"She does," I say, annoyed. "She has me."

Pat's grin slips away and he gives me a look, one of respect. He holds up his bong. "You want a hit, Mary?"

I shake my head. "Oh, no, thank you," I say. The guy in the monster mask snorts. I worry for a second he's laughing at me, because I sounded too polite and straightlaced for Pat's weed-smoking invitation.

Then I realize he's just watching the movie, the girl getting chopped in half. I'm about to cover my eyes when I notice how fake it all looks. The blood like ketchup, the guts like spaghetti. I laugh too.

There wasn't a haunted maze when I used to live on the island. It started after I moved away. The same entertainment company that puts on the carnival in the summertime runs it. They've leased a big field on the rural side of T-Town, where some people still have farms.

"Well, that blows," Kat says, when a parking attendant waves us away from the entrance. The lot is full. We have to drive about six blocks before we can find an open spot. The maze opens two weeks before Halloween, but according to Kat, most people wait until tonight to go.

Kat and I walk together. There are a ton of people out, either walking toward the maze or heading back to their cars. Absolutely everyone's in costume. There's a lot of energy. The closer we get to the maze, the more screaming you hear coming from inside it.

The maze is as big as a football field. They make the whole thing out of hay bales, stacking them ten feet high so you can't see over the tops. The company set up a few big stadium lights so people won't trip over each other, but there aren't enough to light the place up. There's a PA system that's playing spooky organ music. We're not even inside yet and there are already people in scary costumes wandering around trying to freak people out.

I link my arm through Kat's. She feels strong and solid next to me. "I'm scared!"

Kat looks at me with a surprised smile. "You stick with me, kid," she says, patting me on my head.

We get in line. You have to sign a waiver to enter the maze, promising you won't sue if you have a heart attack.

"I wonder what kind of costume Alex is wearing," Kat says, out of the blue. I shrug my shoulders. "Probably something lame."

"I hope Lillia's thing with the kids went okay," I say.

"I'm sure it was fine. Cho's as type A as they come. I guarantee she didn't leave anything to chance."

"Maybe we'll see her tonight. Maybe she'll want to hang out with us. You know, if Rennie's still being mean to her."

"Yeah," Kat says, but she sounds doubtful. I don't know why. I feel like Lillia's made a real effort to stay friends with us. Way more than I expected back in September.

"I'm sure she'll at least say hi," I say, and knock into her playfully. Then I feel a tap on my shoulder. I spin around and come face-to-face with a cute boy. Well, at least I think he's cute, based on what I can see through his mummy bandages.

"Hey," he says to me, "aren't you in my English class?"

"I don't think so."

He rubs his chin and looks at me skeptically, like I might be lying to him. "You sure? I could have sworn that you were."

I shake my head. "I have Mrs. Dockerty, third period."

He frowns. "Oh. I've got Mr. Frissel."

"Honest mistake!" I chirp, and turn back around. Kat's moved a few steps ahead in the line, so I hurry to catch up with her.

Kat cocks her head toward me. "Why didn't you keep talking to him? Go back and give him your digits!"

I shake my head. "He thought I was someone else."

Kat looks at me, slack jaw. "He was flirting with you, dummy! That English class garbage was the icebreaker, the opening line to get a convo going. Hello!"

"What?" I turn around and the mummy boy is standing in a circle of his friends, looking at me, but his eyes quickly go to the ground. I spin back to Kat and whisper, "Oh my gosh!"

Kat laughs. "Innocent little Mary. Do you see what I've been talking about now? You've gotta put yourself out there more. Who knows? You could have a boyfriend by Christmas."

The thought makes me warm inside. Me? A boyfriend?

"You need to quit with this whole meek routine. This bumbling shy shit. You're not twelve years old anymore. You're seventeen!" Her eyes go to my chest. "Look. You've got boobs. And guys love boobs!"

"Quit it!" I say, laughing, and wrap my arms around myself.

Kat shakes her head. "I won't quit it. Own the fact that you're a smoking hot girl who any guy would want." I open my mouth to say something like *No guys want me!*, but Kat shoots me a look, so I keep my mouth shut.

But really. They don't. At least they never have before.

Or maybe it's that I've never even tried to get a boy to notice me. A boy who wasn't Reeve Tabatsky.

It takes me until we reach the front of the line to work up the courage to glance over at mummy boy again. He's still looking at me, and this time he doesn't play it off like he's not. He gives me a sweet smile.

I manage to give him one back before I totally lose my nerve.

But it's something!

There are two huge strobe lights going at the very entrance of the maze, flashing so fast it makes it nearly impossible to see what's right beyond the first bales of hay. We take a couple of steps inside, to the first big intersection. You can go left or right, or keep heading straight.

Kat grabs my hand. "You're freezing." She pulls me along with her to the left. "Now, stick close to me. Suckers are going to jump—"

Right then two ghouls leap from the shadows. I scream and start laughing, while Kat practically leaps into my arms.

"Personal space, asshole!" she screams at the ghouls.

"Are you okay?" I ask her. "Do you want to go back through the entrance?"

She gives me a face like I'm being stupid. "They caught me by surprise, is all. Come on. This shit is going to get tiring real fast. And the sooner we get to the end, the sooner we can hook back up with Ricky and the guys."

I pat her on the back. "O-kay, Sister Katherine."

We only take a few steps before I feel someone come up alongside us as if she were part of our group. Kat notices her too, and we both turn and look. This is an older woman, but she's dressed up like a little girl in a blue dress, white lace-trimmed socks, and black velvet buckle shoes. She's carrying around a doll covered in fake blood, and she holds it up to us. "My dolly's sick!" she cries in a weird, whiny voice. "Help my dolly!"

Kat lets out a shriek I didn't know she was capable of, high and shrill and raw. She drops my hand and takes off running.

"Kat!" I'm laughing so hard. "Kat!"

I push my way in the direction Kat ran off, but it's hard with all the other people in the maze. I take a left, then a right, and head straight right into a wall. I walk backward out, and someone taps me on the shoulder. "Kat?" I say, but it's just a psychotic farmer wearing bloodstained overalls and carrying a pitchfork. I mean, another one of the workers.

He spins me around, and when I take a step forward, I realize I have zero idea where I've come from and where to go next.

"This way, you guys!" a girl's voice calls out.

It's not Kat. It's Lillia.

I stumble in the direction of her voice, but it's hard to tell exactly where she is, with the music and the other people screaming and laughing.

I take a couple of turns, but I don't hear Lillia again. It's dizzying, and the flashing strobe lights are starting to give me a headache. I shout, "Kat? Kat?"

Another ghoul jumps out at me, and this time I scream. He grabs my arm and tries to keep me from getting away from him. I shake him free and quicken my pace down a long maze alley. I need to find Kat. I don't want to go through this thing alone. It's definitely way scarier when you're by yourself. And Kat's probably having a heart attack right now, for all I know.

I take another left and walk for a few feet until I hit a dead-end hay wall. I shake out my hands and try to calm myself down. Am I ever going to get out of here?

Then I turn around and run right into Reeve Tabatsky.

I mean that literally. I run right smack into his chest. The force sends me stumbling backward a step. Reeve's crutches clatter down on the ground, and he totally loses his balance with his bum leg. Thankfully the maze alley we are in is narrow, and one of the hay walls breaks his fall and keeps him from hitting the ground.

"Shit," he says.

"I . . . I didn't see you," I say.

"Are you okay?"

It takes me by total surprise, Reeve asking me this. My cheeks heat up bright, but I lean down and pick up his crutches for him so he won't see it.

"Don't worry about me," I say, the words tumbling out of my mouth super fast and nervous. I can't believe I'm finally face-to-face with Reeve, having an actual normal conversation with him. After all these years, here we are. I straighten up and ask him, "How's your leg?" Reeve doesn't take the crutches from me, so I lean them against the hay wall for when he's ready.

He says, "It's fine," but I don't believe him. He looks like he's in serious pain. I can see it all over his face. His teeth clench as he bends over to check his black soft cast and adjust the Velcro straps.

"Should, um, I get someone to help you?" I take a step back and give him some room. I hope I haven't messed up any of the progress he's made in the pool.

"No, don't," he says, quiet. Reeve pushes a hand through his hair, composing himself. He says with a groan, "It's my own fault for coming to this stupid maze anyway." He reaches for his crutches, slides them under his arms.

I can tell he's about to walk away from me, but I don't want him to. I'm not ready for this moment to be over. Not yet. It's like when we rode the ferry together. I'd wish and wish and wish the ride could last a little bit longer. Even a minute longer.

I reach out and touch his arm. His shirt is so unbelievably soft, and I feel his bicep underneath. It's big and tight and cut, probably from the weeks he's spent on crutches. I say, "I'm sorry you got hurt at the dance." And despite everything Reeve did to me, it feels good to apologize. Because I truly did not mean for him to be hurt so bad that his whole life might be screwed up forever.

He shrugs his shoulders. "Shit happens, you know?"

"Yup," I say, nodding, because it is true. "Shit happens." It happens to all of us.

There's an awkward second, where neither of us knows what to say. Reeve rustles his hand through his hair. "I should go find my friends. Hope you make it out of here alive." He positions his crutches and goes to take a step forward, but I shift my body so he can't. It gives me a surge of adrenaline.

"It's, um, been a long time, huh?" The words get kind of caught up in my throat.

Reeve's head falls slightly to the side. "Yeah . . ."

The wind picks up and blows my hair around. I tuck as much as I can behind my ears. "I've always wondered if you ever thought about what happened." Reeve lets out an awkward laugh and then blinks a few times. I can't tell if he's embarrassed or blindsided. "If you felt bad about what you did."

And then I wait, because it's the perfect opening. I'm giving him the best shot to apologize to me, to finally take responsibility for his actions. To make things right between us, once and for all.

Reeve's eyes narrow in confusion. He's trying to place me.

Which throws me off. Sure, I'm wearing a Halloween costume, but it's weird. It took him five seconds to call me Big Easy at the dance. Does he really not recognize me now?

"Calling a girl Big Easy because she's fat—do you not know what that does to a person?" Reeve's whole body stiffens, and he stares at me hard, this time with cold eyes. I feel him peeling back the layers I've got on. The makeup, the leather pants, the crazy hair, until I'm stripped clean to the bone. I'm shaking. Shaking like a leaf in the wind. "You were such a bully back then. Aren't you sorry? Even a little bit?"

He wets his lips and growls, "Go fuck yourself."

I can feel myself start to crumple and I worry my legs might give out. Reeve pushes past me and down the long corridor.

"I'm sorry," I call after him. I don't even know why. But I immediately hate myself for saying it. Because those are the words *I* deserve to hear. Not him. Only I'll never get an apology from Reeve, because he isn't sorry.

Not one little bit.

And then I feel it coming. A tidal wave. A tsunami. The surge inside of me. Anger, sadness. Like on homecoming night. I close my eyes, but I don't see darkness. I see the hay maze lighting up, walls of fire penning in all these people.

Oh God, oh God.

I have to get out of here before I explode.

CHAPTER THIRTEEN

KAT

I'VE GOT MY BACK PRESSED UP AGAINST A WALL OF HAY bales, and the sticks are pricking through my nun habit. It's a dead-end part of the maze, but I don't care. I'm hiding so no ghouls or zombies or whatever can get me from behind. Every so often, I crane my neck and peer around the corner and keep my eyes peeled for Mary.

Obviously I'd find her faster if I actually *looked* for her, but I'm not moving from this spot. Mary can come to me. I didn't pay thirty dollars to die of a heart attack in this damn maze.

I hope she's having fun. Kid deserves to have a good time.

I'm glad that little doofus in the mummy costume was trying to chat Mary up while we were in line. She could use a boost to her self-esteem, big time. Sure, I'm no guidance counselor, but Mary needs to realize that she's not the girl she used to be.

A pack of people creep past the alley where I'm hiding out. A girl in a ballerina costume breaks off from the group and heads toward me, walking cautiously on her tiptoes. She's got on a pink leotard, pink tutu, pink everything. Of course it's Lillia.

"Lil," I say, stepping out of the shadows.

She jumps and screams a horror-movie scream, but she's smiling, too. Scaredy-cat Lillia loves this stuff—who'd have known? She must think I'm one of the workers, because she's about to run away, back to her friends. But then I say her name again and she stops cold. It takes her another second to recognize me, I guess because of my costume.

"Kat! Oh my God! Is that you under there?"

"Taketh not the Lord's name in vain!" I say in a booming voice.

She giggles. "Where's Mary? She was coming with you, right?"

I nod. "Wait till you see her costume. She looks amazing. I'm talking leather pants amazing." As I say it, I realize that I wish it were the three of us hanging out together tonight. But I push the thought out of my mind, because it doesn't make sense to feel sad about something you can't do shit about.

She's here with her other friends. I quickly change the subject. "Did everything go okay at the elementary school tonight?"

"It was fine. I think the kids had fun. The parents were happy."

"Cool." I felt bad, seeing how stressed Lillia was all week. "Hey. You know, I would have come and helped. But you didn't say anything, so—" Her cheeks get flush, so I back off. "I'm not upset or anything," I clarify. "I mean . . ." I don't know what I mean. I'm babbling.

"Don't worry. It all worked out. I didn't think to ask you, though. I know it's not your thing. But thanks for offering to help"—she smirks—"when it's too late to actually, you know, help."

I touch a finger to her shoulder and make a sizzle sound. "Nice zinger, Lil. I like how I'm rubbing off on you."

She looks like she's about to make another joke at my expense when we hear Reeve say, "Shit!"

His voice sounds like it's coming from the other side of the hay wall.

We both roll our eyes, because Reeve's such a douche, but then there's Mary's voice, all tiny and small and Mary-like.

"I . . . I didn't see you."

In half a second, Lillia and I both have our ears up to the wall, listening.

Lillia whispers to me, "Mary's talking to him."

I whisper back, "Eff talking. Kick him in the nuts!"

That makes Lillia giggle.

We both gasp when we hear Mary say, "Calling a girl Big Easy because she's fat? Do you not know what that does to a person?" Lillia grabs my arm and starts hopping up and down excitedly. I can't believe it. The kid's really going for it!

Then we hear Reeve say, "Go fuck yourself."

Lillia's hands fly to her mouth. Fucking Reeve Tabatsky. He's as much of an a-hole as he was before his accident, if not a bigger one.

Lillia and I wait to hear what she'll say back.

And then Mary says, "I'm sorry."

Lillia closes her eyes and drops her chin to her chest.

Damn.

We see Mary sprint past our alley.

I go to race after her, and Lillia makes a move like she's going to come with me, but I shake my head. "No. Stay with your friends. We shouldn't let anyone see the three of us together!" Only, she doesn't listen. She runs right alongside me.

"Mary!" We're both screaming her name, pushing people out of our way. I see her pink-streaked hair a hundred feet or so ahead.

Finally we catch up. Lillia grabs hold of Mary's shirt. "Mary!"

Mary spins around. She's crying. She tries to tell us what happened, but she can't get the words out.

"We heard it. We heard everything." Lillia gently pushes some of Mary's hair out of her face. "You look amazing, by the way."

The compliment doesn't even register on Mary's face. It's blank. Like she has PTSD or something.

I turn her by the shoulders and make her look me in the eye. "What do you need us to do?" I say, quick. "Just tell us."

I think she's going to answer me, but instead she breaks free and runs off.

We let her go.

"This feels wrong," I say, and chew on my finger.

Lil's perfect ballerina bun has unraveled. Strands are falling out of the coil, but she doesn't seem to notice. "We've got to give her space if that's what she wants."

"I guess . . . But what if she does something to herself?"

Lillia looks unsure now too. "Oh my God. Do you think?" She takes a deep breath and sighs. "Poor Mary."

I don't even know what I'm doing, but I lean in, like I'm going to give Lillia Cho a hug. And she leans in, like she's going to give me one back.

"Lillia! Lil! We're lea-ving!"

It's Ashlin.

"Go," I whisper. "I'll see if I can find her."

Lillia frowns, but she walks backward away from me.

"We'll go over her house tomorrow and check on her."

I nod my head.

As I head toward the maze exit, some ghost gets in my face. I've got so much anger inside, I shove him and say, "Enough already." A few people look at me like I'm insane. And that's exactly how I feel. Insane with worry for my friend.

CHAPTER FOURTEEN

LILLIA

I HEAD TOWARD ASH'S VOICE AND RUN INTO HER AND a few of the girls from the squad. She's all tipsy and happy, and she shrieks my name and threads her arm through mine. I guess because Rennie hasn't caught up yet, she can be as friendly as she wants and act like nothing's wrong. I couldn't care less about any of that right now—all I care about is that Mary is okay. I wish I could help Kat look for Mary, but I don't even have my car. It's still at the elementary school.

Everyone's heading for the parking lot, and then we'll drive over to party in the big cemetery in Canobie Bluffs. People are starting to pile into cars, and I spot Reeve alone, leaning against Alex's SUV, staring off into space. Just the sight of him makes me sick.

I can't help myself.

I break away from the girls and march right up to him and say, "Hey. Reeve."

Reeve turns to me and smiles. The freaking jerk actually smiles. "Hey, Cho. Are you headed to the cemetery?"

My voice shakes as I say, "You're cruel. I knew you could be mean sometimes, but I never knew you could be so incredibly cruel."

Bewildered, he says, "What are you talking about?"

"I heard you," I say. "I heard what you said to that girl in the maze. 'Go *eff* yourself'? Seriously?"

"Wait a minute—"

"What did she do to you to deserve that?" My voice is getting louder and louder.

His face goes hard. "Don't worry about what girls I talk to. That's none of your concern."

"I'm not *concerned*—"

"Then mind your own business."

I want to scream, *It is my business!* but I can't and still protect Mary. So instead I say, "You know what? I'm glad you broke your stupid leg. I'm glad you can't play football and that no college wants you on their team anymore. You deserve everything you're getting, because you're not a good person."

Reeve goes the color of a sheet, but I don't let myself feel bad for him. Instead, I give him the dirtiest look I can conjure up, and then I turn on my heel and run toward Ash's car.

CHAPTER FIFTEEN

MARY

I TEAR THROUGH THE OPEN FIELD, WEAVING BETWEEN rows of parked cars and clusters of people, trying to put as much distance between me and the maze as I can. My heels keep getting tripped up by field rocks and the soft ground, and at some point I end up falling to the ground in between two cars.

I want to get right back up, to keep going, because the woods are only a few feet away. But I'm completely exhausted. Luckily, there's no one around to see me. So I sit there on my knees in the dirt and cry.

Go fuck yourself.

That's what I came back to hear Reeve say?

That's what I deserve, after everything?

After a few minutes of sobbing, I hear Lillia's voice. At first I think she's calling out for me. But then I realize she's screaming at Reeve.

I stay low and use the car for cover, peering through the windows. I end up spotting them a few rows away. Lillia and Reeve, toe-to-toe. I can't make out what she's saying, so I stay crouched down and scurry from car to car, trying to get closer to them.

"You know what? I'm glad you broke your stupid leg. I'm glad you can't play football and that no college wants you on their team anymore. You deserve everything you're getting, because you're not a good person."

Oh, Lillia. You are a true friend.

She walks away from Reeve. I watch closely for his reaction. To hear him defend himself. To hear what kind of jerky thing he'll yell after Lillia.

Except he doesn't do anything. He just stands there, watching her go.

And most shockingly of all, he wipes his eyes on his sleeves.

It's another punch to the gut. Reeve couldn't care less about seeing me and the nasty thing he said; he didn't even care enough to apologize. But Lillia Cho calls him a bad person and he's in tears.

I know why. Reeve likes her.

He might even be in love with her.

I hate that I'm jealous, but I am. I really, really am. It's sick. I'm sick.

I want to go home but I can't. Not when I'm upset like this. Not when I still feel like I could explode at any second. I stand up, wipe the dirt from myself, and head straight into the woods.

CHAPTER SIXTEEN

LILLIA

CANOBIE BLUFFS IS THE OLDEST CEMETERY ON THE island; there are gravestones that go back to the 1700s. All the old Jar Island families have plots here. Lots of weird names like Ebenezer and Deliverance and Jedidah. The boys are throwing around a football, using the tombstones as markers. Someone put on Michael Jackson's "Thriller," and Rennie and Ash and some other girls are putting on a show, doing the zombie dance. Rennie's got on a sexy nurse costume and sheer white thigh-highs with red seams up the back. A few weeks ago I would have been front and center, right by Rennie's side. Now it's me alone on a blanket sipping Ash's "witch's brew"—basically rum punch with cinnamon sticks and oranges and cider. It's so sweet; I've been drinking it like it's Kool-Aid. That, and I have nothing else to do but drink. There's no school tomorrow or the day after because of parent-teacher conferences, so I might as well.

Reeve's sprawled out in the center of the other blanket, his legs stretched in front of him. He's surrounded by junior girls in slutty costumes. Slutty cavegirl, slutty mouse, slutty Pocahontas. They're practically feeding him grapes. I can't believe I ever in a million years felt bad for him. He's horrible, a monster. For him to talk to Mary that way, after all he's done to her . . . it makes me want to puke. I'm glad I said something to him in the parking lot. It felt good to give him a piece of my mind.

The song changes, and Rennie comes running up to Reeve, making room for herself on the blanket and edging the other girls out. "Do you need anything?" she asks him. "We have snacks and stuff."

"Is there any beer?" he asks.

Rennie's head bobs up and down and she scampers over to the cooler. Ugh. It makes me sick to see her wait on him hand and foot. Puke puke puke.

She brings him a beer and he looks at it and goes, "Is there no Bud Light?"

"'*Is there no Bud Light?*'" I mimic to myself. I call out, "Reeve, how about you get your lazy butt off the ground and go look for yourself? Last I checked, you're not a paraplegic! It's a broken left fibula!"

Reeve whips his head around and throws me the meanest look ever. Like I care. "Shut your mouth, Cho," he says warningly.

I'm about to take a sip of my witch's brew, but before I do, I say back, "No, you shut yours." He thinks he can push around whoever he wants. Well, he's not pushing me around. He should know that by now.

Suddenly Alex plops down next to me, breathing hard from running around. "Did you see that play?" he asks me, blocking Reeve from my view. "I almost made it all the way down to the end zone. Beat three guys with my spin moves before I got tackled."

I sigh. Sweet, dear Alex. Alex who made sure there were enough cupcakes for the little kids, and he never ever did anything to hurt me. He shows up for me every time. Sighing again, I let my head droop onto his shoulder. "You are so nice," I whisper.

"Are you drunk?" Alex asks me, a little amused and a little concerned and mostly surprised.

"Yes. No. Okay, yes."

"You never drink," he says.

"I did," I say, sitting up and looking at him. It takes a couple of seconds for him to come into focus. "One time I did and it was the worst, worst mistake of my life. Sometimes I think . . . sometimes I think I'll never be the same." My eyes keep closing on their own. "Never mind. I shouldn't have said that. My eyes are sleepy."

Alex takes the thermos out of my hands and puts my head back on his shoulder. "Are you cold?"

I shake my head. I'm not. The punch is very warmth inducing. Plus I put an off-the-shoulder sweatshirt over my leotard. It's still ballerina-ish, though, like I got back from rehearsal.

"Warmth inducing?" Alex says.

I clap my hand over my mouth. "Did I say that out loud?"

"Yeah," he says, laughing. I tilt my head up and look at his face. His eyes are so nice.

"So nice," I say, touching his glasses.

"Thanks," he says solemnly.

I shiver, and Alex shrugs out of his suit jacket and drapes it over my shoulders. "Feel free to lean against me," he says. So I do. I let my weight fall against him, so relaxed. Boneless, almost. He puts his arms around me, and I feel safe, like the safest I've ever felt. It's the exact opposite of that bad time.

We watch as PJ kicks the football high into the air. "Field goal!" he crows.

Derek goes, "No, dude, the end zone is the Zane plot." He

points to a collection of moss-covered white stone crosses, dead center in the cemetery.

The Zanes. That must be Mary's family. I didn't realize they were old-school Jar Islanders.

They argue back and forth, and I say to Alex, "I can't believe that next Friday's the last football game. Are you upset you guys aren't going to playoffs?"

"No way. The season could've been over when Reeve got hurt, but we turned it around. I'm proud of what we pulled off. And you know what, it's awesome Lee got to play so much this season. He's really come into his own. I bet you next year the Gulls make it all the way to state."

"You're such a good guy," I say, nodding to myself. I glance over at Reeve. He's struggling to his feet, balancing on one crutch. Rennie says to him, "Where are you going?"

His face is red. "Home. This sucks."

Rennie makes a pouty face, but he isn't even looking at her. He's already leaving, swinging away on his crutches. "Reevie, just stay a little longer," she pleads. "I'll drive you home in a bit."

I call out, "Byeeee! Don't let the door hit you on the way out!" and then laugh hysterically.

He ignores me and lurches off into the night. As soon as he's gone, Rennie comes over and gets in my face. She hisses, "Are you serious right now?"

Before I can say yes, I am totally 1,000 percent serious right now, Alex says, "Dude, she's drunk. She doesn't know what she's saying."

"I do too!" I say, poking him in the chest. I sit up straight and say to Rennie, "You bailed on the Fall Fest and then you made it so no one else would help me."

Rennie closes her eyes and shakes her head. "I'm so sick of listening to you, you whine and cry and pout. Poor little Lillia needs *so much help*. She can't do anything for herself, she needs everyone to rescue her. Your whole damsel in distress routine is getting old, Lil."

I feel like she's slapped me across the face. All I can do is stare at her, stunned.

Alex gets to his feet. "Why are you being such a bitch?"

Rennie smiles and waggles her finger at him. "Right on cue, puppy."

The boys have stopped playing football. Someone has turned the volume down on the music. People are looking at us. But I don't care who's watching.

"*Oh* . . . damsel in distress," I repeat. "Like when I was calling out for you to help me that night at the party." I watch the realization dawn on her face, that I actually took it there. Back to that night at the rental, with Mike and Ian. The thing we were never, ever supposed to talk about again. "But wait—you said you didn't hear me, right? Or you did, and you were just too busy with your guy?" As soon as the words are out of my mouth, I realize I'm shaking.

Rennie's face turns to granite. "You're clearly wasted, and I don't know what you're talking about, but we are so done," she breathes. Then she turns on her heel and stalks off in the direction Reeve went.

Alex puts his hand on my shoulder. I'd forgotten he was still there. "What the hell was that about?"

I don't answer his question. I just say, "Can you take me home?"

CHAPTER SEVENTEEN

MARY

WHAT FEELS LIKE HOURS LATER, I STUMBLE OUT OF THE woods and onto a residential street. I'm not sure what time it is, or even how long I've been out walking. The moon is still high in the sky, and there's no sign of dawn.

From the look of the houses, quaint cottages on tiny plots of grassy marshland, I think I might have gotten all the way to Canobie Bluffs, which means I'm on the complete other side of Jar Island from where I live. It's going to be a long walk back to Middlebury. And the thought of doing the big hill in these heels, well, it makes me want to cry all over again.

But I can't, even if I want to. I don't have any tears left.

The only thing I have to be grateful for is that I didn't hurt anyone. I . . . I couldn't live with myself if I had. The energy I felt tonight, it was like homecoming times a hundred. Even now it's not all gone. I can still feel some of it inside me, churning, like the ocean at low tide.

I'm walking in the middle of the street, wishing I could close my eyes, snap my fingers, and be in my bed. It's quiet out in the neighborhood. The trick-or-treaters are long gone. Nothing but the last of the summer locusts that haven't died and the occasional car a few streets away. Nearly all the houses have their lights off. You can tell the ones that are empty summer rentals—they don't have pumpkins or mums or any fall decorations. Everyone else is asleep, so it must be late.

I walk for a few blocks. Then a car turns down the street and catches me in its headlights. It slows down as it passes me. Then stops.

I can't see who's inside; the glass is tinted. The window reflects my face, the punked-up, tearstained Halloween version of myself. Luckily the tears haven't done much damage to my makeup. If anything, they make me look more tough. But it's completely fake, because I'm not tough. I'm not strong. I'm an epic mess.

The driver's-side window dips down.

"Hey, biker girl."

It's the boy. The boy from the maze line. His mummy bandages are off, unrolled in a pile on his passenger seat. Now he's in a long-sleeved JAR ISLAND HIGH CROSS COUNTRY T-shirt and jeans. Without the bandages I can tell for sure: He's cute. He's black, light-skinned, light eyes, dimples. He's lean and tall, too tall for his car. His knees nearly touch the steering wheel, even though he's got his seat all the way back.

He might even be taller than Reeve.

"Can I give you a ride somewhere?" I walk around the front of the car, eclipsing one headlight and then the next. He reaches across and opens the door for me, like a gentleman.

"My name's David." He clears his throat. "David Washington."

"Doesn't ring a bell."

"What's yours?"

I turn toward the window, so I don't have to look at him. "Elizabeth" is what I say. It just comes out, and I'm glad. I don't want to tell this guy anything about me.

Jokingly he asks, "Did you get lots of Halloween candy tonight, Elizabeth?"

"Nope," I say with a sigh. "In fact, my Halloween was the exact opposite of sweet."

"Well, let's fix that right now." He points down at the cup holders in his console, which are both packed full of goodies. "Pick anything you want."

I can't remember the last time I ate candy. But why should I even care about getting fat again? It's not like Reeve is ever going to look at me.

I pick out a lollipop for myself, then slowly unwrap it. The bulb is bright pink. I put it in my mouth, and it tastes so so sweet it's almost sour. David gives me a funny look. "I haven't had candy in forever," I explain. And then, because that doesn't make much sense, I add, "I used to be fat." He laughs, as if I'm making a joke. I twirl the lollipop in my mouth, let it dissolve. "It's true. And I used to get teased all the time. Bullied, actually."

David looks slightly uncomfortable at that. I wonder if maybe he's bullied people, in his lifetime.

I turn and face him. "Do you think I'm pretty? My friend thought you were flirting with me at the maze."

David looks taken aback. "Yeah. You're pretty. Real pretty."

"Well, I don't look like myself tonight," I tell him, with more urgency than I intend. "I don't wear this much makeup."

He shakes his head. "But that's the point of Halloween, right? To wear a disguise?"

I realize that I have been wearing a disguise. I might not look like the sad little fat girl anymore, but that's definitely who's underneath it all.

He looks nervous. I can tell he's not sure what to say. "You know what? I used to have a lazy eye. I had to wear a patch for three years to build up the muscle." He smiles as he confesses this. "Can you pick which eye? I bet you can't."

I stare into his face. His handsome face. I can't tell, so I don't even try to guess. Instead I say, "Can you take me home?"

David does most of the talking on the drive. He moved here from California two years ago, with his mom, after his parents got divorced. Mostly we talk about how weird it is to live here. I appreciate that David doesn't bash it. He's not like Kat, who I know can't wait to move somewhere else, because everything about Jar Island annoys her. David is very measured. For example, he hates the fact that there is no good Mexican food, which I guess is a California thing. But he loves that he can still surf here.

He offers to give me a lesson.

At a red light he takes one hand off the steering wheel and slips it into mine. "Your hands are so cold." He seems embarrassed; the words kind of fall out. I fight the urge to pull my hand away. I think, *This is who I was supposed to be. A girl who isn't afraid to flirt with boys, a girl who is confident and fun and wants to have a good time.* And really, I never used to be shy. Not until Reeve broke me.

I have him drop me off in front of my house. He pulls up to the curb, puts his car in park, and then leans over.

He kisses me.

I kiss him back.

It's my first kiss, my very first one. David puts a hand through my hair and gently cups the back of my head. His mouth tastes sugary, like candy corns.

I kiss him because this is the life I should be living.

Except the only part that feels good is the part of him wanting me. I only wish I could want him back.

He pulls away from me and says, quietly, "I'm going to look for you at school on Monday, Elizabeth."

I don't say anything. My eyes are on the clock—it's almost midnight. David closes his eyes and leans in for another kiss. Slow motion, movie style.

This time I turn my head.

The disappointment on his face is immediate.

"I should go," I say.

"Wait. Give me your number." He turns to the backseat, looking for his phone.

In those few seconds I bolt from the car and run up to the house. I don't like David; I don't want to kiss him. This isn't my life; this isn't who I am. I'm not . . . normal. I can't pretend I am, not even for a night.

I sneak in the back door. I figure Aunt Bette is already asleep, but then I catch sight of her in the living room, peeking out the curtains.

"Were you *spying* on me?"

Aunt Bette gasps like she's been underwater. She spins around and stares at me. "Who was that boy?"

I'm annoyed that she was watching me. It's creepy! Don't I deserve some privacy? Like Kat said, I'm a teenager now; I'm not a little girl anymore. "He's no one. I'm going to bed."

Aunt Bette follows me up the stairs. "I know you missed out on having these kinds of experiences, and my heart breaks for you, but this needs to stop."

"What has to stop? Why can't I kiss a boy if I want to? Or hang out with my friends? I made one mistake a long time ago and you won't let me forget it!"

Aunt Bette reaches out to touch my arm, but then pulls her hand back fast, like I'm raging hot. "You have so much anger inside you. It . . . radiates."

I stare her down. "You know what? I am angry. At you." I fold my arms. "What are all those books in your room? Are you putting spells on me?"

"Mary, I—"

"Those freaky strings you've got hanging up on your bedroom wall. What are they for?"

Aunt Bette is shaking. "Mary. It's for protection."

"What do you mean, 'protection'?" Aunt Bette looks like she doesn't want to tell me, which makes me want to know even more. She starts backing up through the hall, but

I keep closing the distance. "What are they *exactly*?"

Aunt Bette puts up her hands. "They aren't working, anyway."

I scream, *"What are they?"* at the top of my lungs.

Aunt Bette sinks to the floor. "They're binding spells," she tells me, in a whisper of a voice.

Binding? My mind immediately flashes back to that morning when I couldn't open my bedroom door. And the way that smoke made me feel so sick.

Could her spells have worked?

I shake these insane thoughts from my head. How could I believe this nonsense for even a second? Aunt Bette isn't a witch. These aren't actual spells. She's just . . . crazy.

I crouch down so I can look her in the eyes. "Aunt Bette, you need to get out of the house. You need to start painting again. You need to go out and live your life, not try to keep me locked up in here with you." Aunt Bette cradles her head in her hands. She won't look at me. There's no reasoning with her. I don't even know why I'm trying to talk sense to a crazy person. "I want that string thing taken down. Tonight. And I want you to stop burning your little smudgy things, the chalk stuff . . . it stops, or else I'm going to call Mom and Dad and tell them all about the weird things you've been doing to me."

She starts crying. And maybe it makes me a terrible person, but I don't want to hear it. Not tonight, when my heart is already broken.

Actually no, it's not just my heart. It's my whole life that's broken.

CHAPTER EIGHTEEN

KAT

I WAKE UP TO THE SWEET, SWEET SMELL OF TOASTER waffles. Usually, I have to wait until Saturday to have breakfast with my dad, but we've been given Thursday and Friday off for some kind of teacher conference. I drove around trying to find Mary last night. I even went to her house, but the lights were all off. I just hope she made it home okay. I grab my phone and fire off a quick text to Lillia, about going us to Mary's house later to check on her, and then head downstairs in my big sleep shirt and socks.

"Did you have fun last night?" my dad asks as I step into

the kitchen. Of course Pat isn't awake. He's not up until noon, whether or not it's a weekend.

I give Dad a quick hug. He's always been a big guy, Dad-shaped, and it's satisfying to wrap your arms around him. "Not really," I say, because honestly, last night sucked a nut. I know it's not totally my fault, but I feel guilty for leaving Mary on her own in the maze. If I'd been with her, standing next to her, that shit with Reeve never would have happened. Not without me breaking his other leg.

I pour us each a cup of coffee. I like mine with milk; Dad takes his black with two teaspoons of sugar. I secretly give him only one teaspoon, though, because his doctor wants him to cut back. Dad sets our plates down on the table, along with the butter dish and a jar of raspberry jelly. I prefer my toaster waffles with jelly, not syrup, and I've made him a convert.

"Any trick-or-treaters come by last night?" I ask.

"Just the two girls down the street."

I drop into my seat. "What were they dressed as?"

Dad hunches over his plate, his classic eating posture. "Princesses, maybe? I don't know. They looked like pink disco balls to me."

"I hate that pink garbage," I say. "It offends my inner Gloria Steinem. Aren't there any little girls left in the world who want to dress up like race-car drivers or doctors?" I lift the lid off the butter dish and frown. The butter is sprinkled with someone else's crumbs. And there's gunk from older butter sticks congealed on the bottom, because the dish hasn't been washed in a while. I take my knife and scrape the stick into the trash, put the butter dish on top of the pile of dirty dishes already filling the sink, and then get a new stick out of the fridge. It can stay in the wrapper for now.

Dad looks up. "You okay?"

"Fine," I say, and reach for the jelly. The jar is sticky, and the lid isn't on right. This is Pat's doing; he always makes PB and Js when he's high. I set it down on the table with a thud.

"What's the problem, daughter?"

"Nothing," I say, even though I clearly am pissed. "How's the canoe? You going to finish it this week?"

Dad nods. "The guy who bought it doesn't even want to sail it. He wants to hang it on the wall in his beach house. Isn't that nuts? All that money for a decoration. She's seaworthy, though."

I'm not listening. I'm looking around our kitchen. It's freaking gross. A pile of unwashed dishes in the sink, old newspapers and mail stacked on the counter, the front of the stove splattered with hellfire chili.

Dad downs the rest of his coffee. "You cheated me out of my sugar, Katherine." He pushes back from the table, and that's when I notice what he's got on his feet.

"Daaaad, what the hell?" I start laughing. "You'd better not go out in public like that."

He looks back at me, confused. I point to his feet—he's paired a black athletic ankle sock with a light blue dress sock that's supposed to be worn with suits.

Dad shrugs and gets the sugar bowl. "I couldn't find clean socks that matched—so what? What do I care? I'm not looking to impress anyone."

Poor Dad. It's true. He's not looking to impress anyone. He hasn't had one single date since Mom died. Not that I'm jonesing for a stepmom, but it's been five years now. I don't want him to be alone forever. He deserves a good woman.

I guess the problem is that we both know there isn't a woman out there that could ever be better than Judy.

"I'll do the laundry today." It's not like I have set chores or anything, but I tend to take care of the laundry, because I'm the only one who gives enough of a shit to sort colors.

Dad waves me off. "Kat, I know you're busy with school. Don't worry."

He's right. I have been busy. But that's not a good excuse. I need to make time to help out around the house while I'm still living here.

I hammer my two waffles, finish my coffee, and then go on a cleaning tear. I wipe down the kitchen, do dishes until the drying rack is full, change out the towels in the bathroom, put in a load of laundry for Dad. All the while, Pat is asleep on the couch in the den. When I come in with the vacuum, he barely rolls over.

Freaking scrub.

I get so pissed, I ram the vacuum cleaner into the couch and basically shake him awake.

"Oh, pardon me," I say in my bitchiest voice, when he finally opens his eyes.

"What's your problem?"

"You need to start helping out around the house more."

"Whatever, Kat. Go take a Midol. Shouldn't you be at school anyway?"

He reaches for the afghan but I pull it off him. Freaking scrub is in his tighty-whiteys.

"There's no school today! Look around, Pat! Our house is a shithole. What would Mom say?"

"Mom wouldn't say anything. She'd clean it up."

"Yeah, well. Guess what? I'm not Mom. And I'm about to peace out for college, and I don't want to have to worry about you and Dad living in a pile of garbage!"

Pat stretches his arms over his head and growls. "Fine. What do you need me to do?"

I point down at the coffee table. It's covered in Pat's racing magazines and some carburetor parts laid out on a greasy page of newspaper. "Clean up your shit."

Pat sniffs the air. "Is that toaster waffles?" He groans to his feet and shuffles out of the den.

I go to my room before I explode. I pick up my phone. It's been almost two hours, but Lillia hasn't texted me back. I text her again, and then get dressed. When she still hasn't responded, I start calling her over and over.

She finally picks up on the fourth try. Her voice is scratchy. "Hey," she says. "What time is it?"

"Almost noon. Why are you still sleeping?"

She moans. "I'm hungover."

I don't know why, but this pisses me off. "Well, I'm going to Mary's house. You coming?"

"Of course I'm coming." She starts coughing. Or maybe dry heaving. I can't tell. And it makes me feel bad. "Do I have time to shower?"

"Sure. I'll pick you up in twenty."

To kill time, I head to Milky Morning and pick up three cupcakes, one for each of us. I stop and get Lillia a bacon, egg, and cheese sandwich, too, because the grease will be good for her hangover.

On the way to pick up Lillia, I try calling Mary's house, to tell her we're coming, but no one answers. Shit. I get this nervous feeling in my stomach. What if her fight with Reeve sent her off the deep end again? What if she . . .

I don't even want to think about it.

Lillia's waiting for me on the front steps. She's got on a pair of loose-fitting jeans and a hoodie, and sunglasses over her eyes. Her hair is still wet. She walks slowly up to my car, like she's a zombie. I give her the egg sandwich. "Here."

"Oh, awesome," she says. "You're the best, Kat."

"Wild night?" I ask, watching her out of the corner of my eye.

"A bunch of people went to hang out in the cemetery. I got a little tipsy . . . I kept yelling at Reeve about what a jerk he is until he finally left."

I give Lillia a high five for that.

"I got into it with Rennie, too. We're officially frenemies now." Lillia smiles, but I can tell her heart isn't in it. "It's the end of an era, Katherine."

I can't help but feel a surge of vindication. Rennie's pure evil. Lil's much better off without her.

Tremulously Lillia says, "I'm just glad we found each other again. I don't know what I would do if I didn't have you and Mary."

Gruffly I say, "Well, that's not something you have to

worry about," and Lillia smiles a real smile this time.

"Were you able to find her last night?"

"No."

"Shoot." Lillia takes a bite of the sandwich while I drive us to Middlebury. As she's licking her fingers, she says, "I hope she's okay?"

"She'll be okay."

"No . . . I mean, like, I hope she's *mentally* okay?"

I get quiet because I'm not sure.

"I was thinking maybe we should try to get her to talk to someone."

"Like who? A guidance counselor?" I think immediately of Ms. Chirazo and shake my head like a big *Hells, no.* "We'll keep a closer eye on her. If things get bad, okay, we'll force her to talk to someone. But I don't think we're at that point yet." At least, I hope we aren't.

Lillia looks unsure, but she nods. "Okay. Deal."

We drive to Mary's house. I don't see her aunt's car in the driveway, thank God. We go up to the front door and ring the bell a few times, but no one answers. I've got a bad feeling in my stomach when I say, "Maybe she went out for breakfast?"

Lillia calls out, "Mary! Mary!"

"I'm around back!"

Lillia and I walk over to the garage. Mary's inside, her bicycle turned upside down. She's greasing up her chain.

The garage is dark, save for one raw bulb dangling down from the rafters. The place is full of stuff. Furniture covered with sheets, a telescope collapsed and leaning against an old bureau. "Wow. There must be an entire house worth of stuff in here."

"It's mostly my family's things," she says. "From when we moved."

I walk over and look at the telescope. It's super nice. High end. "They didn't want this?" It seems crazy to me that a family would leave all their things behind. But then again, I'm not rich. Maybe Mary's family has money.

Mary shrugs. "Dad liked to try and spot whales from the front window. There's no ocean view where they live now."

"We brought cupcakes," Lillia announces, and takes the box from my hands.

I take a seat on some old patio furniture. "We wanted to make sure you were okay, after what Reeve said to you in the maze last night."

Mary stands up and pulls her hands inside her sweater sleeves. "I'm embarrassed that you guys heard all of that. How I apologized to him."

I say, "You have nothing to be embarrassed about. We're proud of you for calling him out on his shit. You did good, Mary."

"I guess." Her bottom lip starts quivering, but she bites on it to make it stop. "I don't understand why I can't get over it." Mary wrings her hands. "I've been trying so hard . . ." Her voice gets all shaky. "I've been trying to join clubs at school to give myself something to focus on, start thinking about my future. But even though I've been working to put myself back together, I'm always seconds away from falling apart. I had the worst fight with my aunt last night. I know it's terrible to say, but part of me wishes I'd just gone through with killing myself, because this is no way to live."

In that moment, all the air is sucked out of the garage, and I'm suddenly aware of how fast my heart is beating. This is our worst nightmare come true. I glance over at Lillia. She's fiddling with the strings on her hoodie. She doesn't know what to say.

Neither do I.

It's too quiet. So I say, "Mary, this isn't a case of 'if at first you don't succeed,' okay?" My bad joke tumbles out along with a hollow, nervous laugh. Lillia shoots me a look, but what the hell? I didn't see her opening her mouth. "You need to quit saying that kind of stuff."

I don't even know if she hears me, because she's so upset. Her whole body has crumpled, like all the bones holding her up have gone soft. I push my bangs out of my eyes, lean forward, and tell her, "You've been through a lot, but someday this isn't going to seem so devastating. Next year you'll be a senior, and after that you'll head off to college. One day you'll look back on this shit and laugh." I wish I could give Mary more hope than that, something that could help her in the here and now, but that's all I've got.

In her quiet way she says, "The funny thing is that Reeve wouldn't care if I died or not. Do you know how that feels, after everything I've been through? And it's not because he's heartless. He does care about some people." She lifts her head and looks at Lillia. "But not me."

Lillia gives her a puzzled look. Pleadingly she says, "Mary, you can't do this to yourself. He's not worth it." She pushes her hair over to one side. "Like, not at all."

Mary locks eyes with Lillia. "I heard you guys last night in the parking lot. I heard the things you said to him. Nobody's ever stuck up for me that way before, not ever. You've been like a big sister to me. Both of you."

I'm touched, but I don't like the way she's talking. It's as if she's saying her good-byes.

Lillia gives her a shaky smile and tries to say something, but

Mary keeps talking, and her voice gets louder, more intense. "Did you know that Reeve cried? He cried after you told him off in the parking lot. That's how much he cares what you think of him."

I watch the shock cross Lillia's face. "Reeve cried?"

Mary nods her head. "It's because he likes you."

Lillia shakes her head fast. "No, no, no. Please don't say that."

"Wait a minute," I chime in. "Remember at the dance? How he kissed you in front of everybody?"

"He was on ecstasy! I gave it to him, remember! He would have kissed Mrs. Dockerty if she were onstage with him!"

"Wait up," I say. "I remember when you first moved here, and there was a barbecue at Reeve's house. You said you wanted a hot dog. There was one left and I was about to put it on my plate, and he practically clotheslined me out of the way."

Lillia blinks. "What are you even talking about? Hot dogs?"

Mary's eyes are practically glowing, she's so excited. "Oh my gosh, I got it! Reeve gets everything he wants. But not this time. We have the one thing he'll never get. You."

Lil's mouth drops open. "Even if what you're saying is true—and I don't think it is—but if it were, if Reeve did like me, I'd never give him the time of day. Never ever ever." She shudders.

I kind of love the idea of Reeve pining after a girl he can never have. And I'm about to say so, but Mary leans forward as she says, "Him liking you and you not liking him back isn't enough. Don't you see? The thing that made it so bad for me was that Reeve made me believe there was a chance. He drew me in; he spent all that time with me; he told me his secrets. He made me feel special. He made me think I had a chance."

I grimace.

"So when he betrayed me that day, when he pushed me in the water in front of those boys from our school, I was blind-sided. I broke into a million pieces. Because it was all a lie, every moment we'd spent together. He didn't care about me, not at all. Not one bit. He used me for his own entertainment, so he wouldn't be bored on his ferry rides." She clears her throat. "Reeve broke my heart, and now you've got a chance to break his. Will you do it, Lillia? For me? Please?" Mary's voice breaks on the word "please."

Lillia's pinky finger goes to her mouth, and she chews on her nail. "Mary . . . I want to help you. I do. But . . ." Her voice trails off, and then she sighs. "Rennie would make my life a living hell for this. Things are already so bad between us . . ."

Mary nods sadly. "No, I understand. I wouldn't want you to get hurt."

"Hold up, you guys!" I shout, charging in all excited like the bull I am. "Lil, if you get Reeve to fall in love with you, you're *untouchable*. Nobody could say dick to you if you were Reeve's girl! He's the fucking king of the island."

"And then what happens to me when I break up with him?" Lillia challenges. "Where does that leave me?"

I smile a wolfy smile. "I'll tell you exactly where that leaves you, Cho. That leaves you as the Head Bitch in Charge. Any girl that could reel in Reeve Tabatsky and then reject him is the *boss*, dude. People might not like it, but they're sure as shit gonna respect it. It's a power move, the ultimate power move. Shit, I wish I could be the one to pull it off."

Lillia shakes her head slowly. "I said some really horrible things to him last night. I don't think he'll ever forgive me for that."

"If you apologize, he will," I say. "Guys like him, they love a little push-pull. They don't want it to be too easy. Tell him you're sorry and it'll be fine. Right, Mary?"

Mary nods.

Lillia goes silent, and I can tell she's thinking it over. She lifts her head and sucks in her lips. "Rennie would be hella pissed." A grin blooms across her face. "Okay," she says at last. "I'll do it."

"Are you sure?" Mary asks her.

Lil lets out a deep breath. "I'm in."

Mary practically sags in gratitude. "Thank you. Thank you, Lillia."

I grab Lil's shoulders and give her a shake. "Yes! Lillia Cho, HBIC!"

She laughs, and I grin at Mary. A hopeful smile is spreading across her face. "Operation Break Reeve's Heart begins on Saturday!" I crow. "My house."

"Why not right now?" Lillia asks me.

I shake my head. "First we need ammo. I'll show you on Saturday after I'm done retaking the SAT. Just you wait, my pretty."

CHAPTER NINETEEN

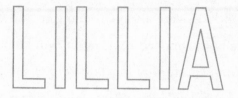

I park a block away from Kat's house, to be on the safe side. The houses are a lot closer together here, and mostly split-levels. There aren't the big hedges and gates that the houses in White Haven have, so everybody can see everything. Rennie lives pretty close by, and Reeve does too, so I'm not taking any chances. On Jar Island, you never know who's watching.

I ring the doorbell, but no one answers. The plan was to meet here after Kat took the SATs. You couldn't pay me to take them again, even if I was guaranteed a perfect score.

I wait before I ring it a second time. A minute goes by and still nothing. The light's on in the kitchen, though. Somebody's home. Gingerly, I touch the door handle, and it's unlocked, the way it always was. "Hello?" I call out, opening the door a crack. "Kat?"

When we were growing up, Kat's house was like that— neighborhood kids were always running in and out the front door, and nobody minded. My mom would have been all, *Would you mind taking your shoes off at the door, and also, does your mother know you're over here, and who wants some Greek yogurt with blueberries?* At Kat's house it was a free-for-all; we would stuff our faces with Cheetos and Mountain Dew and play video games for hours and nobody would bother us. It was kid heaven.

"Hello?" I call out again.

A guy's voice says, "It's open."

I venture into the kitchen, and there is Patrick, sitting at the table, eating cereal without a shirt on, even though it's well past lunchtime. He looks sweaty and dirty, like he just got back from riding around on his bike. His shoulders are freckled the way I remember, but he's not so skinny anymore—still lean, but stronger looking. His eyes widen for a split second; then he grins. "What are you doing on this side of the island, little girl?"

My throat feels dry all of a sudden. "Hi, Patrick."

He drawls, "Are you here to see Kat, or me?"

I feel myself blush. "Kat. We—we have a project at school. Did she finish the SATs?"

"Yeah. She ran out for something. Cigarettes, I think," he says, and then he starts eating his cereal again, like it's perfectly normal that I'm in his house and he doesn't have a shirt on. With his mouth full he asks, "Want some cereal?"

"What kind?"

"Your favorite," he says, and he points to the seat next to him. "Sit down."

Even though I had chicken salad on a croissant an hour ago, I sit down, and he gets up and brings a box of Trix, which *is* my favorite, a jug of milk, and a spoon. He tips more Trix into his bowl and pushes it so it's between us.

"Bon appetit, Lil," he says, handing me the spoon.

And then we're both eating Trix, from the same bowl, and he smells like outside and wind and motor oil.

I can't believe Patrick remembered that Trix was my favorite. I haven't seen him in years, and also he goes to college now, so why should he remember anything about me?

It's funny, because even though my crush on him was so long ago, sitting across from him now at Kat's kitchen table, it feels like yesterday that I loved Patrick and that Rennie and Kat and I were best friends. *RKL till we die.*

He's telling me about some philosophy class he's taking at the community college, and I'm nodding hard like I'm paying attention, but all I can think about is how his eyes are green like evergreen, same as before—when Kat comes home. She looks surprised to see me, even though we said we were hanging out this afternoon.

Leaning against the doorway, she says, "What are you guys doing?"

"Eating cereal. What does it look like?" Patrick says, and I giggle.

Kat shoots me a strange look. "Bring it up to my room, Lil." Then she heads down the hallway.

I stand up. "Do you mind?" I ask him. "If I take it with me?"

"Be my guest," he says.

Cradling the bowl against my chest, I say, "Thanks for the cereal, Patrick."

"Anytime, Lil." He winks at me, and I press my lips together so I don't smile. Then I trail after Kat, to her room.

"What the hell was that?" Kat asks me. She's lounging on her bed with her shoes on. Ew.

"What?" I say, sinking onto the floor. I know we were supposed to be keeping everything on the DL, but it's not like it's my fault Pat is home.

"You know what," she says, smirking at me. She shakes her

head. "That lowlife is skipping class again. Such a loser. I have no idea why you were always so gaga over my gross brother. He goes to JICC; isn't that beneath you? 'Cause it's sure as shit beneath me."

Stiffly I say, "I was never *gaga* over Patrick. Also there's nothing wrong with community college. He says he's probably going to transfer soon anyway." So I guess Kat's known all along. I never told her I had a crush on Patrick; I only told Rennie, who swore up and down she'd never tell. Yet another betrayal.

Kat snorts. "Oh, sweet naive Lil. He ain't going anywhere. He has, like, two credits. He'll be stuck on Jar Island for the rest of his damn life."

"How did the SAT retakes go?"

"Hell if I know."

I concentrate on eating my cereal fast, because it's getting soggy. "When's Mary coming?" I ask, wiping milk off my chin.

"I think she said she had to do something with her aunt first, and then she'd either get a ride from her or bike over."

"Cool," I say. I drink my sweet cereal milk, and then I put the bowl down on the carpet. I take off my flats and crawl onto the bed next to Kat. She scoots over for me. Staring up at the ceiling I say, "So, um, did Patrick ever say anything about me?"

Kat busts out laughing and hits me over the head with her banana pillow. I laugh too, and then I burst out, "I can't believe

Rennie told you I liked Patrick when she explicitly promised she never would. She swore on her mom's life!"

Giggling, Kat says, "Even if she didn't tell me, it was so obvious. You used to think up excuses for why we should have sleepovers over here instead of at Rennie's!"

"Well, that was partly because of Shep." My mom is supposedly allergic to dogs, so we've never been allowed to have one, no matter how much we beg. I think it's because she doesn't want a dog on our white furniture. Sitting up, I call out, "Shep! C'mere, Shep!"

Shep comes bounding into the room, and he jumps on the bed and kisses my face. I hug him to me. "Hello, sweet boy," I say in his ear.

"Remember those skanks Pat used to bring home?" Kat asks me suddenly. "They were always way older and they'd smoke inside the house. Remember that one time?"

Of course I remember. I was thirteen during the height of my Patrick crush, so I guess he was fifteen or sixteen at the time, and the girls he hung out with seemed like women to me. They had boobs and they cussed and they rode around on the back of his motorcycle.

There was this one girl, Beth. It was the middle of the day, and Rennie and Kat and I were in the TV room blasting music, practicing a routine from one of those dance movies where peo-ple have dance-offs in the rain in a parking lot.

"Lil, you have to roll your hips back like this," Rennie instructed me, demonstrating.

She and Kat started doing it together in perfect unison. "Loosen up, Lil," Kat said. "You're too stiff."

Haltingly, I tried to follow their lead and get the motion. That's when Patrick and Beth came in. They burst out laughing, and I stopped immediately, but Rennie and Kat ignored them and kept on going, even when they sat down on the couch and watched.

Beth had auburn hair; it was long enough to put in a ponytail, but barely. She had on a ton of eyeliner and no lipstick, and a big black T-shirt with slashed arms that she wore as a dress. She looked like she was twenty-two even though she was probably only eighteen. "Look at those little hoochies in the making," she cracked, lighting up a cigarette. Her voice was low and husky.

Patrick snorted, and I lowered my eyes. Through my lashes I sneaked a peek at her. She had her legs stretched out on the cof-fee table even though she still had shoes on. "Let's go upstairs," I whispered, but Kat ignored me.

"We're hoochies?" Kat said. "Look at you. Where are your pants? In the back of somebody's truck?"

Beth guffawed with hoarse laughter and took a drag of her

cigarette. She looked sexy when she did it, like she was in a movie.

"Excuse me, but you're not allowed to smoke in the house," Rennie said, her hands on her hips.

Patrick tapped a cigarette out of Beth's box. "Go play outside, little girls. We want to watch TV." They smirked at each other.

"We were here first," Rennie said.

Patrick gave her a threatening look, and Kat said, "Fine, fine. We're going." To us she said, "Come on." At the last second she snatched Beth's pack of cigarettes and made a run for it with us close behind her. We ran out the screen door and I could hear Patrick's roar.

I never felt more my age than that moment. I wanted to be eighteen and not thirteen. I wanted Patrick to look at me like he was looking at her.

And more than anything, what I wanted was to ride on the back of Patrick's motorcycle. Once, to see what it felt like to go that fast, with only him to anchor me to the world. My parents would have sent me to a convent if I'd ever even said that out loud. They'd made me promise I would never ride on Pat's motorcycle; that was the condition of me being allowed to hang out at Kat's house.

I've never broken a promise to my parents before, but if

Patrick asked me to go for a ride on his bike right now, I'd do it. I wouldn't even hesitate. To be that wild and free. I want to know what that feels like.

We're eating candy-apple popcorn and listening to music—Kat's favorite band, but it's making my head hurt, it's so loud—so we don't hear Mary when gets here. She bounds into the room, her cheeks all rosy and pink, already so much better than she looked on Thursday. "Mary!" I sing out.

"Hi, hi!" she says, coming over by the bed. She's about to sit down with us when Shep bares his teeth and growls at her.

Kat grabs him by the collar and gives him a shake. To Shep she says, "Cut that shit out." To Mary she says, "He's harmless, I swear."

Mary gives a nervous laugh and sits on the floor. "Dogs usually love me."

"I can kick him out," Kat offers, getting up.

"No," I protest. "Let me cuddle with him. Mary, he won't come near you."

"Fine by me," she says, giggling. "Nice doggie."

Shep darts under the bed, and I crawl over and try to lure him out with a handful of popcorn, and he looks tempted but doesn't come out. I offer Mary the can. "It's so good," I say, dangling it in front of her.

Mary makes a face. "You only like super-sweet things, Lillia."

"That's cause I'm so sweet," I say in a singsong voice. She smiles back at me, and I climb into Kat's hammock.

Kat snorts and goes to her closet. She throws me a shopping bag of clothes. "Here. Ammo."

Before I even open it, I say, "Just so you know, I'm not wearing fishnets."

"There aren't any fishnets in there, you beotch." She plops down on her bed and watches me as I start going through the bag.

A pink strapless corseted top. A lacy black corseted top. Cream thigh-high socks made out of soft yarn. A bandage skirt so short it might even be a tube top; I can't tell. The socks are kind of cute, but this other stuff looks like Frederick's of Hollywood. Totally not my style.

"Kat, did you steal all this?" I ask. I'm mostly kidding.

Kat rolls her eyes. "You know I don't steal, beotch. That's your girl Rennie. Oh, and BTW, you owe me a hundred and sixty bucks."

I lift up a stretchy long-sleeved minidress. It's basically a ballet leotard. "I'm not wearing this!" I shriek. "I'll look like a prostitute."

"I have that in purple," Kat says, glaring at me.

Whoops . . . "It's not really my look," I say. "I mean, I'm sure you look amazing in it. But it's not me." I spot a black lace corset at the bottom of the pile. "You expect me to go to school in lingerie?"

Kat scoots over to the edge of the bed. "So what! You're gonna look hot. You strut into school wearing that and some high-ass heels, and Reeve's head will be spinning. All you have to do is wear the clothes; then you catch his eye. Next comes physical contact, a touch on the arm, a hand on his knee. Then you talk to other guys and inspire jealousy. It's simple."

"Um, excuse me, but I know how to talk to boys," I snap. As if I need Kat to give me advice on how to get a boy to notice me! I add, "For your information, I set a student-council record last Valentine's Day for most roses ever sent to a girl at Jar High." True, a dozen were from my dad, but I got roses from boys, too. I even beat out Rennie. She kept saying how I wouldn't have won if it haven't been for my dad. Now that I'm thinking of it, I'll beat her this year too. I'll do whatever it takes, talk to ugly freshmen dorks if I have to.

Kat heaves a sigh. "Fine. If you're not going to wear this stuff, then what do you have in mind?"

I pop some popcorn into my mouth and think. "Well, I have this cute blouse with a bow at the collar; I could wear that with these amazing gray flannel shorts that roll up on the bottom. I saw them online last night."

Mary and Kat exchange a look.

Kat leans forward. "Listen. The way I see it, you're more of a Jackie O type. You're classy and refined and stylish."

I give her a nod. "True, true, and true."

Rolling her eyes, Kat continues. "But we need you to be a Marilyn. Sexy. A bombshell. Like, we don't want Reeve to want to bring you home to his mom. We want him to *want* you. Hard-core obsession want. Blue balls want—"

"Okay, okay! I get it!" Giggling, I fall back into the hammock. "But you guys, he's *so* gross. I'll be throwing up in my mouth every time I have to pretend cozy up to him."

Kat tosses the stretchy dress at my head. "At least try it on."

Mary says, "Yeah, Lil. Anything's going to look pretty on you."

I groan.

"Lil, trust me on this. I know what I'm talking about. Do you know how many lead singers I made out with this summer? Four! There were hotter girls there than me around, but I'm the one they picked out of the crowd. You wanna know why? Attitude. It's all about attitude. You act like you're the shit and guys are so dumb they'll totally believe it."

She's completely right. Look at Rennie. Rennie's all attitude. Whatever she wants, she gets. She has the whole school under her spell. Forget Marilyn. I'll just channel Rennie.

I pick up the dress. "So what do you guys want me to wear first? This streetwalker dress or this bra top?"

Mary squeals, and Kat's eyes gleam as she says, "Definitely the dress."

When we pull into the school parking lot on Monday, Nadia sees her friend Janelle and gets me to drop her off by the front entrance. I take my time parking and then fixing my hair in the rearview mirror. I put it in my mom's hot rollers before I went to bed and then I slept on it so it wouldn't be too bouncy. *Bombshell hair*, Kat kept saying last night. This isn't exactly bombshell hair, but it's fancier than my normal style. I dab some pink gloss on my lips, too.

When I step out of my car, I make sure to keep my trench coat buttoned and tied tight around my waist. Right as I close the car door, I spot Kat watching me from across the lot, hanging on the chain-link fence. She shakes her head and mouths, *No coat*. I mouth back, *I'm cold*, and I shoot her a pleading look, but she shakes her head again. She mouths, *Marilyn*. Slowly, I peel the coat off and stow it in my trunk.

I make my way across the parking lot and into the school. I'm wearing my highest heels, the pale pink patent-leather ones from homecoming. I walk up the steps carefully so I don't trip and fall. The dress is super tight but also totally comfy, because it's basically spandex. It barely covers my butt and it makes my boobs look huge, which never, ever happens. I hope I don't get sent home for wearing it. My mom would probably faint.

Right away I can sense people staring, but I look straight ahead, head up, shoulders back. A sophomore girl whispers to her friend, "Damn . . ." and a couple of boys whistle. I walk like I don't hear them; I walk like I own this school.

This must be what it feels like to be Rennie.

I drop off my bag in my locker and only carry a purse, which is way sexier and more Marilyn than my school bag. I touch up my lip gloss, too. There's five minutes before the bell rings, which means that Reeve will be by the vending machines with Alex and PJ like every morning.

Which they are; they're leaning against the wall of lockers, eating donuts, except for Reeve, who has a protein bar. No Rennie, thank God. My heart is thudding in my ears as I wave hi and sail past them. I go straight for the vending machine. As I punch the numbers for chocolate donuts, I peek in the glass to see if Reeve is looking. He's not. He's polishing off the bar. I notice too that he doesn't have his crutches anymore. And he's traded in his soft cast for a walking boot.

PJ lets out a low whistle and calls out, "What are you all dressed up for, Lil?"

Turning slightly, I say, "I have to give a presentation in French class." Which would totally make sense if I were giving a presentation on the Moulin Rouge.

"*Très bien*," PJ says appreciatively, and I give him a curtsy.

My dress is too short for me to bend down and pick the donuts out of the slot. Luckily, Alex comes right up beside me. "You look—wow," he says, in a low voice.

I can feel myself blushing. "Thanks."

Alex stoops down and grabs my donuts and hands them to me. "Wow," he says again. His eyes are wide, and he's staring at me.

I try not to smile. I can't remember—should I have already attempted physical contact with Reeve, or do I go straight to making him jealous? I don't even know if he's looking at me.

I'm about to sneak a quick peek at Reeve when I see Rennie coming down the hall with Ashlin. Quickly, I link my arm through Alex's. "Walk me to class?" I chirp.

"Sure," he says. "I'll be your bodyguard."

Reeve's looking at me now. His eyes flicker over me and then, just as quickly, away from me. Completely disinterested. He's not even making an obnoxious joke about the way I'm dressed. He wipes off his mouth and tosses the wrapper in the trash without another glance in my direction.

Maybe he's still mad about the things I said to him on Halloween. Crap. If this plan of ours has any chance of working, I'm going to have to eat humble pie and apologize to him, which is the last thing I want to do.

At the lunch table, I'm all set to sit next to Reeve and make amends, but when I get there, he's already sitting at the end and Rennie's next to him. Her eyes go huge when she sees me in my getup, and I have to resist the urge to cross my arms over my chest.

I slide into the seat across from her. My plan is to pretend our Halloween fight never happened, because what other choice do I have? "Hey, guys," I say, opening my bottle of blueberry white tea.

She acts like she didn't hear me, which is fine, and then she puts her head on Reeve's shoulder and says, "Do you want me to get you something from the lunch line, babe?"

"Nah, I'm good," he says, shaking a box of Muscle Milk.

"Okay, I'm gonna get some fries. I'll be back in two secs." Rennie practically skips over to the lunch line.

When she's gone, I lean forward and quickly whisper, "Hey, um, I'm sorry for those things I said on Halloween. I think I had too much to drink."

My little apology barely registers. He says flatly, "Yeah, ya think?"

Clearly, Reeve's not going to make this easy on me. How very Reeve of him. I swallow, lower my head, and then look up at him through my lashes. I've got to put on an Oscar-worthy performance here. In a contrite voice I say, "Reeve, I really am sorry. I should never have said that stuff to you . . . especially since you came to Fall Fest and tried your best to help me out, even with your injury." I reach out and touch his arm lightly.

Reeve moves his arm away from me. "I didn't come to Fall Fest to help you out. I did it because I made a commitment to the kids." He tips back in his chair.

This isn't working, like, at all. I'm going to have to change tactics. Maybe tell the truth a little. "I don't know if you've noticed, but Rennie and I are sort of in a fight. It's been . . . hard, and I think I took it out on you because you were there. So, I'm sorry. I promise I didn't mean any of those things I said." Well, that part's a lie.

Reeve shrugs and takes a swig of milk.

Gee, thanks for being so understanding, Reeve. Thanks a whole bunch.

CHAPTER TWENTY

MARY

IT'S AFTER FIVE; EVERYONE'S ALREADY LEFT SCHOOL for the day. We are sitting in the last two rows of the auditorium. Lillia's next to Kat, who's got her combat boots up on the seat in front of her, and I'm perched backward on a seat in the row in front of them.

Lillia unwraps a light brown Tootsie Pop and waves it around. "First lick?" she asks me and Kat. We both shake our heads.

"Update!" Kat shouts, clapping her hands. "Update! Update! Update!" I clap along with her, because this is super exciting. It's the thing I've been looking forward to all day.

Lillia swirls the lollipop around in her mouth. "Well, I pranced right by him before homeroom and he barely looked at me. It was actually kind of insulting, now that I think about it. I mean, yeah, I screamed at him on Halloween, but he's a guy. Aren't guys supposed to always be horny? Like, he's hooked up with every girl in school but he can't give me the time of day?" She sighs. "And after I spent all that time on my hair and makeup too."

"He was probably trying to hide his boner," Kat says, chewing on her fingernail. "You look fierce as fuck, Lil."

Lillia laughs. "Um, thanks?"

"In Spanish class I overheard Connor Dufresne describing what you had on today with, like, an insane amount of details," I offer. "He said you're the hottest senior by far. He said—"

"Second hottest," Kat booms, and we all laugh. "Don't stress yet, Lil. We're only getting warmed up. Today was about laying down the foundation. Next we kick it up."

"How?" Lillia asks. "I even apologized to him at lunch and he didn't want to hear it. And he's never alone, what with Rennie the Parasite constantly clinging to him."

I clear my throat. "I know a place where he goes by himself." Looking down, I wind my hair around my finger. "The swimming pool."

Surprised, Lillia says, "Reeve's joining the swim team?"

"No, it's for his physical therapy. He's there every day, ever since he got his hard cast off." I'm sure I sound like a stalker, but whatever. This is too good an opportunity for us to pass up. I fix my eyes on her. "Lillia, start swimming in there with him! It'll be the two of you; no one's there after school."

Lillia's already shaking my head. "Mary, I don't swim. Tell her, Kat!"

"Lil doesn't swim," Kat confirms.

"You don't know how?" I ask.

"I know how, but I hate it," Lillia says, defensive. "And Reeve knows that about me. He'll be suspicious if I start showing up at the pool all of sudden!"

Soothingly, Kat says, "Chill, Lil. Nobody's throwing you in the water today." But Lillia's still shaking her head. And then Kat's face lights up. "Wait! Don't you have to take the swim test to graduate?"

"My family doctor wrote me a note," Lillia says, lifting her chin high. "I mean, my dad did."

Kat's so excited she's practically vibrating. "That's it, Lil! There's your excuse. You're practicing for the test."

Lillia crosses her arms. "I told you, I'm not taking the test! I already turned in the doctor's note from my dad. What am I supposed to do now? Walk into Mr. Randolph's office and tell him that my aquaphobia is miraculously cured?"

"Reeve doesn't have to know you're not actually taking the test! Pretend like you are. All you have to do is paddle on a kickboard," Kat urges. "Like, literally doggy-paddle around the shallow end. And don't forget that Reeve's an awesome swimmer. He set the Jar Island record for breaststroke when he was like, ten, and bitches still haven't beat it yet! Even with his gimp leg, he could swim you to safety easy!"

Stiffly, Lillia says, "I'm not worried about *drowning*."

"Then what are you worried about? This plan is foolproof. If you're in the same physical vicinity as him, the two of you alone? Day after day?" She snaps her fingers. " He won't be able to keep that act up for long."

Lillia looks a little queasy. I guess I can't blame her. Day after day of having to face Reeve Tabatsky in a bathing suit would give me anxiety too. She turns to me, biting her lip. "What are you thinking?" she asks.

I run my hands through my hair. I don't want to put Lillia in a situation she's uncomfortable with, but then again, what other options do we have? "I'm thinking Kat's right," I say at last. "Will you at least try it, Lillia? For me?"

Lillia stares at me and then breaks into a laugh. She nudges Kat and, keeping her eyes on me, says, "How can I say no to that face? I'm not like Rennie. If my friend needs me, I'm there."

Later, when I get home, Aunt Bette is up in the attic. I press my ear to the door and hear the scratching of her brush against the canvas. I close my eyes and smile, relieved. She's painting again, thank God. Aunt Bette is always happiest when she's working. And our house could use that kind of positive energy.

CHAPTER TWENTY-ONE

AFTER SCHOOL LETS OUT, I GO STRAIGHT TO THE pool. The building is empty, and there's a bluish cast because of the lighting. I hate the smell of chlorine. I set my teddy-bear beach towel along with my flip-flops down on the bleachers next to Reeve's walking cast and his towel and gym bag. I'm wearing a white bikini with embroidered daisies and ties on the sides. It's my cutest one. I tie my hair into a bun so it won't get super wet.

Reeve's already in the water. He's got floats attached to his legs, and he's curling his legs inward and outward, grimacing as he uses his arms to push himself forward. He's focusing so hard it doesn't seem like he's noticed me, so I clear my throat. His head jerks up. "What are *you* doing here?" he demands.

"I'm here to practice for the swim test," I say. "It's a graduation requirement."

"Well, don't bother me," he says. "I'm here to work, not to talk. That's why I come here *alone*."

"But *you* asked *me*—"

"I need this lane and I need this stuff here," he says. "Don't touch any of it." Then he goes back to his exercises.

Seething, I grab a kickboard from the stack and make my way over to the pool ladder at the deep end. I start to go down one rung at a time, very carefully. The water is heated, but it still feels icy to me. I've already got goose bumps. This is so not worth it.

And my feet are still planted on the ladder.

If I were to take the swim test, I'd have to dive in and get from one end of the pool to the other two times without stopping to rest. Plus tread water for three minutes, plus float for one minute. I can't do any of those things.

I mean, I know how to doggy-paddle. I don't know the official strokes or whatever, but who cares? I'm not going to drown in my own pool. I don't like putting my head underwater. I don't like not being able to breathe. So sue me. I have plenty of other forms of exercise that I actually enjoy, like cheering, and horse-back riding, and tennis and golf. Why should I be forced to swim?

I hold on to the side for a minute, one arm on the wall and one arm clutching my kickboard. My feet can't touch the bottom, which makes me feel panicky. Whenever I'm in my pool at home, I stay in the shallow end.

Meanwhile, Reeve has ditched the floats and is swimming like he's an Olympian, lap after lap after lap. He barely even comes up for air. He's pushing himself hard, maybe too hard. He's doing the butterfly stroke, and his arms knife through the water powerful and sure, but his leg trails limp behind him. I have to admit it makes me feel better knowing he's here. Like, if something did happen, no matter how much he hates me, he wouldn't let me drown.

I don't think.

I let go of the wall and start using the kickboard, holding on tight. I kick and kick my way down the lane, bobbing above the water, trying to keep water from splashing in my face. This is hard work, plus I keep feeling paranoid I didn't tie my bikini top tight enough. My swimsuits have always been purely decorative; they've never seen this much action. All in all it takes me for-ever—Reeve's done three laps by the time I make it to the end.

Reeve doesn't stop or acknowledge me. I'm floating by the ladder waiting for him to finish like some kind of swim groupie, if such a thing even exists. When he's finally done, he yanks off his goggles and looks up at the big clock on the wall and lets out an annoyed gust of air.

Then he puts his goggles back on and starts doing laps again.

What, since his football career is a bust, he's trying out for swim team now? I look down the length of the pool. It's so long. I'm tempted to go home. But I've only been in the water for like fifteen minutes. I suck in a deep breath and kick off from the wall and start paddling on my kickboard again. I concentrate hard, imagining I am a duck. Kick-kick-kick.

I'm concentrating so hard on making it to the end of the lane that I don't even notice when Reeve leaves.

On Wednesday, I'm wearing my yellow polka-dot bikini, the high-waisted one. Rennie calls it grandma chic, but it makes me feel glamorous, a bathing beauty, like Marilyn. This one doesn't have a tie around the neck; it's an underwire top, so it's more secure.

It's silent in here, except for the sound of Reeve's kicks and splashes echoing against the tiles. I feel glum as I collect the kickboard and climb down the ladder into the pool. Same as yesterday. Yesterday we didn't talk. Not really. And we definitely didn't flirt.

I'm splashing and floating along toward the middle of the

lane when I decide that today will be my last day. I've given it my all. Kat and Mary couldn't ask for more. They'll have to understand that I've done my very best to get Reeve to notice me, but this is pointless. I didn't promise to spend the rest of my senior year on a kickboard.

I'm deciding all of this when Reeve's bored voice calls out, "Why are you here again?" He's hanging on to the side of the pool, shaking water out of his goggles.

"I thought you didn't want to talk," I say, resting my arms and chin on the board.

He ignores that. "You know they're not going to let you use a kickboard in the swim test, right? At least that's how I remember it. But I took it a long time ago. Like freshman year. With everyone else."

"I know that," I snap peevishly, and then I stop myself before I can say anything else. Not very Marilyn of me. This is my chance to make a connection, I have to make the most of it. I take a breath, and in a sweeter tone I say, "I'm just . . . getting used to doing laps."

"What you need to get used to is putting your face in the water," he says, swimming toward me. When he gets close enough, he splashes me right in the face.

"Quit it!" I yell, swiveling around to kick away from him and holding on tight to my board. Oh my God, I hate him so much!

Reeve makes a lunging motion like he's going to dunk me, and I let out a scream. He grabs me by the waist, hoisting me in the air. I've still got my fingers clenched around my board, I'm kicking and splashing as hard as I can, but he doesn't let go. "I said stop!" I scream, and my terrified voice echoes throughout the pool. Not because I'm afraid to be thrown. It's his hands on me where I don't want them to be. It's me telling a boy to stop and him not listening.

It feels worse than drowning.

He lets go and I fall back into the water. When I come up to the surface, he's looking at me like I'm crazy. My heart is racing; I'm breathing hard. Reeve swims back to the other end of the pool and lifts himself out of the water. With his back turned to me, he dries himself off with a towel.

"Don't you ever do that to me again!" I scream.

He turns around and eyes me. "You're going to have to get your hair wet eventually. If I were you, I'd worry less about my bikini and my hair and more about actually, you know, swimming."

My mouth drops open. "Well, I'm sorry I don't own a swim cap and a racer-back Speedo."

He shakes his head at me like I'm some sad case. Then he walks off, and with his slight limp it's more like a strut. The door slams behind him. And my heart is still racing.

That night, I'm digging around in my swimsuit drawer for my black one-piece to wear to the pool tomorrow. Because black says, *I mean business.* It's not a Speedo—it has a halter neck and a little keyhole—but it'll give me better support than a two-piece, at least.

I'm sifting through string bikinis when I find it. Not the black one. The red one. The one I wore that night, the night at the beach house.

My hands shake as I ball it up and throw it into the wastebasket.

CHAPTER TWENTY-TWO

IT'S FRIDAY, AND I'M WANDERING THE HALLS WITH A BATHROOM pass, trying to eat up some of sixth period, when I spot Mary tucked underneath the first-floor stairwell with a book.

"Shouldn't you be in class?"

Mary looks up, startled, but relaxes when she sees that it's me and not a hall monitor. She smiles coyly. "I'm, um, taking a break."

"Like a bathroom break? Or a break like an I'm-skipping-class-today break."

Mary drops her head. "Okay, you got me. I didn't study for

my Spanish quiz. So last period I asked to go to the bathroom and then came here to hide out until next period." She lets out a sigh. "My aunt is going to kill me when she sees my report card this semester. I swear, the only class I'm going to pass is chorus."

"Well, then you made a good decision to cut. But you need to find another place to hide out, stat. The hall monitors always check this spot on their rounds. Trust me, I know." I glance over both my shoulders. "In fact, I'm surprised you haven't been busted already. You should head to the nurse's office and hide out there. Pretend you have cramps or something."

"Thanks," Mary says, and stands up.

"How are things with your aunt? Any better?"

"A little bit. She's started painting again, but she's still not speaking to me." Mary shakes her head. "It's funny. I never remember fighting like this with my own parents. I feel so . . . unwelcome in my own house, you know?"

I lean against the banister. "Hey, you want to do something tonight? You and me?"

Mary brightens. "Like what?"

"How about we go for a drive."

"Sure. That'd be great."

"Cool. I'll pick you up at nine." I'm about to walk away, back up to the second floor, when I say, "Wait. Where's your hall pass?" I hold mine up. It's a big wooden carving of the symbol for pi, some ugly thing one of the remedial shop kids must have made for the math department, probably for extra credit.

Mary looks confused and says, "Uh-oh. I guess my teacher last period forgot to give me one."

"Well, then don't walk up by the science labs. I just came from there and there's a hall monitor lurking right past the doors. Take the back door by the gym and walk past the library to the nurse's office."

"Got it," Mary says, and spins in the other direction. "Thanks. I've never had detention before."

I roll my eyes. "Of course you haven't, sweetie."

I wake up to Shep licking my face. I leap off the couch and run over to the window. It's already dark out.

"What time is it?"

Pat checks his phone. "A few minutes after ten. Why?"

Shit! Shit shit shit!

"Where you off to?" he asks as I run through the kitchen, looking for my boots by the back door.

"Out," I say. Thank God the car starts. I drive so fast to Mary's house. What a jerk I am, to be late for a thing I invited her to! Ugh. At a red light I try calling Mary's house, but the line is busy.

When I get there, she's on the curb, waiting in the dark. She's got on the same dress she wore to school today, a little flowered thing, underneath her parka.

"I'm so so sorry I'm late," I say, jumping out of the car. I open the passenger-side door for her gallantly, because I feel like a total piece of shit. "I fell asleep watching TV. I tried calling your house, but the phone was busy." I wince. "Have you been waiting out here long?"

She gives me a tiny smile. She doesn't seem mad, which is a relief. Mary might be the most forgiving person I know. "I knew you'd come."

Mary and I drive around for a bit and listen to music. After a few laps around the island, I get hungry. The only place open this time of year, at this time of night, is the Greasy Spoon, a twenty-four-hour diner in T-Town. It's never hopping, because the food isn't good, but there are a few not-too-god-awful things on the menu.

I pull up and park around the side. The lot is strangely crowded. Hopefully I won't have to wait long for my food. "You want anything?"

Mary yawns and shakes her head no.

I walk inside and order at the counter. Coffee, black with two sugars, and a cinnamon doughnut. I'm waiting as the lady punches in my order when I hear her voice. Rennie.

I turn my head and there she is, sitting at the end of a long table in the middle of the diner. It's like the entire Jar Island football team is here. And all the cheerleaders, too. I see Lillia huddled laughing with Ashlin and a couple of other girls on the squad. Each of the girls has a long-stemmed red rose sitting in her water glass. They're all still in their cheering uniforms except for Rennie.

I remember now. Tonight was the last football game of the season.

I look back and Rennie is staring at me. We lock eyes, and I immediately look away, because I don't want to get into any shit right now.

"Oh, look! It's Kat DeBrassio!" she says it in a false whisper, and everyone turns in her direction. "Hey, should we ask her to come over and sit with us?"

I can tell by the way her words slide out of her mouth that she's been drinking. I bet she's pissed that our team actually did okay without Reeve. Alex sees me, they all do, and he tries sticking a menu in front of Rennie's face, to get her to look at something. She swats it away.

I turn back to the counter and give sharp eyes to the waitress. Can she pour my freaking coffee already so I can get out of here? I wonder if this kind of shit will still happen after we've graduated. If whenever I come back home to visit, I'll always have to dread running into Rennie on the island somewhere.

"Kat, are you like stalking me or something?" Rennie says. "How many times do I have to tell you . . . I'm not a lesbian!" Rennie cackles like a hyena. "Loser trash."

That's it. I turn to say something back, but I don't have to. Lillia sets down her menu and says, "Rennie, you're just pissed that we all got roses from our players tonight, and Reeve couldn't even be bothered to show up for you."

You could hear a pin drop. Rennie's jaw goes slack. Everyone at the table turns to face Lil, who for a second looks as surprised as everybody else. Rennie's face turns bright red, the brightest I've ever seen on a person, then she looks around to see if anyone is going to have her back. But Ashlin avoids her eyes. And all the guys are uncomfortably looking away. The other girls on the squad too. Then she waves her hand at one of the waitresses and says, "Can we *puh-lease* order," in her most whiny, impatient voice. She takes a sip of her water, and her hand is shaking.

Lil doesn't look at me. Or maybe I don't give her the chance. I turn back to the counter, take my stuff, and walk out of there as fast as I can.

I go outside and Mary sits up. "Hey. You okay?"

"Yeah," I say, smiling, because holy shit. "I'm good."

CHAPTER TWENTY-THREE

MARY

I'VE THOUGHT ABOUT QUITTING YEARBOOK committee a few times, but I keep telling myself to stick with it, even though I haven't gotten to do any photo collages yet. It's hard, because the fun jobs are already taken, and even if you ask if you can help, they pretend not to hear you.

The only person who hasn't totally ignored me is a sophomore named Marisa Viola. She goes over all the page proofs, looking for formatting errors or misspellings in the text. I pulled a chair up to her desk and read over her shoulder. She's super fast, and she's circling things in her red pencil before I can even notice them, but I think it's still good to have a second set of eyes looking out for mistakes.

After our Monday meeting, I decide to pop over to the library so I can take out one of those grammar and punctuation books. That'll definitely help me do a better job.

On my way there, I pass by the gym offices. Coach Christy's door is open. She's having a heated conversation with someone. And then I see Rennie, sitting on her knees in one of Coach Christy's chairs. She ducked out of yearbook early. All Rennie does is obsessively look through homecoming pictures and leave early. I swear, I don't understand why she even bothers.

As soon as I pass by, I press myself up to the wall and listen.

"Rennie, you didn't even show for the entire last month of our cheer practices," Coach Christy said with a sigh. "You're not exactly in good standing with me right now. You understand that, right?"

"Why do you think that is? Because of Lillia! How could I be around someone who'd steal homecoming queen from me?"

I hear Coach Christy's chair creak, like she's leaning way back. "I don't know how many times I have to tell you this, Rennie. I counted the ballots myself. I was the only one to touch them. Lillia Cho won homecoming queen fair and square."

I expect Rennie to back down, to listen to reason, but the exact opposite happens. With an unwavering voice, she says, "I won homecoming queen. I did. I've asked, like, everyone who they voted for, and like ninety-nine percent of the population said me. All I'm saying is that if we had a revote, you'd see. I'll pay to get the ballots printed up myself!"

"Rennie, please let this go. You and Lillia have been friends for a long time. You don't want to let something as petty as who won some cheap plastic tiara ruin your friendship, do you?"

Rennie laughs. She laughs and it sends shivers down my spine. "There is no friendship. And you can tell me all you want that perfect little Lillia had nothing to do with me getting screwed over that night, but I'll never believe you. Also, you suck as a cheering coach and your routines are all tired and nobody likes the music you pick for the halftime routines!"

In a flash Rennie's flying past me down the hall.

It scares me to know that Rennie figure out what we did. But thank God there's no way she can prove it.

CHAPTER TWENTY-FOUR

LILLIA

MONDAY AFTERNOON I'VE GONE UP AND DOWN THE length of the pool twice before Reeve even arrives. He doesn't get in the pool; instead he stands there watching me, eating an apple. I don't look up or acknowledge his presence. I keep doing what I'm doing. "You should point your toes," he says, chewing loudly. "Make your body longer."

"Excuse me, but I don't think you're allowed to eat in here," I huff. "And aren't you supposed to be wearing that walking cast?" He's dragging it behind him.

"I'm building up my pain tolerance." He tosses the apple

into the trash can. A perfect arc. I don't have to look to know it lands inside. Carelessly, he throws his towel on the bench where my stuff is. Then he dives into the lane next to mine, instead of the one on the far left the way he's been doing. My whole body stiffens. "Well, then you'll have no one to blame but yourself if you reinjure your leg." I don't need him critiquing me or giving me swimming advice. But I do try pointing my toes a little as I swim to the ladder, and I guess I can feel a very slight difference.

I scramble over to my towel because I'm freezing cold. I'm wrapping the towel around me like a blanket when he suddenly swims under the dividers and over toward me like a shark. He hoists himself out of the water, not bothering with the ladder. He hasn't done a single lap.

Silently, I hand him his towel. He looks at me right in the eyes and says, "You know what? I wasn't going to say anything . . . but yeah, Lil. Let's talk about my injury. Let's talk about how this all went down."

Oh my God. Please. Please no. "I have no idea what you're talking about." I turn to leave, but he grabs my arm.

"I know it was you who put something in my punch at homecoming."

It feels like the floor is coming out from under me; my knees are weak, and I'm two seconds from passing out.

"Tell me why," he says, his voice harsh now. His green eyes are boring into mine, and I'm looking back at him, trying not to flinch, trying not to give anything away, forcing myself to maintain eye contact. Don't they say liars can't look you in the eye?

I try to shake him off, but his grip is too strong. "What punch? What are you talking about? Let go of me!"

He doesn't let go. "You don't remember giving me a cup of punch? We were sitting at the table. You were bitching at me for leading Rennie on. Then we made nice and cheersed cups. You don't remember any of that?"

I say, "Reeve, you were wasted at the dance!"

His eyes narrow. "No, I wasn't. They did a drug test on me on the hospital. It came up positive for MDMA."

"I don't even know what MDMA is!" I cry.

"It's ecstasy. And you know that because you're the one who put it in my drink."

I force a swallow. "You were drunk by the time you got to Ash's house. I saw you guys drinking out of a flask, you were drinking in the limo, you were drinking at the dance! How can you be so sure that the punch I supposedly gave you had that MD whatever in it? Because I know so many drug dealers!"

"I know where you got the drugs." Reeve's mouth gets hard; his eyes narrow. He spits out, "Those guys you met on the beach were drug dealers! Rennie took me to their house so I could score weed for our fishing trip."

Wait. Reeve doesn't know. Not really. But my whole body goes cold anyway.

"Oh, you didn't know the guy you gave it up to was a drug dealer?"

It's the way he says it, the way he looks at me. With such disdain. Disgust.

Rennie told him. He knows everything. A hotness rises up inside of me then, and I slap him across the face as hard as I can. He stumbles backward, and there is a red imprint on his cheek from my hand. We stare at each other. His face is shocked; mine must be blank, because that's how I feel. Numb. I say, "I didn't get any drugs from those guys. You have no idea what you're talking about."

"Then explain it to me," he says.

"Didn't Rennie already tell you?" I say. In this moment I hate her like I've never hated anyone in my entire life.

"No. She didn't tell me anything. I saw it with my own eyes. I was there that night. At that party."

"I don't believe you."

"It was that house over on Shore Road. A piece-of-shit rental my dad manages. I rolled up over there after Alex's party died out. I saw you and Ren doing Irish car bombs on the kitchen table, and then I saw you guys go upstairs with them."

I'm reeling. He was there. He saw.

I start to turn away from him, wrapping my towel tighter around me. "Then you already know."

"Yeah, I know you're not the goody-goody everyone thinks you are."

I stare him down, my chin quivering with the effort of looking at him and not crying, not running away. "Then I guess you also know that I was so drunk I could barely keep my head up and that Rennie was right across the room, with the other guy. That I think I said to stop, I think I did, but I can't be *sure* I did." Then I do start to cry, because I can't anymore, I can't keep it inside me.

Reeve recoils. "I—I didn't know any of that." He lifts his arm like he's going to try to touch me, but I must flinch, because he drops it.

That was my secret, mine and Rennie's. It wasn't for anybody else to know. Especially not him. I cry harder, my tears mixing with the pool water dripping from my hair.

"I'm sorry," Reeve says. "Please don't cry."

I sink down onto the bench. He doesn't make a move; he just stands there awkwardly. "Then don't talk about things you don't know for sure," I say, wiping my cheeks with the corner of my towel.

"You're right," he agrees quickly. "I'm a dick. I never should have brought it up."

I'm still crying; now that I've started, I can't seem to stop. Tears roll down my cheeks, and I keep wiping them away with my towel.

"Lillia . . . if I had known you were that drunk, you have to know that I would never have let you go upstairs with that guy. I'd have stopped you." He squats down in front of me so we're at eye level, and he balances his hands on my knees. When I flinch, he quickly backs away and balances his elbows on his thighs. He pleads, "Please stop crying."

I nod. I let out a big breath of air. There's an odd sense of relief in telling someone. In saying it out loud. I feel . . . a little bit lighter. A little tiny bit. But it's something.

We stay like that for what feels like a long time, and then he shifts, and I can tell his leg is bothering him. "Does your leg hurt?" I ask. My voice pings off the walls; it's like the room isn't used to sound anymore, we've been quiet that long.

"Not at all," he says.

I stand up and offer him my hand, which he takes. He stretches his leg out, massaging it. "You shouldn't push yourself so hard," I tell him. "You should listen to your doctors."

Reeve shrugs his shoulders, and his back muscles ripple. "I have to push myself if I want to get a scholarship."

Sniffling, I say, "Well, hasn't your physical therapist told you you'll make it worse if you overdo it? I'm sure he has. Or she has. If he or she's any good."

"Oh, so you're a doctor now too?" Reeve says, smiling slightly. "Looks like we've got another Dr. Cho on the island."

I start to dry my hair with my towel. Then I sit down and open up my bag, pulling out my leggings and my zip-up hoodie. "I hate going outside in the cold after swimming. It feels like I'll never be warm again."

"See, that's why you should be wearing a swim cap."

I shudder. "Never. I would look like a peanut head."

Shaking his head at me, Reeve says, "Princess Lillia. Always so vain." He sounds gentle, though. Affectionate. He sits down, near but not too near. "Then let's not go yet. Wait for your hair to dry more."

So that's what we do. When I'm in my car, I text Kat. I don't explain exactly how it happened, but I say that I'm finally getting somewhere.

CHAPTER TWENTY-FIVE

KAT

TUESDAY IS OUR THIRD MEETING OF THE COLLEGE prep group. A few kids have dropped out, which I totally don't get. Hello! It's essentially a get-out-of-class-free card every couple of weeks.

Alex is already there, clicking away on his laptop. I sneak up behind him to scare the shit out of him, but then I notice what website he's looking at.

The University of Southern California.

Funny. I thought Alex was only applying to two colleges. Early decision to the University of Michigan, and Boston College as a safety.

He clicks a drop-down menu with all the undergraduate majors listed and selects the songwriting program.

Before I can say anything, Ms. Chirazo walks over to us. Alex quickly closes his laptop, as if he was looking at porn or something. I pull out the chair next to him and take a seat.

"Okay, you two. I've read both your essay drafts." She sets the papers down on the table, Alex's and mine. Alex's doesn't have much written on his. A couple of check marks in red pen. Mine is covered in scribbles.

Damn. I snatch it away so Alex doesn't see.

"Alex, I love what you're exploring here. I think you make a strong thesis about how class and privilege disappear on the football field, and success hinges only on hard work. But I want you to make sure that you aren't too critical of your parents' wealth when you relate back to your own life. I'm hoping you can temper some of those places to sound a bit more grateful for the opportunities you've been afforded."

Alex nods. "Sure, of course."

I slump in my chair. I thought Alex's essay was fine, it was well-written and tight, but I also know exactly what Ms. Chirazo is talking about. There were a couple of points where I felt like he was being kind of a doof. Where he'd say things like, *I never knew how rich my family was, and how that might make people think of me differently.*

Come on, dude. Your SUV costs more than a year's tuition at Oberlin.

Ms. Chirazo turns her head to me. "Now, Kat . . . I was surprised by your essay."

"Pleasantly surprised?" I say it with zero enthusiasm, because I already know she hated it.

I wrote about how freaking bizarre it is to grow up in a place like Jar Island. How it shelters you from the outside world. I talked about my friendship with Kim, how music has made the world seem a lot bigger. I talked about how ready I am to get the eff out of here and start living my life. Obviously not in those exact words, but it was pretty much an indictment of this place. It was a counterpoint to Alex's essay. It's kind of hilarious, how Alex and I basically wrote about the same thing. It's not like we planned it.

"I thought Kat's essay was great," Alex says. "Jar Island *is* a weird place to live, and that should help her stand out."

Bless his bleeding heart.

Ms. Chirazo's glasses are on a chain around her neck. She puts them up on her nose and reaches for my paper. "I agree. I'm not saying that your essay isn't good, Kat. It is. I don't know that I've ever seen Jar Island in quite the way you present it." She starts turning pages, and presses her lips together tight. "My biggest problem is that it doesn't tell me much about you. It's more about this place. And remember, we're trying to make the admissions committees think of you as a real person." She sets the paper down and turns her chair toward me. "Have you considered writing about losing your mother at such a young age?"

My jaw drops. Did she really go there? I swear to God, Ms. Chirazo freaking gets off on the fact that my mom is dead. She brings it up every freaking chance she gets!

"I considered it, and then decided against it," I say, using all my energy to sound calm and not rage on her. That's probably what she wants. For me to explode so she can force me to go to more counseling sessions.

"Would you mind explaining your rationale?"

I huff. "Look. I have a lot of reasons, but I'll give you one. I don't want to use the fact that my mom died to get people to pity me. Not to mention I'm pretty sure I'm not the only high school senior in the United States to have lost a parent. It's not as uncommon as people think. And there are kids out there with way, way worse problems than I've got. Trust me." I say it pretty bitchy. "So I don't need to use it. My grades are stellar, and I'm pretty sure I killed it on the SATs last time."

"Your academic record is great, Kat. Especially the fact that you've accomplished what you have in light of your situation."

"My situation," I repeat, my lip curling.

And then I feel it. Alex's hand on my knee, underneath the

table, where no one else can see. He gives my leg an encouraging squeeze, a sign to breathe, to not let this upset me so bad, to not explode on this lady in front of the whole room.

I lean back in my chair and say, "Fine. I'll consider it. Whatever."

"I don't mean to upset you, Kat. But please do think about it. You can write about your mother without exploiting her memory. I think you owe it to yourself to speak about that experience and how you derived so much strength from it."

I force a tight-lipped smile as Ms. Chirazo gets up, pats me on the back, and moves on to the next group.

"Thanks for that," I say to Alex, under my breath. "If you hadn't been here, I'd have gone off on her."

He bumps my leg under the table. I wonder if he'll say anything comforting, if he'll ask about my mom, or try and talk me into writing that kind of essay. But all Alex says is, "Any cool bands playing this week?"

I think about telling him that I'm going to a show with Ricky, to see if it might make him jealous. But I decide against it . . . because what if Alex is asking because he wants to hang out? We've been having a good time together lately, like last summer.

I decide to play it coy. "There's a band coming Thursday that I might want to see," I say. "What are you up to?"

"I'm going to Boston with Lillia. We're leaving first thing

tomorrow morning. Taking two days off from school."

Huh. Never mind. "Shit. I forgot. I have a date Thursday night, actually. He's in a band. Lead singer. They're pretty big in Germany."

"Whoa. Cool."

"Yeah, I know right?" Lillia didn't tell me about any special trip with Alex. "What are you guys heading to Boston for?"

"We've both got prelim interviews with alums." He sighs. "It ended up being this whole fight between my mom and my dad. If he had his way, I'd only apply to Michigan. But my mom said I should at least visit my backup school. Between us, I think she wanted to go shopping."

Okay. So it's not like a romantic trip or anything. "You should probably check out Berklee, too."

"Huh?"

"It's the number-three music school in the country. I think they might have a songwriting major too." Alex's face gets tight, and I suddenly feel guilty, like I've said something I shouldn't have. "Sorry. I saw over your shoulder."

I wonder if Alex is going to try and deny it. Which would be weird. I mean, what's the big deal? "I don't think so," Alex says quietly. "There probably won't be time."

"How you guys getting there? Driving? Leave a little earlier, then. Or come back a little later. Whatever."

Alex grimaces. He leans forward and whispers, embarrassed, "We're taking a private charter plane. I'd be fine with driving. But my dad's already out of town, and he thinks my mom is a terrible driver, so he told us to take the plane. He pays to be a part of this service, so it doesn't actually cost us anything."

A private plane. Jesus.

The bell rings. "Welp," I say, and quick pack up my stuff, "you two kids have fun." But I don't mean it. Not at all.

CHAPTER TWENTY-SIX

LILLIA

IT'S TUESDAY, AND SCHOOL'S ALREADY LET OUT. I'VE been in and out of the pool, and now I'm studying for AP US History on the bleachers while Reeve does more laps. I figure this way we can walk out together; I can give him a proper good-bye. You can't flirt with a boy if he's underwater and you're on dry land.

Reeve has a clipboard lying on top of his gym bag. I glance over at it and recognize the bubble loops of Rennie's handwriting right away. She's still plotting all his workout sessions. I smile smugly to myself. She'd kill to be here with him. But she's not. I am.

Though it's obvious Rennie doesn't know anything about our after-school meet-ups. If she did, she'd drain the pool. I guess Reeve hasn't mention it. Me.

After half an hour or so, Reeve finally climbs out of the pool. "I'm starving," he says, stretching his arms out and shaking water from his ears. "Wanna get pancakes or something?"

My heart skips a beat. This is the first time he's initiated an actual hangout. This is real progress. Ever since our fight, things have felt different.

Casually, I look up from my textbook. "Hmm, I don't know. I'm nowhere near done studying. Don't you have a US History test on Friday too?" I'm in AP and he's not, but I'm pretty sure we both have a test on Friday, when I'm back from Boston.

Reeve shrugs. "I haven't been to class in a couple of days. I've been doubling down in the weight room. Now that I have my walking cast, I've been working on my sprints. That way, when the doctor gives me the okay to go full-throttle, I'll be ahead of the game."

"Are you serious? Then you'd better start studying, like, yesterday!"

"I'm not worried. I have a great memory," he tells me. Tapping his head he boasts, "Like a steel trap."

"Okay, so what year was Shays' Rebellion?"

"Um . . ." Reeve leans forward and peeks at the notebook in

my lap. "1786." A droplet of pool water from his hair splashes onto the page.

I shove him away. Crossly, I blow on the page and say, "Reeve! You're getting my notebook all wet!"

He sits down next to me. "Come on, this is boring. Let's get out of here. I'm starved."

Pancakes do sound good. We could go to the Greasy Spoon. They serve real maple syrup there. But this test is important. It's practically a midterm.

"I have to finish my note cards." I reach into my backpack and pull out a chocolate chip granola bar. "Eat this for now," I say, handing it over and going back to my book.

Abruptly he asks me, "Why are you being so nice to me?"

I look up, surprised. Nice? It's a granola bar. "Because we're friends."

"Friends?" Reeve scoffs. "Admit it, Cho. You've never liked me."

Whoa.

I mean, it's pretty much true. But I never thought Reeve noticed whether or not I liked him, much less cared. And it's not like I've always *hated* him or anything like that. At least, not before I met Mary.

I quickly try to string some words together. "Yes I did!" I shake my head. "I do."

Reeve doesn't look convinced. Impulsively I hold my hand out to him. "Well, we're friends now, aren't we?" He cocks his head and gives me a nod, and I say, "So shake my hand!"

He finally takes my hand and shakes it and says, "Does that mean you're going to help me study this week, friend? Tomorrow, postswim library trip?"

"Oh . . . I can't. I'm leaving in the morning for Boston for a college trip."

"You too? Lind told me he's going to visit schools in Boston this week."

I hesitate. "Yeah . . . he's going with me." I quickly add, "With our moms. They're the ones who set the whole thing up. I didn't even know about it until a week ago. We're all staying at our apartment in the city."

I don't know why I'm explaining it to Reeve. It's not like it's his business. And judging by the bored look on his face, it's not like he cares. "Have fun," he says, yawning and stretching his arms over his head again.

"We will," I say. I'm annoyed now, and I can't pinpoint the reason. I snap my book shut and put it back in my saddlebag. "I should get home and pack." He'll probably meet up with Rennie now. I don't even know what the deal is between those two. I wonder if they've DTRed or whatever.

"Your hair's still wet," Reeve protests.

"I'll be okay. I'll run to my car." I throw on my hoodie and tie my towel around my waist.

Lazily, Reeve reaches over and pulls my hood up so it's covering my head. "Why do you need, like, ten hours to pack for two days?"

"It's three days, actually. We're not coming back until early Friday morning. Besides, my mom made reservations for us at fancy places, so I have to figure out what I'm bringing. And these interviews are important. I need to look my absolute best."

"Sounds fun," he says, rolling his eyes. "Are you guys going to go to a ballet too? Maybe an opera?"

"Maybe!" I screw up my lips tight. "And maybe we'll go to a Red Sox game! My dad's friend has box seats!"

Reeve busts up laughing. He's laughing so hard he can't talk.

"What? What?" I demand, my hands on my hips.

"Lillia, Lillia, Lillia. Baseball season's over, girl. You guys aren't going to any Red Sox game!" He shakes his head, holding his sides, guffawing. "You two nerds have fun, though."

I want to push him off the bleacher. And then it occurs to me. It's the second time he's told me to have fun.

Which is boy speak for "I'm jealous." Reeve is jealous! Of Alex. Of me and Alex, together.

It's working. The plan is working!

I pack my bag up and say, "So are we getting pancakes or not?"

"I thought you had to pack," he challenges.

"I might have time for one pancake," I say, giving him what I hope are flirty eyes.

Reeve stands up, stretching. "All right. Whatever Princess Lillia wants, she gets." But I can tell he's happy, because he puts his hands on my shoulders and gives them a quick squeeze.

CHAPTER TWENTY-SEVEN

WEDNESDAY NIGHT, I'M STILL THINKING ABOUT WHAT Ms. Chirazo said about my college essay. Maybe I'm being stupid. I should do whatever the hell it takes to take to get into Oberlin and score some good financial aid. Ain't no way private planes are in my future. And I don't know why, but no matter how many beers I drink, I can't stop thinking about Alex and Lillia jetting off together this week.

"Let's go hot-tubbing!" I suddenly announce to everyone in the garage. "Who's in?"

Ricky, Skeeter, and a bunch of other guys look my way. "Where?" Ricky says.

I turn off the radio. "I know a place. A mansion. And it's completely empty tonight." Seems stupid to let Alex's house go to waste.

"But it's kind of cold out," Skeeter whines.

"That's why we're going in a *hot tub*, dummy."

"I don't want to get arrested," Ricky says.

I walk over to him and pull on the strings of his hoodie. "You won't. I'm telling you. No one is home. And the kid has no neighbors."

Ricky shrugs. "Okay. I'm in."

It's me, five guys, and one of their girlfriends who bugs the shit out of me so I never bothered learning her name. Pat stays back. He says he wants to keep working on his bike, but I know the truth: He has a thing with hot tubs. They skeeve him out. The heat, the germs, all the bodies cooking together in one big bathtub. I don't blow up his spot, though, mainly because I don't want to gross everyone else out.

Which affords me a real opportunity. Tonight, I'm going to let Ricky get what he's been after. The kid's been flirting with me for weeks. And I could use a good make-out. I don't even care that I have school tomorrow. I haven't kissed a boy since . . . Lind. I think about calling to invite Mary, but decide against it. It might scare the poor thing to see my moves in action.

We put two sixers of beer in a plastic bag, hop on a bunch of bikes, and tear over to Alex's place. The lights in his house are all on, like someone's home, but I know it's empty. I have to drag Ricky up the driveway.

"You sure about this?" he keeps saying.

I crack open a beer and take a sip before offering it to him. I get close to his face and say, "You know it." I like flirting with Ricky. He's sweet. He's two years older than me, a year younger than Pat. We were both at Jar Island High together at some point, but back then he was dating someone else. Sarah? I forget. Anyway, he dumped her this summer, after she cheated on him with her professor at the JICC. That's the kind of shit that goes on in our community college, which is why I need out of here.

The fence is locked, so we have to climb on top of the trash cans to get over. As soon as we land on the other side, the backyard lights automatically turn on. My heart stops, and I'm just waiting for a siren or something. We all hold still, and then they click off. "See?" I say, trying to sound nonchalant. "It's fine."

Alex's pool is closed for the season, half drained and covered with a tight tarp. Oh shit. I take off the cover of Alex's hot tub, and thank God it's full of water. It's a pretty pimped-out model, with buttons that make different colored lights go on and a built-in stereo. We all get in, crank the jets, and it doesn't take long before it gets toasty. Ricky doesn't have a bathing suit, so he goes in in his underwear. He's wearing black boxer briefs, and he looks freaking hot. His body is cut, you can see every ab muscle, and he's got a wicked scar from when he got his appendix removed.

I'm in my black bikini and a black tank. I push Tim's girlfriend out of the way so I can sit next to Ricky.

"This place is sick!" one of the guys says.

"Damn, I wish I was loaded," says Skeeter.

It sort of pisses me off, because most of these dudes will never have money, will never get to experience this side of Jar Island living. Unless they become pool boys. Which some of them might.

Tim asks me, "You know the guy who lives here?"

"Yeah."

Ricky says, "You ever hook up with him?"

"Hell, no," I lie, because I know what my friends think about these kinds of people. They aren't like us. Though it may be racist, or classist, or whatever . . . it's freaking true. Alex isn't like me. After all, he's in a goddamned private plane, going to visit a school where his parents will most likely make a huge donation to get him accepted. I don't know why he's even in the college essay class with me. He doesn't need a good essay when he's got a blank check. I finish my beer and throw the empty can in the yard, like I don't give a shit. I get close to Ricky. He puts his arm around me for like a second, but then takes it back.

Um, weird.

I get a stomach cramp. Have I read the signs wrong? Is Ricky not into me? I don't know if I could take another Alex Lind scenario. A guy who's only being nice, not actually pursuing me. My ego ain't indestructible.

I look across the hot tub, at all of my brother's friends, watching us.

Oh. Okay. That I can work with. He wants to be alone with me.

"Shit," I say suddenly. Everyone gets real quiet.

"What?" Ricky whispers.

"I think I heard something." I climb out of the water. Damn, it's bitter out. My whole body is steaming.

"What? I didn't hear anything."

Dummy. I grab Ricky's arm. "Come investigate with me."

He gives me this pleading look, then glances over at the rest of the people in the hot tub. But they're all back to giggling and speaking in whispers. They aren't paying attention to us at all.

"Hurry up!" I growl. I'm freezing my ass off.

We walk out of the main yard and around to the side of the pool house. It hits me how awesome it will feel to kiss Ricky, basically right in front of Alex's bedroom. I push him up against the wall and say, "So, we gonna do this or what?" But it doesn't sound as sexy as I want it to, because I'm shivering so damn hard.

His lips stop, like, millimeters away from mine. "Everyone's right over there, Kat."

I put my hands up on his shoulders and drape myself against him, boobs pressed up against his chest. If nothing else, it'll warm me up. "What are you worried about that for?" I whisper. My breath comes out in puffs. I close my eyes and wait for him to plant his lips on mine.

Nothing.

When I open my eyes, Ricky's looking at me with these pathetic puppy-dog eyes.

I let my arms fall to my side. "Seriously, Ricky? You're blowing me off right now?" My voice is much less sexy. It's straight-up pissed off.

Ricky shrugs. "Come on, it's cold. Let's get back in the hot tub."

I walk away from him, teeth chattering so loud it's all I hear. The last thing I need is to get hung up on another ball-less guy.

Ricky tries to guide me to face him. "Kat, wait."

I'm already gone, headed to the hot tub. But instead of getting into the water again, I grab my shit from one of the outdoor lounge chairs. "Hey. The cops drove by and flashed their lights in the yard. We'd better bounce. Now." Ricky comes back, he hears me tell this lie, but he doesn't call me out on it. Everyone rushes out of the water and heads barefoot back to where we parked the bikes.

I follow them out, but at the last second I glance over my shoulder at all the shit we left around Alex's yard. The empty beer cans and the cigarette butts.

"You coming?" Ricky asks me.

I don't answer him. And he doesn't ask again before he leaves me behind.

I find a trash bag inside one of the garbage cans and start walking around the yard, using my cell phone light to find the trash in the grass. Not long into it, snow begins to fall. My shirt is soaked; I don't even have a ride home. FML.

CHAPTER TWENTY-EIGHT

LILLIA

IT'S SNOWING OUTSIDE. TEENY TINY FLAKES THAT barely stick, but it looks beautiful. I always did love Boston in winter. The city looks like something out of a Charles Dickens novel.

We're waiting for a table at Salt, my mom's and my favorite restaurant. They have the best lobster bisque; the waiter serves it tableside in a silver urn. We had a seven o'clock reservation, but Mrs. Lind took so long getting ready we missed it, and now it's almost eight and we still haven't had dinner. I feel faint.

"This is ridiculous," Mrs. Lind says loudly, so everyone can hear. She's in a fox-fur coat and black stiletto boots that go up past her knee.

"They should have one for us any minute," my mom says. "I see them clearing a table for four now." Even though she sounds as serene as ever, her lipsticked red lips are a thin line, and I know she's annoyed.

"We've been waiting for half an hour," Mrs. Lind huffs. "On a Wednesday."

"It's a five-star restaurant," my mom reminds her. "And this isn't the island."

Mrs. Lind shakes her head from side to side, her coppery hair swishing around her shoulders. "I'm going to say something to the hostess."

"Celeste," my mom pleads.

Luckily, the hostess comes over to us then and says our table's ready. "At last," Mrs. Lind huffs, and Alex and I exchange a look.

It's been like this since we got here—just shy of tense. Like, my mom wanted to stop by her old interior-design office before dinner, so she and I could say hi to Bert and Cleve, her friends who've known me since I was a baby. They're partners, and they travel all over the world getting inspired by rugs in Marrakesh and ceramic tiles in Provence. They send Nadia and me the nicest Christmas gifts—lavender oils and crystal bracelets and jars of Dead Sea mud.

But we couldn't go because Mrs. Lind was all, *Grace, we need to stop by Hermés before it closes; I want to get your opinion on that end table I've got my eye on.* So we did that instead. Alex kept making a pretend gun with his fingers and pretend shooting himself in the temple. I kept lingering by the enamel bracelets, hoping my mom would notice and add one to my Christmas wish list. I super-casually pointed out one I liked and she was like, *Not going to happen, Lilli; you do not need a six-hundred-dollar bracelet.* Mrs. Lind tried to tell the saleswoman to add it to her bill, and my mom said absolutely not, which Mrs. Lind made a face at. I felt guilty about that, because if I'd known how much it cost, obviously I never would have said anything. Though I had to admit, wearing it to school and seeing the look on Rennie's face would have been worth the six hundred dollars.

And then, when we were touring the BC campus, my mom wanted to look at the library and the art building and Mrs. Lind kept complaining about her feet hurting. I knew what my mom was thinking because I was thinking the same thing—why would you wear four-and-a-half-inch stiletto heels on a campus tour? So impractical.

The hostess ushers us toward the back, to a sleek leather banquette. I sit down next to my mom, and Alex and his mom sit down across from us.

Mrs. Lind picks up the wine list. "Red or white, hon?" she asks my mom.

"I might have a glass of sauvignon blanc," my mom says, reaching over and tucking my hair behind my ear. To me she says, "You look so pretty tonight, honey."

"Oh, Lil's always a knockout," Mrs. Lind says. "God, I wish I could still dress like that."

I smile a humble smile, through my lashes. I did take extra care with my outfit. I feel like on Jar Island it's whatever, but people get more dressed up in Boston. They care more. I've got on a snug heather-gray sweater dress with a white patent-leather belt that cinches around my waist and a pair of platform booties that I bought for this trip. I curled my hair and pushed it all over to one side in a low ponytail. When I came out of the bathroom, Alex told me I looked nice. He was wearing a navy cashmere sweater, but after he saw me, he went and changed and put a light blue button-down and a tie underneath.

As soon as the server comes over, before he can say a word, Mrs. Lind says, "We'll have a bottle of sauvignon blanc and a bottle of Veuve Clicquot."

My mom looks alarmed. She's not a big drinker. "Celeste, I don't know—"

"Live a little! We'll let the kids have a sip of the champagne.

The wine is for us." Mrs. Lind winks at me, and Alex and I shrug at each other.

"A tiny sip," my mom says to me.

Alex and I drink a thimbleful of champagne each, and our moms finish the bottle. With each new glass they get sillier and sillier, and the tension from before fades away.

"To the future!" Mrs. Lind says, waving her glass in the air.

"To our babies!" my mom says, clinking her glass to Mrs. Lind's.

Mrs. Lind touches the top of Alex's head. Mournfully she says, "Where have our babies gone?"

I swear, everyone in the restaurant is looking. That's when they start sharing stories about us. My mom tells the table about the time she took me to the zoo. I was scared of all the animals, and when Mom paid for me to ride one of the elephants, I completely lost it and peed on him.

"She ruined her dress," my mom chokes out, sputtering with laughter. "It was the sweetest dress, too—it was white, and it had a lace pinafore and puffy sleeves. I bought it in Paris when she was tiny. . . . She looked like an angel in it. Lilli, do you remember that dress?"

I cross my arms. *"No."* In a lower voice I say, "Please, no more stories, Mom."

"Ooh, wait, I've got a good one," Mrs. Lind shrieks. She

proceeds to tell us about how hard it was to get Alex to stop breastfeeding, and the whole time Alex is glowering at her like he wants to take her out with his salad plate.

While the moms are busy cracking up, Alex kicks me under the table. He mouths, *They're so wasted.*

I mouth back, *I know.*

We share a secret smile, and I wonder—what would it be like if we were here together? At the same college, I mean. I think it would be like having a piece of home with me.

The next night, Alex and I are hanging out in the den of my family's Boston apartment, the TV flashing a show that neither of us is really watching. I think it's because we're so beat. Thank God we go home tomorrow. Even if I have to go straight to school.

Alex is in the middle of the couch, his legs folded underneath him, in a pair of his track pants and an Academic Decathlon T-shirt from last spring, when we lost the championship by two stupid questions. I'm draped sideways on my dad's favorite leather armchair in leggings and a baggy sweater, under one of the snuggly cashmere throws my mom is obsessed with. She's bought at least ten of them, all in cream.

We're flipping through the glossy university brochures that we got on our tours today, laughing at the obviously staged photos. We went to Tufts in the morning, BC in the afternoon; then we split up so Alex could go suit shopping and I could go to Wellesley, the girls' school.

"Oh, come on," Alex says, and presses his lips together to stifle a laugh. "Lil, tell me what's wrong with his picture." He turns the brochure around and points at a page-size photo of a student in a lab coat and goggles, proudly holding up an empty glass beaker.

I crack up when I figure it out. "Oh my gosh. They couldn't even put anything *inside* the beaker? Don't they have a prop guy or an art director?"

Alex starts laughing so hard he can't breathe. "It's like, dude, I don't know what you're smiling about. You're going to fail your experiment unless you put something in that beaker." He shakes his head and then puts the brochure down on the coffee table with the others. "Pass me a cookie?"

I toss him a new sleeve of Chips Ahoy!, since mine has only five left inside. The brochure in my lap shows pictures of students in their dorm rooms. There's one where four girls are smiling up from a pair of bunk beds inside a room that looks about as big as a prison cell. "I don't know how I'm going to live in a dorm. My bathroom is bigger than that room we saw today." I take the last sip of milk in my glass and kick off my blanket. "You want something to drink?"

Alex nods. "Water, please. You'll probably join a sorority, don't you think?"

I shrug. "Maybe. It depends on where I end up, I guess. What about you? Do you think you'll pledge a fraternity?"

"Ah, I don't know. I think a lot of those guys are meat-heads." Alex watches me get up. "Maybe you could live here. This apartment is sick, Lil."

"Shhhh," I say, and nudge my chin toward the hallway where the bedrooms are. My mom's in the master bedroom; Mrs. Lind's sleeping in the guest room. "Mom's already freaking out about me leaving, and my dad would love to keep me under lock and key here with him."

Alex reaches for the remote and puts on sports. "I doubt anything will wake our moms up tonight."

He's probably right. They popped open a bottle of red wine once we got back at the apartment. I swear, they've probably consumed more alcohol in the last two days than the freshmen we saw in the dorms. Their wine glasses are on the table, still relatively full, with two different colors of lipstick on the rims. I stick them in the dishwasher, empty what's left from the bottle, and put that in the recycling bin. Hopefully, my dad won't be mad at my mom for opening it. Every word on the label is in French. He keeps all his best wine and champagne here.

On the way over to Tufts this morning, I could tell my

mom was getting annoyed at Mrs. Lind. Mrs. Lind was running the GPS on her phone, trying to navigate us out of traffic, even though my mom knows Boston like the back of her hand and obviously had the best way to get across town. Mom had wanted to get us there early, so we could park at one end of the campus and walk to the admissions hall, but Mrs. Lind kept saying that the spots Mom tried to park in were too small for our SUV. We were almost late, so Mom used the valet parking at a nearby restaurant and tipped the guy big since we weren't actually eating there.

It takes me a few tries to remember which kitchen cabinets have the glasses. I pour us both waters. I haven't been to the apartment in over a year, but Dad's here all the time, working at the hospital. We have a cleaning lady, and a person whose job it is to keep the house stocked with food and stuff, so he doesn't have to worry about anything. God forbid he'd actually have to go to the store and buy a carton of milk.

When I get back to the den, Alex is staring out the windows at the city below. I put our glasses down and stand next to him. It's snowing again.

"It's pretty out there," I say, leaning forward so my forehead is against the glass. We're on the thirtieth floor of a huge high-rise, and you can see everything. It's still another couple weeks until Thanksgiving, but lots of people have holiday lights already strung up on their roofs or their balconies. The trees down in the park are all bare and spindly, and the sky is super inky black with flecks of white. The people walking around look like tiny ants.

Alex turns to me with a big grin on his face "You want to go for a walk or something? I'm not tired."

"Now?" It's after midnight, and I'm basically in my sleeping clothes. "But we've got school tomorrow." Plus, my feet kind of hurt from all the walking we did today. I've got two blisters coming, one on each pinkie toe. I didn't want to wear heels, but Mom insisted because I was going to an interview. And when we were strolling around Wellesley's campus, she leaned in and whispered, "Never, ever, ever, Lillia," and pointed to a group of girls who were walking to class in PJ bottoms and slippers. I rolled my eyes, because yeah, right, like I would ever.

"Come on, Lil. Let's have an adventure without any chaperones." He groans. "This was supposed to be a trip about our futures, but I haven't felt more like a little kid in a long time."

I laugh. I know what he means. Both our moms were completely on top of us today. They asked, like, double the questions Alex and I did on the college tour. Mom picked every restaurant we went to, not that I minded. I love the homemade gnocchi at Sorrento's. I sometimes ask Daddy to bring it home for me when he takes the hospital's private plane, but it never tastes the same when it's not fresh fresh fresh. And Mrs. Lind kept fussing with Alex's hair or his tie.

I'm about to admit to Alex that I've never actually walked around Boston alone, and definitely not at night. But he looks so excited, and I'm not that tired either, especially not after all those sweets. So I say, "Okay."

I tiptoe into my room, trade my leggings for a pair of jeans. I put some Band-Aids on my pinkie toes and slip on a pair of boots. Before I walk out the door, I grab my phone and I see that I have a text from Reeve. It says, *So did you and Lind go to the opera or are you having a spa day?* I laugh out loud at the thought of Alex and me getting mani-pedis in matching robes. I text back, *Spa day. Duh!*

When I come out, Alex has cleaned up our mess in the den. He's changing in the corner, where he's put his duffel bag full of clothes. He's wearing jeans too, and he's putting on a pair of sneakers, but he doesn't have a shirt on yet. I can see every muscle in his shoulders and arms. I pop around the corner and pretend like I don't see him, and give him a few seconds of privacy.

We're so quiet as we sneak down the hall and open the front door. Alex shushes me as I unlock the dead bolt and slowly pull the door open. Once we're in the elevator, I let out a deep breath. We walk past the doorman together and out onto the street. Alex gives me a high five.

Boston is even prettier at night. It's an old city, with a lot of charming details, like gas streetlights and wooden signs.

"I like this city," Alex says. "So much to see and do. I'll probably die of boredom in Michigan. "

"Do you think that's where you'll end up going?"

Alex shrugs. "My dad's donated a bunch of money. And his best fraternity brother is on the board of directors. I think it's inevitable."

I rub his arm. "You'll make the best of it," I tell him. Because that's the kind of guy Alex is.

Our apartment is somewhat close to Harvard Square, so that's where we walk to. At first I'm a little scared, because there aren't a ton of people out, and the street we take has a bunch of dark alleys. I keep close to Alex, my arm threaded through his. But the closer we get to the school, the more kids we see out on the streets. I guess it doesn't matter that they have class tomorrow or that it's snowing out. We follow a flow of them to a street where there are a lot of bars.

He takes my hand so we won't lose each other in the crowd. "They should put this on the tour," Alex says with a laugh.

I start to say something back when a pack of drunk frat

guys stumbles out the double doors. A wave of nausea and abject fear crashes over me, and I freeze up. For a second I think I see him. Mike. But then he turns around and it's not him after all.

"Are you okay?" Alex asks me and gives my hand a tender squeeze. I can barely hear him through the sound of my own heart beating in my ears.

What if I did run into Mike? Would he remember me? Would he apologize for . . . what happened? Or does he think it was nothing? That's probably it. He probably doesn't even remember me.

My chest feels so tight it's hard to breathe. Amherst is a few hours away from Boston. That's what I say to calm myself down. But they could be here. It's not a crazy idea; it's totally possible. I bet lots of college kids come to Boston to party.

Maybe I don't want to come to school in Boston. Maybe I'll apply to a school on the West Coast—UC Berkeley maybe, or UCLA. I'll run as far as I have to to never see his face again.

I think I finally get what Mary has been going through all these years. Why she left, and why she came back. She wants closure. It's not something I'll ever get, but I can to help her get hers.

"Are you okay?" Alex asks me again.

I nod. "Let's keep walking, okay?"

My pace is decidedly quicker, but Alex keeps up with me fine.

When I get back to my room, I check my phone and there's another text from Reeve. It says, *What are you up to for real? Bored out of your mind?* I text back, *We just got back from a walk in the snow! So beautiful here!* There. Let him chew on that.

CHAPTER TWENTY-NINE

KAT

On Friday, Alex and I are supposedly working on practice resumes, which is stupid because it's not like college apps even ask you for a resume. But Ms. Chirazo keeps saying "in the real world" you need them, so we might as well get some practice in.

But I start to freak, because when it comes down to listing all my extracurriculars, my resume is looking pretty thin. Pretty much just my name and GPA. Oh yeah, and my summer job at the marina. I quick put that down too. I sneak a peek at Alex's, and he's got all kinds of shit on there—interning at his dad's company, academic decathlon, volunteering at an animal shelter in Boston, some choir.

I lay my head down on my notebook and close my eyes. I still haven't revised my essay to include stuff with my mom. I know Ms. Chirazo is pissed about that. She didn't even act excited when I mentioned that I think I did well at my SAT retest a few weeks ago. Hopefully I'll crack 1900, by the grace of freaking God. That will put me a few points over what you need to get into Oberlin. But this, this resume shit, it's a problem I'll have to work on.

When Ms. Chirazo leaves the room to take a phone call, I lean into Alex and say, "Hey, how was Boston? Did you check out Berklee?"

Alex looks up from his paper. "Nah, I didn't get a chance. Our schedule was packed."

"Alex, you dummy! Why didn't you at least stop by?"

"I didn't see the point."

"What? Why not?"

Alex leans back in his chair and taps the table with his pencil. "If I were going to apply to a music program, I'd do USC. Los Angeles is, like, the center of the music biz. And the emphasis there is more on contemporary songwriting, not classical, which is what I'm interested in." He shakes his head. "Anyway, there's no point, because I'm not applying to any music programs."

"But you love music."

"Sure. But, like my mom was saying, it's not like you're guaranteed a record deal or anything like that if you graduate from a music program. If I do a business program, I'll be set. And I could still take a music class as an elective."

I give him the side eye. "Business? Since when do you care about business?"

"I have to think long-term, Kat. And with my dad's contacts, I could—"

"But you want to write music." I shake my head. "And sure, nothing is guaranteed, but that's what makes it awesome, you know? The fact that it isn't!" I glance around the room. Everyone's looking at me. Probably because I'm getting loud. I lower my voice and say, "You've got to go balls to the wall because you love music. Fuck everything and everyone because you're going to give it a shot regardless."

Alex wants this. I can tell, because he doesn't say respond right away. He stares off into space for a second, working it over in his head. Then he frowns and says, "You know, even if I got in, I doubt my parents would pay for it. They don't exactly envision a life for me as a starving artist. My dad's always talked about me working for his company when I graduate college."

"Alex, I hate to be the one to break this to you, but you're fucking rich. You're going to have money no matter what. You already have a safety net! Your parents aren't going to let you starve in the street. Apply to USC. What can it hurt? Maybe you won't get in. I don't know. Maybe you suck. I've never heard your stuff." I elbow him and he laughs. "Stop being such a little bitch and give it a shot. What do you have to lose? So they reject you. So what. Then you pick yourself back up and you go to business school like your daddy wants. But you'll never know unless you try."

"I guess."

I think about mentioning how I've heard Oberlin has a kick-ass conservatory, but I swallow it down. My life is complicated enough. I put my hand on his back. "Go for it. Balls to the wall. California or bust!"

He scratches his head. "Maybe I'll look at Berklee. At least if I went to school in Boston, I'd have Lillia there."

I feel a pinprick in my chest. "Dude, you said USC is the program for you. Don't shoot for second best because of a girl."

Alex looks startled. "What? That's not what I'm saying."

"Oh no?"

"No! Geez, lower your voice, Kat. I like Boston. And we just . . . we had a fun time hanging out. That's it."

"Friends," I say. "That's what you guys are. Like you and me."

He cocks his head to the side and looks right at me. "I've never hooked up with Lillia."

I lean back in my chair, pleased. "Send in the USC application, Alex. You need to start going after what you want."

Ms. Chirazo comes back in and shoots me a warning look like she knows I've been goofing off. Of course she's only looking at me and not Alex, because she thinks Alex is a freaking redheaded angel.

CHAPTER THIRTY

MARY

I HANG AROUND AFTER SCHOOL ON FRIDAY TO GO TO a Spanish tutorial that Señor Tremont is holding in advance of our midterm. I get to the classroom first and worry for a second that maybe I got the date wrong, but then ten other kids from my class arrive and sit in the same seats as they do in sixth period. They're the students I'd expect to see here, ones who never, ever, ever talk in class. Like me. We've all perfected the art of staring down at our desks when Señor Tremont asks for volunteers to do conversations with him.

The only one who isn't here is Señor Tremont.

Ten minutes go by, then fifteen. The halls have emptied out and quieted; the noise comes from outside. I unzip my school bag, open my Spanish textbook, and review the stuff Señor Tremont covered in today's class. But the others are way less patient. After twenty minutes, one of the other kids makes a big, huffy show of standing up. He says, "What the eff, man?" and a few others push back from their desks, ready to follow him out.

But then Señor Tremont bursts through the door with a cell phone in his hand. He shouts excitedly, *"Mi esposa está teniendo un bebé!"* the words coming out faster than the dialogue in the Spanish soap operas he lets us watch on Fridays.

The students stare at each other like *Huh?*, because we don't have a clue what Señor Tremont is saying. Did he forget that this is a remedial session? Señor Tremont doubles over laughing and translates it for us.

"My wife is having a baby!"

With this news, the entire mood of the room shifts from annoyed to happy in a second. Everyone claps for Señor and cheers him on as he shoves his papers into his briefcase and sprints out the door. The whole thing brings tears to my eyes; I'm not sure why. Maybe because I have this feeling that Señor Tremont will be a good dad. Or because I miss my parents. It's probably both.

On my way out of the classroom, I see Lillia down at the other end of the hall. I can tell it's her because of her hair. No one in our school has hair as long and as shiny as Lillia Cho.

I open my mouth to call out for her, but then change my mind. Lillia's probably on her way to the pool to swim with Reeve. I hang back but keep her in my sights. And I follow her, to be sure.

Lillia walks through the snow to the new pool building. She doesn't use the same side door we used to, back when she, Kat, and I would meet up to plan our revenge schemes, back when the pool was being renovated. Instead she follows the sidewalk to the main double doors at the front of the pool building. By the time I reach them, I see Lillia make a left into the girls' locker room.

I should go home. I know I should. Only something is drawing me into the building. I've wanted to sneak in and watch them before, many times, but I've always managed to talk myself out of it. Maybe because Lillia's told me plenty about what goes on with her and Reeve when they swim together. She's happy to share the details. And I'm happy to hear them.

But suddenly I need to see it with my own eyes. Them together. While she's changing, I hurry down the hallway into the pool area. The whole space is finished now, and it looks beautiful. They've installed the diving board, painted a big seagull mascot on the far wall. The entire ceiling is glass, and it lets in a ton of light. It bounces off the cool blue water.

Off to the side of the diving board is the utility closet where Kat, Lillia, and I once had to hide out from a construction worker. I wish I could duck inside there, but there's no way. Reeve's down at the shallow end, doing high knee lifts. He'd definitely see me.

I glance in the other direction and see a row of metal stadium bleachers bolted along the wall, running almost the length of the entire pool. Quickly, I duck underneath them. Lucky for me, someone has stacked up a bunch of blue kickboards, which gives me enough cover if I kneel down on the floor.

Perfect.

For a few minutes I have the chance to watch Reeve alone. He's working hard out there. And though he's lost a bit of the muscle from early in the football season, I like his body even better now. It's less bulky, more lean.

After he finishes a set of his exercises, Reeve swims over to the entrance and looks down the locker room hallway. He's waiting for her.

Then Lillia comes into the pool. She's changed out of her school clothes and into a black one-piece. It's definitely not something she'd ever be caught dead wearing on the beach, but it still looks great on her. If I didn't know she couldn't swim, I'd think she was there to lifeguard. She sits on the edge of the bleachers right in front of where I'm hiding, and tucks her hair up into a white swim cap.

"Yo, Cho," Reeve calls out. "You're late."

Lillia doesn't answer. Even though there's a ladder that's closer, she walks down to the shallow end of the pool and climbs into the water there. She's timid, and she reacts like it's freezing cold.

As soon as Lillia is in the pool, Reeve abandons his own exercises and starts instructing her. He helps her practice floating, with his hands underneath her back. He has her practice her arm movements in the shallow end. Every exercise he gives her, he watches her intently, like a coach. He corrects her plenty of times, which definitely seems to frustrate Lil, but when she can't see it, he's nodding and smiling like she's perfect.

For a while I close my eyes and think about that day when Reeve shoved me into the water. Would it have happened if those other kids hadn't been there? I bet it wouldn't have. I bet we would have ridden the ferry home together, like always. I feel the tears come out of my eyes, and I let them fall.

When I open my eyes again, Reeve is out of the water, drying off right where I'm standing. Close up, I can see he still has a few scars from homecoming night, places where the glass cut into his skin. The skin in those spots is pinker than the rest of his body. Pink and pale and almost translucent.

I wipe away my tears with my sleeve.

"I'm going to go get changed, Cho. Why don't you take the kickboards out and do some laps in the deep end?"

Reeve leaves, and Lillia goes to do what she's told. But when she comes over to grab a kickboard, she sees me and almost screams.

"I'm sorry!" I whisper.

"Mary!" She looks over both her shoulders. "What on earth are you doing here?" And then, I think, the answer comes to her. She looks suddenly joyous. "Have you been watching the whole time? Did you see how many times he tried to touch me? It's really, really working!"

"Yes, it is working," I say quietly.

Lillia adds, "As a bonus, I've gotten a lot better in the water. I think I might actually take that swim test for real." She shivers, and water droplets fly off her. "It's a win-win!"

I blink a few times. Thank goodness Lillia doesn't know all the things I feel deep down about Reeve. I don't want anyone to know, not ever. "That's awesome," I say quickly, in a whisper. "I'm so glad you're getting something out of this too."

But I'm not sure if Lillia hears me. Her eyes turn to the

hallway. "Crap." She quickly takes a kickboard off the top of the stack and leaps into the pool awkwardly.

Reeve enters a few seconds later, fully dressed. "You punking out on me, Cho?"

"No. I . . . I just . . . I don't like to go to the deep end when I'm by myself."

Reeve crouches down at the edge of the pool. It takes some effort; I can tell his leg is stiff and sore from the workout. Plus he has his walking cast back on. He says, "Don't worry. I'm right here." And then he adds, "You owe me an extra lap for that," but he says it in a tender, joking way.

Lillia uses the kickboard and works her way down to the opposite end of the pool. Reeve walks alongside her, every step of the way. His leg has gotten better. Stronger.

As soon as I get my chance, I run out of the pool, and all the way home. I'm the one who's in deep water. I'm the one who's sinking.

CHAPTER THIRTY-ONE

LILLIA

WHILE I DRY OFF, REEVE GOES TO THE PARKING LOT and starts my car so it's warm for me. I didn't even have to ask him to, which is a great sign.

I gather up my stuff and meet him out there. I keep my eyes peeled for Mary, to see if she's still around, but she's nowhere to be found.

Reeve's taken the icer and chiseled the frost off my windshield. Reeve's truck is also turned on, and frostless, parked right next to mine. But he's waiting in *my* car, sitting in my driver's seat, listening to my music. I force the grin off my face and hop into the passenger side. "Hey," I say, pointing the vents so they're blowing right on me. "Thanks for starting my car up for me."

"No problem." He doesn't make a move to get out, so I stay put too. Abruptly he says, "Hey, you never told me how Boston went."

"Oh, it was good. My interview with the Wellesley alum went really well. The interviewer used to visit Jar Island when she was growing up, so we had that in common."

"Cool, cool." Reeve drums his fingers on my steering wheel. "So did Lindy finally man up and make his move?"

My eyes go wide. I mean, we did kind of hold hands. But it's not like that's a *move* move. I'm not going to tell Reeve that, though. Better he thinks Alex did. "Why? Are you jealous?"

Reeve makes a "pfft" sound and looks out the window. "Is Lind jealous of our pool time?" he counters.

I force a swallow. "He doesn't know about it." I want to tell Reeve, *Please don't say anything,* but I can't do that. Instead I think fast and say, "Does Rennie?" even though I'm pretty sure of his answer.

Reeve scrunches up his forehead. "Nah. I haven't mentioned it."

"Okay."

"Okay."

So neither of us has told anyone. Rennie and Alex don't

know. But I'm dreading the moment they do. Because this is happening. The train is on the tracks, and it's speeding up.

Reeve takes his hands off the steering wheel and lets them fall to his lap, where he fidgets for a moment. Then he looks at me, and I can tell he's about to say something. Or do something.

I panic.

I whip out my cell, pound out a fake text, and tell him, "I should get home. Maybe I'll see you this weekend?"

He bites the inside of his cheek and says, "Sure. See you, Cho."

On Saturday, on my way out of Milky Morning, I run into PJ. "Hey, stranger!" I say, as he holds the door open for me.

He holds his hand up for a high five and says, "See you tonight, Lil."

I hand him my box of muffins to hold while I zip up my puffer. "What's happening tonight?"

"Ren scored a ton of free booze. We're going to meet up in the woods by her house. She didn't tell you?"

"No," I say. "She didn't." Neither did Ash. At Rennie's command, I'm sure. If that's how Ren wants to play it, so be it. Two can play at that game.

"What time are you guys meeting up?" I ask him.

"Nine."

"It's so cold, though," I say. "We'll freeze out there."

"The booze will keep us warm. Besides, where else are we gonna go?"

Lucky me, my mom and Nadia are off island at a horse show. They won't be back until tomorrow afternoon. My mom wanted me to stay at Rennie's or ask Carlota to stay over, which I told her was ridiculous—I'm seventeen, and in less than a year I'll be away at college. I'm old enough to stay by myself for a night. "Besides," I said, "don't you trust me?" My mom caved at that. "Of course I do," she said.

I text Alex first.

It's so cold out. Wanna come over and watch a movie tonight? 9? Bring Derek!

He writes back immediately.

Sounds good!

Next is Ash. I know that if I dangle Derek in front of her, she'll take the bait. She'd blow off Rennie in a second to hang out with Derek. She's been crushing on him since last year, and they've hooked up a few times, but they're definitely not exclusive.

My mom and Nadia are off island tonight. Wanna come over and watch a movie? The guys are coming—Derek too!

Yes! What time?

9

Yay!

Then Reeve.

Movie night at my house if you're interested.

Reeve takes his sweet time writing back. But eventually he does. One word.

Cool.

I jump into action. Carlota was here earlier today, so the house is sparkly clean. But we need snacks.

I bake a batch of brownies, not from scratch, from a box, but it's a fancy brand my mom got from some specialty food store in Boston. It cost eleven dollars, so I figure it must be good. For good measure I throw in a handful of chocolate chips. I grab a not-too-expensive-looking bottle of red wine from the wine cellar, and I set that out too, with some glasses. At the last minute I pop a bag of kettle corn and figure that will be good enough.

Then I run upstairs to get ready. I change out of my school clothes and put on skinny jeans and an off-the-shoulder cream-colored sweater. I dab some Lillia perfume on behind my ears and in the hollow of my neck. No makeup, though, only cherry ChapStick.

Casual.

But I'm excited inside. Excited thinking about Rennie alone in the woods with her bottles of booze, freezing her butt off while she waits for everybody to show.

We're all lounging in the TV room. Ash and Derek are cozied up in our leather armchair with a blanket, where I told them to sit. Alex and I are on the sectional. No Reeve. I guess he met up with Rennie after all. I'm trying not to feel disappointed, when the doorbell rings.

"Who else is coming?" Alex asks me.

"I don't know," I say, and run for the door.

I open it, and there's Reeve in his puffer vest and sweater. "Hey!" I say. I get up on my tiptoes and give him a hug. He looks taken aback, and I smile at him, sweet as cotton candy.

"Lind is here?" he asks me, looking over my shoulder and frowning.

"Yup . . ." Then it dawns on me. He thought it was going to be the two of us. Like maybe a date. Wow. That's good. That's really good. I can't wait to tell Kat and Mary all about it. I link my arm through his and lead him into the house. "Everybody's in the living room."

Reeve follows me down the foyer. "Reeve's here," I announce, even though, duh, he's here; we all have eyes.

"What up, Tabatsky," Derek says.

Alex makes room for him on the couch. When Reeve sits down and starts to put his feet up on the coffee table, Alex says, "Dude, her family doesn't wear shoes in the house."

"Calm down, Lindy," Reeve says. But he obeys; he takes his shoes off.

"You too," Ash says to Derek.

"It's fine," I say, but I'm relieved Alex said something. I hate to be the one going around telling people to take their shoes off; it's so awkward. But my mom will seriously kill me if our white furniture gets dirty. It's like her life's mission is to buy everything in white and then rise to the challenge of keeping it that way.

"Does anybody want any wine?" I ask. I feel so grown-up until I realize I don't even know how to open a wine bottle.

"Yes, please!" Ashlin chimes in.

I fumble with the wine opener until Reeve takes it from me and pops it open in like two seconds without saying a word. Then he pours the wine for all of us. "Where's Ren?" he asks me, setting the bottle back down.

Shrugging, I say, "No idea." I hop up and run to the kitchen and come back with the plate of brownies. "Fresh baked!" I sing out. I shimmy over to Ash and Derek, and they take one and share it.

I come back to the couch and offer one to Alex, who accepts it. Then I put the plate back on the coffee table and sit down between him and Reeve. "So what are we watching? There are a few good things on demand—"

"You're not even going to offer me a brownie?" Reeve interjects. "What kind of hostess are you?"

"You don't eat sweets!" I know this about him, for a fact.

"I don't eat sweets during the season," he corrects. "And the season's over." His green eyes glint as he opens his mouth and says, "Ahh."

I slide the plate in his direction and he shakes his head. "Ahh," he says, patiently.

I roll my eyes and pop a piece of brownie in his mouth. "Diva!"

With his mouth full Reeve says, "Delicious." I give him another angelic smile as a reward.

"These brownies are awesome, Lillia," Alex chimes in.

"I baked them myself," I say. It's not like they need to know they came from a box mix. Grabbing the remote, I say, "I vote we watch this French movie I heard about."

Reeve groans and Alex says, "The one about the cat burglar? They were reviewing that on NPR yesterday. It's supposed to be good."

Reeve mutters, "Why don't you two move into the retirement home already."

"We don't have to watch it," I say. "Ash, Der, what are you guys in the mood for?"

They are whispering to each other and feeding each other brownie crumbs and not even paying attention.

Reeve grabs the remote from me. "Let me put on SportsCenter for a sec."

Holding out my hand, I say, "Give it back, Reeve!"

"I want to check the score on the game," he says.

"Reeve!" I keep reaching for the remote, but he keeps twisting away from me. "Oh my God, I feel sorry for whoever marries you," I say, and then I fall back against the couch and take a tiny sip of wine. I almost spit it back out into the glass. It tastes like smoke to me. Like barbecued wood. I don't know how adults drink the stuff.

I meant it as a joke, but Reeve obviously doesn't take it that way, because without looking away from the TV he goes, "Likewise."

"Come on, man, give her the remote," Alex says.

Reeve tosses it to me and starts looking at his phone while I queue up the French movie and Alex turns on the surround sound.

"Should I dim the lights?" Alex asks me.

Reeve stands up. "I'm gonna get out of here."

"Already?" Derek asks, turning around.

"Yeah. People are hanging out in the woods by Rennie's. Wanna come?"

Derek looks at Ash and says, "Nah. Too cold." Ashlin snuggles closer to him.

Reeve eyes Alex. "Al, I'm guessing you're not going anywhere."

"Yup, I'm good," Alex says, stretching out on the couch.

"All right. I'll hit you guys up after." Reeve shrugs back into his coat and picks up his shoes. "Later."

"Bye," Alex says, settling back on the couch.

"Bye, Reevie," Ash calls.

I can't believe he's leaving. Rennie snaps her fingers and he comes running?

Reeve heads toward the hallway and I follow him. "Why don't you hang out a little while longer?" I ask him.

"No thanks," he says over his shoulder. "Didn't realize I was crashing a double date."

"Don't go," I say, reaching out to touch the hem of his puffer vest. I drop my hand when he doesn't turn around.

He steps back into his sneakers, and then he opens the door, and at first I think he's going to go without saying bye or anything, but he stops and looks back at me. He hesitates, and then in a low, uncertain voice he says, "See you on Monday at the pool?"

Smiling slowly, I nod. Then he leaves, and I close the door behind him and lock it.

CHAPTER THIRTY-TWO

I watch my alarm tick down, and a minute before it's supposed to go buzz, I turn it off. I close the photo albums I pulled out last night and set them on my floor. Then I pull the blankets back up over me. My head finds the still-warm dent in my pillow, and I lie there for a minute.

Since she passed away five years ago, I've made it a tradition to stay up the entire night before the anniversary of my mom's death to think about her. I don't sleep, not one minute. It's like some depressing form of meditation, I guess, but it's how I do. I think about her all through the night.

I can trace that whole last shitty year of her life back to the moment it started, to the day Mom had to drop me off at school early because she had to go off island for an appointment with some specialist doctor.

I think about the day she and Dad sat us down at the kitchen table to tell us. How it didn't look good, but we still needed to have hope. Mom was calm and Dad cried so hard he couldn't breathe, and Pat ran straight out the back door in his socks and didn't come home for three whole days. I felt anything but hopeful.

I think about telling Rennie when we first got the diagnosis. I rode my bike over early, before she was even awake, and basically ambushed her. She sat in her bed, still half-asleep, while I knelt on her floor and cried and cried. There was a sick part of me that was happy to have such a sad story. By then she was already starting to pull away from me. She was completely obsessed with Lillia and creaming her pants over the fact that Lillia was moving to Jar Island full-time after next summer. It's pathetic to admit, but I remember hoping that Rennie might pity me enough to be close with me again, at least while I went through this terrible shit, but my mom getting sick only made things weirder between us.

I think about how Mom was strong for so long, until she couldn't be, and then over a single freaking week she evaporated. Cancer eats you from the inside out, and I watched her waste away to skin and bones, to a hollow body, in literally seven days. The last day, she only opened her eyes once, and I don't know if she saw me standing there, at the foot of her bed. Dad called out her name and Pat said he loved her, but her eyes didn't focus. It was like we all saw the door closing. I wanted to say something meaningful, but I couldn't get it out before her eyes shut again. We brought a stereo into the room and played "Suite Judy Blue Eyes" on repeat.

It was almost a relief to see her go.

All those memories, plus the good stuff from before she got sick, typically take up most of the night. Once the sun rises, I shift gears and wonder how things might have been different if she'd lived. I go through the old photo albums, the letters she wrote to me as soon as she found out she was sick.

I do it all and I never, ever sleep.

The bonus to this is that I can sleepwalk through the actual day it happened. I'm so tired I don't have to feel anything. That means I won't cry in front of strangers; I won't break down. It keeps things nice and tidy.

When I come downstairs, Dad is already at the table, staring over his newspaper off into space. Pat is quietly eating a slice of cold pizza over the sink. Well, as quietly as Pat can eat.

Dude is a wildebeast. This is exactly what this day is like. Our loud, crazy family turns the volume down as low as it can go.

I give Dad a hug, and it brings him back into reality. He taps the newspaper and says, "Found a coupon for the store. Half off a pumpkin pie for Thanksgiving."

Thanksgiving used to be awesome. Mom would entrust me with her recipe box, a wooden thing Dad had made to keep all her index cards. I'd set out the ones we'd need, each one sticky and stained with use. It would be my job to line up the ingredients on the counter for each of the recipes. Sugar yams, green bean casserole, turkey rubbed with sage and butter, cranberry sauce and sausage stuffing.

Needless to say, it's not like that anymore.

Dad tried, and failed miserably, at recreating the family meal the first few years after Mom died. Every time it was a disaster, and he'd feel bad about the money he wasted and how he couldn't survive without Judy, and the whole thing was so awful that we started buying a rotisserie chicken and frozen veggies. The only thing we'd make at home was baked potatoes. And even though it's nearly impossible to fuck up a baked potato, it still never tastes right to me.

Suddenly Dad starts weeping at the table. I wonder what

memory he's thinking about. And like every year that this shitty anniversary falls on a Monday through Friday, I hate the thought of spending this day without him.

Even worse, this time next year I won't be on Jar Island.

"I'm not feeling well," I tell my dad, my voice soft and quiet, like my throat hurts. "Maybe I should stay—"

"Don't even," he says, sniffling.

"What? Come on, Dad." I know the sick sound is gone, but seriously? "I never skip!"

"I know you don't. And that's why you're going to school. Your mother would never forgive me for letting you miss school on her account."

I open my mouth to keep arguing, but Pat shoots me a look. He's right. This day is hard for everyone, and I don't want to be starting shit with my dad. So I trudge back upstairs, get dressed, and head out the door.

One good thing—I don't think many people know that I don't have a mom. Not besides Ms. Chirazo, anyhow. It's not like I come to school and everyone treats me different. Which I'm glad for, because I couldn't deal with any pitying looks. But part of me does wonder if Lillia remembers. If she'll say anything. She wasn't around for the funeral—her family still lived in Boston back then—but they made a donation in my mom's name to some cancer society.

I walk past Lillia in the hall. She's talking to Ash, and she sees me and gives me a tiny smile, but it's the same one I get every day. No different.

I'm pretty sure I've mentioned my mom to Mary, but it's not like I told her the exact day she died.

It's weird, even though I'm totally used to going through this day alone, somehow this year it's worse.

I open my locker door to chuck in my jacket. There's one white daisy inside, laid at the very top of my pile of shit.

Daisies were my mom's favorite flower. Everyone placed one on top of her casket before it got lowered in the ground.

I spin around and look behind me. Who did it? It wasn't Lillia. And it wasn't Mary. She wouldn't know that.

And then, for a second, a split second, I see Rennie peering at me from around the corner of the hallway. Our eyes meet.

The weekend when Mom had her last round of chemo, nobody felt much like celebrating. She'd had gone through the treatments, even though things weren't looking promising.

A month before, her doctor had said something like, "It's your call, Judy." Which is basically the worst thing a doctor can say. It means that even he doesn't have much hope. Still, at dinner we'd had a family discussion about whether or not she should do it. Dad spoke first. He thought she should take it easy, enjoy what she had left, but Mom looked at me and Pat and said, "How can we not try?" Dad started sobbing. We all did. Nobody touched the lasagna.

Mom had her last treatment on Thursday, and three days later Pat had a dirt-bike race. It was his first off-island one since Mom got sick. Usually Pat's races were a family affair, and Rennie would tag along too. Obviously Mom wouldn't be able to go this time, and, unspoken, maybe never again. Pat promised her he'd win her a trophy. He did a good job not crying in front of her. He waited until he was out in the garage to lose his shit.

I loved watching my brother race. Every other racing family knew who he was, because he was that good. We were like minor celebrities on the track. Even when I'd be hanging out on the swings or in line for a hot dog, the other kids showed me respect. But I didn't just go to cheer Pat on. I had a job, too. After each heat I'd wipe Pat's bike down until it shone brand-new. I'd get all the grit off. His helmet, too. Rennie gave herself the job of making sure Pat always had a cold can of Coke.

Dad and Pat had loaded up the trailer. I went to pack a bag of rags, and Dad pulled me aside. "Katherine," he said, setting his hands on my shoulders, "I want you to stay home this time. Make sure your mother doesn't need anything."

This might have seemed obvious, but it wasn't to me. I was looking forward to getting out of our house, away from Jar Island for an afternoon. Also, there was Rennie. "But Rennie is supposed to come with us! We made plans weeks ago! She's expecting us to come get her."

"Sorry, kiddo. Next time." Dad quickly put Mom's afternoon medications inside a teacup. "I'm sure Rennie will understand."

I called Rennie, and she did understand, though I could hear in her voice that she was disappointed. I watched from the front window as Dad and Pat drove away.

"Kat! I need you!"

It was my mom. A side effect none of us had expected was that Mom was now cranky as hell. She'd never been like that before. Everything seemed to bother her. How messy the house was getting, what Dad would make her to eat, the smells coming from Pat's bedroom. I had always been Mom's girl, her baby, but even I wasn't immune. She flipped out when I put some special sweater of hers through the laundry.

Honestly, I was a little afraid of her.

"One sec!" I shouted upstairs. And then to Rennie I said, "Can you come over?" I hoped it was obvious in my voice. I didn't want to be alone with my mom. I needed her.

"Um . . ." I could hear her switching the phone from one

ear to the other. "Actually, my mom needs my help with taking down some wallpaper. Sorry. I'll call you later!"

I was furious. But not at Rennie. At my mom. I blamed her for making my friend not want to come over, not Rennie for being a sucky friend.

I trudged upstairs. Mom was in bed. Her eyes were slits. She'd kicked off all her blankets; she was sweating in the bed. "Can you please turn off the heat. I'm dying!"

"Anything else?" I said it so bitchy. So incredibly bitchy.

"No," she said. "Sorry to bother you." She said it sadly, which I knew was my opening to apologize. Instead I walked out and closed her door, hard.

I blamed the wrong person. Not my mom. She was sick. She needed me. It was Rennie. And maybe if Rennie had been a better friend, maybe I would have had more patience. Taken better care of my mom that day. It's unforgivable, really.

I take the daisy, the one Rennie put in my locker, and I throw it into the garbage can. I don't know if she's still watching, but I hope to God she is.

CHAPTER THIRTY-THREE

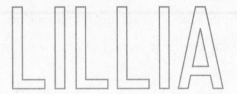

TUESDAY, I'M LATE LEAVING LAST PERIOD BECAUSE OUR test goes long. I run straight to the pool, expecting to see Reeve in the water doing laps. But the pool's empty; he's not there. I wait for a few more minutes; then I go sit on the bleachers and text him.

No pool today? :(
Nah. I'm done with that.
???
Can't talk now. I'm working at my dad's office.
Huh. What does that mean, he's done? With what? With

working out or with me? If we don't swim today, I won't get to spend any alone time with him before Thanksgiving break, because tomorrow's a half day.

I think fast. The only thing for me to do is go to him right now and ask him what he meant. Make a show of how much I care.

I hightail it out of the gym and drive over to his dad's office. It's not far from school. It's a small colonial house. There's a white-and-black sign that reads TABATSKY PROPERTY MANAGEMENT out front.

Reeve's truck is parked out front, no other cars. I flip down my vanity mirror and dab on some lip gloss and fluff up my hair. Then I grab my purse, hop out of the car, and walk up to the door.

Reeve's sitting at a desk; there are keys all lined up in front of him, and he's sorting through them. He looks up and starts to say, "Hi, can I help—" His eyes widen when he realizes it's me. "What are you doing here?"

"I was worried when you didn't show," I say. I scooch closer to him and perch on the edge of the desk, which is when I notice he's not wearing his walking cast. Both feet are in sneakers. "Oh my gosh! No more boot!"

"Yeah. Earlier this afternoon." Reeve keeps sorting keys, making piles, and not looking at me. And he doesn't sound that happy about it.

"So why the face? We should be celebrating! Pancakes on me." I poke him in the side so he'll finally look at me. "I knew all your hard work would pay off."

Flatly he says, "It didn't."

"What? What do you mean?"

Reeve stares straight ahead and says, "I asked Coach if he would time my sprints today. I was pumped to show him how much progress I was making in the pool, and I figured if I could win him over, he'd help me train and maybe make some phone calls for me to the scouts. Tell them I'm back on track, that I'll be in fighting shape by the time spring workouts begin, and to save me a roster spot." He clears his throat, like the words are getting stuck, and I feel my heart sink for him. "Well, it was a complete joke. I'm nowhere near where I used to be. I'm slower than the defensive line, and those guys weigh like three hundred–plus pounds, and there's no way I'll get back to top form in time. It's over. I need to face facts, figure out what I'm going to do now. "

"Wait. Maybe you won't get the top programs, but I thought there were still a few D-three schools," I begin. "Like what about Williams?"

He shakes his head. "I'm not even good enough for a practice squad, Lillia. I'm done. My ass isn't going to college. No football scholarship. I'm staying right here on the island."

I stay still and quiet as he tries to yank open a file drawer. It's stuck, and he pulls on it so hard that the keys he's organized slide together into a heap. Reeve's face goes red; he looks like he's going to cry or maybe punch a wall. "Fuck!" he yells.

I jump in my seat and he shakes his head. "I'm sorry," he says, and he lets out a choked sound. He's crying. Reeve Tabatsky is crying.

I'm not sure what to do. Rennie's so good at comforting him, at saying all the right things. I've never been great at comforting people.

"Don't apologize," I tell him. "You have nothing to be sorry for."

I'm the one who should be sorry. Next fall, Reeve should be a football god at a division one school, doing keg stands and hooking up with random girls. That's his destiny. The thought of Reeve stuck here on the island, going to community college and living at home . . . it's too sad to even think about.

Reeve sinks back into his chair; he hangs his head in his hands, and his shoulders start to shake. He's sobbing like a little boy. Meanwhile I keep my eyes on the floor.

He gets quiet all of a sudden and he says, "Remember what you said to me on Halloween night?"

You deserve everything you're getting, because you're not a good person.

My stomach lurches. "Reeve, I was—"

"No, you were right. I'm not a good guy, Lillia." He wipes his eyes with the backs of his hands. "I did something to someone a long time ago. I hurt someone bad."

"Who?" I breathe. Mary. He has to be talking about Mary.

"A girl . . . The more I think about it, the more I think maybe this is me getting what I deserve, so I can't—I can't even be upset about it." He nods to himself. "In a way it's like a relief. I've been waiting all this time for my punishment. Maybe . . . maybe this is it." He sounds so resigned. So hopeless. It makes my heart hurt.

I rest my head on his shoulder. "Don't talk like that," I whisper. It's crazy, but I feel genuinely bad for him.

He lets me sit like that for a moment and then he says, "Can you please go?"

I sit up straight to look at him, but he won't look me in the eye.

That's when it comes to me. An idea. And before I've really thought it through, I'm telling him a way to fix things.

"We have this family friend. He's my dad's coworker's son. He's a football player. Not a star quarterback like you, but still. He took a fifth year of high school at a prep school, and it was like a whole other year for recruits to check him out." I say all of this super calmly, like he hasn't been crying and he didn't tell me to leave. I say, "You could do that, Reeve. If you train hard, and you get your grades up, I bet you could get a scholarship at a prep school somewhere, and then colleges would look at you again next spring. It would be your second chance."

He lifts his head; his eyes are red. "I told you, Cho. I don't deserve a second chance. I'm no good. You shouldn't even be around me."

"I don't want to hear you talking like that," I snap. I never thought I'd feel this way, but maybe Reeve does deserve a second chance.

Reeve looks startled. Then he says, "Why would some fancy school give me a scholarship? My grades aren't good enough for a scholarship."

"Duh, you're an amazing quarterback. If their team sucks, they're basically paying to make it better by having you go to their school. I could ask my dad to talk to his friend, get more information. This could be your ticket out."

He's shaking his head. "I don't know. It seems like a long shot."

"Don't give up on yourself. All you need is more time to heal and get strong again. Sure, spring workouts in a few months might be too soon for you, but what if you had another year to recuperate? You might not get to go to some big football school, but at least it'll be a real college and not the JICC." Reeve opens his mouth, but before he can answer, I grab him by his shirt collar. "Listen to me, okay? It's worth a shot. I'll help you study, if that's what you're so worried about."

Reeve almost smiles, which makes me feel so good. "Oh yeah? That's generous of you, Cho. Just so you know, I'm actually not a Neanderthal; I'm a pretty smart guy."

"I never for one second thought you were dumb," I tell him, dropping his collar and smoothing it out. And then, like it's already decided, I say, "Tomorrow you make an appointment with Mr. Randolph and see what he knows about this kind of thing. He's bound to have some contacts at prep schools; I think he went to one. Then you register for the December SAT test date."

"I already took the SAT," Reeve says. "My score was fine."

"Fine?" I repeat. I give him a doubtful look.

"Yeah. It was easy. At one point I put my head down and took a nap. I think maybe I had a hangover that day."

"Well, what was your score?" I challenge.

"1920."

Oh. That *is* pretty good. I've taken it three times, and it was only on the third try that I broke 2100. So Reeve is smart. He does have a chance at going to college. "Then take the test one more time. If you scored that high without even trying, who knows what you could do if you studied?"

I tell myself not to feel guilty for helping him. If I can fix this, if I can help make it so he still gets his football scholarship . . . everything will still end up the way it's supposed to. Mary can still have her pound of flesh, and Reeve can still go to college.

I clap my hands together, cheer-style. "So first we reorganize these keys and then we go to the library. And if you do a good job, you'll get a snack after."

Reeve smiles for real this time. "You're a piece of work, Cho. Did you know that?"

I smile back smugly. "Oh, trust me. I know."

CHAPTER THIRTY-FOUR

MARY

I'M PRACTICALLY SLEEPWALKING AS I SHUFFLE DOWN the hall to English class. I can hardly keep my eyes open. I stayed up super late to finish reading *The Scarlet Letter* for today's discussion. I'm too shy to actually talk in class, but Mrs. Dockerty loves to randomly call on the quiet kids.

I should have been doing a few pages a night, but of course I left it to the last minute. It's such a sad story, and I can't say that I enjoyed it. It hit a little too close to home. The scars that Hester carried all through her life, the guilt and shame she felt even though it wasn't her fault. And when she died at the end, I was in tears.

Needless to say, it was not a fun read.

I just haven't felt like doing much of anything since I watched Reeve and Lillia together at the pool. I should be happy. This should be helping me move on.

Only it isn't.

I walk through the classroom door. I'm the first one, which is odd, especially since my last class was on the other side of the high school and it feels like everyone is counting off the minutes until Thanksgiving break begins. Not even Mrs. Dockerty is here yet. She's probably in the bathroom or something. I fall into my seat and lay my head on the desk and rest my eyes for a minute.

I wake up with a start, my cheek stuck to the cover of the paperback. I lift my head slowly, trying to figure out how long I've been out. The class is suddenly full; everyone is in their seats. But there's no Mrs. Dockerty. Instead a man is sitting on her desk. I guess we have a sub. I quickly wipe my mouth and take out my paperback.

"What did you think about Bartleby's decision never to leave the office? Did it make him sympathetic? Or were you frustrated?"

A bunch of hands fly up. I glance down at my copy. I don't remember an office anywhere in *The Scarlett Letter*. Or a character named Bartleby. Maybe I didn't read closely enough?

The sub calls on one of my classmates, who says, "I thought it was annoying. If you're not happy working at a place, why would you stay?"

Another kid across the room says, "He's unhappy, but he doesn't know how to fix it. He's paralyzed. He's got nowhere else to turn. Life at the office is all he has going for him. Without it, he's nothing." This kid doesn't even wait to be called on. Which is crazy. Mrs. Dockerty is very strict about not talking out of turn.

The substitute nods, pleased. He hops off his desk and gives a stack of papers to each row of desks. Once he's up, I see something on his desk. It's a brass name plate. It says MR. FRISSEL.

Oh my gosh, I'm in the wrong class.

I realize this as the papers are being passed to me. The boy sitting in front of me turns around.

It's David Washington, the boy I kissed on Halloween night.

"David," I say, before I can stop myself.

He doesn't answer me.

Maybe because he doesn't recognize me without my makeup and the wild hair?

No, it's worse. He lifts himself up out of his seat and hands the papers to the girl sitting behind me, like I'm not even there.

I get up with a start. "I—I made a mistake," I announce. I grab my things and run out the door. But not to the class I'm supposed to be in. For the life of me, I can't even remember what that is. So I head straight home. It's a half day anyway.

When I get there, I'm still upset, so much so that my hands are shaking as I set my bike against the side of our house. Only one light is on inside, over the kitchen sink. The rest of the rooms are dark, like the sky.

I hear a knock around the front of the house. I edge past the corner and see two of the ladies from the Jar Island Preservation Society, with phony smiles plastered on their faces. They've stopped by before, always unannounced. I already know Aunt Bette will not answer the door.

I was home the first few times they came. We stood together in the doorway as they recommended landscapers who could come help clean up one yard or passed the name of a handyman who might replace the broken shingles in a way that would "maintain the original integrity" of the house.

Sure, our house isn't in the best shape. Not when you compare it to the other homes on the block. This part of Jar Island has the oldest houses; almost half have been officially designated as landmarks. And some people take that designation super seriously, making sure that every detail is true to the period and that any renovations are done with special materials that would have been used at the time, like slate and cedar.

But old houses take a lot of upkeep, and that's never been Aunt Bette's forte. Mine either. The whole place could use a fresh coat of paint. One of the wooden front steps has rotted through. And yes, our yard catches all the dead brown leaves from our big oak, but I don't see what the big deal is. The ground is covered in snow; everything will stay white until March.

Not to mention that all of this stuff . . . it's not hurting anyone. And it's none of their business even if they do want to make it a landmark. This is our house, part of the Zane family since Jar Island came to be. I watch the two ladies retreat slowly down the steps.

But like anything you don't deal with, they keep coming back. We're going to have to do something about them; otherwise they'll just keep coming around.

I plan on saying exactly that to Aunt Bette as I walk through the back door. But I don't, because she's talking on the telephone.

"She's upset all the time. I don't think she knows. There's no reasoning with her. I tried to tell her that she needs to not focus on this Reeve boy. I never told you this because she swore me to secrecy . . ." Aunt Bette pauses. "No. No, of course not. You don't need to come. I've got it under control."

Oh my God, she's talking to my mother about Reeve. I run in the room and stand right in front of her and stare daggers. Aunt Bette's eyes go wide. She's surprised to see me at this time of day.

"Erica, I . . . I have to go." And then she hangs up.

"I can't believe you just did that. You promised me you'd keep that a secret!"

Aunt Bette falls into her seat and starts rubbing her temples. "What does it matter now?"

I completely resent how exasperated she's acting, like my very presence is taxing. "Are you serious? I trusted you!" I say, curt. "And I come home to find you talking about me behind my back? How do you think that makes me feel?"

Aunt Bette shrugs. "I've stopped trying to guess how you feel, Mary. I'm staying out of it."

I point at the phone. "That's not staying out of it!" I am quivering with anger. "And now I'll have to explain everything to them at Thanksgiving."

"Your parents aren't coming for Thanksgiving."

"Why?"

She looks at me and says, "Your mom doesn't have such happy memories of this place." She says it with more than a hint of bite, which I guess I deserve, but it still catches me off guard.

"Call Mom back. Call her and tell her that everything's okay, that they should come for Thanksgiving. Tell them I'm okay."

Aunt Bette stands up. "Nothing would make her happier, Mary, than to know that her daughter is okay. But I'm afraid we both know that isn't exactly true."

After my thirteenth-birthday-party disaster, when the only kid from my class to show up was Reeve, my parents became very concerned. Concerned and smothering.

Dad had the idea to throw me another birthday party, as if the first one had never happened. This new party would be somewhere on the mainland. He had it in his mind that the ferry ride was too much to ask of people. He refused to believe that no one came because no one wanted to be associated with me. He casually suggested that we make it more mature, cooler for a group of budding teenagers. Either roller skating or bowling.

I told him no way.

Mom wanted to start riding the ferry with me, to and from school. She said it would be fun. She'd bring the newspaper with her, or a book. I wouldn't even have to talk to her if I didn't want to. We could sit quietly with each other and enjoy the scenery. I refused, of course. The ferry ride was my time with Reeve. It was the only time I was happy.

Around them I made an effort to not eat as much food at

dinner, and they'd look so hurt when I'd tell them to please not give me so much pasta.

They were trying so hard it made me feel worse. I started shrinking into myself. I didn't want to hang out with my parents or do fun stuff on the island on the weekends. I hated how hard they were trying to fix this for me. It couldn't be fixed. Not by them. And I hated seeing them hurt. I wanted to shield them from the hurt. I could take it. But I didn't want them to suffer.

The worst of it was when the two of them knocked on my bedroom door late one night. The semester had ended at Montessori. I'd brought home a crappy report card. I never got bad grades.

Dad sat on my bed,; Mom leaned against my desk.

He said, "Do you have any interest in changing schools?"

Mom said, "You could go here in Middlebury. You wouldn't have to do the ferry anymore; you could have a brand-new start."

Vehemently, I shook my head from side to side. "I don't want to change schools."

Mom zoomed right along, fixing a bright smile on her face. "Or we can move. Your dad and I have always talked about going back to the city some day. Picture it, Sunday afternoons at the art museum, picnics at the park."

I said it louder. "I don't want to change schools!"

Dad patted my leg. There were tears in his eyes. "We want you to be happy. That's all we want."

"And all I want is to stay at Montessori," I said. With Reeve.

I fall on my bed and stare at the ceiling. Time and time again, I pick Reeve over everything and everyone else. And it's always the wrong choice. It's like my life is a broken record, and even though I can see it coming, I can't seem to jump over the scratch.

CHAPTER THIRTY-FIVE

LILLIA

NADIA AND I ARE LYING ON THE COUCH WATCHING TV, and my mom's on her computer working on her Thanksgiving spreadsheet. It'll be a small Thanksgiving this year. My dad's brother's family is coming from New York City, and our California grandma was supposed to come, but she decided at the last minute she didn't want to make the trip, which upset my mom. Next year, she keeps saying, we'll go to California instead.

A couple of times we've had Rennie and her mom over for Thanksgiving. Last year it was super awkward, because Ms. Holtz kept trying to flirt with my dad's divorced friend from the hospital. Rennie asked me afterward if I thought her mom had a chance with him, and I didn't know how to tell her that he only dates twentysomething Estonian models. I wonder what she and her mom are doing this year.

"Can we have mashed sweet potatoes this year instead of sweet potato casserole?" Nadia asks.

"You love sweet potato casserole," my mom protests.

"All that cream and butter and sugar?" Nadia shudders. "Rennie says it's pure fat."

"You only have sweet potato casserole once a year," I tell her. "You'll live. Besides, Mommy already ordered it."

"I think our family should be eating healthier," Nadia says with a shrug.

My mom sighs. "I can check and see if it's not too late to change it," she says, and goes off to call the caterer.

"Thanks, Mommy!" Nadia calls after her.

Casually, I ask, "What *is* Rennie doing for Thanksgiving?"

Nadia motions for another throw pillow. "She's having dinner with Ms. Holtz's boyfriend and his son. She says that Rick has a friend who's a fancy chef and he's going to cook for them."

I roll my eyes. Rick owns a sub shop and he lives in a one-bedroom apartment right above it. He's a nice guy, but somehow I don't picture him hanging out with fancy chefs. This sounds totally made-up. "When did Rennie tell you this?"

"She gave me a ride home yesterday since you were at the library," Nadia says.

I don't like the way Rennie's been glomming on to Nadia one bit. Twice now she's called the house phone asking to speak to Nadia about yearbook photos or something. I know her; she's doing it to get under my skin. I nudge Nadia's foot with mine. "Don't listen to Rennie on everything. Sometimes she says stuff just to say stuff."

With wide eyes Nadia asks, "Are you guys in a fight?"

"No . . . we've grown apart."

"But did something happen?" Nadia presses. "To make you grow apart?"

"Why?" I ask her, thinking back to our fight in the graveyard. "Did Rennie say something?" She wouldn't dare.

Nadia hesitates for a split second, and then she shakes her head.

"Nadia!"

"She didn't say anything," Nadia insists. "But I've noticed you haven't been hanging out as much."

"Well, nothing happened specifically. We're different people, that's all."

Nadia absorbs this. "Yeah, I guess that's true. Rennie's so . . . sparkly. She makes everything feel like . . . an event. I don't even know how to describe it."

I frown at her. "If Rennie's so sparkly, then what am I?"

Hastily she says, "You're fun too. In a different way."

I don't say anything, but I'm still thinking about it hours later. *Am* I boring compared to Rennie? It's true that I'm more cautious than she is, and I'm not the life of the party the way she and Reeve are. But if I was so boring, why would she have been best friends with me all these years? Because there's nothing Rennie hates more than being bored.

I hate that Nadia puts her on such a pedestal. Like she sees Ren as this magnetic force of nature, and I'm her goody-two-shoes older sister.

If Nadi only knew the trouble I've gotten into this year. She wouldn't think I was so boring then.

My mom always tries to make us get dressed up at Thanksgiving. She says that if we eat this fancy meal in sweats, it won't feel special. We go along with it to make her happy. Nadia's in a strapless green tartan dress with a poofy skirt and a cardigan on top. I have on a mauve knit miniskirt with a sheer blouse tucked in.

My dad's in a dress shirt and slacks; my mom has on a wine-colored knit dress with a cowl neck and a gold cuff. I make a mental note to ask her if I can borrow that cuff, maybe take it with me to college.

The adults are in the living room drinking the wine my uncle brought, and us kids are hanging out in the TV room. We have two cousins on my dad's side—Walker, who is Nadia's age, and Ethan, who is ten. Walker and Nadia are pretty close, even though we don't see them often. Ethan's a brat, but it's not his fault. His parents are always telling him how great he is because he's a violin prodigy.

"How's Phantom?" Walker asks Nadia, adjusting her headband. We're all lying on the sectional, and Ethan's playing video games on his phone.

"He's good! I'm going to show him next month." Nadia spreads cheese on a cracker and pops it into her mouth. "He's the best horse in the world."

I nudge her with my toe. "Don't forget whose horse he is!"

"You hardly ever even ride him anymore," Nadia says. "He's basically mine now. I bet he wouldn't even recognize you.

I frown at her. "I was there last week!" Or was it the week before? She's right; I'm like an absentee horse parent. I've been so busy with swimming and Reeve and my college applications I've totally been neglecting Phantom. Tomorrow. I'll go out there tomorrow and bring him a whole bag of baby carrots and spend the afternoon grooming him.

"Pretty soon you'll be at college and he'll be all mine!" Nadia fake cackles, and Walker giggles.

"You're right," I say. "You have to take extra good care of him when I'm gone."

"I already do," Nadia says, stuffing another cracker in her mouth.

Dinner lasts forever, with everybody making toasts and the dads having a brag war. My dad tells everyone I have a good chance at valedictorian so they'll have to come back for graduation to hear my speech. I have to correct him and say it's salutatorian, and it's not like that's a guarantee. My uncle starts quizzing me on which colleges I'm applying to.

"Boston College," I say. "Wellesley. Maybe UC Berkeley."

My dad frowns. "Berkeley? We never talked about Berkeley."

I take a bite of turkey and stuffing to buy myself time. When I'm done chewing, I say, "It's something I've been thinking about."

Luckily, my aunt saves me by bragging about Ethan winning some violin competition and maybe getting to do a performance at Juilliard.

After dinner, everyone's all cozy watching old black-and-white movies in the TV room. I'm sitting next to my dad on the couch; he has his arm around me, and I have my head on his shoulder. It is nice to have him home.

I've got my phone in my lap, and when it buzzes, I nearly jump. It's a text from Reeve. My dad tries to read over my shoulder, but I scurry off to the kitchen. The text says, *What are you up to?* I write back, *Watching TV with my family.* He writes back, *Same. Wanna come over?*

I read the text over and over. Does he mean come over and watch TV with our other friends? Or does he mean watch TV just us, up in his room by ourselves?

I text him, *Who's coming?*

And he texts back, *Just you.*

Wow. I wonder if his family will think I'm Reeve's girlfriend.

When my dad comes into the kitchen to get more water, I ask him, "Daddy, can I go hang out with my friends tonight?" I don't tell him that I'm going to a boy's house, and that he's the only friend who will be there.

My dad considers this. "Are you bringing Nadia and Walker?"

"Um, no."

"Then my answer is no," he says.

"Daddy!" I make a face at him. My mom would have said yes. I shouldn't even have asked him.

Shaking his head, he says, "Final answer, Lilli. It's Thanksgiving, and your family's only in town for a couple of nights. Come sit and watch the movie with us."

"In a minute," I say in a snotty voice. "I have to tell my friends I can't come."

So that's what I write back, and then I hang around in the kitchen waiting for Reeve to text me back, but he doesn't.

JENNY HAN AND SIOBHAN VIVIAN

CHAPTER THIRTY-SIX

MARY

I DIDN'T EVEN BOTHER GETTING DRESSED ON Thanksgiving. I didn't go downstairs and ask if Aunt Bette needed my help in the kitchen.

But that's where I find her now. At the sink, doing the Thanksgiving dishes.

Or, should I say, *lack* of dishes.

I never expected Aunt Bette would make a turkey, because she is a vegetarian. Thanksgivings with her usually mean a whole lot of vegetable sides. Sugar squash, green beans with almonds, roasted beets, creamy mushroom soup. But tonight she only made a salad. For herself.

She's spent the rest of the day in the attic. Painting. Alone.

"So I guess there are no leftovers," I say, snarky.

Aunt Bette freezes. After a second she drops the dish back into the sudsy water. Then she spins around to face me. I can tell she's mad too. "I didn't make a lot of food, Mary, because you don't eat!"

It wounds me, her pointing this out. This is supposed to be a day of giving thanks, of being with family. It's all wrong.

I fall into one of the kitchen chairs. "My parents should have come. I don't know why they're punishing me like this. They never call me. Never." Aunt Bette bites her lip, like she wants to say something but second-guesses herself. "What? Did they say anything?" Have they been calling and Aunt Bette's not passing along the messages?

She sighs, and I can tell she's trying to choose her words carefully. "I don't know this for sure, Mary, but if I had to guess, I'd say your mom's still upset that you left in the first place."

"I didn't do it to hurt them!"

"Maybe not, but it did. You're her only daughter, Mary. She'd do anything for you! I used to fight with your mom and dad because I thought they spoiled you something rotten. Gave you everything you asked for. I said it wouldn't be good for you. But they didn't listen. They'd bend over backward to give you what you wanted. So can you blame your mom for missing you? You were her whole world!" She turns back around, probably because she can't face looking at me.

"I've been better, though. Since Halloween. Since you took that weird stuff down and quit with your weird spells." I say it, even though it isn't exactly true. I haven't had any more freak-outs, sure. But other weird things have happened.

Aunt Bette looks at me pityingly and whispers, "You don't know what you're capable of, do you? You don't even know what you are."

A shiver rolls down my spine. "Then tell me! Tell me what I am! You're scaring me!"

Aunt Bette shrinks. "You need to calm down."

"You're the one who's making me upset!"

Aunt Bette heads to her room. I follow her, but she's fast. She goes to her room and slams the door. "Go to your room, Mary!" she calls through the door. "Go to your room until you calm down!"

I do the exact opposite. I strike out into the night.

Main Street's pretty dead. All the stores are closed; everything is except for the theater. A few of them are already decorated for Christmas. As people pile out of the theater, I stand by the double doors and watch. Am I really not like them? Am I not normal?

Maybe something happened to me when I was in the hospital for all that time. Even when I try to remember, I can't. Did they do something to me there? Electroshock therapy, or worse? Some kind of experiment or drug that messed with my mind?

Just then I see Reeve and Rennie come out of the theater. He's walking behind her with his arms slung around her neck, and she's laughing. "Reevie, I told you that movie was gonna suck! You owe me another movie."

He shakes his finger in her face. "Nuh-uh. You still owed me for that cheering movie you made me watch this summer."

"Then we're even," she says. She turns her head and then kisses him on the cheek.

I stand there stock-still as they make their way down the street to Reeve's truck. He opens her door first; then he goes around the other side to unlock his. Like a gentleman. I can't believe what I'm seeing. Is Reeve two-timing Lillia the same way he did to me?

I feel the anger, the jealousy rise up in me. Instead of being scared, I decide to try and focus it. I've spent too long trying to ignore what's inside me. To dismiss it. If there is something going on with me, if there's any truth to what Aunt Bette is saying, I need to know.

I stare at the lock on Reeve's door. I stare hard and imagine myself pressing it down.

Reeve struggles turning his key. He can't get the door open. "Ren," he calls through the window. "I think the lock is frozen."

Rennie slides across the cab into the driver's seat and tries to open it from the inside. "I can't get it!" she whines.

Reeve tries his key again. This time I feel the force of it fighting against me. My chest is burning. It's like arm wrestling. I'm losing. I feel myself losing. And then, suddenly, the lock pops up.

I fall against the wall exhausted.

Aunt Bette was right. I don't know what I'm capable of. At least not yet.

CHAPTER THIRTY-SEVEN

I GO TO MS. CHIRAZO'S OFFICE FIRST THING ON Monday morning. Well, first thing after hitting up the computer lab. I've got a stack of warm white pages in my hand.

"Hey," I say, closing her door behind me.

She looks up, startled, holding the cord to an electric tea-kettle that plugs into her wall. "Katherine? Is everything okay?" She motions to an empty chair.

I perch my butt on the armrest and drop the papers on her desk. "I did a draft of a new essay. Sorry. I didn't have a sta-pler or anything." I spot one on her filing cabinet and use it.

Ms. Chirazo brightens. "Is this about . . ."

I nod. "But I don't want to go over it in group."

It was hard enough to write it alone in my room. The entire time, I was crying and feeling so completely panicked by the idea of anyone, especially Alex, reading it that it made me dry heave.

The thing is, my mom actually got into Oberlin. Only she could never go, because she couldn't afford the tuition. If I get to go there, it's like I'm making both of our dreams come true. In some ways it felt cheap to put it in those sappy terms, but it is true. And at the end of the day, I want off this island and into Oberlin with a big fat scholarship, so I'll jump through whatever hoops Ms. Chirazo tells me to. And I've convinced myself that it's not like I'm selling out my dead mom to get there. She'd want me to do whatever it took.

"It might be a little all over the place," I say. "And I'm still not sure I'm going to use it. But . . . I'd be interested in what you think before I send it off this week."

She nods. "Of course. I'll try to have it read by the end of the day."

"Don't rush or whatever. It's fine." But I'm pleased. I stand up. "Thanks, Ms. Chirazo."

CHAPTER THIRTY-EIGHT

MARY

THE CHORAL PRACTICE ROOM IS A WINDOWLESS ROOM directly behind our auditorium. The walls are bright white and completely soundproof, and the door makes a funny suction sound when it closes. As we file in, it's so bright it's like artificial sunshine.

Mr. Mayurnik, the high school choral director, sits behind his upright piano. As the students walk through the door, he plays some jazzy, foot-stomping tune, pounding on the keys so hard the air feels like it's vibrating.

"Welcome back, turkeys!" he calls out as we take our seats. "You survived the slaughter!"

He means it as a joke, but that's exactly how Thanksgiving felt. One hundred percent.

It seems like everyone has been dragging their feet today, our first day back at school after Thanksgiving break. I know I've been. But for me it's not shaking off that happy, overstuffed feeling of too much food and too much sleep. The truth is that I feel empty. Drained. I guess that's why my book bag feels extra heavy on my back, even though I'm carrying the same textbooks as always.

I spent the rest of the holiday weekend practicing. Seeing what I could do. Can I roll that pencil off that desk? Yes, barely. Can I make the wind blow? No. How about the curtains in my bedroom? Can I make them flutter without touching them?

Sometimes.

It feels crazy to be doing this sort of thing, and then to also be here now, back at school, like everyone else.

I am so not everyone else.

A thick packet of photocopied songs has been placed on every other chair. They have green paper covers with holiday clip art on them—holly leaves, a snowman, presents wrapped with bows, candy canes. Pretty much all my favorite things. I think about seeing if I can't discreetly ruffle the pages or something, but I fight the urge. I have to be careful with this secret. Nobody can know. Not even Kat and Lillia.

Especially not Kat and Lillia.

What would they say if I told them? Would they still want to be my friends? If that's how it's going to be, I'll keep it a secret forever. My friendship with Kat and Lillia is the only thing going right in my life these days. But I will tell them what I saw. Reeve and Rennie together.

I take a seat where I normally do, in the last row. Alex Lind comes in a few seconds before the bell rings and sits in the front. When the semester first started and I realized that Alex was taking this class too, I thought about dropping, to be on the safe side. But I don't think he knows who I am, beyond a girl he sees hanging around Kat or chatting with Lillia every once in a while. He's never spoken to me.

After the bell Mr. Mayurnik stands up and speaks to us over his piano. He's tall and broad-shouldered with a shiny bald head and a silver walrus moustache. His ties are always musically themed—piano keys, violin strings, clef notes.

He says, "Okay, ladies and gentleman. From this day forward, you are no longer turkeys. You're little elves now. Not *Christmas* elves, mind you, because this is a court-ordered nondenominational, secular celebration." He sighs deeply. "We should have been rehearsing these songs for weeks already, but the town elders wanted to approve the song booklet, and you know how fast things move in politics." Mr. Mayurnik bangs out a slow scale to show what he means. Do. Re. Mi.

I have to share a booklet with the girl sitting next to me. I lean over her shoulder as she flips through the pages. My favorite classics, like "The Little Drummer Boy" and "Joy to the World" are nowhere to be found. Instead, it's mostly "Winter Wonderland," "Frosty the Snowman." Generic holiday songs. Which is fine. I like those kind, too.

"As always, our class will be singing on Main Street during the Jar Island holiday tree lighting next Tuesday, which means we have a week to get these numbers in tip-top shape. So let's dive right in!"

He tinkles a few keys and we begin our standard warm-ups. It feels good to use my throat, to hear my voice blend into everyone else's.

Afterward Mr. Mayurnik says, "Great. Now that we're good and warm, we need to figure out who will be singing our solos. Can all the sopranos to come to the front of the room."

I'm a soprano, so I stand up. As I squeeze through the rows, I get nervous. Instantly nervous. I do okay singing in the back of the class, but here, with everyone looking up at us, I feel my throat close up. My dad pops into my head, because he always says that I have a pretty voice. So pretty he makes me sing "Happy Birthday" twice before he'll blow out his candles. He doesn't even care that the cake gets covered in melted wax.

But that memory doesn't make me feel better. It makes me feel worse.

I take a spot around the piano and end up standing directly in front of Alex Lind.

Mr. Mayurnik starts playing "Baby, It's Cold Outside." I forgot to take the booklet with me, but I know the words. I try my best to do a good job. Some of the other sopranos, I know they've been in chorus longer. And a few of them are in drama club. They're already practicing songs for the spring musical. *Hello, Dolly!* I would love to be in the spring musical. I can't compete with their voices, so I just try not to mess up.

For most of the song, I stare at the ceiling. But toward the end I look down at Alex. He has his eyes closed and a smile on his face, like we sound really good.

He's nice. Alex Lind is genuinely nice. I know it.

When we finish, everyone in the room applauds. Alex even whistles. Mr. Mayurnik picks Jess Salzar to do the solo, and I'm okay with it. I'm actually kind of relieved. And anyway, she does have a pretty voice.

"Okay, boys. Let's hear it."

Alex and the other guys stand at the front of the room. There are only four of them. Mr. Mayurnik makes Jess stay up at the piano to sing the girl part, and when the boys sing, he listens closely.

I do too.

Alex has an amazing voice. He's not like some of the musical-theater guys in the class, who you know are bound for Broadway. His voice isn't big like that, but you can still pick his out from the lineup of guys. It's just . . . sweet. Earnest. And it's perfect for the song.

And I'm happy for Alex, genuinely happy for him, when Mr. Mayurnik picks him for the solo.

Alex looks shocked. "Me?"

Mr. Mayurnik bangs on his piano. "Yes, you! And a little birdie told me that you're pretty good at playing the guitar, too. Can you read music?" Alex nods. "Great. Bring it with you to school tomorrow and we'll get started on you playing along."

"I don't know . . . I've never played in front of an audience before."

"You'll make all the ladies in the crowd faint! Won't he, girls?"

As if we're all on cue, every girl in the class screams for Alex like he's a pop star or a teen idol or something. Even me. Alex turns redder than a holly berry.

It's a good reminder that nice things do happen to good people, every so often.

CHAPTER THIRTY-NINE

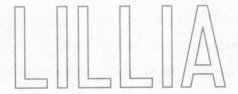

I'VE NEVER STOOD ON A DIVING PLATFORM BEFORE. Reeve wanted me to try it, at least once before the test, but I couldn't bring myself to. My knees are shaking. It's so high up, and the water looks really deep. There's a whole line of us on the blocks. People are crouched and poised in diving positions, everyone except me. I force myself to breathe. I don't have to do a fancy swan dive into the water; all I have to do is jump.

If I can do this, I can do anything. That's what I keep telling myself.

Coach Christy is giving the instructions that I know by

heart—up and down the length of the pool twice, then two minutes of treading water. I fumble with my goggles. They feel so tight around my eyes. I hate wearing them, but Reeve kept saying I would feel more comfortable underwater if I could see, and he was right.

Coach Christy blows her whistle, and I squeeze my eyes shut. The other people jump first; I hear their splashes in the water. I count to three, and then I do it. I jump. I hit the water with a slap. I move my arms; I kick my legs. I try to remember everything Reeve said: Keep your head down, arms against your ears, kick kick kick. I hold my breath for as long as I can before I gasp to the surface; then I'm turning my face back down into the water again. I feel like I'm drowning, but I keep pulling myself through the water until my fingers hit the wall, and then I'm turning around and going the other way.

I don't look over to the lanes on my left and right, because I'm afraid to break up my rhythm, but I'm pretty sure they're already done. I can't care about that, though, I have to focus on myself and not worry about what other people are doing.

You can do it. You can do it.

I feel exhausted by the second time I hit the wall, every muscle in my body is burning, but now I know it's almost over, only one more length of the pool. I take my time now; there's no rush, like Reeve said. Take it easy, one stroke at a time.

And then I'm there. My fingers touch the wall. I made it. I come up for air and cling to the side of the pool, breathing hard. I hear clapping, and I look up—there's Reeve, standing by the bleachers, clapping and whistling. For me.

I can't believe he came.

Everyone else is out of the pool, so Coach Christy comes over with her stopwatch to time me treading water. I keep my back straight and my knees bent and I do the eggbeater kick that Reeve taught me last week. I swallow some water, but I manage to keep my head up.

"Good job, Lil," she says, beaming at me.

The stopwatch goes off, and I can't believe it. I swim over to the pool ladder, and I climb up. My body is so sore, but I feel like a champion. I feel like I can do anything.

Running over to Reeve, I scream, "I did it!"

He's grinning like crazy. "Yeah, you did!" I launch myself into his arms and he lifts me in the air. I feel deliriously, euphorically happy.

We're laughing, but when he sets me back down, there's this long awkward pause of us looking at each other. We both start talking at the same time.

"Thank you—"

"You were awesome—"

We laugh and I try again. "Thank you for everything. I

couldn't have done it without you, Reeve. The whole time, I kept reminding myself of everything you taught me."

"Aw," Reeve says, cocking his head to the side. "Look at that, swimming brought us together." Quickly he adds, "As friends."

Another awkward silence. "Yup, totally!" I say. "Thank you so much."

Reeve hands me my towel from the bleacher bench. "Don't mention it," he says. "Are you gonna go to the library today?"

I shake my head. "No, I have to be somewhere." I'm meeting Kat and Mary in the girls' room at five.

"Ah, okay." He sounds disappointed, which makes me feel warm inside. He reaches out and gives my wet ponytail a playful tug. "Good job, Cho."

"Thanks, Coach." Impulsively I give him a hug, so he knows I really mean it.

CHAPTER FORTY

MARY

I'M PERCHED UP ON THE BATHROOM RADIATOR WHEN Kat walks in.

"Hey, hey, girl," Kat says. She tosses her backpack on the floor and plops down on it. "How was your Thanksgiving?"

"Umm . . . not great." I pick some lint off my sweater. "My parents didn't come."

"Damn."

"Yup," I say, and let the *P* pop. "It pretty much sucked."

The door suddenly bursts open and Lillia comes running in. "I did it!" she screams. "I passed my swimming test!"

I clap my hands and Kat whoops. "Way to go, Lil!"

She's practically hopping up and down she's so excited. "I was so nervous up there on the diving block, but then I did it—I jumped right in! I mean, it took me twice as long as everybody else, but I did it. And treading water was the easiest part, too." She stands in front of the mirror and takes her wet hair out of the ponytail holder. "Reeve came to cheer me on. I was totally surprised." She fishes around in her bag and pulls out an ivory-colored comb and starts combing her hair. "Actually . . . Reeve might have mentioned you the other day, Mary."

I'm stunned. "Are you serious?" Wow. Just . . . wow.

Kat's picking at the soles of her combat boots with a pen, and her head snaps up. "What did he say?" she asks, skeptically.

The comb in Lillia's hand stills. "It was right before the break. He found out he can't play football next year. His leg hasn't healed fast enough." I don't take my eyes off her; I'm hanging on her every word. "He was crying; he was upset. And then he said that he deserved it. He said he had it coming. He said that a long time ago, he hurt a girl really badly and he's never forgotten about it. He said it was almost a relief that he was finally paying for what he did." She turns around and faces us. "He had to have been talking about Mary, right?"

He never forgot me? He really has been thinking about me. I feel tingly all over.

"You don't know that he was talking about Mary," Kat objects. "Did he say her name? Did he say what he did to her? What she did to herself?"

Lillia hesitates. "Well . . . no. I guess not. That's why I didn't say anything. I wasn't sure."

"He's dicked over like ninety-nine percent of the girls in this school," Kat says, her arms crossed. "He could have been talking about anyone."

"Kat," I say pleadingly, "let Lillia finish." I mean, maybe Kat's right. But I don't want her to be.

Lillia's shaking her head. "Guys, if you'd been there, if you'd seen the look on his face, you would have believed him too." She turns to me. "Whoever he was talking about, he was sincere. There was genuine remorse. I honestly think he's sorry."

Kat jumps up off the floor. "Eff that! Even if he was talking about Mary, who cares if he's sorry now? It's too late. Sorry doesn't count for shit. Also don't forget, like, three weeks ago he had a chance to tell her how sorry he was to her face and instead he told her to go fuck herself! He wants to look good in front of you, Lil. He doesn't care about Mary. He's a liar!"

My eyes well up. Here I go again, falling into the same old trap, even though I know better.

"There's something I need to tell you," I say, and my voice

comes out thin and watery. "Lil, I know you said things are going good with you two, but on Thanksgiving night I saw him at the movies with Rennie. It seemed like they were on a date."

"Seriously?" she asks, and I nod.

Lillia frowns. "Oh. Well, I bet he only hung out with her because I couldn't get out of the house." She bites her lip and adds, "He texted me first."

Kat cracks her knuckles. "Even if Ren's sloppy seconds, she's still a threat. The girl is like a pit bull when she wants something. We should seal this deal sooner than later."

"Seal the deal?" Lillia says. "What does that even mean?"

"You guys have been hanging around each other for almost a month now, swimming and studying and shit, but you haven't *done* anything. Like, he hasn't made any actual moves on you yet, right?"

"Right . . . ," Lillia says and she frowns again. "But it's not like we ever decided what I'm supposed to do. 'Break his heart' is kind of abstract, you guys." She folds her arms. "I want a plan, something with a concrete end game for me to execute. I don't want this to be dragging on for another three months."

Kat's nodding. "Okay, okay, so I think it's a three-step plan. You've definitely baited the hook, but I'm not sure Reeve's bitten. So, step one is you guys need a hot French."

"What?" I say. "We never talked about Lillia *kissing* Reeve."

Lillia looks aghast. "French? Like in French kiss?"

Kat laughs. "Come on. Haven't you ever French-kissed someone you didn't like? Close your eyes and pretend he's someone else."

Lillia bites her lip. "I guess . . ."

Hastily I say, "Kat, we shouldn't push Lillia into doing something she doesn't want to do." Kat and Lillia exchange a look, and I realize I sound jealous, so I backtrack. "I mean, if you're okay with it, maybe you could do it at the tree-lighting ceremony. I'll be there, singing with the chorus. Alex Lind, too. He got a solo. It's next Tuesday night."

"He did?" Kat looks surprised. It's nice to have news to share with the group for once, to know something they don't.

"He's going to be doing 'Baby, It's Cold Outside,'" I tell her. "He has a great voice. And he's playing his guitar, too."

Kat smiles to herself. "Nice."

"Lindy must be so happy. But why didn't he say anything?" Lillia pouts her lips and puts on some ChapStick. "You know what, I'm going to get the whole group together to watch him sing. And plus, I want to see you sing too, Mary."

"I don't have a solo or anything," I say. "But it'll be nice having someone in the audience there for me." There's no way Aunt Bette will go. Not that I even want her to.

Kat says, "Lil, this is perfect. Make your move on Reeve that night. Boom."

"Maybe," Lillia says. "If Rennie's not there."

"I thought you said that was no problem."

"She's not. I—I just don't want to do it right in front of her face."

I wish she didn't have to do it in front of *my* face.

Lillia digs her cell out of her purse. "Let me text Reeve, make sure he can come."

We crowd around her as she texts, *Thanks again for coming today, Coach. Do you want to go to the tree lighting on Tues? Lindy is singing a solo, we can surprise him!*

He writes back right away. *Yeah, let's do it. Hey. Are we still studying on Sat?*

As she reads it, Kat wiggles her eyebrows at me.

"Boom. Then you're on to step two."

"Which is . . ."

"Make Reeve think you're his girlfriend through Christmas. Be all cozy and shit so he buys you a present. Then we'll know for sure that he sees you as girlfriend material."

"Do you think he would?"

I think of that day, when Reeve gave me my daisy necklace. How happy it made me. "Yeah," I say. "I bet he will get you something."

Lillia chews on her nail. "Well, what's step three?"

"New Year's Eve. You leave him hanging at midnight."

Kat waves her hands. "Ooh! Even better! You could kiss someone else at midnight!"

Glaring, Lillia shakes her head at her. "I'm not a slut!"

Kat backs off. "Okay, okay. Then leave him high and dry."

Lillia thinks it over. And she starts nodding, slowly. "Okay. Good. And then, January first, I'm done. New year, new start. For all of us."

"Yup. Done." Kat high-fives her for emphasis, and she's about to high-five me when a girl I don't recognize steps into the bathroom. Kat's arm drops and I hurry out before the door slams shut. As I leave, Kat goes into a stall to pee, and Lillia leans over the sink and finishes putting on her makeup.

I'm about halfway down the hall just trying to process what's about to happen, Lillia kissing Reeve, when something tells me to go back. I don't know why; it's just a feeling. So I do. I go back to the bathroom door and press my ear close.

"Did you know her parents didn't even come to Thanksgiving? They were supposed to and then they changed their minds."

Kat. Whispering. About me.

Lillia gasps. "That's horrible. Poor thing. No wonder she was so down just now."

"Shit with her aunt sounds crazy too. If she's not locked up in the attic, she's berating Mary. And have you driven past her house lately? Thing is practically falling down. I don't know if she should be living there anymore."

"Should we try to call her parents or something? Tell them what's going on?"

"But that's the thing. We don't even know what's going on." Kat lets out a long sigh. "I doubt Mary's giving us the full picture of how bad things are. Probably because she doesn't want us to worry. Something is definitely going on with her."

"Maybe we could get her to talk to someone. Like a counselor."

"Yeah. We probably should. It's up to us to take care of her. No one else is."

I run from the bathroom. I know the conversation is them being good friends, but I hate the idea of them talking about me behind my back. And I can't have anyone, not school, not Lillia and Kat, talking to Aunt Bette.

CHAPTER FORTY-ONE

LILLIA

I CAN'T STOP THINKING ABOUT WHAT KAT SAID—how Reeve isn't sorry, how he only told that story to impress me. She made a good point. Why didn't he apologize to Mary when he had the chance? But then I remember the way he looked at me, how he cried like a little kid, and I feel sure that he was telling the truth. And who else could he have hurt worse than Mary?

Only it doesn't matter, either way. Because it isn't my responsibility to make Reeve apologize. Or to try and figure out if he's sorry for what he did. My loyalty lies with my friend. I have to get Reeve back for what he did to Mary. That's all. An eye for an eye, a tooth for a tooth.

A broken heart for a broken heart.

We're supposed to meet at Java Jones at noon. I'm planning to finish up my AP English essay on mother figures within the works of Shakespeare, which is due Monday. I packed a CD-ROM of timed practice SAT questions for Reeve to work on. He's already blown through the two test workbooks I let him borrow.

I decide to go to Java Jones an hour early, because this essay isn't going to write itself, and to make sure we score a good table near an outlet, so we can plug in our laptops in case we run out of battery. Luckily, the one I want is free when I get there. I put my princess coat on the back of a chair and my laptop bag on the other. Then I order a hot chocolate with whipped cream and a peppermint stick at the counter. While I'm looking through my change purse, my phone begins to buzz.

It's a text. From Reeve. *Leg is pretty sore this morning. Don't think I can make it. Sorry. :(*

I frown like the face in his text. I keep telling him that he needs to make sure he's not overexerting himself in the weight room. You can't rush physical therapy. You need to be patient. My uncle broke his ankle running two years ago, and he finished his physical therapy like one week early, and he says his ankle still bothers him when it rains.

I've opened up a text to write him back when I see Reeve drive past the front window in his truck.

What the—?

And then it hits me. Reeve could very well be on his way to Rennie's.

I get my things from the table and leave behind my hot chocolate on my table, to save my spot. "I'll be right back," I tell the barista and step outside. The sun is bright, and I have to shield my eyes with my hand. For a second I think I've lost him, but then I catch sight of Reeve's truck making a left into the ferry parking lot.

Okay. Maybe not.

I hustle down the sidewalk. I'm mad, but I'm trying to stay calm. Maybe he's picking up one of his brothers? I send Reeve an innocent text back. *Should I swing by? We can study at your place.* As soon as I hit send, my heart fills my throat, because I have this terrible feeling that he's about to lie to me.

He doesn't text me back right away, which gives me a chance to catch up to him.

When I get to the parking lot, I'm careful to keep camouflaged behind trees and the ticket booth. Reeve's parked his truck in line with the cars waiting to drive aboard the next ferry. I'm close enough to see him looking at his phone; he's probably reading my text. He writes me back. *I think I should take it easy and ice it for now. I'll text you later if it feels better.*

My body goes cold. Kat and Mary were one thousand percent right. Reeve's not a trustworthy guy, not at all. I'm so mad at myself for falling for it when I know better.

Reeve doesn't see me coming. He's fiddling with his radio. I can hear the music as I get closer. It's hip hop, the volume turned way up. And he's drumming his hands on the steering wheel. Whoever he's off to see, he's sure pumped.

I knock so hard on the glass my knuckles hurt. Reeve startles, and when he sees that it's me, his jaw drops. He fumbles to turn the radio off and then tries to get his window to roll down.

"Hey, there," I say, all fake sweet. "So nice to see that your leg's better." I drop the act, let my smile go flat. "Don't bother texting me later. Or any other day." I walk away.

I hear his truck door open and then slam shut, his feet pounding the pavement. I'm speed walking as fast as I can, but Reeve must be sprinting, even with his bum leg. I let my laptop bag fall on the ground; I don't even care. I don't want to look at him.

Before I know it, Reeve wraps his arms around me from behind.

"Let me go!" I try and break out of his bear hug, but his hands are locked around me.

"Lillia, wait a second!"

I don't wait. I struggle and wriggle to get free until I have no strength left. "Let go of me!" I shriek.

Some of the people in the parking lot have stopped to watch us. "You're making a scene!" he hisses. He's right. I don't want the cops to come; I just want him to let go of me. The only way he'll do that is if I stop.

"Please, Lillia." I go limp and he drops his arms.

I'm panting as I turn around to face him. "Care to explain why you lied to me?"

Reeve sets his jaw. "No. Not particularly." He walks back a few steps and picks up my laptop bag.

I feel something mean bubble up in my throat. The overwhelming urge to tell Reeve everything, how I've been only hanging out with him to hurt him for Mary. How it's all a lie. I've been pretending to like him, when in actuality he disgusts me.

But I can't, because those words won't mean anything. They won't hurt him. Because if Reeve did care, he wouldn't have lied to me so he could sneak off, probably to see some other girl.

"Tell me where you're going." I know I sound jealous. And I hate it.

He hands my laptop bag back to me. "It's better if I don't." I snatch it from his hands and hear the bits of broken plastic shake around. It's broken.

I feel the sting of tears, and my vision blurs. "I hope this other girl knows a thing or two about the SATs. Or else maybe she doesn't care that you won't get into college!" I think of all the time I've wasted, trying to help Reeve. I should have stuck to the damn plan. I bet I could have kissed him weeks ago.

Reeve's face goes blank. "You think I'm going to see another girl?"

I walk away.

He's following me again. He speeds up so that he's standing in my way. "Fine, you want to know where I'm going?" He fishes something out of his pocket. A piece of paper. He hands it to me.

I wipe my eyes so I can read it. There are two names written down, and neither of them are girls' names. And an address for a fraternity house at UMass.

I look up at him, because it doesn't make sense.

His mouth is set in a grim line. "I'm going to whoop those fuckers' asses." And then he starts walking back toward his truck.

It takes me a second to put it together. "Oh my God," I say, staring down at the paper. At the names. Ian Rosenberg and Michael Fenelli. "Oh my God."

And then it's me who's chasing him. "Are you crazy?" I scream.

Reeve doesn't slow down. "I'm an idiot for not thinking of it sooner. That house those turkeys rented, it was one my dad manages. All I had to do was look up the address, and boom.

I found their addresses, their phone numbers, their birthdays. I'm going up there, and I'm going to make them wish they never, ever laid eyes on you and Rennie."

"I don't want you to do that!" The ferry horn sounds and the cars waiting to drive aboard start their engines. "I don't want you going anywhere near them!"

Reeve opens his door. "Why?" he demands. "You don't think they deserve it?"

I struggle to answer him. Because as much as it was the guys, it was my fault too. I was the one who went to a stranger's house. I was the one who got too drunk. I was the one who created the situation where something terrible could happen. And I was unlucky enough that it did.

"It won't change anything!" I reach out and grab hold of his sweatshirt. Two fistfuls. "I am telling you don't go there. If this is for me, I don't want it."

Reeve's already shaking his head. He's not listening to me. "Those guys have to pay for what they did. There have to be consequences. They can't just get away with it."

It's hard to breathe now. "I know you want to help. I know that. But nothing you do can change what happened." I'm trying to stay strong so I can make him hear me, but I can feel myself start to shake. "You going over there, it will only bring everything back for me. All I want to do is forget."

I see him soften a little. "You can't bury it, Lil. It happened. You have to deal with it."

"I know. But let me do it my way." I look up at him with pleading eyes. "Not like this."

We're staring at each other, neither of us blinking, and Reeve finally bows his head and nods. "I just—I wanted to make things right for you." He reaches out and takes my hand and locks his fingers around mine. I let him do it, even though I feel like I shouldn't.

Later, when I think about the look in Reeve's eyes, and I remember what he said about how there should be consequences for the bad things people do, I feel dread, because I know he's right. There will be consequences, for all of us. Maybe me most of all.

CHAPTER FORTY-TWO

During Monday's free period, I head to the computer lab to check e-mail. I have to wait until I'm at school to do it, because our computer at home is slow as shit. It's old to begin with, and then Pat downloaded a bunch of games, aka porn, and now the thing's got more viruses than a prostitute.

As soon as I log in, I get a pop-up window that says I'm running out of available mailbox space. No surprises there. About a month ago my aunt Jackie discovered "electronic mail" and asked for my address. Now she forwards me at least ten messages a day. Poems about angels and cancer-prayer chain letters and articles about new research and treatments. She's unhealthily obsessed with my mom's death. She could use an hour with Ms. Chirazo.

What I don't see, unfortunately, are any e-mails about my early-decision application to Oberlin. I know they have until the end of January to get back to me, but I'm keeping my fingers crossed I hear something before then. Ms. Chirazo loved my new essay. She said it brought tears to her eyes. She was probably hot flashing or something, but it was all I needed to hear.

Later in the day, we have a drunk-driving assembly, which is a lovely way to help ring in the holidays. An older-looking woman in a police uniform is up at the podium, talking in the most sleep-inducing monotone while she clicks through car-crash slides from the 1970s that don't even show you anything interesting, like gore or dead bodies. Just a bunch of wrecked-up and dented metal. She might as well have taken pictures of my garage.

Anyway, somewhere along the line I fall asleep, and the polite applause wakes me up. I open my eyes right as the police officer trips across the microphone cord and nearly falls flat on her ass.

I can't help but laugh. And look around at my fellow classmates to see who else enjoyed this early Christmas gift. Nobody else is laughing.

I meet eyes with Rennie, who has a big smile on her face. As big as mine.

I immediately look away. A sick sense of humor was one thing Ren and I always had in common.

Fuck. I guess we still do.

CHAPTER FORTY-THREE

LILLIA

THE AIR SMELLS PINEY AND CHRISTMASY FROM THE tree and the cinnamon ornaments the church ladies are selling. It smells like it's going to snow any minute. I hope it does. A snow day would be heaven.

There's a nice turnout this year; it seems like half of Jar Island is here on Main Street for the tree lighting, even though it's a weekday. Our school's chorus is in front of the tree, singing "Winter Wonderland," and they actually sound pretty good. They're all wearing Santa hats and red-and-green-striped scarves, and the soprano section has bells. Mary's in the back, and she looks so cute with her hair in braids and her Santa hat perched on top of her head. Alex is up there too, in the front row. His solo should be coming up soon. I catch his eye and wave, and he winks at me and tips his Santa hat.

The song finishes, and I clap and do a quick tuck jump. "Yay, Lindy!" I shout. In my head I add a quick *And yay Mary*.

I'm huddled together with Ashlin; Derek and Reeve went off to get us hot chocolates. Rennie's at work, which is perfect. I don't have to worry about her tonight.

"Lindy looks so cute up there," Ash says, elbowing me. "Like a tall elf."

I dig around my cross-body bag for a peppermint candy. "He *does* look like an elf." And he does look cute in his camel peacoat and his Santa hat and his tartan scarf his mom probably bought him. His cheeks are rosy from the cold, and he has a big smile on his face. I can't help smiling too. To Ash I say, "He has a good voice, don't you think? I can't wait to hear his solo."

"Totes," Ash agrees. Then she leans in close and whispers, "So what's going on with you and Reeve? Are you guys, like, here together?"

I blink. And before I've thought it through, I squeal, "Ew! No." Ashlin looks skeptical, so I add, "No way would anything ever happen with me and Reeve. Not in a million trillion years."

Ash is about to reply, but then her eyes light up and she reaches her arms out and squeals, "Gimme, gimme!"

I turn around, and Derek and Reeve are standing there with the hot chocolates. I worry for a second that Reeve heard me, but he hands me the Styrofoam cup and his face doesn't betray anything.

Then I see her, Kat, across the town square, looking over at us. It's go time for step one.

Oh God.

I switch places with Ash so I'm standing next to Reeve and she's next to Derek.

"It's so cold," I say, wrapping my fingers around the cup. I'm wearing a dove-gray fleece and skinny jeans and riding boots, plus my rabbit-fur earmuffs. I should have brought mittens, though.

When Reeve doesn't say anything, I tug his coat sleeve. "I'm so cold," I repeat.

Reeve rolls his eyes at me. "Why didn't you wear a coat?"

I creep closer to him, huddling for warmth. That's why, Reeve. "Well, my fleece usually keeps me warm enough, but tonight it's *freezing*." I try to link my arm through his, but he flinches like I've burned him.

Then he steps away from me and shrugs out of his puffer jacket. He pushes it at me and says, "There. Now quit complaining. Let's not forget you're the one who made us come to this cornfest."

Why is he suddenly being such a jerk? We had this close moment on Saturday, and now, three days later, it feels like he's trying to push me away. Did he hear what I said to Ash, or is it something else? Maybe I should be relieved, because, fake kiss or not, I won't kiss him when he's acting like a jerk. But I'm not. I'm annoyed. "We're here so we can support Alex," I remind him. "He's your friend too."

Reeve makes some kind of snorty sound and goes back to watching the chorus with his arms crossed. They're singing "Let It Snow." Derek and Ash have migrated over to a tree and they're making out. In public. So tacky. And a total waste of a hot chocolate. Their cups are on the ground.

It's just me and Reeve now. I glance around for Kat again, but I don't see her. There are too many people milling around.

I sneak a peek at Reeve, and he's standing there with his arms crossed and a scowl on his face. I take a sip of my hot chocolate. Maybe I've been imagining this whole thing and he's already over it. "What's up with you tonight?" I ask him, taking another sip. "You're being such a grouch."

He barely even glances in my direction. "Nothing's up with me."

"Is your leg hurting from standing on it too long? We could go find a bench or . . ." My voice trails off. He's not even listening. I bite my lip. If he's over it, then I'm going to be over it first. Whatever *it* is.

I jab Reeve on the shoulder. "Here," I say, shoving his coat back at him. "I'm leaving. Tell Alex I had to go." I start speed walking away from him toward the church parking lot. I toss my cup in a trash can along the way.

"Wait!" he yells.

I don't slow down, I hurry faster, but Reeve catches up with me. Breathing hard, he whirls me around so I'm facing him. His green eyes are bright; he fixes them on me. He doesn't blink once. In a low, urgent voice he says, "I like you. I've been holding it in, for Lind's sake. But I like you. I can't help it." He watches me, waits for me to say something. Do something. "No more games, Cho. You and me—is this real?"

My face is flaming. I know I'm supposed to say yes. Say yes and kiss him. That's the plan. Except the thing is that, deep down, I *want* to say yes. I want so badly to say yes. But I'm afraid. We're suddenly so real it terrifies me.

Seconds pass, and finally Reeve's gaze drops and he isn't looking at me anymore. He's looking down. He's going to back away, he's going to leave, and it will all be over.

"Yes. It's real."

Reeve's head jerks up. "Then—then why did you tell Ash you weren't here with me?"

I don't know what else to tell him except the honest answer. "Because I'm scared." My voice breaks. "I don't want to hurt anybody."

I stand there, shivering. Reeve puts his coat on my shoulders, and I let him help me into it. He pulls me toward him, and then he slides my arms around his neck. "Okay?" he whispers. He's shivering too.

I nod, my heart beating so fast and so hard I can hear it. I think I can hear his, too.

And then he kisses me, and I stop thinking altogether.

CHAPTER FORTY-FOUR

MARY

I SAW THEM LEAVE. AND EVEN THOUGH I TOLD MYSELF not to, I slipped away from the chorus, stepped right off the risers, and I followed them.

Reeve's kissing her, so soft and gentle, like she's a porcelain doll that will break in his arms if he's not careful. She's never looked prettier. Like an angel. Roses in her cheeks, her shiny hair whipping around them. It's like a movie. Two teenagers, kissing in the parking lot, Christmas carols in the background, the tree all lit up behind them.

And then there's me. In the background. In the shadows. Watching.

It worked. He loves her now for sure. The way he's looking at her right now, like she's the girl of his dreams. He can't believe his luck. It's all unfolding exactly the way it's supposed to.

I'm clenching my fists so tight my fingernails leave red crescent moons on my skin. I feel a surge, a heat roar up inside me. As bad as I'm hurting now, he'll hurt ten times worse. That's the only thing that keeps me going.

KAT

I'M SITTING ON THE GROUND, THE COLD SEEPING through the butt of my jeans, in the middle of the damn tree-lighting crowd. I rip off my mittens with my teeth, fold down my combat boots, and check my ankles for blood.

You know, there is such a thing as concert crowd etiquette. Common-sense rules to abide by so that everyone in the audience has a good time. It's true even for punk shows, where people in the pit beat the piss out of each other. So it should definitely be true for this shit show.

I learned about the rules at my very first show at Paul's Boutique. Kim and I were up in the sound booth. She had a bouncer's flashlight with her and kept beaming it on different offenders so I could watch their transgressions live.

It basically boils down to this.

One: Never pretend that you have a friend close to the stage just so you can push up close. People will call out fake names, like, "Hey, Jimmy! I'm coming!" and then weasel their way to the front. It might fool one or two people in the very back, but ultimately you end up at the stage, clearly by yourself, and people get pissed.

Two: Even in the tightest of crowds, you must always respect people's personal space. Like, it's fine to brush up against someone once, but that's it. And if you carry a purse or a bag, you hug it to your chest so you won't knock people with it.

Three: If you're super tall, don't be a dick and stand in front of a short person.

Now, even though it's never come up at any of the shows I've been to, there has to be a rule about how to navigate a crowd when you're pushing a double-wide stroller packed with two screaming babies through a crowd of people like a damn snowplow.

I stare daggers into this Mother of the Year as she coyly spins around and gives me the most pathetic *I'm sorry!* face. Meanwhile, her wailing kids are drowning out the whole damn choir.

I get back to my feet and look for Lillia and Reeve in the crowd, but they've both disappeared. That dummy Ashlin and her meat-bag Derek, too.

I spin around and stand on my tiptoes and try to see where everyone may have run off to, but the crowd is so thick, and the family standing behind me is giving me weird looks, so I turn back toward the concert. Lillia will give us the juicy step-one details later. I know she'll make it happen.

Anyway, I'm interested in hearing Alex sing. I've been trying to get him to play me one of his songs, but he never does. I told him that tonight could be like a practice for his USC audition. He still hasn't sent in his application, as far as I know.

After two boring songs, the band kicks in to "Baby, It's Cold Outside." Alex steps forward, along with some other girl I recognize as a drama geek. He's got his guitar with him, and he starts playing along.

I feel myself smiling. Forget this drama girl. She's coming off way too Broadway, especially since "Baby, It's Cold Outside" is a sexy song. Alex is doing it right. Like how a boy would talk you into something. Sweet, but with something hungry underneath. And he does have a great voice. Clean and bright, and very confident. If he could be as confident in regular life as he is when he's singing, dude would go far.

After he's done, he steps back up on the risers and blushes at the applause. And people are applauding. Not the polite stuff. Like they've seen something . . . special.

Meanwhile, Alex is looking around the crowd, I guess for his friends. But they've all left him.

Poor guy. I don't get why no one in his crew can see how great he is.

Alex's eyes find me. I wolf-whistle and then throw up the rock sign with each of my hands. Like he's a rock star. Or at least on his way to being one.

He breaks into a smile, and despite being freezing, my whole body warms.

I look to give the same rock signs to Mary, because I'm freaking proud of her for getting up in front of everyone like this, but I can't find her, either. Where the hell has everyone gone?

The mayor steps up to the podium and signals for the Christmas tree to turn on. And it does, for a second, before it flickers out. And all the other light too—the streetlamps, the shop windows, the traffic lights—until it's completely dark out. Then everything starts flashing, on and off, like there's some kind of issue with the power.

Damn, does this whole island need to be rewired?

I'm about to run for my life for the second time this year, but then everything clicks back on, good and strong, and everyone in the crowd applauds like it's a true freaking Christmas miracle.

Which, hell, maybe it is. But I'm bouncing out of here either way, to be safe.

CHAPTER FORTY-SIX

LILLIA

I'M AT LUNCH WITH EVERYONE ON WEDNESDAY WHEN two sophomore girls nervously approach our table. They look so young, both of them, in jeans that are way too blue and way too baggy, track-and-field fleeces, and Converse sneakers.

"Um, Rennie? Could we ask you a quick question?" the one with the straw-colored ponytail asks.

"If you're not too busy," the mousy one adds.

Over the past few weeks I've become very adept at pretending Rennie does not exist. Almost as good as she is at pretending that I don't exist. So I go back to the pages of my history textbook and pretend to be utterly absorbed by a portrait of Eli Whitney.

Plus, I already know what this is about.

The two girls produce a clipping and place it down on the table for Rennie to see. From what I can tell without totally obviously looking, it looks like maybe something cut out of a teen magazine. Or a department-store catalog? "We were wondering if this dress would work for your party."

Rennie's New Year's Eve party is all anyone can talk about. It's going to be at her mom's gallery, the last hurrah before Ms. Holtz sells the place. It will be Rennie's pièce de résistance, her masterpiece. It's a twenties theme, and she's pulling out all the stops; she's been hoarding bottles of gin and champagne from Bow Tie for the past month. It's been easy enough with all the company holiday parties they've been hosting; according to Rennie, there are plenty of bottles at the end of the night. And everyone's going to be in costume, too. Girls have been coming up to Rennie showing her pictures of their dresses and getting approval on 1920s hairstyles. I actually spotted her, forehead wrinkled with concentration, reading *The Great Gatsby* during a free period, which is hilarious, because we were assigned that, like, freshman year.

I was the first one Rennie told about this idea, back on the first day of school. Rennie has practically invited the whole school to the party, but she hasn't invited me. She hasn't flat-out banned me, but she hasn't invited me either. I don't want to go, but it's not like I have a choice. It's the final stage of our plan.

Rennie tears into both of the girls. "Are you serious right now? First off, this is a prom dress, not a New Year's Eve dress. And it is not flapper-esque. See the cinched waist? And that awful-looking poufy skirt? It's a lame fifties-housewife costume." She actually crumples up the paper and chucks it on the cafeteria floor.

For as long as I've known her, Rennie has been on me to have a party at my house. I've always said no, because the kind of party my parents would let me have is not the kind of party any of our friends would be interested in going to—i.e., no alcohol, no loud music, no skinny-dipping, no hooking up in random bedrooms. It would be more like karaoke and a cheese plate.

And the truth is, I've never been that into the idea of hosting a bunch of people. It seems so stressful, making sure everybody's having a good time but also making sure they're not wrecking the house. It is a perfect party house, though. My mom designed it that way, with an open floor plan and high vaulted ceilings and plenty of room to move around in. And the movie night I had a few weeks ago worked out fine.

I spend the rest of the day wondering why Rennie is the only one to ever throw parties. Why she and she alone gets to be the gatekeeper to all social activities on Jar Island.

That night, an opportunity arises. We're cooking dinner when my mom suggests the three of us surprise my dad this weekend in New York, where he's speaking at a medical conference. I remind her how I have to work on my college apps, and she says, "Lillia, you hardly ever get to see your dad. This will be such nice family time. We'll see a show, go to brunch, check out that new art installation at the Met. Maybe get a massage. We can do some Christmas shopping too! Didn't you say you need new riding boots?"

I know she thinks she's going to get me with the shopping, but I stand my ground. "Daddy will be stuck working the whole time. It's not like he's going to the spa with us."

"He'll be able to meet us for dinners," my mom argues.

"Mommy, I need to work on my applications. Things have been so crazy with schoolwork that I haven't been able to concentrate on them the way I need to." I mean it too.

My mom sighs. "All right. We'll go another time."

"You and Nadi should still go," I tell her. "I'll be fine by myself, promise."

I can read the indecision on my mom's face. She really wants to get off the island; she'll take any excuse to escape. The winters here drive her crazy. It makes her feel claustrophobic, not being able to leave, with the weather so cold and wet and gray.

Plus, she loves New York. She lived in New York when she was in her early twenties, and she gets all nostalgic when she talks about running around the city with her friends.

Nadia's listening from the couch, and she chimes in, "Please, pretty please, can we still go? I want to go shopping!" Hastily she adds, "And also I want to see Daddy."

"I don't know. A whole weekend alone?"

In a strong, firm voice I say, "Mommy, I'll be okay. I stayed by myself last month and it was totally fine."

"Well . . . I do love New York at Christmastime," she says, looking back at Nadia, who squeals. "The whole city is wrapped up like a present." She looks back at me and says, "You can have Rennie stay over here to keep you company."

"Maybe," I say, and Nadia raises her eyebrows. I turn away and start filling water glasses.

"What's going on with you two?" my mom asks. "She hasn't been around much lately."

"Nothing. We're both just busy."

I can tell my mom was gearing up to ask another question. Time for a subject change. "Mommy, when you guys are in New York, can you pick me up some of that face cream I like from the spa you go to? The one that smells like sugarplums?"

"Maybe Santa will put it in your stocking," my mom says with a wink.

So this is how I come to be having my first ever party party. I tell everybody at the lunch table on Thursday, and the sour look on Rennie's face makes the whole thing worth it in advance. "Friday night, seniors only," I say. "Super exclusive. I don't want any random sophomores or whatever. Only the people we like." *Which means not you, Rennie.*

"Your mom's letting you have a party?" Rennie looks skeptical.

I'm about to snap at her, but then I realize that these are the first words Rennie has spoken to me in over a month. I force a swallow and say, "My mom won't be here. Nadia, either."

Rennie's face gets pinched. "What about booze? Let me guess, this is going to be a dry party. Diet Coke and lemonade, am I right?"

I ignore her and touch Reeve's arm. "Reeve? Can you ask one of your brothers to get me a few kegs for tomorrow? I can pay you after school."

"No prob," he says, gulping down a carton of milk. He wipes his mouth. "Tommy owes me for helping him move last week. Do you want some liquor, too? Something sweet for the girls, like peach schnapps or whatever?"

Hmm. I don't want things to get too too crazy. But Rennie's was watching so I say, "Maybe a bottle of tequila. For shots." To the table I say, "But I don't want it to get, like, out of hand.

Can you guys please help me keep things under control? My mom will kill me if the house gets wrecked."

Reeve nudges my foot under the table, his sneaker to my bootie. "I'll be your bouncer," he promises, giving me a look. "Only VIPs at Princess Lillia's party."

I'm tempted to sneak a peek at Rennie, to see the look on her face, but there's no need. I know she's seething inside. Guaranteed. To add more fuel to the flames I say, "And there won't be a theme. Themes are so over."

"Sounds good," Alex says. "Let me know if I can help. Whatever you need."

"Maybe you can pick up the pizzas?" I ask.

Alex nods. "No problem."

After school Reeve texted me and asked him to help find an outfit for Rennie's party, and I said yes, only because I hoped it would get back to her. So here we are at Second Time Around, a thrift store near Reeve's house that his mom told him about. Reeve's in front of a full-length mirror, trying on a double-breasted pin-striped jacket. "Um, I think that's a women's suit jacket!" I say, and I collapse into a fit of giggles.

"No way," Reeve says confidently. "It's definitely menswear. It just has a sleeker cut."

I come up behind and get on my toes to check the label. Ann

Taylor. "You're right," I say, trying not to smile. "Menswear."

Reeve gives me a suspicious look and takes off the jacket. When he reads the label, he exclaims, "Ann Taylor! My mom shops there." He tosses the jacket to me and I put it back on the hanger. "If I can't find anything else, I guess it'll work. The man makes the clothes; the clothes don't make the man."

I shake my head at him in mock wonder. "I can't even believe how cocky you are." I'm giving him a hard time, but the truth is, it's nice to see him acting like his old self. I hand him a gray checked vest with buttons down the front. "You could wear this with a dress shirt and a tie."

He unbuttons it and tries it on over his shirt. "Not bad," Reeve says, checking himself out.

He does look handsome. Very *GQ*. I take a gray fedora off the hat rack and place it on his head. "Now you look perfect," I tell him, tilting it just so. "Very jaunty. Very Gatsby-esque." His cheeks are smooth; he shaved this morning. And he smells good—not like he doused himself in cologne, but clean, like Irish Spring soap.

"Cool, I'll get it," Reeve says. I can tell he's pleased. He looks at himself in the mirror one last time, and then he takes the hat off and puts it on my head. He's looking down at me, and then he gives my side braid a tug, and I have this strong feeling that he's about to kiss me.

But behind Reeve, across the store, I spot two girls and a guy from our high school picking through the racks. They're drama kids, probably looking for costumes or something. I don't know their names, but I bet they know who Reeve and I are. And if they spotted us kissing, that kind of juicy gossip would be all over the school in a heartbeat.

Suddenly I feel dizzy. I take a quick step back and then dart away from him and head up to the register. Reeve follows, and I tell the girl at the counter, "We'll take the fedora and the vest."

Then Reeve pays, and we walk back toward his truck. The sun is bright out, but it's cold. I tighten the scarf around my neck. I'm about to hop into the passenger side of the truck when Reeve clears his throat and says, "Would you want to come to my family's open house?"

"What's an open house?" Is he *moving*?

"It's a thing my parents do every December," Reeve explains. "My mom cooks a bunch of food, and people stop by all day. Mostly family and neighbors. It'll be, like, my brothers and their girlfriends and my cousins. We watch football and decorate the tree, hang lights on the garage, nothing special."

I wet my lips nervously. "When is it?"

"This Sunday. Drop by whenever. We'll be around all day."

"Okay," I say. I've known Reeve for years, and I don't

remember him ever mentioning an open house. I can't believe he's actually inviting me. It's really sweet. But it's also really real. Like, hanging out with his mom and dad and brothers and their girlfriends? That's something only a girlfriend would do.

Which I guess is a good thing.

Reeve's face breaks into a relieved smile. "Yeah? Okay, cool. You can stop by whenever. I mean, people start coming in the morning, and my mom makes these kick-ass sweet rolls, so maybe come around ten before my brothers eat them all."

"Cool," I echo.

He looks so happy that I wonder if maybe he'll try to kiss me again.

Reeve opens the passenger-side door for me, and I climb in, my scarf trailing behind me. Before he shuts the door, he picks up the end of my scarf so it won't get caught in the door, and he winds it around my neck. Then he runs around the other side and starts the car and turns the heater on. "It'll get warm pretty fast," he tells me, and I nod. I have to keep telling myself that none of this is real; it's all going to be over soon. I can't let myself get swept away because I have feelings for him. I *can't* have feelings for him. I have to control it.

Reeve pulls up in front of my house, and before I get out, he says, "Everything's set with the kegs. I'm going to pick them up tomorrow after school. I can grab the pizzas, too."

Surprised, I say, "Oh, thanks, but Alex said he'd pick them up."

"I'll do it. It's on my way."

"Okay. Thank you. I'll give the pizza place my credit card number when I place the order tomorrow."

Reeve gives me a weird look and says, "I can afford a couple of pizzas, Cho."

Great, now I've offended him. I'm trying to think of what to say to make it less awkward, and then he goes, "I can come early with everything and help you get set up, if you want."

I look at him out of the corner of my eye. "People are going to notice, you know."

Reeve shrugs. "What?"

"Come on, Reeve. I'm just saying that if we want things to stay, you know, between us, we should probably be more discreet."

Reeve reaches out and tucks some of my hair behind my ear. "We're not going to be able to hide this forever."

"I know that. But we can't, like, throw it in everyone's faces either. People will get upset." People, aka Rennie and Alex.

He rubs his eyes. "I'm just going to do what feels right. If people have a problem with that . . . well, then they can go to hell."

I nod. What else can we do? Then I go with what feels right to *me* at that very second. I lean across the center console and give Reeve a peck on the cheek. I do it so quick I don't get to see the look on his face, and then I hop out and run to my front door.

I'm breathless and flushed by the time I run up the stairs and to my room. I'm brushing my hair in front of my vanity when Nadia steps inside in one of our dad's big Harvard sweatshirts and her fuzzy slippers. "Hey," I say. "I thought you were going to the barn."

"I am, later." She comes and sits on my bed and watches me, her arms hugging her knees. "You look happy."

"I do?"

"Yeah. Was that Reeve dropping you off?"

I notice something in her voice. A sharpness. "Yeah. A bunch of us were hanging out downtown and he gave me a ride home because he was on his way over to Alex's."

Nadia doesn't say anything. She knows I'm lying. I know I'm lying. And so the lie just sits there between us. Then she says, "I saw you kiss him."

"On the cheek!"

She shakes her head, looking at me like I am a stranger. "But you know it's not right. Whatever you're doing with him, it's not right."

"Why can't it be right?" My voice sounds weak, desperate.

I hate that Nadia's looking at me like that—like she's

JENNY HAN AND SIOBHAN VIVIAN

disappointed in me. Like I've disappointed her. "Because you know how Rennie feels about him. He's hers."

"No, he's not. She thinks he is, but he's not." I feel tears spring to my eyes as I say, "I don't even know how you can defend her after the way she's been treating me. Have you really not noticed? It's been almost two whole months of her ignoring me in public, talking about me behind my back. And I know you and all your friends have been making decorations and stuff for her New Year's Eve party. How is that supposed to make me feel? You're supposed to be on my side, Nadi. You're *my* sister, not hers."

"It's not about what she's doing. It's about what you're doing." Nadia looks like she is about to cry too.

"Nadi," I begin. I'm not sure what I can say to make this better. Before I can figure it out, my sister gets up and leaves. I call out her name again, but she doesn't come back.

CHAPTER FORTY-SEVEN

KAT

MY FRIDAY NIGHTS ARE GETTING LESS AND LESS exciting these days. Lillia's having a big rager and I'm sitting on the floor of the den, trying to untangle a knot of holiday lights. It's a pretty, glowing puzzle. Pat and Dad went to buy us a Christmas tree from the YMCA with a coupon from the newspaper. Pat was all, "I want one that smells piney. Some of them don't." I put my hands on his shoulders and said, "Tall and cheap, Pat. That's your mission."

It still feels weird to spend money on Christmas trees. Back when Mom was alive, we'd go out "tree hunting." That's what she called it, anyway. I think other people might use the word "trespassing."

After dinner, when the sun had set, the four of us would go for a walk in the woods behind our house. Each of us would have a flashlight. When we'd find a good tree, Dad and Pat would each take a side of an old-timey handsaw, and they'd push it back and forth. Mom and I would quietly cheer them on, mittens dulling our applause, and sip hot cider from a thermos.

This was the only thing illegal my mom ever did. We'd drag the tree back to the house, and the whole time we'd tease her about it. Pat would get quiet and say in a whisper, "Judy! I think I hear sirens!" and then he and I would bust up laughing. But Mom refused, she flat-out refused, to spend money on a tree when the woods were full of them. Never mind that the woods weren't our property. They belonged to the Preservation Society, bought in an effort to keep parts of Jar Island undeveloped.

My cell buzzes on the coffee table. I reach over and click open a text.

Can we talk? Please?

I feel my lip curl up, like I've tasted something sour. This is the second time Rennie has reached out to me. First the daisy in my locker, which was so beyond emotionally manipulative I can't even, and now this. I never responded to the daisy. I've looked straight through her when I've seen her at school. And I'm definitely not going to write back now. I mean, come on. Why the eff would Rennie think that I'd want to open that door again? It was barely a month ago that she was trying to start shit with me at the Greasy Spoon.

I know why she's doing it. She's on the outs with Lillia. She's probably not even invited to the party tonight. If things were okay between them, she'd never reach out to me. Um, yeah. Thanks but no thanks, you witch.

Another text comes, before I can delete the first.

Pleeeease?

Why is she refusing to take the hint? The fact that she keeps trying, even when I've blown her off . . . well, it's making *me* feel bad, which is total BS. Because I don't owe her anything. She's the asshole. Not me. She needs to get that straight.

I write back. *Go fuck yourself.*

I figure that'll be the end of it. But she texts me back again, almost immediately.

One coffee. Java Jones in ten minutes?

My jaw drops. Girl has serious balls.

There's no way in HELL I'm meeting you at Java Jones!!! My fingers tap the screen so hard I'm afraid I might break my phone.

For all I know she could be planning some grand humiliation

of me à la Stephen King's *Carrie*, complete with a bucket of pig's blood that'll crash down on my head when I walk through the door.

Fine. No coffee. Can I stop by your house? For five minutes?

Classic Rennie. She'll browbeat you until she gets her way. She pulled that shit all the time when we were kids. Once, Rennie wanted permission to go to a midnight screening of a horror movie that was rated R for being extra, extra gory. Paige said no, but Rennie kept asking until the answer changed. Which, of course, it did.

I write back. *DIE BITCH!!!!*

Then I cram my cell between couch cushions, because I'm over it. I'm over this damn knot of lights, too. It's Pat's fault; he's the one who chucks them in a bag every year instead of wrapping them up carefully. I dig in the boxes, looking for our tree topper. Instead I end up unwrapping the white porcelain angel from a shell of newspaper. I use the sleeve of my black sweater to dust the windowsill and then set it down. There's a place inside to put a candle, one of those tea lights that come inside a metal cup, but we've never done that. I make a mental note to buy some of those candles. I'm not even sure where we got the angel, if it was ours from before or a gift after, but when I see it, I always think of Judy.

The doorbell rings. Shep slides off the chair and barks his way to the front door.

Oh no. No no no no.

I peek through the curtains and see a white Jeep in my driveway.

Hell no!

The doorbell rings again. And then there's knocking. Impatient knocking.

I stand a few feet from the front door and shout, "Get off my property, Rennie!" through the wood. I wish Shep was a guard dog that I could sic on her.

"Kat, come on. Please talk to me!"

I press my back against the door. She keeps knocking.

This is ridiculous. Rennie's somehow found a way to make me look like the idiot. The girl hiding inside, afraid to face down her tormentor. I swear to God . . .

I pull the door open, hard.

"You have sixty seconds. Go."

Rennie smiles shyly. She's got on an olive-green sweater, dark jeans, and some fringy suede Sherpa boots that look utterly ridiculous. "Hey," she says, casual.

I don't say anything. I stand there and wait for her to start.

Except that Rennie doesn't do anything but stare at me, like she's a person with amnesia, trying to remember who I am.

I burst out with "Say what you've got to say!" to get this moving along.

She bites her lip and nods. "Kat," she says, and then pauses to take a big breath. "I'm sorry." She raises her arms up like she's offering me something, I don't know what, and then lets them fall back limply to her sides.

I laugh, I can't help it, and it makes a cloud in the cold air. "That's it? That's what you came here for?"

She lets out a sigh, and it sounds almost annoyed, like I don't know how hard this is for her. "I know the people I hang out with haven't made things so easy for you. Lillia, Ashlin . . ."

"Don't." I shake my head. I'm shutting this shit down right now. "Don't you dare blame anyone else for what you've done to me the last four years." I don't say it; I growl it.

Her eyes flutter, and then she stares at the ground. "I . . . I . . ."

"Oh, come on." I start pushing the door shut, because this is ridiculous.

Rennie takes a step toward me and uses her foot to block the door from closing. "Wait. Okay. Okay. I wish I could go back to the first day of high school and do everything over. I wish I could take it all back, Kat."

"Well, you can't," I tell her. It's way too late for that.

"I know I can't. And that's what sucks."

I lean against the door. "You know what sucks? Your timing. I love that this apology is coming now, now when your whole circle of friends is completely fucked up and you've got nobody." I'm practically screaming.

She blinks a few times.

"Everyone at school knows, Ren. You and your precious little Lillia are on the outs." I don't know why I say that stuff about Lillia. I've made my peace with her; I've forgiven her. We're cool now. But it's like the anger is still inside me, somewhere, for getting dropped. "You picked her over me, so why would you think I'd give a flying fuck that she's ditched you now?" I laugh, and it sounds hollow, but I don't care. "I love it! Karma, baby!" I try closing the door again.

"Wait! Please, Kat. Just listen to me for a second. Lillia's a duplicitous bitch. It's almost psycho, how two-faced she is. I just never saw it before now!" Rennie looks so convinced, so sure of herself. In her sick mind, Lillia's clearly guilty of something.

I stare at her, mouth agape. "Don't you get it, you little idiot? There's not an apology in the world that could make up for the shit you've done." I can feel my temperature rising, despite the fact that I'm trying to keep cool. "All the lies you've told about me. The teasing, the bullying. I never deserved that. I was your friend. I never did anything to you."

Rennie starts shaking. She wraps her arms around herself tight, but it doesn't make it stop. She stares down at her ugly-ass boots. "Fine. You're right. You're totally, totally right. I'm getting everything I deserve."

I don't comfort her. Instead I say, "Eh, I'm not so sure about that, Ren. I mean, I hope you *do* get what you deserve. I hope things get a lot worse for you."

The words leave a bad taste in my mouth. They are mean, really really mean. Maybe too mean.

I think she's going to look up and tell me to eff off. But she doesn't. She looks up, and she's got tears in her eyes. She takes a step backward, away from me. "Let me say one last thing, Kat. For the rest of my life, I want you to know that I'll be ashamed for not being there for you when your mom got sick. I don't want you to go off to Oberlin or wherever, us never see each other again, and you not know that."

It's hard to make words come out. My throat is so suddenly tight. "Good. You should be ashamed." I can feel my chin start to shake.

Rennie sees this, and her tears come fast. "I'm sorry," she says. And then she's sobbing. She sits down on the step, leans forward and puts her head in her lap, and bawls.

This kind of shocks me. And then I realize I'm getting everything I've always wanted. Not revenge, but an apology. A real one. Except I'm too sad to enjoy it. Things didn't have to be this way.

I sink down too, one step above her, and watch her shoulders heave up and down. It's hard not to comfort her. I end up patting her back. Twice. Damn. I'm only human.

Dad and Pat pull up with a Christmas tree tied to the roof of the car. They see us, and Pat's eyes go wide. I shake my head, so he knows it's okay. He pulls my dad in through the garage.

Rennie lifts her head. "I want to promise you something. I promise on my heart that I will not do one more mean thing to you, Kat. Ever." My throat is dry, so I give her the slightest nod of acknowledgment. "And I wanted to invite you to my New Year's Eve party."

I'm about to say thanks but no thanks to her invitation, but then it hits me. If I'm at the party, then I'll get to see shit between Reeve and Lillia go down firsthand. "Can I bring someone?" I ask, thinking of Mary. "If I don't have anything better to do?"

Rennie laughs at that. "Classic Kat," she says. "Totally. Whoever you want." She stands up and stretches. "There's going to be a bouncer, like at a speakeasy. If you tell him 'My flask is empty,' he'll let you in for free." Her face breaks into a devious smile. "I've even got a special surprise planned for midnight and I want you front and center for the show. Boom boom boom, baby."

I can't help but roll my eyes at her, because dude, she's still so Rennie.

"Listen . . . I do appreciate you coming over," I say gruffly. "And for saying that stuff to me."

She smiles. "It's the least I could do." She scratches Shep behind the ears and then kisses him on the head. "Bye, Kat."

"Bye, Ren."

In a weird way, it doesn't feel like good-bye. It feels like maybe the smallest bit of a start.

CHAPTER FORTY-EIGHT

LILLIA

As soon as I got home from school I locked up the liquor cabinet and the door to the wine cellar; then I made a sign with my calligraphy pen that said *Off Limits* and put it on my parents' bedroom door. I debated putting up a sign on the front door that said *Please Take Off Your Shoes*, but then decided it would be a bit much. If I see people putting their feet up on the white couches, I will politely ask them not to.

I'm wearing the lacy black corset top that Kat bought for me. I haven't had the nerve to wear it until now, but I think that as hostess I'm supposed to look extra special. I'm wearing it with a pleated gray mini and my gold horseshoe pendant. I curled my hair and teased the crown up so it's bouncy and big. The last touch is pale pink lipstick and a dab of perfume.

I see Reeve's truck pull into our driveway and watch him bound up the walkway with four pizza boxes stacked up. I run over to the front door and fling it open before he can ring the bell.

His jaw drops when he sees me. "Damn, Cho."

It's exactly the reaction I was hoping for, but my cheeks still heat up. "Thanks for picking up the pizzas," I say as he steps inside. He hands me the boxes as he slips off his shoes and lines them up against the wall. He's wearing white sweat socks with a gray toe, the same brand as my dad. This makes me smile for some reason.

I can feel his eyes on me as I walk him to the kitchen. I set the pizzas down on the counter. "Thanks again," I say, just to have something to say.

"No sweat."

"Did you get the kegs?" I ask.

"Yeah, they're in the back of my truck."

"I'll help you bring them in," I say.

Reeve lets out a laugh. "They're too heavy for you and me. I'll get PJ to help when he gets here." Giving me the once-over, he adds, "Your skirt's too short for you to help anyway."

I make a pouty face. "It's not that short."

He grins at me. Then he hooks his hands on my hips and pulls me toward him, nice and easy. He keeps his eyes on me, watching me carefully, giving me a chance to stop him if I want.

But I don't. I don't want. I mean I do. Want.

And then he's kissing me; his mouth is soft and sure against mine. He really knows how to kiss.

I don't remember inviting this many people. And I explicitly said no underclassmen, so why do I see junior girls from the squad? This party is so not VIP. And God, being the hostess is probably the least fun thing ever. I'm constantly running around wiping up spills and turning down the music. I haven't even had one sip of alcohol!

Thank God, Reeve is here.

He's standing at the door, barking at people to take off their shoes. "Morrissey, were you raised in a freaking barn?" he growls. Reeve winks at me when he sees me watching.

I'm doing a lap around the downstairs when I see her. Rennie. I can't even believe it, but there she is, drinking a beer, sprawled out on my couch with her high-heeled boots on even though she knows the rules better than anyone here, talking to Ash, who's perched on the armrest.

I'm not sure what to do. If I try to kick her out, it'll be such drama, which is exactly what she wants. For us to have a fight in front of all these people. So I do the exact opposite; I grab a bowl of chips from the kitchen and sail over to the couch with a sunny smile. "Hey, guys!" I plop down beside them.

Rennie gives me a fake smile where only the corners of her mouth go up, and Ash leans over and hugs me. "Lil, everything's a mess," she wails.

"What's wrong?" I ask her.

"Derek told me tonight that he wants to keep it casual; he doesn't want to be in a serious thing his senior year." Ashlin blows her nose with a cocktail napkin.

"Ugh," I say. "That's so Derek."

"Ash, this is the best thing that could have happened," Rennie says, taking a sip of her beer. "Derek isn't boyfriend material."

I push the bowl of chips toward Ashlin. She stuffs a handful in her mouth and says, "But you and Reeve are totally a thing and Lil and Alex are probably going to get together too. Who does that leave me with? PJ?" She makes a disgusted face.

I don't say what I'm thinking, which is, *Um, excuse me, but Reeve and Rennie are so not a thing because Reeve and I are.* I wait to see if Rennie will correct Ashlin, but she keeps sipping on her beer. All she says is, "Aw, PJ is super cute. Don't worry, Ash. You'll find the perfect guy for you like I did."

I stand up because I can't listen to this garbage anymore. "Ash, I'll be back in a sec. I'm going to go make sure nobody's upstairs."

Rennie rolls her eyes. "Nobody's going to have fun if you're running around all uptight like a prison guard. Hello, it's supposed to be a party. Chill out."

I'm about to snap back at her when Reeve comes bursting into the living room. He scoops Rennie up off the couch and throws her over his shoulder like she weighs nothing, which she does. "Put me down, Reeve," she squeals, kicking her feet.

"No shoes in the house, Ren!" he says, pulling them off her feet. Then he tosses her back down on the couch, and her cup of beer tips over and spills everywhere; some splashes on my arm. "Awesome. Thanks, guys," I say, sopping up the floor with napkins.

Reeve bends down and starts helping me. "Sorry, Cho."

"Chill out, Lil," Rennie says, her face red from being held upside down. "It's beer! Beer gets spilled at a party."

"Rennie, I swear, if you tell me to chill out one more time . . ." I say it and I mean it; I'm not joking.

Rennie narrows her eyes at me, and we stare each other down. Reeve tries to put his arms around both of us, but I shrug away from him.

Then Alex wanders in with a paper plate in one hand and a beer in the other.

"Hey!" I say to Alex. "I haven't seen you all night."

Alex swallows his bite of pizza. "I've been around." He takes a swig of beer. "Oh, and I went to pick up the pizzas and they said somebody already got them."

I clap my hand to my mouth. "Oh my gosh! I'm so sorry! I totally forgot to text you."

Alex stuffs the rest of the slice in his mouth. "No worries."

"I'm so, so sorry, Lindy," I say, and Rennie rolls her eyes.

"Yeah, sorry, Lind," Reeve drawls. "I took care of it."

Alex looks from me to Reeve, who is still standing next to me. Quickly I say, "They were on his way to get the kegs, so I thought it would be easier."

"No worries," Alex says again, resting his plate on the coffee table. Then he pulls his wallet from his back pocket, and my stomach twists in a knot. He takes a few twenties from the billfold and holds them out for Reeve. "Here."

"What's this for?" Reeve asks him, his eyes narrowing on the money.

Alex takes a step closer, still holding out the cash. "I told Lil I wanted to take care of the pizzas."

"'I told Lil I wanted to take care of the pizzas,'" Reeve mimics back in a whiny-baby voice. "Too late. I already got it."

Alex's face goes red. I'm about to tell him to let it go, but before I can, he tosses the money on the coffee table. "Keep the change."

Reeve says, "I'm not the delivery boy, you dick."

Alex laughs dryly. "Who knows . . . in a couple of years, you might be."

My hands fly to my face. I can't even believe Alex said that. I've never seen him talk to Reeve that way before. On the couch, Rennie rears up like she's going to tear into Alex.

Reeve's fist is clenched at his side, and I just know he's about two seconds from flattening Alex. I have to do something, fast.

Heart racing, I gather up the bills and hand them back to Alex. Nicely but firmly I say, "Thanks, Lindy, but Reeve's got it covered." Then I let my body fall against Reeve and slide my hand into his.

It's a tiny display, subtle and quiet and barely anything. But it only takes a second before Alex's jaw goes tight. I turn my head and look at Rennie, on the couch. Her mouth has dropped so far open that I can see her molars. My whole body squeezes tight with nerves, but I don't move.

They are all seeing this. Us.

Then Reeve glances down at me, shocked. And definitely not happy. He pulls his hand free from mine and says, "What are you doing, Cho?" like I'm out of my mind, like we didn't have that conversation in his truck, like we've never even kissed. Then with a chuckle and a shake of his head, he steps away from me, picks up Alex's paper plate, and disappears into the kitchen. And I'm left there, standing in front of everyone, with my mouth wide open.

What just happened?

I can't bear to see the look on Rennie's face or anybody's face. I spin on my heels and quickly head upstairs. What was that talk about doing what feels right, and people can go to hell if they don't like it? I was the one who said we should be discreet!

I go straight to my room and close the door and plop down in front of my vanity. My hair looks like crap, super flat but not in the shiny, sleek way. It's probably because I've been running around for the last two hours cleaning up other people's messes. I drag a brush through it roughly, then I put on a fresh coat of lipstick because most of it has worn off. I can feel the music from downstairs pumping through the walls, and I just want to lie down on my bed. I wonder how soon is too soon to kick people out.

I'm sure he did it because he was embarrassed. Because of the thing Alex said about him becoming a delivery boy. Maybe I handled it wrong. I could have given him space, let him do his bravado thing, and waited for a better moment.

God, I sounds like Mary.

Sighing, I head back downstairs to check on things. From the foyer, I hear the roar of a car engine peeling down my driveway. I peek through the curtains. It's Alex's truck.

Great. Just great.

In the sitting room I notice a water ring on the coffee table, and I try to smudge it out. I go into the kitchen to grab some Pledge, and that's when I find Rennie sitting on the floor, her back up against our oven door. Reeve's standing over her.

"Reevie . . . I feel wasted." Her head sways from side to side, her hair hanging in her face. "Will you please take me home?"

I peer at her. She's had, like, two beers. I've seen her finish a six-pack in under an hour and not get tipsy. "Wow, I didn't even see you drink that much," I say.

Rennie's eyes suddenly snap into focus on me. "Maybe someone put something in my drink."

I reel back a step.

Reeve stands up. "Ren, how much did you have?"

"I don't know . . ." Rennie moans, now back to acting wasted. "I lost count." She's totally putting on a show. She's only been at the party for like thirty minutes, and a second ago she was fine. "I'll drive myself home. I don't want to make you leave."

"There's no way in hell I'd let you drive like this," he says, shaking his head.

He helps her to her feet, and then he hoists her up and Rennie wraps her arms around his neck. "You're the bestest, Reevie," she sighs, closing her eyes and snuggling closer.

"Go get your coat. I'll meet you by the front door."

"Okay. Huuuuurry." Rennie wobbles off.

When Rennie's gone, Reeve says to me, "I'm gonna drop her off."

I stare hard and fold my arms. "I don't even know what she's doing here in the first place!"

Reeve straightens and says, "She's here because all of us are, Lil. All her friends. What's she supposed to do? Sit at home alone?"

I feel my lip curl. How many times did Rennie make it so I was doing exactly that! "Can you please not defend her to me?"

"I know she can be a bitch sometimes, but she's a good girl at heart." Reeve runs a hand through his hair, then glances over toward my front door. "Look, I'll drop her off and then I'll come back."

I screw my lips together. "Don't bother. I'm gonna make everybody leave soon anyway." I flick my hair over my shoulder. "Just so you know, Alex left."

Reeve sneers. "Good. Little rich boy punk bitch."

"Reeve!" I glare at him.

From the front door I hear Rennie call out Reeve's name. "Reevie! I'm ready!"

He glances back. "Look, let me take care of this, and then I'll come back to help you clean."

"I can do it myself."

He sighs, exasperated. "Are you mad at me?"

Coolly I say, "Why would I be mad at you?"

Reeve grabs my hand and says, "I swear I'll be right back. Give me twenty minutes."

I want to tell Reeve not to come back tonight, but I can't bring myself to say the words. Because I do want him to. I know I shouldn't, but I do. I can't help it.

I smooth down the pleats of my skirt. "Okay. If you want."

After looking over both shoulders to see who's around, Reeve plants a quick kiss on my forehead. Then he fishes his keys out of his pocket, asks me to save him a piece of pizza, and he's gone.

When everybody else leaves an hour later, I turn down Ash's offer to help me clean up. I hustle her out the door, and then I run upstairs and change into my cute pj's, a pink cami with a bunny print and matching shorts. I feel nervous butterflies as I put on lotion and the tiniest dab of my Lillia perfume at the pulse of my neck. I put my hair up and then I put it back down.

I've never been alone with a boy in my house before. Anything could happen.

I don't want it to go too much farther than kissing. Okay, I *kind* of do, but at the same time I don't. I'm not ready yet. And anyway, I'm still angry. And I'm going to give Reeve a piece of my mind for sure. So I figure we'll stay downstairs on the couch and that will have to be it.

While I wait, I clean up the living room, throwing away plastic cups, wiping down the tables, fluffing up the couch pillows. It's taking so long for Reeve to come back, I even get out the vacuum cleaner. Another hour goes by and the kitchen's clean too; the house almost looks back to normal. I set out two pieces of pizza on a nice plate, not a paper one, and I cover it in plastic wrap so I can heat it up when he gets here.

That's when I get the text. It says, *Stuck at Rennie's. Not gonna make it back tonight.* I read it twice to make sure I'm getting it right. He's ditching me. For her.

Rennie and I never had crushes on the same boys. She had a rotation of boys that she liked, boys who were loud and brash and you never knew if they were making fun of you or if they were serious. She liked the ones who made her feel unsure. Because Rennie was always, always sure.

As for me, the only Jar Island boy I ever had a crush on was Patrick DeBrassio. And even then, it was the kind of crush you have on your friend's big brother, when you're safe in knowing that nothing will ever come of it. I was his little sister's friend, a baby.

So Rennie and I didn't have crossover crushes, but there was this one time it almost happened. It was that summer before ninth grade. This was when Rennie and Kat and I were still friends. But this happened on a day when it was just Rennie and me.

There was a new boy scooping ice cream. He was there for the summer, but he looked young like us; he couldn't have been older than fifteen. He had dirty-blond hair and a small mouth, and he was wiry but you could tell he'd be tall and strong one day. I'd seen him twice already, and both times I made Nadia go in front of me so he could be the one to take my order. I liked his dimples, and I liked how careful and precise he was with the ice cream scooper. All of his scoops came out perfect.

That afternoon there was a lull. I was trying to decide between strawberry basil ice cream or blueberry sorbet, and I was working up the nerve to ask if I could try a sample of both, when Rennie leaned on the freezer and asked him, "How old are you?"

Rennie had been doing that a lot this summer—talking to boys we didn't know, boys who were on the island for the week, the month, the summer at most. Kat would join in sometimes, but it always made me feel shy.

His head jerked up; he'd been wiping the counter. "Why?"

"Because I know for a fact that you have to be sixteen to work here, and you don't look sixteen." She said it in her ballbustery way, but with flirty eyes. The Rennie signature move. Rennie was so confident, even then, that he'd want to talk to her, that he'd be intrigued by her gutsiness and attitude.

"How old do you think I am?" he asked her.

"Fifteen, tops," she said. "So how old are you?"

"Fifteen," he admitted. "I got the job because my uncle owns the place. I'm here for the rest of the summer. How old are you?"

"Fourteen," Rennie said.

He finally looked over at me. I'd been staring into the glass freezers, my arms wrapped around me, pretending not to listen. "I've seen you here before," he said. "You got blueberry last time, right? With sprinkles?"

I nodded.

On the way home I said to Rennie, "I can't believe he remembered me."

She said, "Of course he remembered you. There are, like, no Asians on the island."

I looked at her to see if she was joking, but she was already onto the next thing. It was true that there were hardly any other Asian families on the island. But she'd never brought it up before. My being different from her.

She hooked up with him later that week. It was on a day that I was at the barn. She got mad because I told her I couldn't go to the beach because I had a horseback-riding lesson. I don't remember the boy's name. I couldn't even get mad about it, because what would I have done with him? It's not like I would have made out with him on the docks like she did. I wasn't allowed to go on dates.

The thing I remember about it was how it made me feel when she assumed the only reason he would remember me was my Asianness. Like there was nothing else special or worth remembering about me. The idea prickled under my skin and stayed there for a long time.

CHAPTER FORTY-NINE

KAT

Lil mentioned something about maybe hanging out this weekend, but I was still surprised when she texted today asking if Mary and I wanted to sleep over. That was something totally new. I texted back sure, why not, and I dug my sleeping bag out of the garage. I think the last time I went to an actual sleepover was back in the day when I was friends with Rennie.

Pat couldn't drop me off. Our car was busted again. There were a few guys in our garage. Most of them were drinking. Ricky wasn't. "Okay. Guess I'll walk."

I'm about halfway down the driveway when Ricky comes after me.

"I was actually about to head out, so I can give you a ride if you want."

I stare him down. "Thanks but no thanks." I don't need the charity.

"Kat, wait."

"What, Ricky?" I make sure I sound bored, uninterested.

"You're ignoring me. Why? Because I wouldn't kiss you?"

Damn. He doesn't beat around the bush. Well, neither will I. "What makes you think I wanted to kiss you? Don't flatter yourself."

Ricky laughs. "Um, you pushed me against the wall and you were about two seconds from eating my face off."

I sneer. Who does this asshole think he is? "You must have been dreaming."

"Look. Do you want me to come clean?"

I stop walking and spin around. "Speak."

"I do like you. I've liked you for a while."

"Then what's the problem?"

Ricky makes a half turn to the garage. "It's Pat, okay? I tried to come correct, tell him how I felt about you, but he told me to step off."

"Shouldn't I be the one to make those decisions?"

"He wasn't saying it to be a dick. But you know, you're applying to that fancy college, and I don't think he wants anything to distract you. Plus, he's my friend. If he draws that line, I ain't going to cross it." He shakes his head. "Anyway, what would we have together? A few months, tops? And then you'd leave? I don't want to . . . you know, fall for you any worse than I already have."

Okay, seriously. That is sweet of Pat. But also, what the hell is he doing, sticking his big nose into my affairs? He can't bother to pick his shit up around the house, but he needs to weigh in on who I can and can't hook up with?

In some ways it's a blessing in disguise. 'Cause I like Ricky, but I for sure haven't fallen for him. Not the way he's talking about.

I give him a peck on the cheek. "Friends?"

He looks glum, but he offers up a weak smile. "Yeah. Friends."

Mary's waiting on the steps when Ricky drops me off.

"Hey," I say. "Why are you outside?"

"Hey, yourself," Mary says, cocking her eyebrow. "I don't think Lil's home. I've been knocking forever, but she hasn't answered."

"Huh."

I ring the bell and a few seconds later Lil throws the door open and offers a tired smile. "Hey, guys." She's wearing a big

Harvard sweatshirt and leggings and thick socks. No makeup. Her hair up in a towel. Guess she was in the shower.

We come inside, and it takes me forever to unlace my combat boots. Taking shoes off and on is annoying. The people in my family will pass out in bed with their shoes on.

When I've finally got them off, Lillia leads us through the foyer to the kitchen. I lift myself onto the marble kitchen island, and Mary sits at the table.

"So how'd it go last night?" Mary asks.

Lillia tugs on the sleeves of her sweatshirt so her hands disappear inside. "Not awesome. You guys, there's no way we're making it to New Year's Eve. I . . . I think it's over."

I roll my eyes. "You've said that, like, ten times, Lil!"

Lillia shakes her head defiantly. "It's different this time. I think Reeve was jerking me around me from the start."

Mary folds her arms. "No way. He's in love with you, Lil. I've seen it with my own eyes."

"Mary, he's been playing me the same way he played you! And you were right to be worried about seeing him and Rennie at the theater." She yanks at her hair. "God, I was so stupid."

"All right, all right," I say. "What happened? Did he not show up to the party?"

"No, no. He came. And things were going well . . ."

"And?" Mary leans forward, looking tense as hell.

Lillia's face turns pink. "See, we had this talk the other day. About taking things public. Letting our friends know we're together. He was the one who was pushing for it!" She bites her bottom lip. "So when I saw an opportunity last night, I went for it. In front of everyone. Alex. Rennie. Everybody."

Wow. I have to hand it to Lil. She really is all in. Girl went the extra mile.

"But then he freaking denies me. He leaves me hanging in front of everyone!" Lillia turns to Mary, her eyes wide. "All night I thought about you, Mary. And that day on the ferry. How humiliated you must have been." She shakes her head. She can't even finish her thought.

"And he pulled the same exact shit with you," I say.

"Pretty much." Lillia bites her bottom lip. "And then, to add insult to injury, Rennie pretended someone put something in her drink so Reeve had to take her home. He said he was going to come back, but then he didn't."

That for sure sounds like a Rennie move. And then I wonder—will Lil feel weird about Rennie coming over to my house yesterday trying to make amends? I'm about to tell her about it, but like a downplayed version minus the tears, when Mary says, "Rennie's a witch."

Lillia looks like she still can't believe it. "I don't even care about Rennie. Reeve's a world-class manipulator. Every single thing that comes out of his mouth is a lie." She swallows. "Not that I haven't been lying too, obviously. But if this whole thing had been for real, I could've gotten hurt, you know?" Then she lets out a long sigh. "The way I tried to defend him to you guys that day in the bathroom. God, he totally had me fooled!"

"Player got played," I say, nodding. "Damn."

To Mary, Lillia says, "I'm so sorry I couldn't make this happen for you. I tried though. I really, really did."

It's weird, but I swear Mary actually looks relieved. "Lillia, don't talk like that," Mary protests. "I'm so grateful for everything you've done. It couldn't have been easy for you to pretend the way you did for so long."

Lillia's eyes flutter. "Whatever. It's no skin off my back." And then she downs the rest of her drink.

Mary tugs on a lock of her hair. "I can't believe it. Things were going so well. The kiss in the parking lot . . ."

"I know," Lillia says. "He even invited me to his family's open house tomorrow."

"Wait, Reeve invited you to his open house?" This is the first I'm hearing of this. "I used to go to that shit back in the day."

"Yeah, well, clearly that's not happening." Leaning her elbows up against the counter, Lillia asks, "What *is* an open house anyway?"

"People in the neighborhood stop by and kick it throughout

the day." I pick at my nails. "My mom and dad took me a couple of times. You watch football, trim the tree, eat food." Then I look up and say, "Yo, it would seem to me that if Reeve's inviting you to this, it's a BFD. How many girls do you think he's ever introduced to his mom?"

"I've met his mom before," Lillia says. "We've hung out at his house plenty of times."

I wave her off. "Yeah, but this would be in the context of, 'Mom, Dad, Grandma, Uncle Chris, Aunt Linda, this is the girl I'm seeing.' I doubt he's *ever* done that before." Lil opens her mouth to argue and I add dreamily, "Reeve's mom is a bomb-ass cook. . . . Every year she makes this sick chowder with scallops and all kinds of seafood. Like shrimp, clams . . . Speaking of which, do you have anything to eat? I'm starving."

Lillia rummages around her fridge. "I've got leftover pizza, Brie, hummus."

"I'll take some Brie," I say. I never say no to cheese.

"What about you, Mary?" Lillia asks, setting a wedge of Brie on a wooden cutting board. She goes to the cupboard and brings back a box of water crackers and a jar of Nutella.

"I'm not hungry," Mary says, keeping her head down. "I just can't believe it's over."

Me either. I would have bet my life on the fact that Reeve liked her. Then again, I wasn't here last night.

Lillia rolls her eyes. "It is what it is. And I'm glad it's over with. Now I don't ever have to be nice to Reeve Tabatsky again for the rest of my life." She picks up the remote. "Let's watch a movie, something girly."

I groan and Lillia throws a pillow at my head.

We're in Lillia's room, listening to music and talking. It's getting late; it's almost two in the morning.

Mary's lying on the floor with her blond hair fanned out around her. Abruptly she says, "Do you guys think Rennie and Reeve hooked up last night?"

Lillia shrugs. "Probably."

"Why?" Mary wants to know.

"Psh, Reeve is a man whore," I say. "So, yeah, more like definitely."

Delicately, Lillia dips her finger into the jar of Nutella. "You have to be careful, Mary. Promise me that you won't just hook up with some random guy unless you know you can trust them."

I roll my eyes and take a swig of my beer. "Chill out. Mary's still in the V club like you, so don't you worry."

Lillia goes still all of a sudden. Her face is white.

"What's wrong?" I ask her. "What did I say?"

Lillia shakes her head. She looks like she's going to cry.

"It's okay," Mary whispers. "You don't have to say."

Lil's voice comes out strangled. She can't even look at us. "I'm not a virgin anymore. I—I lost it to some guy I didn't even know."

I'm sort of in a state of shock. Lil? Hooking up with a rando? "For real? You? I could never picture you hooking up with a random dude. I thought you were saving it till marriage!"

Tears start rolling down her cheeks, and I feel like a dirtbag. Mary gives me an admonishing look, and I shrug back helplessly. What's wrong with me? Why do I always say the first stupid shit that pops into my head?

"I was saving myself," Lillia chokes out. "Maybe not till marriage, but at least for someone I loved. Someone who loved me."

I reach out and give her leg a sympathetic squeeze. "My first time sucked too, Lil. It was in this guy's basement, and his mom kept banging on the door because she wanted him to mow the lawn."

Lillia cries harder. Her shoulders shake, and her hair covers her face.

I don't know what to say to make her feel better. Hurriedly I add, "You know what? I think that even if it's with someone you love, the first time still basically sucks."

"But—I don't even remember it," Lillia weeps. "I was too drunk. I didn't even want to do it. I—I kept calling out Rennie's name for help, but she didn't answer."

Mary and I look at each other in horror. Oh my God. "Lil,

that was rape," I say. "That wasn't just a bad first time. That was straight-up rape."

She's shaking her head. "No, it wasn't like that. I didn't, like, push him off of me."

"You didn't push that effer off because you were too drunk!" I yell.

The louder I yell, the quieter Lil gets. Her voice sounds feeble when she says, "He was drunk too. I don't even know if he heard me say no, that's the thing." She's curled up, hugging her knees to her chest, her hair falling around her face. "I doubt he thinks it was rape. I don't even know if I think it was rape. I went upstairs with him; I kissed him back. I didn't scream for help or anything."

"Lil, if you weren't in your right mind to say yes, that means it was rape, I'm telling you! That's like the very definition of rape!" My blood is boiling; I can literally feel it boiling. I jump up and start pacing around. I'm going to take this guy down. "What's his name? Tell me his name, and I'll go over there right now with my boys." Pat would come; so would Ricky. I can get a whole posse together. I'll get my old baseball bat out and smash this guy's whole house to smithereens—

"Kat, sit down," Mary says, fixing her blue eyes on me.

I'm startled by how firm her voice sounds, so I sit my ass down. "We can't let him get away with it!"

"It's not up to you," Mary says. "We do what Lillia wants."

I open my mouth to argue with her, but then Lillia speaks up. Gratefully she says, "Thanks, Mary. I . . . I appreciate it. And Kat, I appreciate you too. But what I really want is to forget the whole thing happened. It was a mistake, and it's over. I don't want to let it affect me any more than it already has."

I nod, because I get that. Then I say, "Wait a minute, you called out for Rennie? She was there too?"

"Yeah. It was this summer; we met these two UMass guys on the beach . . . they had a party." Lillia swallows. "We drank a lot, I don't really remember much of what happened after we went upstairs with them. But Rennie was in the room with me; she had sex with her guy too. We left before they woke up."

"So was Rennie raped too, then?" I ask her.

"I don't know. I don't know if what happened was rape, or if things just went too far, or what. Rennie and I never really talked about it again after that night." She wipes her eyes with her sweater sleeve. "I can't even believe I'm telling you guys this."

"We're your friends," Mary says, crawling closer to her. "You can tell us anything."

"But shouldn't we . . ." I hesitate. "Call the cops or something? Report the guy?"

"There's no evidence," Lillia says. "I didn't get a rape kit done. I didn't have any bruises on my body. It would be his word against mine, and I don't want to go through that. I don't want my parents to have to go through that. I don't want them to ever know that happened to me." She lifts her head and meets Mary's eyes. "I want them to still see me the same way. You know what I mean?"

Mary nods. "I know exactly what you mean."

"Lil, maybe you should talk to someone," I say, and I feel like the world's biggest hypocrite, because it's not like I'm some big believer in talking out my feelings. But this is serious. "Like, I don't know, a counselor. Or a therapist. Not Ms. Chirazo, but a legit therapist, someone with a degree, someone who knows their shit. Maybe they can help you."

"Maybe," Lil says, but I can't tell if she means it. Then suddenly she says, "I will if you will, Mary."

Yes! Lillia! Perfect, perfect timing. Girl does not miss a beat!

Mary reels back like Lillia slapped her. "I don't need to talk to anybody."

Wetting her lips, Lillia says, "You've been through a lot."

I quick jump in with, "And I know things aren't so great at home with your aunt right now . . . it could help to have another person on your side."

Shaking her head, Mary clenches her fists inside her sleeves. "Can we talk about something else? Please?" She closes her eyes, like she can't even bear to look at us.

This time, thank God, I know to keep my mouth shut.

CHAPTER FIFTY

I WAKE UP TO THE SOUND OF MY PHONE RINGING. I'm buried under my comforter, and it's dark in my room because the shades are all drawn. Blindly I sit up and start pawing around my bed for my cell phone. Then the ringing stops and I lie back down. And then the ringing starts again.

Kat's sprawled out on the floor on her sleeping bag, twisted up in my baby blanket. She groans loudly. "Somebody turn that shit off!"

From my love seat Mary lifts her head and asks, "What time is it?"

"Too damn early," Kat growls.

I finally find my phone at the foot of my bed. It's Reeve. I sit up quick. "It's Reeve, you guys!" I yelp.

Kat jumps onto my bed and Mary rushes over and kneels on the floor beside us. Everybody's wide awake now. "What do I do?" I ask them. Panic is rising in my chest. "Should I pick up?" Yesterday I fully accepted that I would never speak to Reeve Tabatsky again in my life. But I didn't think for a second that he'd call me.

"Put him on speaker!" Kat orders. "Be brutal, Lil!"

My hand is shaking as I answer it. I click speaker. "Hello?"

"Hey, what's going on?"

I say, "Who is this?" in a fake sleepy voice, and Kat falls over laughing silently. Mary's crouching at my side, her eyes wide. I don't even know if she's breathing.

"It's Reeve!" And I can tell he's annoyed. "Why aren't you here yet?"

"I just woke up. I guess I overslept. Sorry." I keep my voice indifferent and un-sorry.

He huffs, "Well, can you come over now?"

My heart does a little ping. I take a deep breath and try to conjure up some of the anger I felt when he didn't come back the other night, but it's gone. Proof positive that this whole mess has gone too far.

Awkwardly I say, "I'm not really feeling it."

At this, Mary covers her mouth with her hands and Kat's literally rolling on the floor, kicking her feet in the air. There's a long silence, and Reeve doesn't speak, and I think maybe he already hung up.

But then he says, "I'm coming over," and my heart stops.

"Wait!" I say, but he's hung up for real this time. I drop my phone and look at the girls in horror. "Oh my God. Oh my God. What am I supposed to do now? He's coming over here!"

Kat's doing a dance, running in place. "Hells, yeah! Let him! It ain't over till the fat lady sings!" Kat boogies over to my window and peers outside. "He's still on our hook. I mean, what else would he want?"

"I don't know what he wants!" What does it matter? He's coming. He'll be here in like five minutes! And I'm not going to answer the door looking like a pile of crap. I run to my bathroom and splash cold water on my face and brush my teeth as fast I can. I throw off my sweats and put my cute cami-and-shorts set back on.

Out in my room, I hear Kat and Mary debating how I should handle things.

Kat says, "I think she should be mean when she first answers the door, then look upset, then be sad. You know? To make him feel extra bad?" She calls out to me, "Lil, do you think you could squeeze out a few tears?"

And then Mary says, "I don't think she should cry. I think she should get mad. Maybe she could even slap him?"

Kat busts up laughing.

Quietly I say, more to myself than anyone, "I think I just want to get this over with."

When I come out of the bathroom, Kat and Mary are already downstairs hiding in the foyer. They're crouching behind a chaise longue. "Guys, what if he tries to come all the way inside?" I say, pulling on a hoodie. "He'll see you."

"But we want to hear everything," Kat whines. "Don't let him past the front door and it'll be fine."

"I'm nervous," I say, putting my hands on my cheeks. My hands are cold but my cheeks are burning up.

"Don't be," Mary says. "You've been perfect so far."

The doorbell rings, and my stomach drops. "Damn, did he fly over here?" Kat whispers.

I look at Mary for reassurance, and she nods at me encouragingly. "Crush him, Lil." I answer the door.

Reeve's standing there in jeans and a button-down and a puffy vest. "Why aren't you dressed?" he demands, jamming his hands into his jeans pockets.

"I told you, I overslept," I say. I let my hair fall in my face.

"Yeah, I know. I heard you on the phone. What did you mean when you said you weren't feeling it?" He looks genuinely disappointed, which throws me off for a second.

"I didn't even know if I was still invited," I say.

His eyebrows knit together. "Why?"

Is he being dense on purpose? "You never came back the other night."

Reeve lets out a breath. "But I told you, I had to help Rennie get home! You saw how drunk she was."

"Oh, please. Rennie was playing you, and you let her."

"I couldn't just leave, Cho. She woke up her mom to say hi to me, and then they dragged out all these old photo albums of us when we were kids."

He's telling the truth, I can tell. And it does sound like something Rennie would do, especially knowing that I was sitting at home waiting for him. I force this thought aside and in a bored, blasé voice I say, "Whatever."

Tightly he says, "Ren means a lot to me. She's been there for me every time I've ever needed her. I don't want her to get hurt. You of all people should get that."

I cross my arms. "What's that supposed to mean?"

"Lind! You're always so concerned about his feelings."

How dare he throw Alex in my face? "Yeah, I am concerned about Alex's feelings. I care about him, because he's my friend. *He's* been there for me every time *I've* needed him. That's the kind of person he is. He's good."

Reeve stiffens and I feel a surge of satisfaction. Be jealous. I hope you choke on it.

I keep going. "And yet I was still willing to let Alex know that we were together at my party. Despite knowing it would hurt him, I was willing to do it. Unlike you. You talk a big game, Reeve, but when it comes down to actually doing something, you punk out."

"I didn't punk out! But I didn't want to throw it in their faces!"

"You mean you didn't want to throw it in Rennie's face. Since she's your girl and all."

Reeve shakes his head and exhales loudly. "That's not what I'm saying and you know it!" He looks away. "Can you just . . . can you go get dressed and come with me and we'll talk about it later? My mom's expecting you."

My heart plummets. Oh God. His mom? All I want to do is run upstairs and put on something nice and go with him. If Kat and Mary weren't standing on the other side of this door, maybe I would.

But I can't. They're here, and this is fake and I just can't.

"I don't think so," I say, lifting my chin high. "Honestly, I don't feel like coming over and doing the whole family thing today. We're not boyfriend and girlfriend or anything."

He pales. "Are you serious? Come on, Cho. If you want me to, I'll call Rennie right now and tell her how I feel about you."

"That's not necessary." I start to close the door in his face, but he reaches out and blocks it with his arm.

"Wait! You're right. I was a coward. I should have been the one to tell her weeks ago. I got scared, Lillia. Please, give me another chance. Let me prove it to you." He tries to grab my hand but I pull it away and shake my head.

I can't even look at him.

Because this *is* real. He's not playing me. One look at his face, at the hurt and the desperation in his eyes, and I know it's real.

I also know that I can't do this anymore. I have to finish it now. If I don't break it off right this very second, I'll never be able to do it. It's better this way—it really is. The longer this thing goes, the harder it will be, for everybody. It's already gone way too far.

I've fallen for the one person I shouldn't have. For the boy who broke Mary's heart. For Rennie's one true love. For Alex's best friend.

It has to end here. Now.

I take a breath. "You've already proven who you are, over and over again. The crazy thing is, I've known it all along. But these last few weeks, I've tricked myself into believing that there was something more to you than the self-centered jerk I've known for years. Maybe . . . maybe because I felt sorry for you." I shake my head. "But you are who you are, Reeve. And the fact is, you'll never be able to treat me the way I deserve to be treated. You don't have it in you. So let's just stop here. You're probably as tired of pretending to be a good guy as I am of pretending to believe it."

The words come out of my mouth, but they don't sound like me. I don't sound like me. Probably because I know it's all lies.

But I can see that they're lies that Reeve believes. He swallows them whole. His eyes go blank. Empty. He completely shuts down.

That's what hurts me the most, how easily he believes, and I know it's because deep down it's what he believes about himself. I've preyed upon his deepest fear and used it against him, and I think that's maybe the biggest betrayal yet.

Still, some part of me is expecting him to fight back, to tell me I'm wrong. Because, the Reeve Tabatsky I know never gives up. But I'm hoping this time he will.

Leave, just leave.

And that's exactly what he does. Without another word, he turns around, walks to his truck, and drives away.

I close the door, and Kat's jumping up and down, and Mary's staring at the door, stunned.

"I'm sorry," I say. "I couldn't wait until New Year's Eve."

"Screw New Year's Eve! The ball dropped here and now, baby!"

I'm almost afraid to look at Mary. If this isn't enough for her, I don't know what else I can do. I feel like I've died a little inside.

"Oh my God," she says, the words trickling out of her mouth

like honey. "I felt it happen." Mary focuses on me, then touches her hand to her chest. Her eyes flutter as she says, brightly, "I actually felt his heart break."

I force myself to smile.

The girls leave my house late in the afternoon. By that time, the sick feeling that's been inside me ever since Reeve drove away has turned into full-on nausea.

It makes my stomach lurch, replaying it in my head. The things I said. How cruel I was to him, how cold.

Mary and Kat played the whole thing out over and over to each other, mimicking Reeve in the deepest guy voices they could put on: "My mom's expecting you." I swear, they must have said that a hundred times, laughing harder and harder.

They wouldn't have laughed if they'd caught a glimpse of him from their hiding spot. They didn't have to see the hurt in his eyes. Not like I had to.

Right after Reeve drove off, Kat took my cell and placed it on our kitchen island, where the three of us could stare at it. She said they shouldn't leave yet, because Reeve would definitely call before he got home. In fact, she said, we should all keep our voices down, in case he was circling the block.

Of course he wasn't. He didn't come back; he didn't call. I knew he wouldn't.

An hour later, Kat painted us a picture of Reeve stewing, picking up and putting down his cell phone like a tortured man. He'd surely call me after lunch. When that hour came and went, Kat changed her mind and said that I'd definitely hear from him before they had to go. As Kat rolled up her sleeping bag, she swore up and down that Reeve would totally text me before it was time for bed. Or tomorrow, at the absolute latest.

Kat put on her boots and loaded her stuff in her arms. Before she and Mary headed out the front door, she called out from the bottom of the stairs, "If he calls tonight, memorize every word he says so we can all have a laugh!"

As Mary slipped on her shoes, I held the front door for her. "I can't thank you enough for what you did," she said, tears shimmering in her eyes.

I swallowed hard and said, "You're welcome. I'm just glad it's over."

I'm lying on my couch with a pillow over my face.

I know it was my choice to get it over with, but now I'm wishing I had done it differently. Like I could have waited until I was at the open house. Alone, without an audience. I could have let him down easy. I could have said, *I care about you a lot but I think we're better off as friends.* Kat and Mary wouldn't ever have had to know the specifics, only that I'd done the deed as promised.

Sure, he'd still be mad, but he wouldn't have a reason to hate me. The thought of Reeve hating me . . . right now I can't think of anything worse.

It's only three o'clock. Reeve said himself that people stop in all day long at his family's open house. If I hurry, I could still go over there and talk to him. Make him understand. We can't be together, but I can still take back the terrible things I said.

I run upstairs and turn on the shower, dancing from one foot to the other until the water gets warm. But shoot, I don't have time for a shower! My hair takes forever to dry!

I turn off the water and plug in my curling iron instead. While it heats up, I dash into my closet and throw on the royal-blue silk shirtdress I bought as a backup for college interviews. I pair it with my nude pumps and the string of mini pearls my dad bought for me when I turned sixteen. I curl the ends of my hair, and then put on mascara, a touch of pink blush, and a plain glossy lip.

I check my reflection in the foyer mirror before I run out the door. I look festive, feminine, and mature. Which is great. I want to make a good impression on Reeve's mom. Who knows what she must think of me now, showing up hours late.

I'm about halfway to T-Town when I remember that I can't go to his house empty-handed. I do a U-turn in the middle of the street, and a bunch of people honk, but I don't even care. Milky Morning is already closed, so I go to the florist next door and have them wrap up their biggest red poinsettia in cellophane. It's more of a centerpiece than a houseplant, the kind of thing you'd see in the lobby of a hotel. It's oversized and set in a beautiful pot made to look like a vintage mirror. The thing costs over a hundred dollars with tax, but whatever. I ask the guy to load it in my passenger seat.

I get to Reeve's house close to four o'clock. I'm relieved that there are still loads of cars there, so many cars there's hardly anywhere to park. I pull across the apron of his neighbor's driveway, completely blocking their minivan in. I'll move my car as soon as I have a chance to tell Reeve that I'm sorry.

The plant weighs a freaking ton, but I manage to carry it up to his front door. I hear the party going on inside, people cheering at something on television. I set the plant down on the ground, run my fingers quick through my curls, and ring the doorbell.

Okay, Lil. Showtime. I'm nervous, but I'm excited, too. To make things right, to fix what I've screwed up. To feel like myself again.

The door opens, and it takes me a second to recognize the person who answers.

Rennie. She folds her arms across her chest. She's dressed in a football jersey and a pair of leggings, bare feet, her hair pulled up in a sloppy bun at the tippy top of her head. I feel completely ridiculous and wrong in my fancy clothes.

"I can't even believe you'd have the nerve to show up here," she spits out.

"I need to talk to Reeve," I say.

She lets out a harsh laugh. "You think he wants to talk to you? He's through with you. He finally sees you for what *you* are. A fucking bitch."

Helplessly, I look past her into the den, hoping he might see me standing here and change his mind. Or at least give me a chance to explain. But the den is full of boys, Reeve's brothers and some other men I don't know. Nearly all of them are wearing the same jersey Rennie has on; all their eyes are pinned to the television screen. Behind that is the Christmas tree, every single branch decorated. On the coffee table I see Rennie's seven-layer taco dip, the one she always makes for sleepover parties in her mom's blue casserole dish. And in the back of the house I see Reeve's mom in a holiday apron and flannel slippers, stirring a big stockpot.

I call out Reeve's name and try to edge my way past Rennie, but she pushes me so hard I stumble in my heels and almost fall backward. She says, "You're not welcome here. Reeve hates you now just like I do."

"He can tell me that himself," I say, craning my head to see inside.

"He's not downstairs," Rennie informs me, as she slouches in the door frame to block my view. "We're upstairs in his room." She over-enunciates the "we're" part to make absolutely sure I hear it. I hear it, of course, and my imagination goes wild. Of Reeve and Rennie lying in his bed, his head in her lap, her running her hands through his hair, and suddenly they start to kiss. Reeve knows exactly how to hurt me best, and so does Rennie. And I bet both of them wouldn't hesitate to do it. "You should know better than to compete with me, Lil. You know I always win."

I lift my chin. I'm not going to grovel at Rennie's feet, like she's the lady of the house and I'm a beggar off the street. "Tell him I stopped by." I try to pick up the poinsettia to push it inside the house, but Rennie shakes her head and starts closing the door.

"They have a cat, and poinsettias are poisonous to cats."

A woman's voice behind her shouts, "Who's at the door?"

Rennie calls out, "Nobody," as it shuts in my face.

On my way back to the car, I tell myself that this is for the best. Reeve and I are done. I'm finally off the hook. And even though it's a huge relief, I still cry my eyes out the entire way back home.

CHAPTER FIFTY-ONE

MARY

KAT AND I ARE STANDING NEAR THE START OF LILLIA'S block. She's on the phone with Pat. She's been trying to get him on the phone for the last few minutes.

"Yo! What the hell! You're supposed to come pick up me and Mary from Lillia's, remember?" I can hear Pat's voice on the other end. He doesn't sound as chilled out as he was on Halloween night. His voice is sharper, more stressed. "Are you serious?" Kat makes an unhappy snort, and silently mouths to me that the car isn't working again. Then she screams, "Call a damn mechanic, then!" into the phone. Pat shouts something back, and Kat hangs up on him.

"Fool needs to get his ass back to trade school." She tucks the phone into her jean pocket. "I could try Ricky, but I think he's working, and anyway only one of us can fit on his bike. We can walk back to Lil's house and get her to drive us."

"Or we could walk," I suggest half-heartedly. I figure Kat will ixnay that plan right away because it's far for both of us, and it's kind of cold out. I don't mind it but she doesn't seem to own a proper winter coat. To fight the falling temperatures, Kat keeps layering on sweatshirts and thermals and her army coat. She's practically bulletproof at this point.

"All right," she says, "we can head up the State Road and split off near the high school." She unrolls her sleeping bag and wraps it over her shoulders like a big cape. "We've got plenty to talk about anyway."

So we start walking. At first we walk quick, but then we're slow and leisurely about it, as if this were a summer afternoon. It's pretty out. The sky is heavy with the threat of snow, and every so often we pass a house lit up with holiday lights.

The whole way, we go through Lillia's decimation of Reeve. Second by second. Kat has a great memory; she remembers more details than I do. I was so nervous, hoping things would work out the way we'd planned. So I am her captive audience, clinging to every moment.

"I only wish I could have seen Reeve's stupid mug when Lil

JENNY HAN AND SIOBHAN VIVIAN

shut him down!" Kat whoops. "Damn. You think Lillia's parents have surveillance cameras?" She turns and faces the wind, and it blows all the hair straight off her face. "I feel like rich people always have security cameras. Plus, her dad's a little psycho protective over her."

"They might," I say with a laugh. "We should ask her!"

Kat takes out her phone and texts Lil. "Tell you what, Mary. If they do, I'm going to get you a copy of that shit on infinite loop, so you can watch the moment of Reeve's heartbreak over and over and over again, whenever you want. Merry Christmas, baby. You've been such a good girl this year."

"Uhh," I say, and giggle. "Have I?"

Kat laughs. "Maybe not by typical Santa standards, but you definitely deserve this." She gets suddenly serious. "I hope this helps you. Makes things better."

"It has, Kat. More than you even know." As soon as I say the words out loud, they feel true.

Kat pumps her fists. Then she starts to sing, "Heartbreaker, love taker, don't you mess around with me," and her voice carries on the breeze. We pass a house where a man is up on a ladder, hanging lights, and he almost falls from the shock of it.

Hopefully, Lillia will text back, because I would have loved to have seen Reeve's face too. Even so, I know it worked—my plan worked. Reeve's heart is broken. There's no doubt about it.

The whole thing reminded me of that day down at the docks, when Reeve told all those guys that he wasn't my friend. My heart broke that day for sure.

Now we're the same.

"Oh, hey. How old is your aunt Bette? Does she have any dresses from the twenties?"

"Kat, she's not that old! She's only forty-six."

Kat guffaws. "My bad. I just thought she might have some vintage stuff you could borrow for New Year's Eve."

I swallow. "You don't mean Rennie's party?"

"Um." Kat looks blankly at me for a second, then starts shaking her head. "Here's the thing. I overheard someone talking about the bouncer password. Everyone at school will be there. I was thinking it'd be fun to crash. She won't even notice us."

"What about Lillia? She won't want to go there."

"We'll convince her. What else is she going to do?"

When we get to the high school, Kat waves good-bye and heads toward T-Town. I pick up the bike path and head home.

I can feel it, inside. The peace and the quiet where the rage used to be. It's like the lowest of low tide; all that bad stuff has gone out to sea. And then, I realize. I can go home now.

Not to Middlebury. *Home* home. Back with my parents.

Now that Reeve's gotten his, now that I've got closure, what's keeping me on Jar Island? I love Lillia and Kat to death, obviously, but they're both out of here next year. It's not like I've made a ton of other friends. It's the perfect time to say good-bye to Jar Island. I came, I saw, I conquered. I'll leave after New Year's. My past is really the past. I'll finally get to leave it behind.

I feel a twinge, thinking about leaving Aunt Bette behind, especially the way the house is. And the way our relationship is. But maybe she can come with me. Why not? She could use getting off this island as much as I could. Mom and Dad could hire someone to work on the house while it's empty, get it back to tip-top shape by summer.

Yes, this is the plan. I stop at the water, watching a ferry chug off. I imagine being on it, sandwiched between my mom and dad. All of us so happy, back where I belong. With my family. With my life on track.

I fight the urge to immediately tell the girls. I don't want to upset them, or let them try to convince me to stay, or at least to finish out the year. I feel the sort of peace that comes from any good decision. It's the right thing to do.

Aunt Bette gets a call after dinner, and I can tell right away that it upsets her.

"What is it?" I say.

She sinks into a kitchen chair. "One of the galleries where I sell my paintings is closing down. They want me to come pick up my work tonight." She glances at the clock and rubs her temples. "Now, actually."

"Gee. Nice of them to give you a heads-up." I say it sarcastically, with a mean laugh. But Aunt Bette doesn't even crack a smile. "I'll go with you," I tell her. "You might need help carrying stuff."

She shakes her head. "Oh, Mary, I don't—"

"It's no trouble. I'm finished with my homework." That's a lie, but whatever. How long would this take? As weird as things have been between us lately, I'm still worried about her. She might need me. She doesn't have friends like I do, to have her back.

Anyway, there's something about this that feels like good timing. Now that this gallery isn't showing her work anymore, well . . . what reason does she have to stay?

I meet Aunt Bette in her Volvo. I was thinking she'd change into a pair of pants and a nice sweater, but she's still in her housecoat. And her hair is wild. I don't think she's combed it today. And maybe not yesterday either.

Her hands are trembling. We're driving kind of fast, taking the turns too sharp.

"You're nervous."

She glances at me out of the side of her eyes. "Mary. Please.

Do not say a word, okay? Not to me, not to the owner. I want to get in and out of there as fast as I can."

"Okay. Sure. You won't even know I'm there. Promise." Hopefully, I won't have to say anything. But if I need to, I'm not going to hesitate. I learned that from Kat.

The gallery is down in T-Town, at the end of a small stretch of businesses. There are about half as many stores here as there are on Main Street in Middlebury, and none of them are as nice. Of all the parts of Jar Island, T-Town probably gets the least amount of tourists. It's more a place for the locals. So I'm not surprised the gallery went under.

The gallery is a white building on a corner. It has a big window in front, and across the bottom of the glass, in gold-stencil, it reads *art in the jar*, lowercase letters because I guess that's the thing? A temporary wall is directly behind the window. I figure that's where they hung the best paintings. It's bare now, pock-marked with nail holes.

The front door is propped open. I can see a ladder inside, a bunch of drop cloths, open cans of paint. There's a woman sitting cross-legged on the floor in the center, her hair tied back in a black scarf. She's thumbing through some papers inside a cardboard box.

Aunt Bette turns off the car and takes a few deep breaths. She walks in. I watch her from the car. The woman doesn't smile;

she doesn't even seem to say hello to Aunt Bette. She just points toward the back.

I get a twinge in my gut. A not-good feeling. I decide to walk in.

"I'm here to help my aunt," I say as I come through the door, but the woman doesn't acknowledge me. I step past her and head toward what looks like the main gallery space to my left.

Only this gallery isn't one big room. It's a lot of small rooms. I'm trying to figure out where Aunt Bette went to, and I end up getting turned around. I'm about to step through another doorway, when I realize I'm back at the main entrance.

"She looks like a witch!" a girl whispers. And then two people laugh.

I crane my neck around the door frame. Sitting with the woman is Rennie Holtz.

Oh my gosh. This is the gallery that Rennie's mom owns.

"Like a homeless witch! I wonder if she got here by broom."

Her mom lets out a laugh that sounds like a goose honking. "Quiet, Ren."

Then Aunt Bette comes into the room. She's got her arms full of her paintings. She's about to scurry out when Rennie's mom stands up. "Um, Bette? I wondered if I might give you some unsolicited advice."

Aunt Bette doesn't answer her right away. She walks toward

the door and peeks outside at her car. I guess she's looking for me. And when she doesn't see me, her eyes dart around the gallery. I duck out of sight.

"Bette?" Rennie's mom says again. I hear Rennie snicker.

"Yes. Yes. Sorry."

I edge my head around the corner again.

"I had a lot of trouble with your new work. To be frank, it was making some people uncomfortable. I'm not saying it isn't intriguing. It is. But I don't think that kind of darkness is what most buyers are looking for." My eyes narrow on the canvases in Aunt Bette's hands. They are all muddy, dark, haunting. Slashes of blacks and grays. Nothing like her old paintings. It looks like the stuff of a madwoman. Painting hasn't brought her back to the real world; it's drowned her further in darkness. "You should go back to those darling lighthouses and seascapes."

Aunt Bette's face hangs. "I don't paint to sell. I paint my world. And this is what it's like now." She turns to leave.

Rennie's mom mutters, "She's gone off the deep end."

"Cuckoo!" Rennie says. And they both crack up laughing.

I am about to flame.

I look around the room. I want to do something to make them stop. I narrow my eyes on the open paint cans on the floor and will them to tip. *Tip tip tip tip.* They start to shake.

"Mary!"

Aunt Bette shouts from the front door. Rennie and her mother look wide-eyed.

I rush out past them and follow her to the Volvo.

"I told you not to come inside!" Aunt Bette is furious. "What's the matter with you?" Her hands squeeze the steering wheel so hard the skin turns white.

"I finally understand, Aunt Bette. I can make things happen."

"You shouldn't be doing any of that. Whatever you've been doing. You need to stop."

"They were calling you crazy! They were saying you're a witch, that you've lost your mind. And, anyway, I've been practicing. I can control it." I take my seat and fold my hands calmly. "Aunt Bette, I've decided it's time for me to leave. Right after New Year's."

I wait to see if Aunt Bette will say anything. If she'll try to get me to stay. But if anything, she looks relieved.

"Yes, Mary. I think that would be the best thing for us all." Then she rolls up her window tight, sealing us both inside like in a tomb.

CHAPTER FIFTY-TWO

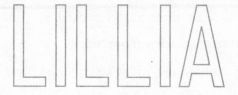

IT'S TWELVE FIFTEEN ON MONDAY AND I'VE BEEN dreading this exact moment since I woke up this morning. The lunch table.

I would love to sail right past and sit with Kat and Mary, but Mary doesn't even have the same lunch as me, and Kat never eats in the cafeteria. And the main reason I have to sit at our lunch table is because if I don't face them today, I'll never be able to sit at the table again. That's my table, and Ash and Alex and PJ, they're my friends too. I will go in with my head held high, nose in the air. Untouchable.

Rennie and Reeve can't hurt me because they can't touch me.

This is what I tell myself as I walk into the cafeteria. Thank God Ash is with me. She and Derek got back together sometime over the weekend, so she's even more bubbly than usual. I'm wearing my best I-couldn't-care-less-about-you outfit—that high-waisted bandage skirt Kat bought me, plus a silky black blouse with lipstick print that I tucked in, plus sheer black stockings and suede platform booties.

Mercifully, Rennie and Reeve aren't sitting down yet. Maybe they won't show. I eat the Cobb salad my mom packed for me and listen to Ash chatter about how romantic Derek was when he asked her to get back together. "He showed up at my house with flowers, and he would not take no for an answer, Lil," she says, sighing happily.

"What kind of flowers?" I ask. My heart's not in it, but I'm at least trying.

"Pink carnations!"

That he probably got from the gas station on the way to her house.

"So sweet," I say. Then Ash spots Derek in line for food and she runs over to him.

I see Rennie and Reeve heading toward the table; Rennie's got her arm linked in Reeve's. Even in heels she only comes up to his elbow.

I keep focused on my salad, and I don't look up when they sit down. I just dip each individual lettuce piece into my honey-mustard dressing with my fork. If I keep at it, I won't have to look up for all of lunch.

Then Alex comes walking over. I wonder if he and Reeve are still mad at each other or if they made up already, the way boys do. Or maybe he hates me too now, for the thing with the pizzas and for holding Reeve's hand in front of him. I hold my breath as he sets his tray down and sits in the seat across from me. "You look nice," he says, taking off his cable-knit sweater.

I smile at him gratefully. "Thanks, Lindy." Thank you so much.

At the other end of the table, Rennie's practically sitting in Reeve's lap. She's whispering and cooing to him, and he puts his arm around her.

I keep concentrating on cutting my lettuce into tiny pieces and dipping each one into the dressing.

Derek plops down with a tray full of french fries and says, "Yo! Did you guys hear about how Mr. Dunlevy got a DUI over the weekend?"

"Yeah, I heard," Rennie says. "Coach Christy was pissed. I mean, he gets paid extra to teach us driver's ed."

I take another bite of salad. Chew. Chew. Chew.

"Lil, weren't you and Reeve in driver's ed with him last year?" Alex asks. "Did he ever smell like booze?"

I shrug. Reeve shrugs too. Neither of us says anything.

"Huh," Alex says, and there's this slight edge in his voice. He's looking at me, and then he jerks his thumb in Reeve's direction. "You were so chummy-chummy at your party on Friday. And now you can barely stand to look at each other. What gives?"

I almost choke on the piece of hard-boiled egg in my mouth. It tastes like dust.

Lazily, Reeve says, "Lil and I remembered that we don't actually like each other," and Rennie smiles a cat-that-ate-the-canary smile, which makes me see red.

Across the table, Reeve's and my eyes lock for a second, and it's like the rest of the cafeteria goes silent; it's only us looking at each other. And then it's over. Reeve shakes his head and chuckles. Like he couldn't care less.

After lunch, I'm walking to my next class when a sophomore girl comes running up to me with a thick manila envelope.

"Lillia, you don't know me but . . . I was hoping you could give these to Rennie for me. She said she wanted them in an e-mail, but my computer broke and it was just easier to print them out. I haven't seen her yet today, and I don't want her to think I'm slacking."

"Okay," I say slowly, and take the envelope. It's heavy.

"Thank you!"

I quickly duck into the bathroom and open it. It's stuffed full of pictures from homecoming. Sophomores arm in arm posing, sophomores on the dance floor. Sophomores shooting the homecoming court from the gym floor.

Yeah, Rennie's on yearbook committee, but only to make sure no bad pictures get in of her. What would she care about these pictures of other people? You can see Rennie's sparkly silver dress in a few of the shots, see us all in the background, but mostly we're just blurry.

I shove the envelope through the slats in her locker door, not even caring if some of them rip.

CHAPTER FIFTY-THREE

MARY

IT'S WEDNESDAY AFTERNOON, LAST PERIOD, AND I'm standing in the parking lot in front of Reeve's truck, concentrating with all my might.

But it's hard, because I'm so happy. Seeing Reeve these past few days walking around school, pretending like he doesn't care when I know the truth because I can see right through him. He's miserable, and I'm loving every second of it.

The door doesn't move. I concentrate harder. If only I knew what the inside of a car lock looked like, then maybe I could picture it clicking open.

Openopenopen.

I need to get inside Reeve's car before school lets out, so I can leave him a gift. It's my daisy necklace, the one he gave me on my thirteenth birthday. Once upon a time it was my most prized possession; I never took it off, not even to take a bath. I found it the other night when I was packing. I hadn't seen it since homecoming night. The perfect parting gift.

I want him to see it hanging from his rearview mirror and think of me. I know he won't make the connection, that I am the reason he is hurting right now, that I am the one who is behind it all. But I hope there will be a flicker, a shadowy hint of an idea, an idea that will grow and fester long after I'm gone: *You are suffering right now for of all your past sins. This is what you deserve.*

Either way, I'm done with it. I don't want it anymore.

I slide my hand into my coat pocket, take the daisy charm into my hand, and squeeze it as hard as I can. As hard as it takes to turn coal into a diamond.

Click.

Both truck doors, the passenger side and the driver's side, spring open hard and fast, like they are spring-loaded. It makes the entire chassis rock. Reeve's car alarm wails. I don't have much time.

I climb into the front seat and loop the chain around Reeve's rearview mirror. I give it a flick, so the daisy charm swings back and forth like a pendulum, dead center in the middle of his windshield.

Then I slide out and walk away, without bothering to close the doors, as the high school begins to empty out.

CHAPTER FIFTY-FOUR

KAT

IT'S ONE MORE DAY UNTIL CHRISTMAS BREAK, AND school is basically a joke. I've seen a movie in three of my classes today. Not that I'm complaining.

I take my lunch to the library to check e-mail, which is my new routine since sending in my early-decision application. You're technically not allowed to eat or drink in the library, but I'm stealth about it. I have my chicken wrap tucked up the sleeve of my flannel shirt and an open soda inside my book bag, which I keep upright by anchoring it between my feet.

I've got two e-mails. One forwarded warning about

violence against puppies from my aunt Jackie, and one from Oberlin.

I stop breathing and click, and my eyes pop all over the screen.

"Oh God. Oh fuck. Fuck fuck fuck fuck."

The librarian rushes over immediately. I think she's been waiting for weeks to catch me on some rule break, so she can toss my ass out of here. I swear, the woman wants this damn library all to herself. "You cannot use that language in here, Ms. DeBrassio. I'm going to write you—"

I don't even wait for her to finish saying whatever the fuck she's saying. I push back my chair, hoist my bag up on my shoulder, and book it to Ms. Chirazo's office. I burst in without even knocking.

She's with another student. A pudgy freshman in a striped polo shirt. They both turn and look at me, shocked. I don't realize right away, but a steady stream of upended soda is dripping out of my bag.

"Fuck!" I scream out at the top of my lungs, because that's the only word I can think of. And then I start crying like a baby.

Ms. Chirazo isn't even fazed. If anything, she's a guidance machine. "Kat, take a seat right now," she says in a voice like a drill sergeant. I collapse into the empty chair next to the pudgy kid, wrap my arms around my head and moan. Ms. Chirazo turns to the boy and says, "Billy, I'll come find you later."

I shoot Billy whatever-his-name-is dagger eyes. "You didn't see this," I growl.

Ms. Chirazo follows him to her door and closes it so hard her papers flutter. Then she rushes to my side. She doesn't go back behind her desk. She takes the seat next to me, the one Billy vacated. I wipe the snot from my nose on my sleeve, but more drips out.

"What happened?"

I want to look at her, but I can't. "I didn't get into Oberlin, that's what happened!" Saying it out loud is like a freaking bitch slap.

"Did you get a letter from them?"

I shake my head. "No. It was an e-mail. From some automated robot. It wasn't even personalized or anything. Cruel bastards." I can barely choke out the words. "I told them in that damn essay that this was my dream. I told them that my mom is dead, and that I was going to live her dream for her. And they don't even have the decency to send a personal response?"

"What did it say, exactly?"

I glare at her, fire in my eyes. "Are you fucking deaf? It said I didn't get in!" Immediately I want to take it back. I don't want to be a bitch to Ms. Chirazo. I shouldn't have cursed at her. She's been good to me.

Ms. Chirazo doesn't yell or throw me out. Instead she

motions me to stand up. Then she ushers me to sit behind her desk. She leans around me and opens up the Internet on her computer. "Show me. Show me exactly what they sent you."

I do. I pull the damn e-mail up so she can see it for herself.

She reads it a lot more carefully than I did. It takes her a few seconds to talk. "Kat, this just says you didn't get in early decision. Your application got pushed into the general pool. You still have a chance."

Maybe I should feel better at this, but I don't. "If they don't want me early decision, they don't want me period."

"That's not true. Not at all. In fact, it says here that you can still update your application. We can pump up your extracurriculars, try to find you some additional opportunities to round you out. I've looked at your application myself, and that's your only weak spot."

"What am I going to do? Put out a hit on the student council president?"

"Not funny, Kat."

"I'm just saying. It's too late."

She walks over to her filing cabinet and shuffles some papers around. "We did get a request earlier this week from Jar Island Preservation Society. They're looking for office volunteers after school and on the weekend."

I don't want to hope, but this is better than nothing. "All right."

"Excellent. I'll call them today and ask when you should start.

"I'm sorry I cursed at you."

"You were upset. I understand. I'm glad you're expressing your feelings." She pats me on the leg. "In the meantime, you'll go ahead and apply to your safety school just in case. You're a tough girl, Kat. Don't lose your head now."

I never thought I'd say this, but thank freaking God for Ms. Chirazo.

And then it hits me.

"Hey, Ms. Chirazo. Do you have, like, set students you deal with? Or can you talk to anyone who might need help? Because I have this friend . . ."

Later that day, a note from Ms. Chirazo is delivered to my eighth period. Turns out the Preservation Society wants me to start today. So I head over there after school. Why not? I've got nothing to lose. And, if anything, I feel like I owe something to her, for working so hard to help me.

It's a nice building, on the strip of fancy stores in White Haven. White wood with black trim and lots of old leaded-glass windows that have bends and dimples in them. They've got bundles of balsam branches hung around the doorway and laced through the iron step railings, and it makes the air smell freaking fantastic. I spot a plaque on the way in. Bronze. It says this building was once the town meeting hall, back in the 1700s.

Inside, the space is big and open, with hardwood floors so shiny I can see my reflection in them. Every wall is covered with red exposed brick, and they've got town artifacts hung up, like a moth-eaten old flag and a weathered wooden boat paddle. Every few feet there's a large oak desk. Vintage lightbulbs with the twisted orange filaments dangle down from the ceiling. The whole place reeks of money.

I don't like it right away. Something about rich-people causes makes me itchy. It's like they're looking for ways to use their money to ease their guilt.

I walk up to the first desk I see. There's a woman there, talking on the telephone. She's got on a fuzzy cream sweater, pearl earrings, and a huge honkin' diamond on her finger.

She sizes me up—my messy hair, the rips in my jeans, the combat boots—and offers a tight smile. Into the phone receiver she says, "Of course we're worried about the house. It's absolutely charming. And with all your family history there . . . Now, we've made several attempts to reach out to your sister, and . . . there's no other way to put this, except to say that she's not well. And the house is clearly suffering because of it." The lady's voice is hella high-pitched and whiny. She mm-hmms a bunch of times to the voice on the other end of the call, but she's clicking through e-mails or something on her laptop, so I doubt she's even listening. "Yes, well, we are willing to help in whatever way possible. If the house proves too much for your sister to care for, then we'll be happy to make you a very generous offer. Yes, well, of course. We look forward to hearing from you and are happy to assist in any way we can."

The woman hangs up the phone and lets out a pained sigh.

"Tough day on the job?" I ask.

She chuckles dryly. "You could say. Now, may I help you? You've been waiting so very patiently, and I appreciate that."

I want to say, *You don't need to be so condescending, you bitch,* but instead I smile. This woman must think I'm some kind of feral cat in from the streets. "Ms. Chirazo from the high school called about me today."

The woman eyes me. I guess however Ms. Chirazo pitched me, I'm not exactly measuring up. "Of course. Yes. Well, we're happy to have you, Katherine." She gets up from behind her desk. "Let me show you to the basement, where you'll be working."

Of course.

She ushers me down a creaky stairway. The basement has not received the same designy care as the upstairs. There are no windows, and the ceilings are so low we need to hunch if we don't want to knock ourselves out.

"You'll need to go through these documents, scan the front pages, and then save them to the hard drive." She shows me a thing that looks like a paper shredder. "It goes quick; you slide the documents through this and the scanner takes a picture. Try to get them to go in straight. And be extra careful with any paper that's turned yellow."

"What is all this stuff?"

The woman laughs through her nose. "A little of everything, really. Town charters, newspapers, land surveys." She's already halfway up the stairs. "Let me know if you need anything."

I shrug off my jacket. I'd love to bust right up out of here, but I can't. I'll be working here until spring, probably. Ugh. The things I'll do for Oberlin. For fuck's sake.

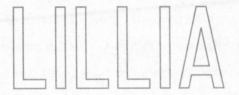

CHAPTER FIFTY-FIVE

MRS. LIND HAS GONE ALL-OUT THIS YEAR. THERE are red-bow-tied waiters walking around passing out fancy little bites like mini lump crab cakes and pear latke cakes with truffled crème fraiche on top, plus there's a carving station and a raw bar and all kinds of chocolate goodies.

It's a packed house, people everywhere. My parents are by the Christmas tree talking to some friends from the yacht club. My mom looks so beautiful tonight. She's wearing a white dress that drapes on the side, and she got her hair done in an updo. She tried to get Nadia and me to go with her and get our hair done too, but Nadia hates the way anyone else does her hair, and while I would normally jump at the chance to get a blowout, I wasn't in the mood.

I'm in that blue silk dress again, the one I wore to Reeve's open house. I put my hair in a ponytail and I've got on my platform booties because they're my most comfortable dressy shoe. It's not like I'm trying to impress anyone tonight.

I'm sitting with Alex on the comfy couch in the living room, sharing a chocolate tart with whipped cream on top. He snuck us some mulled cider, too, although I doubt our parents would care. I don't know where Nadia is—probably playing Guitar Hero in the pool house with Alex's cousins. We're the only kids still hanging around, only I guess we're not kids anymore. That's what Alex's mom said, that we should stay and socialize with the adults because we're practically adults ourselves. I'm hoping my parents won't want to stay too late, because we only took one car.

"Why so glum, Lil?" Alex asks me. "Christmas is in three days."

I've got a forkful of chocolate tart halfway to my mouth. "Glum? I'm not glum. Sorry if I seem that way . . . I guess I'm just tired. I went to the barn really early this morning."

"How is Phantom?"

"Oh, he's good." I take another forkful of tart. "I can't believe you remember his name."

Alex gives me a wounded look. "Of course I remember. I've seen you compete. Remember, back in freshman year? You used to ride, like, every day. Phantom was all you talked about."

I laugh. "I guess I was kind of a horsey girl for a while there." I reach over and grab my clutch off the coffee table. "I got you something for Christmas."

Alex chews fast and swallows. "No way."

Shyly, I nod. "I wanted to say thank you. You've been so great to me this year." I pull out the present from my clutch. I could barely fit my lipstick and compact inside with it because it takes up so much room.

Alex looks touched. He turns the whole thing over in his hands, and I'm glad I took special care in wrapping it up. I used a special shiny gold foil paper and tied it with a cream silk ribbon. He opens it slowly, careful not to rip the paper. He pulls out the long, whiskey-colored piece of leather and stares at it without saying anything.

"It's a guitar strap," I say, because maybe he thinks it's a belt? I take it from him and turn it over. "I had them emboss your initials in the leather. I picked the font out myself. Anyway, the lady said it's adjustable, so you can wear it high and tight like Johnny Cash, or low like the punk-rock kids do." I hand it back to him. "I wasn't sure what style you're into."

"Lil," he says quietly, and then looks up at me. "This is so cool."

I beam a smile. "Really? You like it?"

Alex nods, but then suddenly stands up from the couch and stares across the room.

I look up, and there's Reeve, wearing his puffy vest and standing in front of the buffet table with a beer in his hand. He's cutting himself a piece of the pork tenderloin and eating it with his fingers.

I stand up too, my heart pounding. "Did you invite him?"

"No," Alex says.

Now Reeve's taking a swig of the beer, finishing it in one long gulp. He's looking around the room; he hasn't seen us yet. But he spots Alex's uncle Tim, and he goes up to him and claps him on the back so hard that some champagne tips out of Uncle Tim's flute.

"Shit. He's drunk," Alex says, and strides across the room. I follow him. He goes up to Reeve and puts his hand on his shoulder. "What are you doing here, man?"

Reeve turns around unsteadily. "Your mom let me in." Then he sees me standing behind Alex. "Whaddup, Cho."

"Hey."

Alex starts hustling Reeve out of the room and out the back door, toward the pool house, with Reeve protesting and stumbling all the way.

Reeve pushes Alex away from him when we're outside. "What

the hell? I'm not welcome at your house all of a sudden?"

"Hey, hey, hey," Alex says. "Just chill."

I wrap my arms around myself, shivering. I left my coat inside.

Reeve juts his chin at me. "What is it you have against winter coats?" He starts to shrug out of his vest.

"I'm fine," I say.

"'I'm fine,'" he mimics back. Then Reeve's lip curls. "Whatever. Freeze to death, then. See if I care."

My eyes well up. He's being so mean. Is this how it's going to be with us now?

"You should go," Alex says, stepping in front of me.

Reeve throws up his hands. "So much for bros before hoes." He yells out toward the pool house, "Merry Christmas, kids! Santa's getting his ass kicked out." And then he stumbles off toward the gate.

Nadia and a couple of Alex's older cousins have come outside; they're watching us from the front of the pool house with wide eyes.

I take Alex's arm. "He shouldn't drive," I say. "He's drunk."

Alex doesn't make a move; he just watches as Reeve stalks off. I push Alex in Reeve's direction as hard as I can. "Hurry, Alex!"

Reluctantly, Alex follows him. "Give me your keys. I'll drive you home."

Reeve tosses his keys out onto the lawn. "Nah, I'll walk."

"Reeve!" I call out. "Let him take you."

But he's already halfway down the street, his black puffy vest blending into the night sky. I go looking for his keys, but it's too dark. Alex comes back to my side and shrugs. "Give me your phone," I say to him, and he hands it to me. I use it like a flashlight and I comb through the grass.

Behind me, Alex says, "We should go back inside. It's freezing out here. I'll find them in the morning."

I ignore him and keep searching. My fingers finally close on the hard, cold metal, and I clutch them in my hand. Then I hold them up in front of Alex. "You should go after him. He's drunk; it's going to take him hours to get home with his bad leg. He could get hit by a car."

Alex's face is impassive. "He's not going to listen. He's too stubborn. He'll be fine."

"Please try."

Alex stares at me for a second, and then he says, "What's going on with you guys?" He runs his hands through his hair and squinches up his face, like he's afraid to hear the answer. "Please don't lie to me."

I don't say anything. I don't want to lie to him. I feel like I've been lying to everybody lately, and I'm sick of it. Alex deserves better than that.

"We've . . . hung out a few times."

Alex watches me intently. "Did you guys hook up?"

I take a deep breath. "We kissed. But that's all over with. It was a stupid mistake." Alex stares at the ground. He won't look at me. "I'm sorry."

"You don't have anything to be sorry for," Alex says, finally looking up. Thankfully, he doesn't sound angry. Just bummed. He takes the keys from me. "Thanks again for my present."

"You're welcome." I watch as he jogs over to Reeve's truck, parked in front of Alex's neighbor's driveway. He gets in and drives off.

Nadia comes running up to me and asks, "What's going on?"

"Nothing," I say, putting my arm around her. "Let's go back inside."

The next day, I'm lying on the couch, watching TV and texting with Ash, when my dad comes into the living room and sits down next to me. "What are you watching?" he asks me.

I don't look up so I can keep texting. "I don't know, some Christmas special."

What the h happened at Alex's?? I heard Reeve showed up wasted and Lindy kicked him out!

Not really. Is that what people are saying??

Ren said she had to pick up Reeve off the side of the road!

Of course he called Rennie for a ride. Of course he did.

"Have you finished your Wellesley supplement yet?" my dad asks me.

"Yup, pretty much," I say. It's almost true because it's almost done.

Casually he says, "Do you want me to take a look at it before you send it off?"

"That's okay," I say. "I already showed it to my guidance counselor."

What was he even upset about?

No clue. What did Ren say?

She made excuses for him as always. He's got her on the hook.

So true.

"It wouldn't hurt to have another pair of eyes."

I finally look up from my phone. "Daddy . . . I don't even know if I want to go to Wellesley."

Frowning, he says, "I thought we all agreed you'd at least apply."

"I'm applying, but even if I get in, I don't know if I want to go there." I scroll Ash's and my text conversation and reread what she wrote. "Just because Mommy loved it at an all-girls school, that doesn't mean I will."

"I want you to apply so you have the option," my dad says. "Understood?"

I nod. Fine. I don't even know if I'll get in, so whatever.

He clears his throat the way he does when he's uncomfortable. "The other night at the Linds . . . was that friend of yours drunk?"

I keep my eyes down, but my heart jumps. "What friend?"

"Reeve. That's his name, right?"

I'm surprised my dad knows his name. My mom probably told him. "No, he wasn't drunk." My dad looks skeptical, so I say it again with more emphasis. "He wasn't drunk, Daddy! He's not like that. He's an athlete."

"All right, all right. I trust you. I just want you to be careful of who you hang out with. Right now you should be focused on your college applications and finishing out senior year well. Don't get complacent."

I want to snap back at him, but I don't, because that's not done in our family. You don't talk back. It makes me mad when my dad comes home and tries to play the part of the involved parent when he's hardly ever even here. He doesn't have the right to tell me what to do. Calmly I say, "I am very focused on my applications, Daddy. In fact, I'm going upstairs to finish my common app right now." I stand up.

"That's my girl," my dad says, giving me an approving nod.

When I get up to my room, I flop down on my bed and call Ash.

I can hear her munching on something. "I think Ren deserves better. He's been stringing her along since we were kids. She gives him whatever he wants and he takes, takes, takes. It's like the freaking Giving Tree."

I would hardly call Rennie a Giving Tree, but I don't say so.

Ash continues. "He's all about himself. He couldn't care less about anyone else."

I don't know if that's true. In fact, I'm sure it's not.

I remember the first time I ever met Reeve. It was back when our house was being built. Nadia was little then. I was seven.

I never saw the house that used to be there. Just pictures of it. It was a two-story house with a wraparound front porch, decorative shutters, and a big iron weather vane. It wasn't at all my parents' style. But my mom was set on the spot. It was a large plot, two acres, with a perfect view of the sea. The man who lived there wasn't even planning to sell, but Dad had a lawyer send him a letter and he offered a ton of money.

The day after Dad and Mom signed the papers, they had the house bulldozed.

This was back when White Haven wasn't all megamansions. I mean, the houses were definitely big, but I don't remember many of them having in-ground pools or elevators or five-car garages. It was more about the land. There was a lot of space between the houses, privacy, and they really did have the best views on the whole island. I guess in that way it was destined to end up the way it did. Owned by rich people.

Anyway, since my mom was the one who worked on the plans, she liked to visit the site and see how things were progressing.

One time she took Nadia and me with her.

When we got to the site, they'd poured the concrete foundation and had started framing out the rooms with two-by-fours. There were at least ten pickup trucks parked on the lawn and one big yellow dump truck.

"Oh good Lord," Mom muttered. "We'll have to resod the whole front lawn."

I remember being totally amazed by how big our house was going to be. We'd only ever lived in apartments. Granted, they were luxury apartments, but you still had people living right on the other side of your walls. This house was humongous.

There were a bunch of workmen milling around. They all seemed to have big round stomachs. I held Nadia's hand and stood close to my mom, while she talked to one of the contractors. Even though it was hot out, Mom wore a black suit and heels, and she kept her sunglasses on even when we were inside the house.

She was arguing about the staircase. She kept pointing to her plans, telling him he needed to follow her directions or else she'd hire another crew. The man scoffed. "We're the only crew on the island." My mom said, "I'll send them in on the ferry and rent them a house." And that basically shut him up.

While my mom was getting stern with him, he kept looking down at me and Nadia. I think he didn't like being yelled at by a lady, and especially not in front of children.

And then, suddenly, I felt a big slap on my back.

"Tag!"

I spun around. There was a boy a little taller than me, with a big smile that showed nearly all his teeth, rocking his weight from one foot to the other.

"Reeve!" the man yelled. "I told you to stay put in my truck."

"You have *children* running around this work zone?" my mom said, exasperated.

"He was supposed to be at football camp, but my wife apparently wrote the wrong date on the calendar. And she's away visiting her sister, so . . . I did what I had to do."

Reeve blinked at me a few times. Then he slapped my arm and said, "Tag," again. And then he added, "You're it," and said the words slowly, as if I didn't understand English.

"I know how to play tag," I said, as mean as I could. I hated when people did that, assumed that because I was Asian, I didn't know English. It drove me crazy.

"Doesn't seem like it." He hustled backward away from me.

I dropped Nadia's hand and sprinted after him.

Mom and the man shouted after us, but I didn't stop. I wanted to catch him so badly.

Though the man had said Reeve wasn't usually on site, he sure whipped around through my house like he'd been there before. He knew all these places to twist and turn. He jumped over a pile of wood, ducked under two sawhorses. He was quick, but I was too. I would have been faster if I hadn't had on dress shoes.

He was almost in my reach when he twisted into a door frame. At the very last second it was like he changed his mind, he didn't want to go through. But I was already on top of him. I crashed into him and tagged him as hard as I could, and he went flying into the room, skidding across the floor.

It was freshly poured wet concrete. He left the craziest skid mark.

I gasped.

"Damn it, Reeve!"

I turned around, and there was Reeve's dad, red in the face. He stepped into the room, big boot prints on the concrete. I guess he didn't care about ruining it, since Reeve had already taken care of that. He picked Reeve up by the back of his shirt, like cats do to their babies. Only he wasn't gentle. He looked like he was going to kill Reeve. And Reeve looked scared. His whole face changed.

My voice came out in a squeak. "I—It's my—"

It was my fault, I'd pushed him, but Reeve didn't let me say it. "Sorry, Dad. I'm sorry. It's my fault."

Mom and Nadia came up then, and they gasped too.

Reeve's dad, seeing them, set Reeve down. "We'll fix this right up—no charge, of course." He glared down at Reeve. "Get in the truck. Now," he said through gritted teeth.

"Yes, sir," Reeve said.

I felt so bad. Mom put me and Nadia in the car. As we drove away, I saw Reeve sitting in the bed of his dad's truck, like he'd been told. He didn't look scared anymore.

He grinned at me.

CHAPTER FIFTY-SIX

KAT

CHRISTMAS MORNING, MY PLAN WAS TO WAKE UP early and make pancakes for everybody. But I stay up late watching *A Christmas Story* with Pat the night before, so I end up oversleeping. It's after ten by the time I finally get out of bed.

I put my grubby terry-cloth robe on over my T-shirt and trudge over to the kitchen to make myself a cup of coffee, and I'm surprised to see Dad and Pat at the kitchen table. Pat's got his head bent over a bowl of leftover soup, and Dad's drinking coffee. "Merry Christmas, DeBrassios," I say, my voice scratchy from sleep. "I was going to get up early and make pancakes, but—"

"But you're a lazy little shit?" Pat finishes, slurping his soup.

I grin and pour myself a cup of coffee. "Like my big brudder."

I take my coffee into the family room and turn on the Christmas tree lights. It's bare under the tree. We already did presents last night, as is the DeBrassio tradition. I got my dad a new fishing pole I'd been saving up for, and I got Pat a vintage Italian motocross decal off the Internet from some guy. My dad gave me a hundred-dollar-bill, and Pat said he'd give me my gift later. Like hell. Pat's all about rain-checking gifts.

I turn on the TV, and it's *A Christmas Story* again. It's the end of the movie, where they're at the Chinese restaurant and the waiters are singing "Deck the Halls" and they can't say their *l*'s. It's racist as shit, but it's still a good movie.

Then Dad and Pat come in, and Dad says, "Katherine, I think there might be one more gift for you under the tree."

"Get your eyes checked, old man!" I tell him, pointing to the bare rug.

"Pat!" Dad barks. "You were supposed to put it under the tree this morning."

"Chill out, chill out," Pat says, and he goes to his room and comes back with a box wrapped in Santa Claus paper. He hands it to me. "Here."

I look from Dad to Pat. "What is this?"

Dad's grinning. "Open it."

I tear into it—it's a new laptop. My jaw drops. "No way."

"It's for college, Katherine."

JENNY HAN AND SIOBHAN VIVIAN

There's a huge lump in my throat and tears are pricking my eyelids. "How — how did you even afford this?"

"I finished that canoe last week," Dad says, beaming at me proudly. "And Pat helped."

I stare at Pat, who is standing against the doorjamb with his arms crossed. "For real?"

"Yeah, dude. I worked my ass off to kick in on this, so you better not fail out of Oberlin." Pat shakes his finger at me.

I wipe my eyes with the back of my arm. "I haven't even been accepted yet." I should tell them about the whole early-decision beat-down I suffered, but I don't have the heart.

"You're getting in," Pat says.

"Even if I do get in, it's so far away. . . . Maybe I'd be better off going to school somewhere nearby, so I could still come home and help out around here."

"No way," Dad barks. "You're out of here as soon as you graduate. Your mother wouldn't have wanted it any other way."

I can barely see him through my tears. "Thanks a lot."

Pat leans forward and says, "Dad and I can fend for ourselves. Your ass is going to Oberlin. You're gonna get straight As, and then you're gonna get rich at some fancy job, and when you do, you're gonna send lots of dough home to us."

I laugh. "You're still gonna be living at home in five years? Loser." Then I stand up, and on shaky legs, I hug them both.

CHAPTER FIFTY-SEVEN

LILLIA

CHRISTMAS DAY PASSES IN A BLUR. WE GO TO church in the morning like always; then we come back, and my dad makes a Korean rice-cake soup and my mom bakes frozen cinnamon rolls she ordered from Neiman Marcus. We eat them as we open presents. I get a new laptop and a mint-and-lavender cashmere sweater and new riding boots and little things like my favorite perfume and the sugarplum face cream from New York.

I should be happy, because I love presents and I'm getting

everything I asked for and more. Nadia is squealing over every one of her gifts, hugging our mom and dad each time she opens something, taking her time getting through her pile so she can make it last longer. I can barely muster up smiles and thank-yous. I'm the worst daughter ever.

My parents definitely notice. They keep shooting each other concerned looks. At one point my mom sits next to me on the chaise and puts the back of her hand to my forehead to check if I have a fever.

I didn't think it would be this bad. That I'd hurt this much over something that was supposed to be fake.

When all the presents have been opened, Mom gives a nod to my dad, and he steps out of the room. When he comes back, he has two huge boxes in his arms. Nadia jumps up and tries to take one of them, but Dad says, "These are both for Lillia."

I open them. It's a brand-new luggage set from Tumi, both hard shell in gleaming white. One large roller bag, one smaller roller that will fit in the overhead.

"For college," my dad announces. "Wellesley has some amazing study-abroad programs, you know."

I don't even have the energy to say anything back to that. That I'm still not totally sold on Wellesley. I just nod and click the suitcase latch open and closed a few times.

"Your father picked the set out himself," Mom says. "He figured you'd like the white." She rests her hand on my knee and gives it a hard squeeze.

I automatically look to my dad. "I love it."

"Merry Christmas, princess," he says.

CHAPTER FIFTY-EIGHT

MARY

IT'S FINALLY NEW YEAR'S EVE.

Snow is coming tonight, a few inches. And the wind is howling. Rennie's party will still go on for sure. I just hope the ferry runs tomorrow. I can't wait to see my mom and dad.

I have a special outfit planned for the trip home. Pencil skirt, heels, a cream-colored blouse. I want to look beautiful and mature when they see me again; I want them to see that, see how I've grown. They mean well, but they've always babied me so much. When I go back with them, I want them to treat me like a teenager and not a kid.

But first I have a party to attend and two very special people to say good-bye to.

I take my time doing my hair and makeup. I paint my lips ruby red and put my hair in a bun. I put on a dress I found in my closet—it's white with gold bangles and beads and a drop waist. I scramble around for my gold slingbacks.

The doorbell rings. Geez, those preservation ladies won't quit. I figure Aunt Bette won't answer like usual, but the doorbell keeps chiming, insistent.

Weird.

Eventually, I hear Aunt Bette open the door.

"Erica?"

I freeze.

"Oh my God, Bette. Look at this place."

That voice. I haven't heard it for so long.

My mother. She's . . . she's here! I leap up and hurry down the stairs and when I see her, I stop short.

Mommy?

There she is, standing in the foyer in a long black coat. Her hair is gray, almost as gray as Aunt Bette's. How could she have aged overnight? I haven't been gone that long.

"What's that noise?" my mom asks.

"It's Mary," Aunt Bette says.

My mom says, "Bette, please. Please stop torturing me like this."

I stop dead in my tracks. Something is wrong. Very wrong.

I can feel the heat and the panic rising up inside me. The picture frames on the staircase walls start to shake, and I have to tell myself to calm down, just calm down.

Calmdowncalmdowncalmdown.

"You need help, Bette," my mom says, and she sounds like she's crying. "I'm taking you away from here. This house is making you sick. Those preservation people have been calling, and with good reason. Look at this place!"

"No no, I'm fine, Erica," Aunt Bette says desperately. "Mary wants to leave! I'll be better when she's gone!"

"This house is in shambles, and you're—you're not well," my mom chokes out. "You can't stay here any longer."

Aunt Bette backs up. "You should see her, Erica. Talk to her. Tell her about Jim. Maybe that will help her."

"Bette . . . please stop it," my mother says, and her voice sounds pained. "Stop talking about her."

Jim's my dad.

What's going on? Did they have a fight? Did they get separated in the time that I've been gone—is that why they haven't been back to visit?

"We're leaving. Now." Mom has the door open. I stare at it

and force it closed. She's shocked as the knob flies out of her hand. The door bangs shut, and the dead bolt clicks.

Aunt Bette cries, "Mary! Stop! You're going to scare her!"

Ignoring her, I run to my bed and grab my suitcase and go flying down the stairs and out the door. "Mommy! I'm coming with you! Don't leave without me!"

But then I hear the back door opening. I go to my window and see my mom with her arm around Aunt Bette, trying to walk her to the rental car. They're leaving? Without me?

I race back downstairs and out to the car.

My mom is sobbing. She doesn't even look at me. "Bette, please, please, get in the car."

I run up to her. "Mommy!" I scream. I'm howling now, and the shutters on the house are opening and closing, faster and faster. I can't stop it; I can't control myself.

"Oh my God!" my mom screams, and she jerks the passenger-side door open and pushes Aunt Bette inside. She runs to the other side of the car and stumbles and falls to the ground.

I run after her, sobbing. "Mommy, Mommy, Mommy," I cry. "Don't go. Don't leave me. I want to go home!"

Her eyes widen in shock. "Mary, is that you?"

"Don't leave me," I beg. She struggles to get up, and I wait for her to hug me, to hold me to her close. *It's been so long, Mommy.*

But she doesn't move toward me, she runs to the other side of the car and gets in. I pound on the window so hard the glass starts to crack.

"I'm sorry," she weeps. "I'm so sorry. I can't stay." Her hands shake as she starts the car, puts it in reverse, and drives away.

CHAPTER FIFTY-NINE

LILLIA

I WASN'T GOING TO GO TO THE PARTY. KAT KEPT texting me, telling me to come and that she and Mary would protect me from Rennie tonight. But then this afternoon I got a text from Rennie herself. It said, *New Year, new start? Come tonight.* Then she sent me a picture of her hand holding a cherry Blow Pop. Her manicure looked awesome. It was all pale pink glitter, like sparkly cotton candy.

So I'm going. I don't want to be the only one in the whole school missing out. My sister will be there. Even Kat and

Mary are going. What else am I supposed to do? Go to dinner with my parents?

A few months ago it would have been Rennie and me getting ready for this party together. We'd be blasting Madonna and fighting for the mirror, going back and forth over a crimson-red lip versus a brick-red lip. Instead it was me by myself. No Nadia, because she got ready with all the freshman girls at Janelle's house. Just me.

I found my dress at a vintage store online. I was worried it wouldn't fit, because sizes were different back then, but when it came, it was perfect. It's emerald-green silk, tissue thin, with a drop waist and a low V-neck and a back that dips low in an *X* that looks like cobwebs, delicate and fine.

I put my hair in my mom's rollers and then I styled it in a bob. It kept falling out, so I stuck a bunch of pins in it. Dark red lipstick was the final touch.

When I walked down the stairs, my dad came out of his office to hug me and tell me how beautiful I looked. And also to tell me to remember my special curfew for the night, two a.m. and not a minute later. He told me not to drive home, to take a taxi or to call and he'd come get me. "The streets aren't safe on New Year's Eve," he said. "Too many people driving drunk." I rolled my eyes and kept saying, "Yes, Daddy. Sure, Daddy."

At a stoplight, I text Ash to see if she's there so I don't have to walk in alone. She texts back and says she's already inside. I text Alex too, only he doesn't text me back right away. We haven't talked much since his holiday party, since I told him that I kissed Reeve. Things were already a little weird between them, and I can't help but think that that probably made things even worse.

There's no parking in front of the gallery, so I park two streets away, and then I regret borrowing my mom's strappy rhinestone heels. They're Manolos, and I'd always thought shoes that expensive would be more comfortable. But they're not; by the time I get to the party, my feet hurt so bad I just want to take them off.

The gallery name had been scratched off the glass, and there's a FOR RENT sign in the window. From the outside it looks so . . . desolate. You can't see much inside. All the windows are steamed up.

There's an actual bouncer at the door. I recognize him from Bow Tie; he's one of the line cooks. I can't believe Rennie got him to blow off his own New Year's Eve in favor of standing in front of her mom's gallery all night for a high school party. He goes, "What's the secret word?"

"Moonshine," I say, and for a split second I fear that Rennie's changed the word and I'm not even going to get in to her party.

Then he nods and says, "Ten bucks."

Ten bucks? I've never, ever paid to go to one of Rennie's parties.

"I'm a senior," I tell him. "And I'm a friend of Rennie's. We've met before, at Bow Tie?"

"Everybody's a friend of Rennie's tonight," he says, and looks past me, over my head, to a group of kids coming noisily down the block. "It's ten for seniors, twenty for juniors, thirty for sophomores—"

I'm 1,000 percent sure Ash or any of our other friends didn't have to pay, but I don't want to stand out here arguing with him. It's humiliating. "Okay, okay. Whatever." Luckily I have the cash my dad gave me for a cab. I pluck a twenty out of my beaded clutch and hand it to him.

He pulls a wad of cash out of his leather-jacket pocket and hands me back a ten. "Have fun."

I make my way into the gallery. I've seen it empty before, when Paige was switching out one show for another, giving the walls a fresh coat of white paint so the art would stand out. But Rennie's transformed it. She's set up a bar over by where the cash register used to be, and another one of the workers from the restaurant is there mixing drinks in a crisp white tuxedo shirt and black bow tie. Drinks are being served in actual glassware, probably from the restaurant too. No plastic Solo cups. Pretty metallic garlands crisscross the ceiling in all different colors. They look vintage. There are helium balloons, too, clusters of white and silver and gold with matching ribbons, floating across the room. I look down and see that Rennie's painted the floor, alternating black and white zigzag stripes. She's made a bunch of centerpieces for all the tabletops: bouquets of cream-colored feathers, some dipped in gold and silver glitter.

Even I have to admit, this is her best party yet.

The place is packed; it's so dark it takes a second for my eyes to adjust. No Kat or Mary yet. I spot Nadia and some other girls from the squad huddled together on a couch in the corner. Nadia waves, and I wave back.

And then it's me, standing alone.

I get a pain in my stomach. Is this how it's going to be all night?

I take a deep breath and then fish in my clutch for my lipstick and my compact. That's the thing with dark red lipstick. You have to make sure it's always on nice and thick and rich; otherwise it looks like you've been eating a popsicle or something. I touch up the corners of my mouth, and as I put everything back into my bag, I feel my phone vibrate.

It's Alex.

You look amazing.

I smile and click my phone shut. I look around for Alex and spot him over by the bar, leaning against the corner, sipping something brown from a glass. He lifts his glass to me and I laugh. I can't help it. He's wearing a button-down and suspenders and a hat his mom must have found him. He looks adorable.

He makes his way through the crowd over to where I'm standing. As he walks, I see him reach for something inside his pants pocket.

"You left our party before I could give you your Christmas present the other night." He comes up next to me and holds out his hand. In his palm is a small orange box with a narrow brown ribbon tied around it. The ribbon says *Hermès*.

I can't believe it.

Alex puts the box in my hands. "Open it, Lil."

I untie the ribbon and open the box. It's the bracelet I wanted, the one I saw in Boston. White, enamel, perfect. "Alex, this is way too expensive! I can't accept this."

"You said you wanted it, remember?"

"I know, but . . ."

He smiles, pleased. "So I want you to have it." Alex takes the bracelet out of the box and puts it on my wrist.

"I can't."

"Why not?"

"Because . . . it's too much."

"Don't worry about that. I used the money my grandma gave me for a new guitar." Alex shoves his hands in his pockets. "Actually, there's something I've been meaning to ask you. About that weekend in Boston."

I give him a quick, nervous nod.

"If . . ." He looks down, and then back at me again. "Remember when we went on that walk, in the snow? If I would have tried to kiss you that night, would you have let me?"

My mind flashes back to that night. How beautiful it was, in snowy Boston. How I felt so safe with Alex. How easy it was with him, especially compared to Reeve.

I think I would have. Maybe.

I'm about to tell him so, but then everything falls away and goes to static because over Alex's shoulder, across the room, I see him.

Reeve. On the couch, next to a girl who at first I think is Rennie, but then see is not. She's a sophomore; I think her name is Kendall. He's wearing the outfit we bought together. He looks so good it makes me feel sick. She's wearing a feather boa around her neck, and he keeps playing with it.

Our eyes meet, and then deliberately he looks away. He says something in Kendall's ear and puts his hat on her head, and then she scoots onto his lap. I can feel all the blood rush to my face.

I break away from Alex. "I have to go."

Alex's face falls. "Are you not even going to answer my question?"

"I . . . I can't right now."

I look over at Reeve again; I can't help it. He catches my eye again, and this time, takes a big sip of his drink, and then puts his hand on Kendall's thigh.

I have to get out of here. I start backing up, pushing people out of my way.

I stumble toward the hallway. Then Reeve pops up in front of me, blocking my way with his arm. "Excuse me," I say icily.

"Oh, so we're still not speaking?" Reeve oh-so-casually crosses his arms and leans against the hallway wall.

I glare at him. "Why would we need to speak? We don't even like each other, remember?"

Reeve gives me a condescending smile, like I'm just a silly girl and he's so mature and above it all. I try to push past him again, hard, and his smile drops. He says, "Look, I was pissed that you blew me off, but I'm over it now, so you don't have to run away every time you see me. I won't bother you anymore. It's cool."

"Awesome," I say.

Reeve reaches out and touches the bracelet on my wrist. "Nice bracelet," he says.

I know he's being insincere, but I still say, "Thank you."

With a smirk he adds, "Lind must have worked really hard to save up for that for you."

"He did." I should smile and leave it at that, but I can't resist adding, "Classy of you to be talking to another girl at Rennie's party." I throw a pointed look in Kendall's direction. "Or are you and Ren already over? Why am I not the least bit surprised? How very Reeve of you, already on to the next." I'd assumed the reason Rennie invited me to her party was so that she could flaunt her relationship with Reeve in my face. But maybe not. Maybe they're over and done with too.

Reeve's not smiling anymore, and I know I'm getting under his skin. "Like I said a million times, Rennie and I are just friends."

"Oh," I say dryly. "You must mean friends with benefits."

Reeve puts up his hands. "Believe what you want. I don't care."

"I'm believing what she told me, you dummy. I saw her at your house! She was more than happy to throw it in my face."

"When?" he demands.

"That day. The day of your family's open house."

Reeve jerks in surprise. "You came?"

I look around and spot Rennie in the crowd, surrounded by guys from the football team. So she didn't tell him I came by. Big surprise. Not that it makes a difference. It's all over and done with now.

I shrug. "Yeah, I stopped by. Rennie told me you didn't want to see me, so I left."

Reeve's staring at me. "Are you serious right now? You came to my house?"

"It wasn't a big deal," I say, and I try to duck under his arm to get past him.

But he backs up and blocks me again. "Wait! I don't know what Rennie said to you, but I spent the whole day alone in my room, pissed at you for bailing on me. I wanted you there, Lil. Only you."

For a second I close my eyes, and then I open them again. "It doesn't matter anymore."

Which is when Kendall makes her way over to us and says, "Hey, Lillia. What's up?" She puts her head on Reeve's shoulder, which he immediately tries to shrug off.

"Hey," I say. I've got my eye on the front door. There's a line of people coming into the party now, so I can't get out through the front. I'll just go out through the back. I flash a quick smile at Kendall and say, "Have fun, you two!" and squeeze past them both.

I'm halfway down the hallway when I hear Reeve coming up behind me, calling my name. He yells out, "You still like me. I know you do. So I reject our breakup on the grounds that this is a bullshit misunderstanding."

I stop and turn around and face him. "We're not broken up, because we were never together." And we can never *be* together.

"You like me! Admit it, Cho."

God, I hope Kat and Mary aren't here yet. If they see us like this, they'll want to start the ruse up again. I can't do it anymore. So I say it again, more calmly. "Reeve, I don't like you."

"Yes. You. Do." Reeve takes my hand, and I try to pull it away, but this time he won't let go. "You like me, and I like you. So can we just—can we stop with the games and be together already?"

"What about your girl Kendall?" I challenge.

He makes a dismissive sound. "I was talking to her to make you jealous. It worked, too."

He pulls me closer and closer to him until we're close enough to kiss. "It doesn't have to be this hard, you know."

I'm about to deny it when suddenly he cups his hands to my face and kisses me. I try to resist for like a second, and then I kiss him back because this is what I've dreamed of for days. My hand snakes around his neck to pull him closer, and his hair feels so soft against my fingertips.

Then I hear a gasp. I break away from Reeve, whose arms are cradling me against the wall.

"What the *fuck*?" It's Rennie, standing at the other end of the hallway, staring at us. Stunned. She points at me, her arm shaking.

Reeve turns around and sees her and says, "Hold up, Ren."

She backs away from us, into the kitchen. I follow her, with Reeve at my heels. "Rennie . . . ," I start to say.

She pushes me to the side and pounds her fists on Reeve's chest. "You picked *her* over *me*?" Rennie lets out an angry sob and steps away from him. "She's not who you think she is, Reeve. Sweet, innocent Lillia? What a freaking joke. She's a slut."

"Don't talk about her like that," Reeve warns.

Rennie ignores him and advances toward me. "I let you be my little shadow, I took you under my wing, I basically made you!" Rennie's whole body is trembling with rage. "You would be *nobody* if it weren't for me."

Reeve tries to get in between us. "Ren, stop it. Lillia didn't steal me, so don't put the blame on her. You know I love you, you know I do. But it was never gonna be like that with us."

"Don't you dare defend her to me!" Rennie screams, whirling on him. "You can't see her for what she really is!"

I take a raggedy breath and step toward her. "Rennie, you've got it backward. You're the one who's always wanted what I have, not the other way around. Our whole lives, you've been jealous because I have what you want."

Her mouth twists into a sneer. "I can't believe this. I can't even believe you're turning this around on me right now."

I wet my lips. "You know what? I think that on some level you were glad about what happened that night with those guys."

Rennie's eyes dart over to Reeve and then back to me. "Shut up," she warns. "Don't say another word."

"I think you were glad because it brought me down to your level," I say, my voice shaking. "I wasn't innocent Lillia anymore. I wasn't a princess, or a virgin. I wasn't special. I was like you. Both of us damaged goods."

Rennie's hand strikes lightning fast, slapping my cheek so hard I rock back onto my heels and almost fall. Reeve yells, "What the hell, Ren!" And he pulls me away from her and stands between us.

Black mascara tears run down her face. "She doesn't care about you! Trust me."

I shake my head over and over. I'm crying now too. "That's not true." Despite everything I've done, that isn't true.

A guy in suspenders stumbles into the kitchen and says, "Whoops, I thought this was the bathroom."

"Get out!" Rennie screams, and the guy runs off. As soon as he's gone, Rennie starts up again, advancing on me this time. "I'm telling you, she's not who you think she is, Reeve. She's an evil, lying bitch." She takes a deep, satisfied breath. "And I have proof!"

Oh my God. Oh. My. God.

I feel dizzy. Rennie knows. She knows what I did at homecoming. But how?

"Reeve, please go," I beg, trying to push him out of the room. "Just go." I'm pushing with all my might, but he won't budge.

Her face is bright red. "You could have killed him, Lillia!"

"Please, Reeve!" I'm begging, trying to steer him toward the door.

Reeve stands there like a statue, his arms crossed. "What are you talking about?"

Rennie sobs to him, "I'm the *only one* who's been there for you. After you got hurt, nobody gave a shit about you but me. I was the one who was at the hospital every day. That's how much I care about you."

The muscle in Reeve's jaw twitches. Stonily he says, "If you cared that much, you would have told me that Lil came by the day of my open house. But you didn't. You saw how upset I was, but you said nothing." To me he says, "Let's go."

Desperately Rennie cries, "Wait! Wait." She stumbles in her heels and straightens up again. "I was going to drop this bomb at midnight, but screw it." She doesn't take her eyes off me as she says, "You want to know why you fell off the stage? Lillia drugged you at homecoming. She put something in your drink. I found a picture of her doing it!"

Everything goes slow-motion for me. As I turn my head to look at Reeve, I feel like I'm underwater.

Rennie is panting. Waiting for Reeve to say something. "Let me show you the photo. I'll show you. I'm not lying, Reeve! I've never lied to you." She smirks at me. "Guess what, Lil? Your perfect life is over. You're going to jail, you stupid bitch."

It's over. I'm done for. Reeve, my friends, my whole entire life is ruined.

Reeve's face is expressionless. He doesn't look at me. Then, in a low, measured voice, he says to Rennie, "I don't need your proof. I already know what happened at homecoming."

"*What?*"

"It was a stupid joke that went wrong. She wasn't trying to hurt me. So drop whatever shit you were planning and leave it alone. I'm serious, Ren. If you ever want to see me again, you'll let this die this right now." He holds out his hand to me. "Come on, Lil."

"Reevie, no!" Rennie cries. "Please!" I let him take my hand and lead me out of the kitchen and down the hallway where people are crowding around. They stare at us as Reeve pushes through to make a path for me. I see Alex in the crowd of people, and I have to look away.

When we're outside on the street I say, hiccupping, "I forgot my coat."

"Stay here. I'll get it." He shoulders his way back inside, and I'm left alone with the bouncer, who's smoking a cigarette.

He eyes me. "Damn. Did you get into a girl fight?"

I touch my cheek. It feels warm and pulsey against my hand. "Sort of. But it's over now."

CHAPTER SIXTY

KAT

I SWIRL THE INCH OF WHISKEY IN MY TUMBLER, AND the ice cube clinks against the glass and slowly, slowly dilutes the amber into honey. I take a small sip and it burns the back of my throat in the way that only primo-quality whiskey can.

The DJ goes from a popular rap song to a snappy old jazz tune. He's been mixing it up like that since I got here twenty minutes ago. It's weird but it works. The kids who are grinding on each other on the dance floor transition into more jaunty shakes and shivers, and it turns the crackly song into something sexy and current. I nod my head to the beat, smile, and take another sip.

I have to admit it. The New Year's Eve party is as epic as Ren promised it'd be. Which is saying something, because I've been burned plenty of times by Rennie's overhype. Once, when we were eight, she made a big deal about inviting me to spend the weekend at her grandma's "summer home on the river." It turned out to be a retirement community on the edge of a sludgy creek. We both got ringworm when we held our noses and waded in up to our ankles in a case of double-dog dare.

I remembered that weekend while I was getting ready tonight. It felt good to focus on something nice from back in the day and not totally hate Rennie with all my being. I'm not forgiving her for the shit she put me through. I can't flip the switch like that, even if I wanted to. But I definitely prefer a scab to a bleeding wound.

I touch my head and make sure my hair is still in place. It took me so damn long to get my finger waves to work. I had to wash my hair in the sink twice and start over. The whole time I was thinking . . . How good can a high school party actually be? I had no clue. Just like Mary, I'd never really been to one before.

I've heard about Rennie's infamous parties for years. Rolled my eyes while other people told stories of her bashes rotten with pilfered booze and barely legal shenanigans. But tonight I have to hand it to her. Her party is truly, all-out, undiluted Rennie Holtz. Crystal punch bowls, vintage barware, linen napkins. The DJ, the bouncers, everyone in costume. And not lame versions of costumes either, the way some people phone it in for Halloween. All the invited guests have stepped up their game tonight. If I hadn't done the damn finger waves, I would have looked like a jerk.

It's insanely impressive, especially because it's not like Rennie has the money to buy whatever she needs to do it up right. It must have taken serious work to pull off something so luxe on the cheap.

Rennie should do this for a living. Party planning, I mean. No joke. I'm going to tell her that when I see her.

As crazy as it is for me to admit: I'm actually happy I'm here.

The whole afternoon I steeled myself for the inevitable dirty looks, the "Why the eff is that piece of trash here?" whispers. Everyone knows Rennie and I have a past. And even though I'm dressed the part—my hair, a black slip, fishnets, and a silver cigarette case—they'd know I didn't belong. Not really.

Turns out I didn't have anything to worry about. Everyone's been . . . nice to me. They've said "Whassup, Kat!" and "Happy

New Year!" and "Yo, DeBrassio!" Some girls even hugged me. These are all people I haven't talked to in forever. People I've ignored, I've iced out for the last four years. Everything's thawed tonight.

Just like that.

I take another sip of my whiskey and push through the crowd toward the front of the gallery space. The plate-glass window is fogged with condensation, and I wipe at it so I can see outside. Where's Mary? She should have been here by now. There's a line of people trying to get in, kids shoving their hands into their blazers and girls shivering in whispery dresses. I catch myself grinning. They probably don't know the password.

I feel something tickle my arm. A feather.

I look over and see Ashlin.

"Hello," she says, slurry, and takes a dainty sip of her champagne out of a glass flute. Ashlin's dress is short and completely covered in pale pink sequins. It's skin tight, and her freaking huge boobs look like they're going to spill right over the top. She has a black mole drawn on her left cheek, and her eyelids are bright with glitter.

"Yo," I say, and shrug the strap of my slip back up onto my shoulder.

She tickles me again with a feather. It must have fallen off her purse. The purse looks like a pink baby chicken, tiny and covered with feathers. "Um, just curious, but does Rennie know you're here?"

I stare her down. This freaking bimbo. Is she seriously that dumb? Does she think I would show up here if I wasn't specifically invited?

But I haven't seen Rennie tonight. Not yet, anyway. I get a knot in my stomach. I wonder if this isn't a trick about to blow up in my face That midnight surprise she wanted me here to see.

Suddenly I see Reeve and Lillia push out the front door.

What?

And then Rennie's behind them, running after them. She's quiet, not saying anything, but I can tell she's upset. Reeve and Lillia are gone, and Rennie stops in the center of the dance floor. Nobody even notices her. Nobody except Ashlin and me.

Rennie magically turns to us and walks over, looking suddenly unsteady on her high heels. As she gets closer, her chin starts to quiver, and I know tears are about to drop. I take a step to the side to give her room to approach Ashlin.

"Ren!" Ashlin says brightly, because she's an idiot. "Let's dance!"

Rennie pushes right past Ashlin and practically falls into my arms. I glance behind me, trying to look out the window to see where Reeve and Lil went, but it's fogged back up.

Ashlin is next to us, swaying drunkenly and looking

confused. And then I see other people, people around the room, starting to notice us. Notice Ren.

"Kat. Lillia did it. Lillia's the one who drugged him." She can barely make the words. She is grabbing me tight with her fingertips. And she is shaking.

I pull her toward the bathroom. "Come on."

On our way, we pass Alex. I smile politely, but Rennie spots him and says, "Your girl is a two-timing slut whore!" And Alex looks dumbfounded.

In the bathroom, I lock the door. I pour out what's left of my whiskey and fill the cup full of tap water and hand it to her. "Now what the hell is going on?"

Rennie takes a few small sips, but with her tears, she almost chokes. "She knew. She knew I loved him and she stole him from me. That bitch gets everything she wants! How is that fair? How is that at all fair?"

I swallow the urge to tell Rennie about our plan. To confess to her that Lillia doesn't actually want anything to do with Reeve. It would make it all better, stat. But I don't say anything because . . . has Lillia gone rogue? I thought we were done with that shit after Lillia stood Reeve up for his mom's open house. Did she figure out a new, better way to hurt Reeve? Maybe she hasn't had a chance to tell us what it is yet.

"Calm down, calm down," I say. "What were you talking about out there? What about . . . drugs?"

She looks up at me from the floor of the bathroom. Her eye makeup is two huge black smudges. She opens the bathroom sink cabinet and pulls out a stack of pictures. And there it is, a picture from homecoming. Two girls, arm in arm, smiling together. It takes me a minute to notice what's happening in the background.

It's Lillia slipping the liquid E into Reeve's drink while he looks in the other direction.

I grab the towel rack to steady myself.

"I told him and he didn't even care! He wants to be with her. They freaking ran off hand in hand!"

My head is spinning, and it's way too fucking hot in here. "Ren, I don't know what this proves," I say, even though it basically proves everything.

She lets out a bitter bark of a laugh. "Look close. She's got some kind of vial in her hand. It's got to be liquid E. There's only one place to get drugs like that. That piece-of-shit skank Kevin. He sells to the guys at the restaurant. I bet if I ask him, he'll remember selling it to some Asian girl."

Except Kevin didn't sell it to Lillia. He sold it to me.

Oh fuck.

I check my phone for a text from Lillia. Nothing. Does she

not realize that everything's about to blow up in our faces?

There's a knock on the bathroom door. I scream out, "Damn! Someone's in here!"

"Kat?" It's Alex. "Um, is Lillia in there with you guys? Or did you see her leave?"

Rennie throws her head back and explodes. "Alex, Lillia doesn't give two shits about you! Get it through your thick skull, you dumb-ass! She's with *Reeve*. You're just her lap-dog!"

Rennie opens her mouth to scream at him again, but I cover it with my hand and open the door a crack. Alex is standing there, mouth hanging open. I say to him, "Sorry, can you just give us a minute?" and then I close the door again.

Rennie wipes under her eyes. "Lillia's so done. If Reeve doesn't care about what she did, everyone else here will. They'll all hate her just as much as I do. Where's Nadia? Did you see her out there?"

Oh shit. I've gotta contain this.

"Let's just get out of here," I say. "If we hurry, we can catch up to them." I expect Rennie to fight me, but she doesn't, and that makes me feel sad for her. She holds out her hands, and I pull her up like a rag doll. "Where's your purse?"

"I didn't bring one."

Shit. I didn't drive here. Pat dropped me off. But I don't

want to waste the time it's going to take to text him to pick us up. "Did you drive?"

Rennie nods. "My Jeep's parked out back. The key's inside it."

I open the bathroom door a tiny crack and peek out. Luckily, it's near midnight; people have started moving into the main room of the gallery. Ashlin is handing out noisemakers. Alex is standing in the party, but his eyes keep moving from the front door to his cell phone.

I take Rennie by the hand and run for the back door. We go outside and it's bitter cold. I stop her from getting into the driver's seat. "You're too upset," I tell her. "I'll drive."

The air seems to be rousing Rennie. Her eyes are dark with anger and her fists are clenching and unclenching.

I turn the car on and blast the heat, even though it's cold at first. The whooshing sound makes it so neither of us has to talk. I gun it out of the parking lot, and as I turn past the party, I look again for Mary. Where the hell is she?

Rennie says, "Where do you think they went?"

"I don't know," I say truthfully. "Let's swing by my house and regroup. We'll figure out what to do."

Rennie stares out the window; her eyes are laser beams. "When I find them, they're so dead." Every car that passes, she looks to see who might be in it.

To be honest, I feel bad for her. Not getting to enjoy her

own party after she worked so hard on it. I don't even know what to believe right now, but I can't help feeling pissed at Lillia.

This better be a huge misunderstanding. I can't even think about the alternative, if Rennie somehow has this right in her head. If Reeve and Lillia have something real going, I'll kill Lillia myself. Because doing that to Mary would be the most fucked-up thing in the whole world.

We get to my house. Rennie and I both get out of her Jeep. She slams her door loud, and with too much force. She's still pissed. Really really pissed.

"Give me my keys," Rennie says. "I'll drive by the cliffs. You check the dunes."

I have this feeling, this terrible feeling that something bad is going to happen.

I squeeze my hand around her keys. The ring is full of charms and shit that dig into my hands. "Are you sure you're okay to drive? You're so upset. And you've been drinking."

"I'm fine." She takes the keys out of my hand. As she does, she looks up at me and gives me a half smile. I get the feeling that she's happy I'm not giving her a guilt trip or a hard sell or offering to sleep over so I can babysit her. We never had that kind of friendship anyway. So it seems weird to try and have it now.

I get in my car as Rennie peels out down the street.

But I don't drive to the dunes, like she wants. I drive back to the party. I have to get those pictures, before anyone else finds them.

I hope Lillia knows what she's doing. 'Cause if she doesn't, we're all dead.

CHAPTER SIXTY-ONE

MARY

I DON'T KNOW HOW I MAKE MYSELF GET UP OFF THE ground and go to Rennie's party. I'm in such a fog; I feel like I'm floating outside my body, watching myself move down the streets. Snow is falling in tiny gentle flakes, dusting the ground and the trees and the dead grass. I can't even feel the cold. I try to swallow, but my throat is closed. What happened to my dad? Why didn't my mom let me go with her?

My powers couldn't stop them from leaving me.

When I get down to T-Town, I break into a run, all the way to the gallery. I need to find Lillia and Kat. They'll help me.

They'll help me find my mom and Aunt Bette.

I reach the gallery door and come face-to-face with a bouncer in a black pinstripe suit and black fedora pulled low over his eyes. I think about trying to slip right past him, but he's so big, he fills the door frame like a human wall. Just beyond him I hear music and laughter and merriment, and it makes my chest hurt, because I'm so far from any of that right now. I doubt I'll ever laugh again.

"I need to find my friends," I say, desperate.

He doesn't say anything, doesn't even raise his chin so I can look him in the eyes.

Crap. The stupid speakeasy password. What was it? I had it written down, in my purse. I rack my brain but I can't hold on to any thought. It's all a jumble. "Please, sir. Please. This is an emergency."

Again the bouncer doesn't say anything. I wonder how many kids he's turned away tonight. People Rennie didn't think belonged in her company. I pull on my hair, hard, but it doesn't hurt, and I concentrate all my energy on willing myself to remember. "I know there's a password to get in. My friend told me. I . . . I even know the special one where I don't have to pay a cover charge. Rennie invited us herself. But I—I . . . My friend Kat, she's definitely inside. She has short brown hair." The bodyguard arches his back into a deep, long stretch, and then fishes a flask out of his jacket pocket.

I think about trying to ask for Rennie, but she probably wouldn't let me in. Not after the way I acted when Aunt Bette came to the gallery to get her paintings back. I can't even bribe my way in with money because I don't have a red cent on me.

It finally comes to me. "Moonshine! Moonshine! Moonshine!" I shout it as loud as I can, but the bodyguard still pretends not to hear me. It's like I'm not even standing in front of him. My lips quiver and the tears come. What's happening? "Please," I'm begging. "Please let me in." Only it's no use.

I stumble backward away from him and try peeking through the foggy glass in the front window. I don't see Kat or Lillia inside, can't make either of them out in the crowds of revelers. But I know they are here. I can feel it. I sit down on the curb and touch for my heartbeat, because it feels like it's pounding in my chest, but I can't feel a thing.

And then, suddenly, I turn my head back to the gallery door, and there's Lillia standing out front on the curb. She's shivering in a thin dress and her stockings. Is she looking for me? She must have felt that I needed her.

I step toward her, but then Reeve appears, carrying her coat. He wraps her in it. They run across the street together, and Reeve picks up Lillia and puts her inside the cab of his truck. They seem like they're in a hurry.

JENNY HAN AND SIOBHAN VIVIAN

They kiss on the lips before they drive away. A tender, slow, warm kiss.

Oh no. Oh no.

I turn around; I'm spinning. I sink to the ground. I don't understand. How could she do this to me?

I'm still sitting on the curb when, from out the back of the store, I see Rennie's white Jeep goes flying down the road in the other direction. Kat's behind the wheel.

I lift a shaky hand and push my hair behind my ears. I've got nowhere to go, no idea what's going on. My whole world is falling apart.

Maybe I can catch Mom and Aunt Bette before the ferry leaves. I can make them take me with them because I definitely cannot stay here. So I run. I run as fast as I can, my shoes slipping on the slick roads, and scream, "Wait for me! Wait for me!" until my throat is raw. I know they won't hear me, I'm too far, but I have to do something.

I get to the ferry landing. Normally bright, tonight it's cloaked in darkness. I search the parking lot, but it's empty. A thick metal chain ropes off the entrance. All the white lights running along the planks are turned off. The ferry has stopped running. Mom and Aunt Bette must have boarded the last one.

They're gone.

I drop to my knees and let out a wail that makes the trees

tremble. I'm done. I've got nothing left inside. I can't do it anymore. I can't go on like this. I rise to my feet and head up the hill. I know what I need to do. I should have done it a long time ago. And this time, there'll be no one to stop me.

A white Jeep pulls up beside me. Inside is Rennie. I can tell she's been crying, the way her makeup raccoons around her eyes.

"Are you okay?"

I stumble up to the Jeep. I see myself reflected in the glass. I'm not in my party dress, but in a pair of still-damp jeans and a wet white T-shirt, speckled with gravel and dirt, clinging to my rolls of fat. I look down, and there are my old sneakers, soaked through with water.

I try to answer Rennie but I can't. I'm choking on my tears.

She tells me to get in. I don't move. She opens the door for me and I finally climb in.

"Where do you live? Where are your parents?"

I try to answer her, to make words, but nothing comes out of my mouth. It's like I'm choking. Like something is around my neck, squeezing it closed. I can feel my eyes bulge out of my head. My lungs burn for oxygen.

Rennie's scared; I can tell she's scared. "Just breathe. It's going to be okay. Just breathe."

"Breathe! Breathe!"

I want to. I want to suck in a deep, cool breath, but all I can feel is the burn of the rope around my neck. I'm dizzy from lack of oxygen. That and the way I've been swinging, to and fro from the beam in my ceiling, before she cut me down.

"My beautiful baby!" Mom sobs. She leans forward; she kisses my face. Hers is wet with tears. "Why? Why would you do this to yourself?"

I turn to Rennie and am finally able to choke out, in a strained whisper of a voice, "Reeve." Rennie's eyes go wide. "Reeve did this to me. This is his fault."

I watch her hands tighten around the steering wheel. She can't look at me; she's too frightened. "I . . . I'm taking you to the hospital."

"Hold on, baby!" Mom is screaming herself raw. "The ambulance is coming! Hold on. I've got you."

I try to, but it's hard. I feel myself slipping away. I don't want to die. I don't want to die. But that's exactly what's happening.

And then, with one last rush, I'm pulled out of my body

and up to the ceiling. I can see my mom holding me as the ambulance arrives. I see them grab at me, but my mom won't let me go. She knows. She already knows what I apparently didn't.

I'm dead.

"What are you doing!" Rennie screams. She's terrified. She's scooting over as far as she can away from me. She's not looking at the road, not looking at the turns.

I feel myself heat up, a fire. Hotter than any other time before. I close my eyes and everything goes white, like the center of the sun. I barely hear Rennie, because this is it. My chance to finally jump the scratch. It's a relief, to do it. To finally let go.

JENNY HAN AND SIOBHAN VIVIAN

REEVE AND I DRIVE AROUND IN SILENCE, EXCEPT FOR a few times when one of us says, "Oh my God," because of how crazy this all is.

I don't ask where he's going. I just let him drive.

We end up parking in the woods. It's so dark and quiet. Reeve pulls to a stop and clicks off his headlights, but leaves the car running so it can stay warm.

Not that it matters. For once I'm not even cold. It's like we're in our own real-life snow globe.

He unbuckles his seat belt and then I unclick mine, too. And in a second we are completely going at it. I am pressing my lips as hard as I can against his, and his arms are around me, squeezing me so tight. I feel a rush of everything I've been trying so hard to hold back. And I can tell he does too.

I can't kiss him enough; I can't hold enough of him in my hands.

I pull his coat off his shoulders and then I wriggle out of mine. Reeve lifts me clean out of my seat and puts me in his lap, my back pressed into the steering wheel. The horn keeps honking, but neither of us cares.

He pulls his face away from mine and says, in a panic, "After I left your house that day, I went up to my room and lay in my bed listening to depressing music."

I keep kissing his face. His eyes, his cheeks. "Like what?"

His eyes roll back in his head. "Like . . . um . . . damn." He laughs nervously. "Radiohead . . . Beck. I don't remember now."

I plant kisses on the side of his neck, up to his ears.

Reeve shivers. "If I had known you came over, I would have run downstairs. I would have showed you off to my whole family." He pushes me away suddenly, so he can stare me straight in the eyes. "I want you to know that I didn't invite Rennie. She came on her own."

I drop my head to his chest and cling to him. I don't want to,

I don't want to do anything to ruin this moment, but I have to confess. I have to be true to him. "That stuff she was saying at the party . . ."

He lifts my face to his. "Forget it," he says.

"Reeve, please. Let me finish. I—"

"Don't. Just—don't. Don't tell me. I don't need to know what happened before. I just need to know that you're with me now."

"Yes." I hesitate, and then I just say it. "I'm yours."

A smile spreads across his face and his mouth comes up my neck and over my lips and then we're kissing again. His lips are urgent, like all we have is tonight. And I don't even remember what I was going to say anymore, it's that good. We kiss over and over and over again. This time there's no one around to stop us.

CHAPTER SIXTY-THREE

KAT

IT'S EASY TO GET THE PICTURES. I SNEAK IN TO THE gallery, grab them out of the bathroom sink cabinet, and sneak straight back out. And then I go find my brother.

Pat and all his friends are camping. I know roughly where the spot is, a wooded clearing near the bluffs that he found on one of his dirt-bike rides. I park as close as I can get, on the side of the road, and head through the woods in my dress and my heels. The trees are so dense the snow barely hits the ground.

I find them. They've got a fire going, and everyone's festive and drunk and cold as shit.

"Kat," Pat says, standing up from the log he's sitting on. "What's up?"

I walk straight up to the fire and toss the stack of Rennie's photos on the flames. "Someone pour me a whiskey."

Ricky passes me his bottle. I down what's left in one thick, smoky gulp.

I sit quietly for a while, while everyone else parties. Every few minutes I send Rennie a text like, *Where are you?* and *Let me know where you are?* and *Rennie, WTF?!!*

Then, through the crackle of the logs and the conversation and the Led Zeppelin, I think I hear a siren. Like a fire truck or an ambulance. I can't tell. But it sends a shiver down my spine. I glance down at my cell. Rennie hasn't answered my texts, not a single one.

I've got a feeling. A bad feeling.

"Everyone shut up a second!"

Pat laughs at me. He's sitting across the fire on his sleeping bag, cooking some nasty-looking hot dog on a stick. "You hear Big Foot out there?"

The rest of the group either laugh at his lame joke or ignore me and keep talking.

I take a few steps away from them and strain to hear. Now it sounds like two sirens. Maybe even three. I run over to the radio someone brought and shut it off in the middle of a killer

Led Zeppelin guitar solo. Someone whines. I say, "I'm not kidding! Shut up."

I guess something in my voice tells them to take me seriously. They shut their traps. And then we all hear it. Like every fire truck in Jar Island is on its way to something bad.

"Ricky!"

I'm running over to his bike and putting on a helmet as fast as I can. No one knows what to make of this, but Ricky, bless his heart, doesn't hesitate a second. He roars the engine and we peel out, sending a spray of dead pine needles and snow.

We drive toward the sound. It's not far off. But we can't get close. One of the fire trucks has blocked off the road. I climb off the bike and run to the side of the road where a fireman is pulling caution tape across the pass. A jagged cliff, a few hundred feet in the distance, seems to glow. My eyes trace the light down its jagged edges to the water, where a bright orange ball burns in the cover. It . . . it looks like the water is on fire.

"What happened?"

He gives me this look, like I'm some stupid rubbernecker wanting the gory details. "There's been an accident." And then he turns his back to me.

I grab his arm. "What? Who was it? Was it a white Jeep?"

As soon as I say the white Jeep bit, he spins around, his face completely different.

I fall to my knees and let out a howl like a wild animal.

CHAPTER SIXTY-FOUR

LILLIA

WHEN I WAKE UP, IT'S JUST GETTING TO BE LIGHT outside, and I'm leaning against Reeve's chest and his arms are around me. The clock on the dashboard says 7:07. Oh God.

I try to sit up, and Reeve stirs but doesn't wake up, and he doesn't let go. He holds me tighter, and for a second I let him. My parents are going to kill me.

Was it worth it? I look up at Reeve; his eyes are closed and his lashes are long and his hair is all mussed in the back. He looks like a little boy. Yes, it was worth it. I know now that I can't *not* be with him. It will be hard, but I'm going to have to explain it to Mary and Kat so they understand. That I didn't plan for anything like this to happen . . . but it did happen. They'll have to, they just will.

I sit up and gently shake Reeve's shoulder. "Wake up, Reeve."

He opens his eyes, and he smiles. Then his eyes widen. "Shit."

"My parents are going to kill me. I was supposed to be home by two." I slide away from him and start looking for my clutch. I find it on the floor by my shoes. I check my phone—eighteen missed calls, all from home. "Oh no."

Reeve starts up the truck, and reverses out of the woods and onto the main road in one swift move. "I'll get you home in six minutes. We'll explain that we fell asleep; it'll be fine."

"You're not explaining anything," I tell him. "You're just dropping me off. I'm talking to them alone." I check my hair in the mirror. A mess. I start running my fingers through it, trying to untangle the ends. I'm starting to feel queasy, and it's not just my parents. Every time I think of Mary, I feel an ache inside. And the way I left things with Rennie . . . it's all such a mess.

Reeve reaches over and grabs my hand. He laces his fingers around mine and says, "Ren will get over it eventually. I'll talk to her. She can't stay mad forever."

I let out a laugh. "Do you know Rennie at all? Of course she can."

Confidently he says, "Not at me. We've known each other for too long."

"Okay, then, she'll forgive you and she'll go on hating me." As soon as I say it, I know that's exactly how it's going to go. Reeve's just a guy; he's not her best friend. He didn't betray her the way I did.

"I won't let her hate you, Cho," Reeve says, and I start to smile, but then stop.

"And Mary. Mary's going to be so upset," I whisper.

Reeve asks, "Who's Mary?"

"She's my friend." We're pulling into my neighborhood now. Later, if my parents ever let me out of the house again, I'm going to tell him everything. The revenge pact with Mary and Kat, the ecstasy at homecoming, the plan to make him fall in love with me—all of it. I know he doesn't want to hear it, but it's the only way. And when he understands how badly he hurt Mary, he'll go to her, and he'll apologize. He'll want to make things right.

When we turn onto the road to my house, I see it—a police car in our driveway. Oh my God. My parents put out an APB on me.

Under his breath, Reeve says, "Uh-oh." He pulls into my driveway. Worriedly, he asks, "Are you sure you don't want me to come inside with you? Blame it all on me."

I'm already opening the passenger door. "Just go. I'll call you later." I hop out of the truck and run for the front door. I don't look back, but I hear his car drive away.

Breathless, I run up to the door and slip inside the house. My dad is pacing by the fireplace, my mom is crying on the couch with Nadia in her arms. A police officer is sitting on the couch. "I'm so sorry," I begin. "I fell asleep—"

I stop talking because my mom lets out a choked sob and my dad has the strangest expression on his face. He runs over to me and grabs me in his arms and hugs me to him tight. Hoarsely he whispers, "Thank God you're okay. Thank God. We thought—" He can't even finish the sentence.

"What's happening?" I ask. Then I look over his shoulder at my mom and Nadia on the couch. My mom's crying; so is Nadia. She's smoothing the top of Nadia's head and rubbing her back.

"Lillia," she manages to say, and holds her arms out to me.

I'm scared. I've never felt so scared. "Daddy?" I pull away from my dad and look up at him. "Tell me what's happening. Is it Grandma?"

My dad closes the front door and tries to maneuver me toward the couch. "First sit down, honey."

I'm shaking my head. "No. Tell me now."

He puts his hands on my shoulders. The lines around his eyes look deep in this morning light. He looks so tired. "It's Rennie."

My heart drops. *No no no no no.*

"She's been in an accident, and we didn't know if you were with her. She—she died, Lilli."

I feel my legs go out from under me. My dad rushes to lift me up, but he can't. I can't move. This isn't happening. This is a dream. Rennie can't be dead. It's not possible.

JENNY HAN AND SIOBHAN VIVIAN

CHAPTER SIXTY-FIVE

MARY

AT DAWN, I WAKE UP AND FIND MYSELF IN A BALL ON the ground. Frosty green grass, dirt, and a touch of snow. But I don't feel cold. I don't feel anything. I lift my head.

What happened?

Why am I still here?

Slowly more things come into focus. Slabs of white marble, brittle bouquets, melted candles. I'm in the big graveyard in the center of the island.

I crawl closer to the gravestone I'm lying in front of.

JAMES GLENN DONOVAN, BELOVED HUSBAND AND FATHER.

I let out a sob. Daddy.

It says he died a year ago. I rack my brain, trying to remember the last time I saw him. It had to have been before I left for Jar Island. But I can't remember anything about that day. I can't hear his voice, or see him put me on the ferry. It's like someone erased my memory, wiped it blank.

I'm still choking back tears when I see it. The gravestone right next to his. It looks old, like it used to be white and now it's grayish.

ELIZABETH MARY DONOVAN ZANE. SLEEP, MY LITTLE ONE, SLEEP.

My fingers reach out. Elizabeth. I say it and I know it's my name.

My family has always called me Mary, because I was named after Aunt Bette . . . but at school, I was Elizabeth.

Elizabeth Zane.

Big EZ.

With a shaking hand, I try to trace my birthday. Thirteen when I . . .

I stumble to my feet and start backing away from the grave, without leaving a single footprint behind in the snow. I spin and run as fast as I can back to my house.

The front door is open. I run inside, up the stairs, to my room.

There aren't any boxes. None of the clothes I packed away. My dresser is covered in a sheet. My bed has no linens. I step into the bathroom. The shower curtain's gone.

The towels, too. I look down into my bathtub. It's full of dust, even though I showered right before Mom came.

But I've been going to school. I've been doing all the normal things a high school girl does. I have friends. I have two friends!

How could they see me if I'm dead?

I go over it in my head. All the people I've talked to . . . Kat, Lillian, Aunt Bette. That's pretty much it.

But wait! Halloween! I talked to other people on Halloween. I kissed a boy on Halloween.

Then I remember what Aunt Bette said to me that night. *On Halloween the line between the living and the dead is blurred.*

I rock back on my knees. Aunt Bette's been trying to tell me all along. But I didn't understand.

And I still don't.

Have I been here this whole time? The mental hospital, the new house, the years I've spent away from here, did I make it all up in my head? Like the bike? My clothes?

Is none of it real?

And the biggest question of all . . . If I'm dead, why didn't I go to heaven? Or hell? Or just disappear? Why can't I leave Jar Island?

I squeeze my eyes shut, throw back my head, and scream a scream that doesn't end.

CHAPTER SIXTY-SIX

KAT

IT'S DINNER TIME AND I'M PARKED A HALF BLOCK away from Lillia's house, chain-smoking with my car windows rolled up tight. The snow hasn't stopped falling since last night, and my windshield is almost completely blanketed white.

I've been waiting an hour for her to come home. I'm not sure where she is. Maybe at Rennie's mom's apartment, comforting her. Maybe with Ash, or some of the other girls from the cheerleading squad, holding each other and crying.

My heart hurts bad. Rennie and I were friends for a long time.

Even with our break during high school, I know our friendship was deeper and longer and eclipsed anything she had with anyone else.

I can't even go over to her apartment. It's not like I have a right. It's not like anyone would think to check on how I'm dealing, or give me a shoulder to cry on. No one is explaining to me why this happened, what was the cause of the accident, what the fuck we're all supposed to do now.

I've texted Lillia maybe ten times, and she hasn't written back once. Not one fucking time, when she knows that Rennie was my best friend too.

Maybe she's still with Reeve.

I don't feel like I can even go check on Mary until I talk to Lil so she can explain what the hell is going on.

I let my head fall against the windshield and my eyes close, but as soon as they do, the tears come flooding back. This is all fucking crazy. It's insanity.

I haven't slept. Not a wink. Just sobbed and smoked, sobbed and smoked on repeat since I saw her Jeep burning in the ravine.

I glance at the dashboard clock. It's five p.m.

Rennie's been dead fifteen hours.

Fifteen hours ago. I was the last person to see her alive. I gave her her keys. I left her drive.

I start shaking, shaking and crying, and my head hurts so

fucking bad. I stick my hand in my pocket and take the Valium that Pat handed me when I first tried to lie down, after we'd gotten home from the woods. Lord knows where he even got it. I wash it down with a sip of cold gas-station coffee.

I guess I eventually do nod off, because I don't know how long has passed before I hear a knock at my window.

Lillia.

I lean across the car and open the passenger-side door. She climbs in. The skin around her eyes is pink and her face looks so pale.

"Sorry I didn't text you back," she whispers. "I was with her mom. She . . . she's in really bad shape."

I just stare at Lillia, because I don't know what to say. She starts crying. Quiet, delicate tears.

"Do they know what happened? Why she crashed?"

"I don't know. The officers aren't saying yet."

"Did you know she had pictures of you putting E in Reeve's drink?"

Lillia pales. "You saw them?"

"Yeah. Rennie showed me after you left. I had to convince her to leave with me and not show everybody at the party. I went back and got them and burned them but I don't know if they're the only copies or what."

Lillia closes her eyes. "I can't even think about that right now."

"Well, you better think about it because if anyone else see those pictures, we're fucked." I feel my lip curl. "What the hell happened with you and Reeve last night?"

Her mouth starts opening and closing, but no words come out.

"For fuck's sake, Lillia!" I shake my head and wrap my hands around the steering wheel. "What are you going to say to Mary?"

"I don't know, okay!" Lillia shouts, wiping her eyes. "I can't even think straight right now."

I rail on. "I hope you don't think that I'm going to be the one to tell her, do your dirty work for you. That's on you."

"Kat, God! Can you just—can you just give it a rest? Rennie's dead. My oldest friend in the world is dead."

I slam my hands on the steering wheel and scream my throat raw. "You don't think I know that! You think you were the only one who cared about her?"

Lillia wipes her tears with the sleeve of her coat. "I can't believe any of this is happening." She turns toward me, eyes sad but hopeful. "I mean, this could all be a bad dream. Right?"

CHAPTER SIXTY-SEVEN

MARY

I'M OUTSIDE KAT'S CAR, LISTENING TO THEM fight. Fight over who's going to have to tell me what I already know. That Reeve and Lillia are together now. A couple.

Maybe they're even in love.

But Kat and Lillia have no idea that I've got secrets too. Big, big secrets. Sure, there's still a lot I need to figure out. What I can do, what I can't. Why Lillia and Kat could see me when nobody else could. That will come in time, I'm sure. Like Aunt Bette said, I didn't know what I'm capable of.

I will soon.

I do know this for sure. What happened last night, Rennie dying, was an accident. But next time it won't be.

I've wasted so much time. Trying to make Reeve feel remorse for what he did, trying to guilt him into an apology. But now I understand that there was no point to any of it. He can never give back what he's taken from me. My family, my friends, my heart, my life. All gone. If he got on his knees and begged me for forgiveness now, it wouldn't be enough. Not even close.

An eye for an eye, a tooth for a tooth, a burn for a burn. A life for a life.

That's how all this got started. And that's how it's going to end.